Praise for *Taking Back the Bullet*

"Masterful storytelling, exquisite character development, so real as to HURT and HOPE, a real page turner. Begs for stage, screenwriters, and visual episodic development a.k.a. TV series . . . Thanks Jim Potter for telling it like it is AND providing us visions of how it could be. Well done!" —Dennis Perrin, educator

"As a former law-enforcement officer, I found the story very relatable as it details the life of a law-enforcement officer and the struggles some face throughout their careers. . . *Taking Back the Bullet* is a journey of understanding, respect, and forgiveness . . ." —Rebecca Schillaci

"I enjoyed the different stories of this book because Tom, James, and Suanna, the three main characters, represent in their own way the different struggles with themselves and society's idea of what is normal." —Sheryl Remar

"Terrific story relevant to today's social issues . . . well written . . . likable characters . . . insightful perspective from an insider in law enforcement." —Karleen Wilson-Moon

"I enjoyed your book. When I am looking for a new read, I always read the first page, last page and choose a random page somewhere in the middle before I decide to buy it. You had me on all three pages. I also like reading a book where you can relate to the characters and the settings in which they live and work. It makes a story more realistic if you can say, 'I am familiar with the area; I know where that town is or I have traveled that street.' It was easy to relate to the characters. In one way or another, I have met them all somewhere in my journeys." —John & Cindy Morrill, 20 years Air Force retired, 17 years law enforcement

" . . . I was impressed with the Native American information as well as the depth of character development . . ." —Judy Hawk.

"Three main characters walk different paths but with the same destination —each coping with his or her self-discovery, self-identity, and self-realization. Much like their earlier counterparts—Huck Finn and Holden Caulfield—their journeys are often joyous, often tedious, and often tragic." —Wynona Winn, PhD, retired school superintendent

"Good story line, building the characters along the way. Great job!" — Diana Dester

"Jim Potter has done it again! After his book, *Cop in the Classroom: Lessons I've Learned, Tales I've Told,* Jim has written another great work. In *Taking Back the Bullet: Trajectories of Self-Discovery,* Jim Potter takes us on an insightful journey into the lives and relationships of numerous characters. Jim is such a talented storyteller that the reader quickly becomes immersed and has a 'bonding experience' with each of the characters, feeling their joy, fear, passion, and pain. Jim's novel speaks to the empowerment of persistence with the characters as they work through their trials. As a therapist, I appreciated the heartfelt struggles from each of the characters and their diversity. I also found value in the novel's understanding of society's misunderstanding of both mental health and other conditions in which people struggle. The novel contains rich exposure to various realities that many of us do not know about . . . but should. When I finished this captivating novel, I was wanting to read the sequel! It was an honor and a wonderful, mesmerizing experience reading this book. Congratulations, Jim!" —Deb Theis, LSCSW, clinical therapist/hypnotherapist

"I finished it last night around midnight. What a great piece of work. It kept me intrigued all the way to the end." —Jane Holzrichter

"Retired police officer Potter's novel centres on very disparate characters and, through the tried and tested means of gradually introducing each one, builds a sense of anticipation about what is going to happen to them. This often-used methodology is not easy to do well, but is superbly handled by Potter who knows how to give enough detail to bring the characters to life, yet not too much so as to slow down the pace of the developing story.

"A climactic event affects the main characters and it is at this point Potter's deep knowledge of people and police procedures really hits home; page by page we read how a seemingly simple, though terrible occurrence, can have huge consequences. To Potter's credit the story does not have a completely conclusive or simplistic ending. Instead it leaves the reader thinking about how the events of a single minute can affect lives forever.

"I would whole-heartedly recommend this book not as a crime novel or even as a novel about crime but as a beautiful and positive affirmation about what it is to be human and how ultimately it is relationships which matter more than events." —Sean McArdle, Winchester, England

TAKING BACK
THE BULLET

Trajectories of Self-Discovery

A Novel by

Jim Potter

sandhenge
PUBLICATIONS

Taking Back the Bullet: Trajectories of Self Discovery
By Jim Potter

This is a work of fiction. Names, characters, places, and incidents either are the product of the author's imagination or are used fictitiously. Any resemblance to actual persons, living or dead, events or locales is entirely coincidental. If you want legal advice, hire an attorney. If you're seeking medical guidance, see a doctor. For thought-provoking entertainment, keep reading.

An earlier version of chapter 9 was published as "Boxing or Bullying—If you had to do it over again, would you still hit her?" in *Cop in the Classroom: Lessons I've Learned, Tales I've Told* (Sandhenge Publications, 2007).

Biblical quotations in chapter 16 from *The Holy Bible*, King James Version. Cambridge Edition: 1769; King James Bible Online, 2017. www.kingjamesbibleonline.org

Cover sculpture, *Tom Jennings*, and sculptures in Appendix, by J. Alex Potter
Cover photo and cover design, and photos in Appendix, by Gina Laiso
Editing and interior design by Jan Gilbert Hurst

Potter, Jim, 1949-
Taking back the bullet: trajectories of self-discovery
Sandhenge Publications, 2017
Hutchinson, KS
Library of Congress Control Number 2017907726
ISBN-13: 9780979069703 (perfect bound)
ISBN-10: 097906970X (perfect bound)
ISBN-13: 9780979069710 (e-book)
ISBN-10: 0979069718 (e-book)
FICTION / Literary. FICTION 1. Police 2. American Indians 3. Mental illness 4. People with albinism 5. Anthropology—Guna in Panama 6. Coming-of-age 7. Stigma, identity, and self-discovery

Printed in the United States
First Edition

Also by the author:
Cop in the Classroom: Lessons I've Learned, Tales I've Told
Under the Radar: Race at School (a play)

For Alex,
creative artist
and
first reader,
who fills our home
with
shapes and texture,
rich color,
and
wondrous characters
with
their own special stories

Acknowledgments

Encouragement can take many forms.

An author, like any creative person, needs space to conjure up ideas. I'm grateful to J. Alex Potter, my wife, for contributing to an inspiring atmosphere in our home.

As this novel developed and she met the fictional characters, Alex manifested them in clay, one by one, until their presence was felt in every room. Our home became an active, stimulating environment as the characters came to life.

I can't think of a more supportive gift than these masterful creations. Thank you, Alex, for sharing your remarkable talent.

A great editor can offer valuable advice that helps shape a manuscript. This is true of Jan Gilbert Hurst. Her meticulous editing has allowed my novel to be dressed up so that it may be seen in public. Thanks, Jan.

The cover photograph and design are credited to professional videographer Gina Laiso. She is also responsible for the incredible photos of J. Alex Potter's jaw-dropping sculptures, located in the Appendix. The photographs are simply stunning! Thanks, Gina.

Jim Potter
Hutchinson, Kansas

Contents

Contents, continued

"Make sure of your target
because once you fire your gun,
you can never take your bullet back."

—Instructor at the Police Academy

•

Book Ins 1

By two in the morning, Jailer Jennings had booked in three DUIs. Eight hours down and four to go before he could go home, catch some zs, then return to do it all over again.

After two years working the jail, Tom Jennings viewed most drunks as clones of their intoxicated peers. He'd heard, "I only had two beers," so often that he no longer shook his head in disbelief or judged them as desperate liars. Instead, he smiled. It was a joke, police humor.

Gazing between the jail bars, sitting at the book-in counter, Jennings was introduced to a cross section of humanity: the criers who might later be discovered hanging with a bed sheet around their necks; the big mouths that talked tough then pissed their pants; the chronic huffers and meth heads with their glazed eyes, mouths ajar leaking spittle; the polite, even apologetic prisoners who could stick you with a pen and sign their name in your blood before you knew it wasn't red ink; the crazies or MIs, dumped into this facility, who were more likely to be victims than perpetrators; and the friendly regulars who greeted you by name, then asked, "When we eat?"

The jail was stifling. Now, even in mid-spring it was already hot. There were no windows to open, just steel walls guarding ancient stale air. Vents, designed for climate control, instead funneled water and sewage out of flooded cells from their deliberately backed-up toilets. And the buzzers, bells, pounding, and yelling were enough to wish deafness from the hearing.

Of course his weight didn't help. Obese, he resembled a mutant Idaho potato in a jiggling gelatin suit. Even in his short-sleeved uniform and without the body armor that patrol officers wore religiously, Jennings could feel the constant trickle of perspiration roll down his fleshy chest.

•

"Cottonwood County Jail, Deputy Jennings," he said into the headset's mouthpiece, husky voice resounding like the DJ he once was.

"Yes, I'm . . . I'm calling about Valerie Popalavata," a woman's voice said hesitantly. "She was arrested earlier. Is she okay? When can she get out?"

"Just a second . . . She can bond out any time as long as she's not driving."

"How does she bond out?" questioned the female caller.

"She can call a bonding company to get her out, and they'll put up most of the money, or she can pay the entire cash bond herself. Or someone else can pay it. Are you that person?"

"I'm Jesse Thomas. How much is it?"

"Five hundred dollars, cash only," the officer replied.

"Where's her car?"

"Hold on. I'm checking . . . Randy's Towing. Do you know where it's at?"

"Oh, yeah. What will it cost to get it back?"

"You'll have to call Randy's. We never know."

"Val and I are roommates. We share an apartment. She's got the only car that's running; now it's been towed, and I don't have the money right now to get her out."

"The bond is $500 if she wants out tonight, or she can wait until court on Monday morning. Once she's out she can call you. I believe she had a cell phone at book in, but if not, we have a pay phone in the lobby. We don't take checks, credit, or debit cards. Cash only."

"Is she okay?"

"Hard to say."

"I mean, is she safe?"

"Yeah, ten-four, she's in jail, safer here than driving around drunk, that's for sure. She's passed out. We've got another one coming in now, so I can't talk anymore. If you want her out tonight, come down with the cash. You can call us from the lobby."

"Thank you. And your name?"

"Deputy Jennings."

"Thank you, Deputy Jennings. I'll talk to you later."

"Good night, Ms. Thomas," he replied and hung up.

•

Jesse's breathing was calm and steady. She was relaxed. She had answers. She could get the money. Valerie would be out in time.

•

"Deputy Jennings," his voice echoed over the jail intercom.

"I'm Jesse Thomas. We spoke earlier. I'm here to bond out Valerie Popalavata."

"I'll be out in a minute. Have a seat if you want."

Jesse thought she knew that voice.

The door opened and the hippo-like mass of Jennings squeezed through, filling the visitor's lobby. The overhead lighting bounced off his bowling-ball head. "Hello, again," he said. "You have the bond for Valerie Popalavata? It's five hundred cash."

She didn't acknowledge his girth, but cranked her chin up two notches. Looking into his eyes, she said. "You're Taz from KZOK!"

"How'd you know?"

"Your voice! I knew it!"

Jesse wore black sweats and running shoes with a Nike swoosh. The light shining on her bright red, shoulder-length ponytail, shot out the back of her ball cap like an arc light in a sustained luminous glow. Her sparkling gray eyes intensified the fireworks while her cheeks displayed faint, captivating freckles like fading starbursts. Tom caught his breath.

"It's been a couple of years now since I was on the radio waves. Beside my mother, you must be one of the few who remember my brief career in radio. This was my slot, middle of the night, past my curfew."

"I called in to request my favorite songs. Nice to finally meet you, Taz, I mean Officer Jennings. Sorry about the circumstances. My friend just wouldn't stop drinking."

"She's still asleep, but we'll take care of this paperwork and get her released. Slow right now, so it shouldn't take too long. You found the money?"

"Yes, I've been saving to fix my car, but I've got to get Valerie out. We have a booth at the art fair this morning."

"Oh! You're an artist. What do you create?"

"Me, sculpture; Val paints."

"I used to work the art-fair security before I was hired as a jailer. I was a police cadet."

"Well, we need to get home so we can get ready, but if you're not sleeping all day, consider yourself invited to our booth. Looks like our sales will go to pay back friends and replenish my sick-car jar."

"I just might do that since you'll be there, but I don't think Ms. Popalavata would be too excited about seeing me any time soon. I did book her in."

"She may not remember. She's been getting worse lately, blackouts. This is it. If she doesn't stop drinking, one of us will be moving out. Too bad. We've been friends since college, and we have the perfect loft apartment."

"I'll take the bond money so you can get her home, but I'd be surprised if she's much help right away; I think she needs to sleep this one off."

As she handed him the cash, she said, "I still can't believe it. Who would have ever thought I'd meet Taz in jail? I wondered what happened to you."

"Me, too. Visit me here anytime, but it's usually crowded and expensive. We provide clothing, meals, and health care, but a downside to being locked up is that every prisoner resembles a die-hard Bronco fan." Jennings chuckled as he prepared to tell the punchline. "The issued shirts and pants are bright orange, the underwear dark blue."

"Inviting," Jesse replied with a wide grin, "but I'd rather see you outside at the art fair."

"I'll get your friend and your receipt."

Jesse offered her hand. "Thanks, Taz," she said, as she raised her chin, made good eye contact, and gave him a light squeeze during the handshake.

•

Tom Jennings, whistling in the shower, was feeling refreshed despite his twelve-hour shift in an oven. He was looking forward to the fresh morning air and talking to local artist Jesse Thomas.

Never before in his two years on the job had he met someone while working the jail and then agreed to meet them socially. These circumstances offered a sign, an invitation for him to get his big butt in gear. This appealing redhead, who had earlier bonded out her friend, hadn't done anything wrong—only right. No harm in him meeting her, he reasoned; it was permitted within departmental policy. She hadn't been incarcerated, and this wasn't even a date. Jesse was looking for patrons to buy her art, and he had money to spend from a lot of mandatory overtime.

Tom took another swish of mouthwash, gargled, and swallowed.

He felt warm, but it wasn't from the shower or from money burning a hole in his debit card. Talking with Jesse got him reminiscing about his days as a DJ at KZOK. That was a previous world of greatest hits, endless all-night activity, and cultlike callers. He missed it. In comparison, his so-called law-enforcement career was a treadmill, seemingly a path to nowhere. Jail was a repetitive hell hole. He wanted to catch criminals, not book them, not feed them, and not nurse them. His career goal was to become the first Cottonwood County K-9 handler.

Because working a dog was a position in the patrol division, Jennings had his mind set on a transfer there, upon completion of his indeterminate jail sentence. However, there was a big hurdle before his dream could come true: He had to lose enough weight to fit in a cruiser. So when the patrol captain told him, "Road officers don't drive cargo vans," every muscle in his body tightened. "Just give me a chance," Tom had retorted, "I'm fat, not stupid!"

Bookends 2

Overhead, downtown, the low, gray, lumpy clouds gathered in patches. Rain was unlikely. Parking as close as he could to Broadway's art festival, he heard a nearby tenor sax. Jennings walked past the barricades and approached the flapping, mostly white tents, eager to see Jesse but not her roommate. On the corner of Broadway and Lincoln a bereted saxophone player, his case open for tips, welcomed Jennings with a nod as the musician slid into some old Grover Washington Jr. jazz. Tom recognized the music, titled "Just the Two of Us," and imagined Jesse beside him. He joined in song as if he were still at home in the shower, declaring his desire to be with Jesse, the special one mentioned in Grover Washington's song.

It was only eight in the morning, but already people were crowding around the booths, allotting little space for others to stop and closely observe the art. The artists in their kaleidoscopic clothing offered contrast to the tents that resembled a photo-shoot backdrop. Customers cradled their purchases against their chests like prized family heirlooms. Tom used an old strategy in working his way through the crowd. He followed those already moving slowly, at times a non-motorized wheelchair or a parent with a child just learning to walk. Now, he mustered up behind a mother pushing a double-wide baby carrier transporting twins.

Tom worked his way back and forth down the rows of tents. He hoped Jesse's art would be something he could identify and enjoy as much as he admired her starburst beauty. He passed more booths. One stall had jewelry, especially rings, made from old silverware with intricate line patterns. It reminded him of the work of prisoners at the penitentiary. When they weren't making sharpened metal weapons called "shivs," they sometimes made contraband rings to sell to rookie guards or visitors.

Another booth had a myriad of framed black-and-white photographs hung on portable walls. No doubt these simple but strong prints had been transported in the colorful old suitcases stacked beside the tables.

Next, Tom saw some pottery and stopped to admire the shapes and glazes. He was promptly approached by a muscular, broad-shouldered woman with dirty fingernails and a hint of a mustache. She was no Jesse.

At a booth without tenting—it stood out from the rest—was a leathery skinned, hunched man with renegade shrubbery eyebrows and nose hairs. He was planted in a rocking chair. Beside him at his feet was a graying pet collie, looking as carefree as a lifelong partner. Before the mixed couple was a table with stacked jars of homemade barbecue sauce. A sign advertised "Roy's of Rose Hill, best BBQ sauce south of KC." It priced different quantities.

"Any samples?" asked Tom, licking his lips.

"Sure enough," the man answered. That's when Tom spotted the bowl of thick, reddish-brown sauce with crackers beside it.

"You'll have to use your imagination of what it's like on half a hog. I've been experimenting on this recipe for three and a half years, and now, finally, it's just right. Perfect. Give it a try. You'll like it."

Tom reached for a cracker and dipped it into the sauce. Both the cracker and paste disappeared into his cavernous mouth. He closed his eyes as he swallowed, then moved his tongue around inside like a vacuum cleaner searching for loose crumbs. He opened his eyes and helped himself to another.

"I like the mix of sweet and spicy flavors. The ketchup and paprika hit the spot. It's good, tasty, and will be perfect on brisket. I'll take three jars."

After Tom paid and was handed a bag with his purchases, he looked across the walkway and saw Jesse staring at him, smiling beneath her sun visor. Blazing side-swept hair covered her left eye, the rest drawn back in her jailhouse ponytail. Silver jewelry that framed her face—large hoop earrings and an elaborate necklace, like a breast plate—reminded him of primitive body armor.

Searching for stray sauce, Tom wiped his mouth with his fingers, then approached Jesse's tent. He gravitated toward her smile, looking for freckles, finding none. Instead, she resembled a delicately painted China doll with reddish cheeks, long dark eyelashes, liner, and eye shadow highlighting her glittering gray eyes.

"Taz! You made it. Thanks for coming!"

"You're welcome. I came to see you and your art. No Popalavata?"

"Hangover, like you said; she wasn't getting up for anything. And we've worked toward this for months!"

"Sell anything yet, or is it too early?"

"It's never too early." Pointing to an unframed abstract acrylic with a black background and red square in its center space, Jesse said, "That one sold first thing to a married couple as I was hanging it. They said it would be perfect in their dining room. They'll pick it up when they leave. What do you think of it?"

"Is it yours?"

"No, Valerie painted it. Do you like it?"

"Not really, but I may need to look at it for a while to appreciate it. I'm here to see your sculpture. Let me look around."

A potential customer squeezed by Tom into the tent's interior and started picking up sculpture, looking at the price stickers on the bottom of each piece. "I'll give you ten dollars for this," she said to Jesse.

"The prices are marked. We don't mass produce this stuff. Each is one of a kind, no blue-light specials, sorry."

"Just askin'," the yard-sale lady said without looking up before hurriedly moving on to the next booth.

Tom watched Jesse from the back of the small booth. When he discovered the barcode tattoo on the nape of Jesse's neck, he knew they had more to talk about than her 3-D art. He was already impressed with her sculpture, all familiar, identifiable animals and people. There was a bust of an alluring, sultry woman with a dove on her shoulder who caught his eye and wouldn't let him go. He'd never felt this from an inanimate object unless you included the pull of music that was as much a companion to him as his comfort food.

Tom wondered how Jesse did this, making a slab of clay into something so real. Transfixed, he looked into the sculpture's sexy eyes and whispered, "Hello, there. How're you doing?" The sculpture, looking heavy yet fragile, returned the greeting. Tom wanted to check her price when he spotted a small sticker beneath her raised shoulder. Printed on it were the letters *NFS*. He frowned momentarily.

"I love this piece. Did you make it?" Tom asked.

"Thank you. Yes, that's Le Chanteuse, or The Singer; she's my idea of a French woman I heard about in a song. She entertains while smoking in a bar."

"Then what do these letters mean? I thought they were initials of the artist."

"Oh, we use the abbreviation *NFS* to tell the customer that the art is not for sale, but after last night I changed my mind. I should have taken the sticker off and put on a price tag. Do you like it? Would you like to take her home with you?"

"Tempting, I'll think about it. My stuff is mostly concert posters. Can you tell me more about how you did it? You say this sculpture was done from a person you imagined in a song?"

"Yes, from my imagination, not from a model or photograph. Most of my work is done that way, although on occasion I work from live models."

"So, you see this person in your head, and then you create her in clay?"

"That's right. I'll ask myself questions ahead of time about how she looks, and then I'll get an answer. Sometimes, though rarely, I'll sketch it first. It's a process that's difficult to explain. Does it sound strange to you?"

"Oh, yeah, ten-four, but it makes sense that you would ask yourself those questions in order to get enough information to begin." Picking up a sculpture of a dog, Tom asked, "What about this dog? Did you know it was a German shepherd when you started on it?"

"On the dogs and cats I usually didn't have a specific breed in mind. I just created the idea of the animal, the feeling of the animal. I was working in a loose way rather than tight."

"I really like the bookend with the shepherd but, sorry, I don't have any use for the other bookend, the cat. How about me switching another dog for the cat so that I'll have a set of dogs? In my opinion, cats are worthless; they don't do anything. You can't go hunting with them, and they can't be trained. They just sit and look at you, or ignore you, and then do their own thing. They don't behave."

"Wow! Tell me how you feel about cats," said Jesse. "Sounds like a control issue."

"Oh, no! I should have kept my mouth shut. I've said too much. Do you have cats? You must have cats. You love cats, and I just insulted a cat person. Well, you know, the cat sculpture is nice looking, very artistic work. If I liked cats, I'd want a bookend that looked just like this one. But to tell you the truth, the best thing about this cat is that it won't screech, scratch, or bite, or assume it's the queen of the universe. It's a good cat. It's under control."

"And what's so good about dogs?"

"Oh, dogs and cats serve a purpose. I've just always had a way with training dogs, especially hunting dogs. For me a dog really is man's best friend. They know when you need cheering up, and they can help you snap out of the blues. Lately, I've been attending agility dog competitions. Someday I plan on having my Lab, Biscuit, compete. Have you ever been to a demonstration or competition?"

"How much is this sculpture of the beautiful lady?" an elderly woman interrupted, another potential customer.

"Five hundred plus tax," replied Jesse.

"She's worth it! I don't have the money, but she's gorgeous! I love her partially closed eyes and that pout. You made her?"

"Yes, thank you. The name of the piece is *The Singer.*"

"Let me look around, maybe I'll get something less expensive. Oh, I love the bookends, especially the cats. Would you consider trading out a dog so I could have two cats?"

Jesse tilted her head, pointed her chin at Tom, and smiled with only her lips—not a glimmer of teeth showing. "I'd be happy to trade out a dog for a cat. Don't you just love cats?"

"How can anyone not love cats?" asked the customer, shrugging and raising her hands with open palms. "A person doesn't own cats. You live with them. They're smarter than dogs. They have a personality beyond slobbering over a tennis ball, and they have a life besides waiting for their so-called master to take them for a walk. I think men have the biggest problem with cats because cats are independent. My first husband never liked cats, and I should have known that the marriage wouldn't work. My mistake was that I listened to my libido, not my cats. Are you married?"

"Oh, no. I've just been out of college for a year. I don't see that happening anytime soon." Again, she looked at Tom. This time she smiled with her teeth.

"Well, my advice is that you take a man home and let your cats decide before you start getting serious. The cats can tell if a man wants to be in charge of the household, meaning you, or if he's open to being a member of the family—pets included. How much for the bookends?"

"They're priced at ninety-nine dollars, but for you I have an art-fair, blue-light special of seventy-five dollars plus tax. Are you interested in taking them home to your feline family?"

"Yes, let me write you a check. Can you package them safely?"

"Oh, sure, I've got plenty of newspaper and a strong cardboard box."

"Ma'am," said Tom, stepping forward, "I'm a friend of Jesse, the artist. If you'd like any help to your car with your purchase, I'd be happy to assist you. I wouldn't want your cats to get broken."

"Well, young man, I just might take you up on that offer. Are you a cat lover too?"

"Let's put it this way, my eyes have recently been opened to the advantages of liking cats. As a man, I'm working on appreciating a cat's independence. They serve their purpose but not a master."

"Aren't you philosophical," remarked the lady. "I'd be happy to have you accompany me and my cats to the car. Just follow me."

Smoke Signals 3

Carl Warrior had graduated, and his best friend Joe Morningcloud was a witness to the miracle. Driving through Lawrence, Kansas, after the ceremony, the young men still sported high spirits.

"Looks like rain," predicted Joe, looking around from the passenger seat.

Carl's opinion differed. "No, just passing over."

"Well, don't wash your car just yet; we'll see," said Joe, standing by his forecast.

"Okay, but I need gas anyway," Carl responded. He abruptly changed lanes and powerfully pulled his dusty, red Camaro into the parking lot of one of Lawrence's look-alike convenience stores. Mimicking the engine's surge, Carl's newly acquired purple and yellow graduation tassel from Haskell Indian Nations University swung from his rear-view mirror and fluttered in the breeze like a festooned kite.

"There's an open pump," urged Joe as new recording artist, Alicia Keys, finished her romantic song "Fallin'." "Regular for a dollar-forty-one isn't bad."

Without speaking, Carl pulled up to the fuel pump, braked, and goosed the gas pedal. The engine roared and just as quickly died as he turned it off, silent as its owner. Only then did Joe observe a vehicle on the other side of the pumps with its open hood giving out smoke signals. It was a sparkling new, black, soft-top Jeep Wrangler, but Joe didn't see anyone in its vicinity. Cocking his head a little to his right, he took in more data from the concrete pavement, noting a puddle of slimy green liquid creeping out from under the front of the wounded vehicle. He stepped out for a closer look. Meanwhile, Carl began fueling.

Joe stood beside the Jeep, watching and listening to its gastric-like groans. During this observation he kept his arms crossed as though he

12

were afraid he might accidentally breach an invisible social boundary. Joe took his eyes off the abandoned vehicle and unconsciously looked at his fingers, rubbing their tips with his thumb. Grease was embedded under the nails of his otherwise clean hands. As he directed his attention back to the Jeep, his face revealed his mind shifting to problem-solving mode and his feet inched closer to the challenge. He popped his knuckles.

"Want to buy a low-mileage Wrangler?" a women's voice beside him inquired.

"Oh, I didn't see you there," Joe answered, surprised, first by her proximity, then by her engaging smile, short golden-blonde hair, blue eyes, and athletic body.

"I know you didn't see me. You were thinking about my Jeep."

"Well, yeah, I'm curious about what happened, and I was thinking about cars I've had that overheated," Joe added.

"This is a first for me."

"Did a radiator hose blow?"

"At first I couldn't see anything but smoke. I thought the engine was on fire! It happened so quickly. This car's almost new. Should it be breaking down already?"

"We can take a closer look now," he said, leaning under the hood and over the engine. The temperature felt like an oven with its door wide open. For a second he compared the heat to that of a sweat lodge at a circle gathering—intense. "Yeah, it's a hose. Old cars, new cars, it happens."

"In new cars? That doesn't make sense."

"I don't have a lot of new-car experience, but they all have their problems. Even newborn babies get sick."

"I talked with the cashier inside. They can sell me gas, junk food, or a ticket to their car wash, but no help with my vehicle."

"Yeah, sounds familiar. If you want a radiator hose, you need to go to another kind of store. But I can fix this for now if it's the only thing wrong."

"Do you really think so? Do you have time to help?" she inquired. "I can call a service company."

"I've got time. Why call Triple A when you've got Uncle Ray?"

"What?"

"Oh, just a saying on the reservation. When you know someone that can fix the car, then why spend the money on a wrecker? Hold on, I'll ask my friend I'm visiting. Here he comes," said Joe, seeing Carl approaching. He carried a jumbo-size soft drink in each hand, and a wad of buffalo jerky protruded from his mouth.

"What's your name?" asked Joe. "I'll introduce you."

"Elizabeth, what's yours?"

"Joe. Nice to meet you."

Carl spoke with an indecipherable, temporary ventriloquist's lisp due to his buffalo jerky. Translated, he said, "Joe, you need another car to fix."

"Found one," Joe answered.

Elizabeth observed Joe's physique. He was muscular and packaged to deliver a punch. His boxer's crew cut contrasted with Carl's long braided hair.

Carl handed one drink to Joe, looked at the woman, and swallowed some jerky. "Looks like a nice Jeep; only the design seems flawed," he said. "Gas mileage can't be too good. The hood being up like that creates some major wind resistance. How's your visibility when you're driving?"

"I'm glad you're having a good day," Elizabeth replied.

"It's a good day to live," responded Carl. "Graduated from Haskell today. We're celebrating."

"Well, congratulations! I go to K.U. We're Lawrence, Kansas, neighbors."

"We *were* neighbors."

"Okay, *were* neighbors. Sounds like you've packed your bags already."

"And topping off the gas tank," Carl concurred. "I'm ready to go home."

After introductions, Carl and Elizabeth conversed while Joe made steady progress on the cracked radiator hose. He had his razor-sharp pocket knife out and was whittling two inches off the defective end of the hard rubber. He planned to reattach the slightly shorter snakelike tube. During the gas pump surgery, Joe said to Carl, "If they don't have a garden hose to hook up, see if you can find a bucket of water to start filling up the radiator."

By the time Carl returned, the Jeep was ready for an invigorating drink. Quenching its thirst after two full buckets, it was soon cooled down and prepared for the road. But its owner was not.

With the Jeep in park, its engine now purring, Elizabeth was giving her thanks for the timely and expert service. She thanked her troubleshooter for his ingenuity and his friend, the funny one, for his conversation. She seemed reluctant to say goodbye.

Speaking to both men, Elizabeth said, "I've already taken up a lot of your time. I know you were on your way to celebrate graduation, but could I buy you lunch just down the street? My treat. It beats the food here. I'm hungry, and I'm really indebted to you."

Carl and Joe eyed each other knowingly and grinned. Facing one another, each made a fist with one hand, raised it up to shoulder level, and as if throwing dice, brought it down to waist level with the thumb extended. In quick succession, they repeated the arm movements, adding the index, then middle finger, while counting in unison: "One, two, three," they whispered, jumped in the air, belly bumped, and roared: "A MAN'S GOT TO EAT!"

●

The waitress read back the lunch orders and disappeared.

"How was graduation?" Elizabeth, the K.U. student, asked Carl, the Haskell graduate.

"It was special for me," answered Carl, "I'm the first one in my family to even attend, let alone graduate from any college. I had some proud—okay, stunned—relatives in attendance and a few back home wondering if it's all worth the trouble. My family tribe drove all the way from Nespelem, Washington. The trip is 1,684.2 miles. Physically, that's six states away; mentally it's much farther—another state of mind."

"Where are they now? Did they go home already?" Elizabeth inquired.

"Oh, no," said Carl. "They'll be at the celebration again tonight. The college has one this time every year. It's called a powwow. Have you been to one before?"

"I have, here at Haskell and Wichita. Will either of you be dancing?" Elizabeth asked.

"Both of us," said Joe. "I brought my regalia."

"The dancers I've seen were dressed in costumes with vivid colors and intricate beadwork," Elizabeth replied.

"You want everything right, it's traditional," Joe said, matter-of-factly, and then added, "I'll dance during at least one session. If you'll go, I'll invite you up to participate."

"I've never done an American Indian dance," replied Elizabeth.

"It's easy," said Joe. "Just do what I do."

"Easy for you to say, but with a good teacher I've got a chance. I won't have to dance backwards in high heels, will I?"

"Don't wear high heels," replied Joe before he recognized her humor.

As they ate their way through their salads, soup, and specialties, they talked about what had brought them to Lawrence. The Wrangler woman shared her family tradition, beginning with her grandfather who attended the University of Kansas. Carl explained that after unsuccessfully starting at another college he was led to Haskell Indian Nations University. It attracted him not only because of its free tuition, but predominately because of its diverse, American Indian, student population and its support system for new arrivals. He was now more confident and prepared to manage a tribal business someday.

Joe noted the scarcity of nearby provisions. The once-full bowl of warm dinner rolls, buried under a starched cloth napkin, was but a memory. Elizabeth wasn't bashful about eating, even though most of her food was an unappetizing, rabbit's garden specialty. But overall, she could pack it down, he thought. His dishware—salad plate, soup bowl, and most recently his dinner plate—once cleared of their contents, had been stolen away by the crafty, pouncing waitress. *Are these dishes needed at other tables?* wondered Joe, as he guarded his last fork and spoon with the pressure of a power lifter's forearm.

Joe explained his lifelong friendship with Carl, who had been closer and more helpful than his own older brothers. He shared that even though Carl was only three years older, he was actually a father figure to him. Despite their geographical distance the last two years, Carl continued to be his guide as he worked toward his dream of being a member of the U.S. Olympic boxing team. "I'm here in Kansas to honor Carl for accomplishing something uncommon among us on the Colville Reservation, a college degree. Congratulations, brother."

"You're making it too, Joe," Carl reminded his companion. "Your boxing is a door opener. Someday we'll be business partners."

"With those muscles," said Elizabeth, "you must train hard."

"I do. It takes work. The long trip here in the van, sitting down so long, was actually a challenge for me. At rest stops I did some running, but it wasn't enough."

The waitress returned with a tray of recommendations for dessert, but Carl interrupted, speaking to Elizabeth. "If you like sweets, you'll have plenty of choices at the powwow later."

"I'm full anyway," she replied, as she quickly raised her hand to her mouth, halting a burp.

Turning to Joe, Carl playfully said, "You didn't come all this way to miss out on some intertribal fry bread, did you?" He thanked the waitress, who turned and walked away, with Joe's eyes hungrily trailing after the dessert tray. He picked up his glass of water and finished it, well aware it was hours before the powwow's grand entry.

"You know fry bread's my weak spot," Joe said, rubbing his stomach, as though he were starving. "So much for my conditioning," he added.

"Fried bread? Like French toast?"

"Greasier and saltier, then you add honey. It plays with your taste buds. We'll get you some if you're going with us," offered Carl.

"You know, I'd like to attend, especially with the two of you. Maybe you can explain some of the cultural traditions behind the dances and costumes. The powerful drumming is amazing, but why isn't there more singing?"

"Here's the first lesson: the dancers usually refer to their outfits as regalia, not costumes," explained Carl. "The powwow is a spiritual gathering with shared food and conversation, with old and new friends, and you're our new friend. You may not always notice, but at each drum there's a lead singer. You're right that not all the dances are accompanied by singing; sometimes the dance itself tells the story, and other times the drumming just overpowers the voices.

"The gathering is interesting because so many different tribes are represented. We're always learning the traditions of others. Just because we're Indian and related doesn't mean we'll know the significance of all the dances. Even though we're members of the Colville Confederated Tribes, our ancestors have traveled different paths. Joe is Nez Perce of Chief Joseph's Wallowa band while I'm Colville and Lakota."

"His parents met at Alcatraz Island during the occupation," said Joe.

"They were visitors, not occupiers," added Carl. "Mom was an urban Indian; Dad was visiting from our rez."

"This is my lucky day," said Elizabeth. "Good thing my car broke down."

"Yes, an all-around special day," agreed Carl. "But sorry, with my family and girlfriend attending, you're pretty much stuck with Joe to talk to tonight. Maybe he'll find the time to tell you about his middle name."

Joe hadn't seen it coming. All he could say was, "Carl . . ."

On cue, taking the bait, Elizabeth asked, "What's your middle name, huh?"

"Oh, Carl needs to be telling you about himself, not about me," cautioned Joe. "Maybe that's why his Indian name is Big Mouth. Please, officially meet Carl Big Mouth Warrior."

Like an older sister breaking up a fight, Elizabeth said, "Come on boys, get along." Turning to Joe she teased, "Your middle name can't be all that bad."

"That depends on who I'm telling. Are you ready?"

"Past ready."

"It's Dancing Feet," said Joe in all seriousness.

"What?"

"Joseph Dancing Feet Morningcloud . . . Happy to meet you."

"Whoa. What a beautiful name! You must be a dancer. Do you have special shoes? Ruby-red slippers?"

"Oh, yeah, real special. My moccasins are wrapped in gray, not red, duct tape. They're from my younger powwow days that Carl was talking about. I'm amazed they even fit. My sister Dawn nearly recycled them into a smelly, rotten purse. You could say I've come out of retirement in order to honor Carl for his accomplishment.

"According to my mother, I earned my name because of my steady kicking while still in her womb," continued Joe. "I was exposed to the beat of tribal drums while still developing. Sometimes I'm surprised I wasn't born holding a turtle rattle. But my father used to give another version. He said that my grandfather Charlie named me later when he saw how quickly I picked up the dance. I'll never know the truth, but I'll always have the stories."

"My first name's Anna," said Elizabeth. "I go by my middle name. I'm jealous; I have such a common name. I was named after some relative I don't even know, an Anna Elizabeth from Rhode Island. Do you think my parents could have been a bit more original? The name Anna seems so plain."

"Yeah, plain like the name Carl or Joe," said Big Mouth. "Maybe someday you'll earn yourself another name."

"It could be a way of honoring your ancestors," suggested Joe. "So, what's your full name?"

"Anna Elizabeth Crandall."

"Sounds important. Were you named after a queen or something?"

"Who knows? Maybe," was her honest response.

"Hey Joe, we're sharing a table with Queen Anna Elizabeth Crandall! How does that feel?" asked Carl.

"Honored!" replied Joe. "I'm feeling really honored to be around important people today." His head nodded, like the slow beat of a drum.

"And I'm ready for some royal treatment at the powwow!" declared Elizabeth. "When do we go?"

The Jayhawk 4

Joe, despite being a visitor to Lawrence, was able to locate Elizabeth's apartment without back tracking. About the time he questioned his visual recall, if he was indeed on the correct tree-lined side street, he saw Elizabeth's four-wheeled friend parked below a giant, weathered cottonwood tree. A once-majestic two-story house still proudly postured behind a wrought-iron fence. It reminded Joe of a residence in Grand Coulee (on the white side of the bridge over the Columbia). Here, before him, two front entrances welcomed visitors from a common raised porch. Elizabeth's converted apartment was accessible from the side of the house, where a steep outdoor staircase ascended to the second floor. It was at the top of these stairs, hours earlier, where Elizabeth had stopped, turned, and waved goodbye after he and Carl had followed her home. Now, as he pulled up to park behind her Jeep—inching closer, just feet away—he noticed the Wrangler's soft rear window was zipped into place. Staring at Joe, centered on the plastic window was a black-on-white, bold bumper sticker with the words: "ALLOW ME TO INTRODUCE MYSELVES." He read it for the second time, focusing on "myselves." He snorted at the humor, thought better of it in case it were true, then wondered how many Elizabeths there really were and which one he would meet next. He found himself eager to learn more about this college-educated white woman whose personality was growing more intriguing by the minute. And . . . she had been to powwows.

After exiting his truck, he unconsciously patted the Jeep like a dear friend and then walked to its front where he bent down, searching the pavement for puddles. Finding it dry, he gave a satisfied sigh and approached the house.

Once upstairs, he found perched on the handrail beside the door to her apartment yet another one of those odd, childlike caricatures; a bird he recognized as the school mascot for the University of Kansas. This one, like all the others Joe had spotted in the last twenty-four hours around town, was colored with a blue body and red head. On its chest were two encouraging words: "Go Hawks!" But *this* wooden likeness had a yellow clothespin representing the bird's beak. Gripped firmly in this was a folded piece of paper identifying Joe as the intended recipient, only it wasn't addressed to him by his first name. Instead, in clearly printed letters, it said, "Dancing Feet." Unfolded, the brief note advised Joe: "Welcome! Dangerous animal on premises. Enter at your own risk. Back shortly. Elizabeth."

This time Joe's face broke into a wide grin, appreciating her playfulness. Yet, despite his belief that this was a joke, he hesitated before opening the screen door. He didn't know what to expect and he liked it. Joe leaned his upper body closer to the entrance, refocusing his eyes, peering past the woven mesh and searching for a clear view inside. There, in the middle of her living room stood a blazing red tent on the wooden floor. It seemed almost alive as its nylon surface pulsated to the rhythmical beat of the ceiling fan overhead. But besides the propeller-like fan, the rippling red, and Joe's rising and falling chest, nothing else in the room stirred. No animal, large or small, was in sight.

Joe grabbed the screen door handle and turned it, prepared for a quiet entry. He thought better of it and knocked deliberately. With his mouth up to the mesh, he called out: "Elizabeth, you home? It's Joe." With no response, he released the catch, pulling the door open far enough to stick his head inside, glancing around for anything resembling a wild, or preferably, tame animal. Joe looked for a dog's food or water bowl as he whistled, and in an encouraging voice said, "Here boy!" Again, nothing in response. Finally, he entered, finding it difficult to take his eyes off the out-of-place, walk-in tent.

From his observation point just inside the apartment's doorway, he became aware of items in the camping tent: a blue, rolled-up sleeping bag, an inviting oversized pillow on top of cushions, an open-faced hardcover book with a flashlight as a bulky bookmarker, and a partially eaten bag of potato chips, its top folded and secured with a plastic clip. Seeing the junk food caused Joe to check in with his internal hunger clock. While sizing up his appetite he smelled the faint aroma of vanilla in the air.

Undecided on whether to sit, stand, or browse, Joe's feet remained planted as he continued his visual journey canvassing the room. One thing for sure about the furnishings: they stood out against the shiny white walls like sculptures on a silent stage. Still, the mismatched furniture couldn't compete with the overpowering red glow of the tent.

Joe wanted to learn as much as possible about Elizabeth before her return, so he continued to survey her possessions on display. He began to his immediate left.

In the corner of the living room was a Cracker Barrel rocking chair. Over it hung a sepia poster of a woman he didn't recognize. Atop her image was a quote: "Never doubt that a small group of thoughtful, committed citizens can change the world. Indeed, it is the only thing that ever has." Then its author, "Margaret Mead (1901–1978)," was identified. Beside the rocker was a flower-patterned couch minus its seat cushions.

A clunky television, reservation-surplus style, rested on a battered trunk in the living room's far left corner. Joe finally moved so he could see the other side of the tent. Against the far wall a closet's sliding door lay horizontally on two thigh-high filing cabinets. The combination functioned as a table, supporting a computer with the screen saver awake and bright. Joe took a half step forward, as if being pulled toward the screen. Elizabeth and a guy her age, tanned, fit, and handsome, were smiling and standing close. Each of them wore a backpack over hiking gear. A sparkling lake with distant mountains or volcanoes completed the picture. It was obvious this was a special moment for the happy-looking couple.

Joe caught himself feeling the weight of a nearby sagging bookshelf that held a substantial number of college textbooks. A hallway began where the bookcase ended and led to Elizabeth's bedroom, Joe surmised. Next, closer, just three steps away, stood a metal chrome kitchen table and three matching chairs colored a shade between rich butter and burning sunshine. Behind this blaze was a rectangular wall opening that resembled a fast-food restaurant's drive-through window without the sliding glass. This perpetually open space began at waist height, part of an extension of the kitchen counter. Finally, to Joe's immediate right, was the kitchen's entrance, welcoming the living room's worn wooden flooring.

Joe stepped over a tire pump and avoided a Ping-Pong ball on his way to the front window. Turning sideways, he slid between the rocking chair and couch where he looked down to the sidewalk and street. He could see his borrowed van and Elizabeth's Jeep through the tree's foliage. Feeling more comfortable in her apartment and with no Elizabeth in view, Joe continued his inspection of the premises, all but forgetting her warning of wild animals. Walking toward the bookcase he stopped to view two worn and faded, cloth wall hangings, each thumb-tacked at their corners. Joe had a strong feeling of their indigenous presence and lively spirit.

The piece of fabric nearest the ceiling had a profile image of some type of bird resembling a hawk sewn into its center. Its visible eye appeared to be staring straight at the viewer as the bird stood with an open beak. Joe couldn't tell whether it was prepared to bite, eat, or speak. Each foot displayed three extended claws. Nearly as large as the bird on the fabric panel were four geometric shapes that resembled four-leaf clovers, Maltese crosses, or a portrayal of smaller exotic birds. If they were birds, their heads and tail feathers were the same shape or form as their outstretched wings.

Joe began an inspection of the second wall hanging, a frontal view of a smiling cat, when two things happened simultaneously. A calico kitten materialized out of nowhere, attacking one of Joe's moccasins, grabbing its shoelace, and pulling it until the single knot came undone. Then, as Joe bent over to watch this playful activity and snatch the kitten from above, the apartment door opened. Elizabeth entered, carrying a bicycle wheel and a cloth bag. Her eyes were sparkling.

"I see you found Gatita, the wild animal! Or she found you. Hope you haven't been waiting long. I ran out of cat food," apologized Elizabeth, as she leaned her bike's wheel against the rocking chair.

Joe stopped breathing and his heartbeat fluttered when he saw her.

"I like your regalia," she added with a smile.

Joe smiled and briefly lifted his foot to display the fringed leggings and moccasins (with no duct tape visible). He tugged down his buckskin shirt. A centerpiece of his regalia was a bone hair-pipe and a brass-beaded breast plate. His short, boxer's haircut was still visible as it had been earlier when he'd first met Elizabeth. Later, at the powwow, he would add his colorful, porcupine-roach headdress. This would trail down from the top of his head to his shoulders.

"Thanks, I've got more parts to put on later. Maybe you can help me."

"Sure," she agreed.

"I've just been here long enough to look around the living room and meet your attacking tiger. What did you call her?"

"*Gatita*, it's Spanish for kitten."

"I think she just woke up. The energetic beast sure likes shoelaces!"

"I'll leave her a dish of this while we're out," Elizabeth said, as she pulled a can of cat food from the bag she'd been holding. She momentarily disappeared into the kitchen, materializing again as Joe viewed her through the kitchen pass-through. "She'll be sleeping again after she eats. I read somewhere that kittens sleep twenty hours a day."

Joe heard the "pop" of the can opening, as did Gatita. The metallic music caused the turbo-charged kitten to race toward the kitchen doorway, sliding into the opening with her back legs soon surpassing the front ones. In an instant, the kitten morphed from a playful pet to a crying baby and back, meowing for her meal. As Elizabeth scooped the cat food into a light-green china dish and placed it on the kitchen floor, she spoke to Joe. "I'll be ready soon. Do you have any last-minute advice on anything I should take to the powwow?"

"They have stadium seating if we don't sit down with the dancers, so we don't need chairs. Carl already gave me our tickets. We'll be invited to buy a raffle ticket or two, but there's no pressure to purchase. Our powwows always have raffles and auctions going on in-between the dancing to help raise money for community projects. The only other thing I can think you might need tonight is a windbreaker. Could rain."

"I'll take my Jayhawk jacket," said Elizabeth. "Are you a K.U. fan?"

"In college sports I'm a Gonzaga Bulldog fan. In professional basketball I follow the Seattle SuperSonics. They have a mascot called Squatch who is supposed to represent Sasquatch or Bigfoot. Now that's a mascot, but I've been meaning to ask someone about K.U.'s Jayhawk. What is it? I've never heard of that bird. Carl's no help."

"You won't find the Jayhawk in *Sibley's Guide to Birds*," she continued. "It's a mythical bird that's half blue jay and half sparrow hawk. The combination of the two means the Jayhawk is noisy and quarrelsome, yet a sneaky hunter."

"Okay, interesting traits. Well, at least the mascot's not a sneaky Redskin or a quarrelsome Indian chief," said Joe, inviting a discussion on Indians and political correctness.

Elizabeth added some history to the mythology. "The term Jayhawk was created about 1848, and used during the 1850s to identify both factions fighting for the Kansas Territory. The question was, 'Would it become a state where slavery would be legal or a free state where slavery would not be permitted to exist?' In the struggle, both sides stole cattle and horses, looted and plundered, murdered unarmed citizens, and burned houses. Despite both contingents being bushwhackers, ambushing one another, the name Jayhawk finally stuck to the Free-Staters. During the Civil War the image of a Jayhawk improved a bit to become a patriotic symbol and first appeared in a K.U. cheer in the 1880s," concluded Elizabeth.

"Did you have to learn Jayhawk history for one of your classes? By today's standards, that background makes the mascot sound pretty violent. Could your mascot be next on the hit list of endangered mascots?"

"Remember, we're talking about a mascot, not a role model," said Elizabeth, pressing a fist to her lips. Joe backed into the living room, giving her room to pass.

"When I'm done telling you about the Jayhawk, you can tell me all about the positive traits of Bigfoot, your wild man mythological mentor," said Elizabeth with a grin.

Joe wondered if he was being quarrelsome, acting like a Jayhawk.

"I didn't have to learn about it, but visitors ask. I think the main thing to remember is that the mythical Jayhawk has its roots in Kansas with individuals fighting for freedom and that it's a fun image, yes, fighting image. It's all about good luck, especially in college sports. Oh, and about selling tons of merchandise for the school, too." Having finished her dissertation, she picked up her purse from the kitchen table, and then her blue and red K.U. jacket from a kitchen chair.

"I'm ready," stated Elizabeth. "Should we go?"

"Almost, or you can tell me on the way to Haskell."

"Tell you what?"

"After looking around your apartment, I've got a few questions. I'm curious about these two wall hangings. They're obviously indigenous, but from what tribe? I don't recognize them. Also, I've got to know why you have your tent set up in here. Does the apartment's roof leak?" asked Joe with a throaty laugh, trying to display a sense of humor as in Elizabeth's bumper sticker and welcoming note. "Oh, and what book are you reading? I saw it inside the tent, but didn't examine it."

Those were the questions he dared to ask. The most important questions, however, would remain unspoken. What Joe really wanted to know was: Who's that guy next to you on the mountain on your screen-saver photo, and what's your relationship? Joe couldn't begin to believe he was thinking about how happy Elizabeth looked with another man. He had just met her a few hours earlier and he was already jealous!

Walking to the wall hangings, Elizabeth explained: "These are called *molas*. They're panels handmade by women from the Guna tribe in Panama, Central America. The textiles are incorporated into the design of the women's shirts or *camisas*, but they're also sold individually like these. I've never been to Panama, but I purchased the art panels last summer when I helped my parents on a medical trip to Guatemala. You like them?"

"Sure do. They have a primitive look to them. But this one here looks like a Jayhawk. They're everywhere!"

"It does. I hadn't noticed that before. About the tent, I got it recently and wanted to get the feel of it," explained Elizabeth as she walked into its close quarters, picked up the book and shoved the bedroll aside. "I'm reading this book in Spanish. It's titled *Donde no hay doctor*. It gives basic medical information to people in Latin America who live in rural areas and may not have access to a doctor."

As Elizabeth put the book back down on the bedroll, Joe, for the first time, noticed the rose-patterned couch cushions that belonged to the bare furniture. He stepped inside.

"It's really comfortable in here, don't you think?" commented Elizabeth, even as Joe, taller, tilted his head to avoid brushing the tent ceiling.

Yes, Joe was feeling really comfortable standing close to Elizabeth, but he knew she wasn't talking about the two of them. "It's comfy," he said as he inhaled the delicious vanilla fragrance radiating from her short blonde hair.

As if on cue to reinforce Elizabeth's remark, Gatita walked proudly into her imperial tent, stopped, and glared at Elizabeth until she returned the bedroll to its proper position. Only then did Gatita complete her mission by stepping up and onto the soft bedroll. The blue sea momentarily engulfed each miniature mitt. She made a full, deliberate rotation, her whiskers hugging her tail, then finally sank into softness. This young princess was ready for yet another nap. Closing her eyes, she whipped her tail once as though dismissing the intruders. "On your way out, don't forget to turn out the lights," her body language commanded.

Elizabeth and Joe took the hint. They were ready to leave. With her K.U. jacket and purse in hand, Elizabeth turned off the lights and the fan, and locked the door twice.

Prank Gone Wrong 5

Prank Gone Wrong?

By Mark Greene, *Cottonwood County News*

"It was only a prank.

"He's just sixteen.

"Tell me, you never did anything like this when you were a teenager?"

Carolyn Odessa, Prairie Grove, mother of a juvenile suspect, was quick to defend, justify, and minimize the behavior of her 16-year-old son. He was caught Friday night fleeing the scene of an incident to which the Prairie Grove Police Department and a city fire investigator responded. The 911 call, received about 9 p.m., originated in the 300 block of East 7th Street, broadcast to emergency responders as "shots fired; house fire."

The first police officer on the scene advised emergency dispatch that the fire department was not needed. The small fire, a paper bag on a resident's porch, was out, but a fire investigator responded and collected evidence.

The 911 caller was a woman awakened by her doorbell ringing then "watched in horror" as flames outside her front window appeared to be engulfing her house as the sound of gunfire erupted outside. She told reporting officers she feared for the safety of her 13-month-old baby who was sleeping in another room.

Preliminary reports recommend the formal filing of two counts of aggravated arson charges.

The paper sack was allegedly set on fire intentionally, causing firecrackers inside the bag to explode on the porch of the reporting party.

The alleged arsonist also received a traffic ticket for attempting to flee and elude officers.

According to Lt. Faye Brown, Officer Tom Jennings, first on the scene, made contact with the reporting party and quickly determined there was no house fire nor armed suspects on the property.

Blocks away, while responding to the residence, Patrol Officer Becka Leigh Razer recognized a vehicle matching the BOLO description broadcast by emergency dispatch. According to Brown, the late model orange Mustang, registered to Shawn Smith and Carolyn Odessa, Prairie Grove, was stopped after a brief chase.

The suspect was interviewed and taken to Intake and Assessment at the Juvenile Detention Center where his parents were called.

The youth was released into parental care late Friday night.

A passenger in the suspect vehicle reportedly ran from the scene and has yet to be identified.

Lt. Brown was not aware of the alleged speeds in the brief chase which took place in the central part of the city. There was no damage to the structure and no injuries according to police and fire supervisors.

Note: This newspaper publication regularly protects the identity of juvenile criminal suspects until they are formally charged by the District Attorney's Office. However, in this report Carolyn Odessa contacted the *News* after reading the online edition and requested she be given the opportunity to be quoted for this evolving story. Dr. Odessa explained the event as a "harmless joke that backfired because of a mistaken address."

Learn more and add your comments at cottonwoodcountynews.com.

Circles Upside Down 6

James sat in an uncomfortable chair among a circle of chairs at the Victim Offender Reconciliation Circles office. He rubbed the back of his neck. His father was positioned to his left, mediator Hameed Khuti to his right. James was quiet as he kept rereading a quotation from a poster on the wall: "An eye for an eye makes the whole world blind. –Gandhi."

Officer Razer walked into the room wearing regular clothes, not her uniform. With Razer were two adults unknown to James. All three were greeted by Nancy, the other mediator.

James held his breath and tried to slow time down as his memory rushed back to the night things happened. He was alternately scared and embarrassed reliving his night of shame, and he was afraid it was about to get worse, not better.

Adults sat down filling all the chairs. James finally met Cindy Walker who looked very pregnant and her husband Jeb who didn't blink or nod; he only glared. James felt the man's jaw clenched so tightly that it morphed into a powerful pit bull unwilling to release James. The boy's primal eyes darted back to the poster and struggled to regain lucidity. He hated being in their cross hairs but grasped for closure to the hunt. Exhausted, ready to capitulate, he sensed hope nearby: his father.

Shawn moved his right arm to the back of James's chair and lightly squeezed his son's shoulder. James glanced to his dad who nodded and mouthed the words, "You'll be okay." His whole body looked encouraging.

James recognized he was surrounded by adults, but he knew that his dad was on his side. He also knew with absolute certainty that, had his mother attended, she would have tried to run the show. Fortunately, as James and his dad prepared to leave the house, his mother received a suspicious death call from emergency dispatch, requesting her skills at the scene. James knew that investigating a death suited her personality much better than being a parent.

Last thing she said to him wasn't good luck or any normal words of encouragement, instead it was her incendiary talk: "If you see Rookie Razer, be sure and tell the darling officer the medical examiner is off to do real police work, not framing innocent children with prefabricated putrid bullshit! Ask her how fair and impartial she is since Cindy Walker is her sister. Funny she forgot to tell us that. Talk about a conflict of interest! The chief agreed with me; she should have never investigated this report. One more thing, tell her to go catch a real criminal."

"Sure, we'll tell her, Mom. Glad you've calmed down. Thanks for your support. We'll miss you tonight. See you later."

The mediators gave a canned speech about their mission and how their purpose was to help victims and offenders deal directly with one another, to make agreements, and to put the dispute behind them. If a consensus couldn't be reached, they would have to send the case back to the courts, but they thought it best to resolve everything as soon as possible.

The white noise of the meeting shifted to a clearer frequency. James picked up the labored breathing of the group. He felt he was under a glaring spotlight. Asked to speak first, he knew the agenda was for him to explain what had happened and how he was part of the incident. He was well prepared because he'd relived the details for months. It was nerve racking but simple: All he had to do was tell the truth, admit it was a mistake, apologize, and his part was over.

James cleared his throat, shuffled his feet, and began. He described receiving text messages from his friends and then discovering the tentacle of toilet paper swaying from his family's trees and decorating their shrubs. He described his mixture of humiliation and exhilaration as he viewed images on YouTube of his house and his new car with their soaped windows and thick layers of shaving cream. He'd been got. But he wasn't laughing when he walked outside and confirmed the images were real, not an altered, Photoshopped video.

When he surveyed the damage, he immediately understood that this was an opening skirmish, that he was expected—no, required—to respond. Once he returned the challenge, he'd post his own results to all his friends, proving himself capable of producing a better, more creative prank. That's why he'd crammed so many firecrackers into the gasoline-soaked bag filled with newspaper; he wanted a shock-and-awe show. It was about get-back. It was about respect. He had to outdo what had been done to him. He had to prove himself like graffiti taggers, that he was no punk. The worse he did, the better he'd be. And it had to be documented. That's why he had asked for assistance from his wing man. He wanted a dependable steady hand on the camera.

With cold eyes, Jeb Walker asked: "How could you firebomb the wrong house, any house?"

"It wasn't a firebombing," Shawn defended his son.

"It was a gasoline bomb used to create fear in my family." Jeb continued. "It was arson. Just because you got the wrong house doesn't mean it wasn't a crime."

Mediator Hameed spoke up: "Okay, give James an opportunity to respond. He has the floor. You'll get your chance."

"Well, I got the wrong address," explained James. "The house I was trying to locate was on west seventh, not east. I'd never been there before, and it wasn't a bomb. I wasn't trying to destroy the house or hurt anyone. I was trying to surprise them."

"Fireworks are explosives," responded Jeb. "The fire was aggravated arson." Raising his voice, with flared nostrils, Jeb declared, "You know you could have killed my wife and children!"

"Honey, we promised each other for the sake of the baby to not get upset. No shouting, remember? Please," Cindy told her husband.

"I wasn't going to hurt anyone," stated James. "The newspaper and paper bag were the only things on fire. I dropped the bag on the concrete porch."

"So you never planned on the flames catching the dry pine needles on fire?" questioned Jeb. "You never planned on the hot ashes being blown onto our roof or in the gutters that held combustible leaves? You never intended to burn our house down? Funny, you never planned on getting the wrong house, but you did, didn't you?"

"Well, the fire was never out of control," James responded.

Jeb jumped up from his seat, leaned into James and screamed: "AND YOU NEVER PLANNED ON KILLING OUR UNBORN BABY?"

Shawn stood up, too. He raised his arm upward like a traffic cop at a busy intersection during a power outage, and shouted, "HOLD ON!" Jeb stopped. Shawn looked at Nancy and promised, "If he yells anymore, we're leaving. We avoided court for this? Are inflammatory accusations part of mediation?"

"Both of you, sit down," directed Nancy. "Facts and feelings are appropriate here, but we want this to be a safe setting for everyone. Jeb, your anger at James is understandable, but I think we can all agree that there was no intention to kill anyone. What do you need from James besides an apology? He's explained what he did and why he did it, how he got the wrong address, and that he felt the fire was under control. He admits to intentionally setting the fire, but says he didn't intend to harm your wife or her pregnancy."

James looked to Jeb and said, "My parents told me that a doctor's exam showed the baby was fine." Before Jeb could reply, James looked at Cindy's big belly, raised his blinking, questioning eyes to hers, cocked his head to the side like an old man with one good ear and asked, "Isn't that right?"

Jeb threw up his hands and spoke to his wife. "Honey, you tell him. He's not getting it."

"James, your parents did pay for my doctor's exam, and—no thanks to you—our baby looks to be doing well," explained Cindy as she smoothed her dress over her stomach while massaging her belly. "But we're here to tell you what you've done to our lives. Your prank turned our world upside down. I was already stressed, under doctor's orders to get plenty of bed rest and to not strain myself. The night you set the fire I'd fallen asleep on the couch in the living room. When I heard the doorbell, I woke up to see flames jumping outside the front window, and I panicked. I had to get Makaley out of the house, but she was barely walking, and I had orders to not lift anything heavy. I didn't know what to do! What do you think you would have done under the circumstances? If you can, put yourself in my situation; what would you have done? If I carried Makaley out of the house, I could have miscarried."

"I . . . I . . . no one told me this part." James turned to Shawn. "Dad, did you know this? I didn't know. I never thought about anything like this . . . I didn't mean for anyone to get hurt." Looking at Cindy, he said, "I wouldn't have ever done this if I'd known it was your house or you might lose your baby. It was just supposed to be a harmless get-back joke for YouTube. This was meant as a joke, but it turned into an accident that should have never happened."

"What would you have done if you were me?" repeated Cindy.

"I suppose I would have looked more closely at the fire and seen that it was only a bag on the porch and that the house wasn't burning down.

I might have used the garden hose to put it out if it was still going, but it was going out pretty quickly."

"And the gunfire I heard? What about that?"

"I guess I would have known it was firecrackers."

Cindy raised her voice. "Well I didn't know it was a little joke fire, and I didn't know they were firecrackers. You knew because you did it. Remember, I was asleep inside my house, on our property. I think you see things as no big deal, and we see them as life-altering events. Our children are everything to us, and you put them at risk.

"If what you did is acceptable behavior for teenagers today, then we're all in trouble. If so, we're wasting our time trying to get you to see how we think, what we've been through. You post a video and impress your friends. If others are hurt, so what, you got your pictures. Maybe I'm naive; I need to believe that most teenagers aren't harming innocent people just to impress their friends. I just don't understand. I never set fires when I was younger . . . Jeb?"

"I'm a correctional officer at the prison. Prior to the night of the firebombing, I'd been threatened by some gangbangers—that if I testified to their drug distribution, me and my family could get hurt. Your prank was no prank to us. On our radio at work I heard emergency dispatch broadcast the call to our house. I didn't know it was firecrackers. I didn't know it was a paper bag on fire. I thought it was gangbangers killing my family.

"You've helped ruin us, boy. We're not the same people we were three months ago. We're unsure of our future, and we want it back." Jeb's voice gained volume and intensity. "You have no idea what you've done to our family! You still think this is a little harmless prank—a joke we should forget. Believe me, it's no joke, and it's impossible to forget! That's why we agreed to meet with you, to try and get you to see that pranks have consequences. A prank to one person may not be perceived that way by others. Do you get this? Do you understand? We never agreed to be participants in your challenge game. You want to be accepted. We want to be left alone."

"Yes, yes, I do understand!" asserted James as tears formed in his eyes. "I never intended for anyone to get hurt, and I'll never do anything like this again, promise! I'm sorry, I'm really sorry. I'm not a bad person. I made a mistake. I'm sorry." He put his forearm over his eyes and sniffed loudly.

"James, come over here, sit down," beseeched Cindy. Nancy silently stood up and exchanged places with James. The teen sat directly to the right of Cindy but he was still next to his father. She grasped his left wrist, and as the group watched she slowly raised it and placed his hand on her belly.

With raised eyebrows Jeb questioned his wife. "Honey, are you sure? This is personal . . . family."

Everyone waited for Cindy to speak, but she had already spoken. Her hand covered the boy's hand.

James didn't move. He closed his eyes. He felt the heat of the flames from the house and heard the popping of automatic gunfire as he escaped into the night. He again heard the police siren and saw the bright, colored flashing lights in his rearview mirror. He felt the pebbles on the pavement dig into his forehead while being handcuffed.

As tears rolled down his cheeks and snot from his nose, James cried and spoke to Cindy. "I feel the baby moving! He's moving, I mean, he's really moving!" James turned to Jeb. "He's alive! He's real!" Jeb softened and exhaled, his shoulders collapsing and his jaw relaxing. At last, things were real to the boy. They were real.

Officer Razer got her turn to speak. "When I stopped your Mustang, I was ready to shoot you. I expected you to be armed and for you to use your gun. I thought you had hurt my sister and Makaley. But when you cooperated, I learned that you were just a scared teenager out having fun. I know you were just as surprised as we were. How did it feel to have guns pointed at you?"

"Yeah! I was really scared! I felt like I was being treated like a criminal, like I was dangerous, down on the ground with my face in the street, and handcuffed. That's when I realized it wasn't a joke. I've learned from this. A prank may not be harmless. It can cause unintentional, serious injuries. That's what I've learned. Thanks for not shooting me Officer Razer. I'm sorry to you, too."

"Officer Razer," said Shawn, "let me second that. Thank you for using restraint the night you stopped my son. After hearing the whole story, I don't see your response as an overreaction."

Nancy prepared the participants for the last portion of the meeting. "All we have left now is to be clear on an agreement, get it written down, and signed. Walkers, tell me if this is correct: You don't want any restitution; instead, your desired outcome is to understand what motivated James; you both want to be assured that this will never happen again—not just to you but to anyone else in the community."

"I agree to all of that—never again," said James with a slow smile.

"We're good," said Jeb with a crisp nod.

"Do you need anything from the Walkers?" Hameed asked James.

"I may not deserve it, but I'd appreciate an opportunity to visit the Walkers, especially after the baby's born," said James.

"Talk to them," Hameed directed.

"I'd like to visit and meet your children someday soon," James said to Cindy and Jeb. "I'd be good to them. Maybe I can help with some yard work, raking leaves, and cleaning the pine needles or leaves out of your gutters. I promise I'll call in advance, no surprise visits at night, and I'll leave my lighter and firecrackers at home!"

"Give us some time to think about that," stated Jeb. "We'll call, but it won't be until we're back home with our new baby. Right now the baby comes first."

"Yeah," agreed Cindy, "I want to have this baby soon and get my hormones figured out before inviting a teenager to our house! We thought we had plenty of time, years before we needed to confront the challenges of sensation-seeking teens in our home. But that's all changed now. Thanks to you our lives have been turned upside down."

Wild Horse Adoption Program 7

Joe Morningcloud and his twelve-year-old daughter, Suanna, walked through the well-manicured prison grounds to enter the horse barn. They each took a deep breath, enjoying the familiar smell of caramel hay with its scent of Vidalia onions. But they were unprepared for what they heard next—the sound of laughter. They followed it until, in the distance, through the south entrance, they saw the outdoor arena with a half-dozen blue-clad men mounted on horses. They stopped and watched, not wanting to interrupt what seemed like training or competition.

That's when Joe noticed two, white, plastic barrels inside the muddy corral. Good-natured yelling mixed with laughter continued, and his eyes focused on one long-legged, broad-shouldered cowboy on a horse. He was trying to rip a soccer ball away from another rider, who carried it low like a half back in football, charging through the opponent's line for tough yards from scrimmage. These men were inmates, working outside the prison walls training horses. Their work was dangerous, but they were playing a game and having fun.

Joe smiled and moved closer. What was this game, and what were the rules? The horseman with the ball and shoulder-length dark hair had his mount intercepted by an aggressive opponent, forcing him away from the nearest barrel, apparently the goal. That's when, for the first time, the offensive player rose up in the saddle and, with back erect, revealed the contour of her breasts. She was no cowboy! Holding the soccer ball in one hand, she yelled at a teammate and threw him a high-arcing over-handed pass. After an easy catch, her colleague galloped toward the goal, stopped a few feet from the open barrel, and lightly tossed the ball in for a score. The result was sporadic cheering from his team and suppressed smiles from the other.

Suanna recognized her rodeo idol. "Dad, it's KD!"

"Good Lord! That's her! Maybe she'll have time to talk to you. If Dusty's here, he can make it happen."

Suanna, dressed in her western gear—including black cowboy hat, blue long-sleeve shirt, blue jeans, and boots—walked directly to the fencing closest to where KD and her horse were participating in the game.

The slim newcomer disrupted the flow of the game. She stood out with her straight, shoulder length, white hair, and very pale skin. The mounted men hesitated and looked again.

Joe watched the arena from a distance. Gradually, he understood more of the rules to the peculiar game, but he reminded himself that he hadn't come to be entertained. He began to observe the horses, not the players, with a critical eye. The purpose of his visit was to see what new mounts would be part of the annual public sale in the wild horse adoption program.

Around the arena, three families, a young couple, and two bearded Amish men studied horses on display while inquiring about their conformation, skills, personalities, and habits. These dozen or so horses stood inside the arena, facing outwards, each one saddled up with their lead rope tied to the corral, ready to be ridden. Joe began his inspection of the attractive Mustang, a bay paint gelding immediately in front of him, judging its well-proportioned and alert body. Held up high, the horse's head spoke volumes, ears forward, nostrils open, receptive to all scents. The rest of his body was in alignment: still, confident, with attentive, not fearful eyes.

After the visual assessment, Joe began to read the poster taped on the corral post nearest the horse. When Joe saw the photo and description, he couldn't help himself; being on prison grounds made him think of wanted posters at the post office, escaped convicts, and TV's *America's Most Wanted*. Then he thought of the journey these animals had taken and how they had been forcefully separated—kidnapped from their families.

Joe knew from experience that both horses and people sometimes had comparable histories and similar characteristics. Both could be peaceful on the outside, but below the surface were potentially dangerous. These guys, the humans around him, didn't seem unsafe, only ordinary—like people he knew who enjoyed riding and connecting with their four-legged friends. But the inmates were, he supposed, on their best behavior. He started whistling; thinking that any day in or out of prison had to be a hundred times better when you were on horseback. On top of that, the bonus was improving communication between you and your horse, developing skills as a rider, and establishing deeper trust in one another.

Joe blinked and again focused on the poster. The laminated picture identified the bay as Muster, a three-year-old with a height of 14.1 hands. Muster was from a capture site at Elko, Nevada. The horse had been in training for only six months and was available for adoption. Muster gave Joe a head-nod, blinked, and whipped his full tail.

As Joe moved to the next available adoptee, a deep chestnut gelding, he overheard a conversation between a man who was a prospective buyer and one of the inmate horse trainers, one whom Joe hadn't previously met. Dressed in familiar denim, work boots, and a red ball cap, he sounded nervous but straightforward. As he spoke, it was as if his words were racing to the finish line.

"It all depends," the trainer answered quickly. "There's no set amount of time it takes to train these horses. It all depends on the horse and the trainer. Everyone's got a different temperament and experience. I've only been at this four or five months, but some of the trainers have been doing this for three, four, five years."

"When you say the horse is trained, what does that include?" asked the visitor. "Is he safe to ride?"

"Before we put the horse up for adoption, it must meet our minimum standards. These are easy mounting and dismounting, knowing the basic commands to walk, trot, and lope, turning in any direction, stopping and backing up on command, and being able to pick up all four feet. We also make sure they'll load and unload from a four-horse trailer," concluded the trainer.

"I don't know that we'll ever have a four-horse trailer," the prospective customer responded, "But I can dream!"

"Me too," the inmate echoed. "On the street I don't even own a horse, but I'll get me one after I'm out and on my feet, that's for sure," he promised. "Since I've trained Slick, who's from the Sweetwater, Wyoming, area, I can tell you a little more about his progress. He picks up his feet really well and has a good stop. He's easy to saddle and is just downright eager to please. Slick's an all-around good horse."

"How about safety? Are these trained wild horses more dangerous than those that have been domesticated longer?"

"First off, I'm not sure there's such a thing as a safe horse. Horses can get scared of things and be uncooperative without us understanding the problem, as they see it. Yeah, you can buy a horse that's been ridden for ten years, obeys commands, and never has thrown anyone; then one day he gets chased by a swarm of bees and tries to jump a fence. These here horses are closer to wild, but I like to think of them as smarter than your average horse. Mr. Davis, that's him over there in the cowboy hat, tells us that they're better communicators than most other horses. The secret is being able to pick up their language. I'm learning more every day. You might want to ask Mr. Davis the question you just asked me about safety. He's the expert. Sorry I didn't give you a better answer."

"Oh, it was a great answer! I know there are no guarantees when riding horses, and I don't want my boy to spend his entire life sitting at home in Bubble Wrap."

Joe liked what he heard. Ol' Dusty did a fine job of getting these young men, many former drug addicts, trained to be trainers. He'd heard some pretty amazing stories in the decade Dusty had been supervisor. Joe just figured that any work detail training horses would have men that already knew a thing or two about them. Dusty said that well over half the men requesting his work detail had never been on a horse in their lives. Yet it was near impossible to get any of them to admit it until some time had passed—until they'd become successful veteran trainers.

Out of the six horses involved in the center of the arena and the dozen other horses on show, one really caught Joe's interest. It was an Appaloosa. Smaller and leaner than most, it was brown with white coat patterns from the hip to the base of the neck. From a distance the four-year-old mare with this "blanket" pattern might fool a poor-sighted novice into believing she was ready for a saddle. Out of all markings, this was the one Joe liked best, especially the spots inside the blanket pattern which reminded him of a real hole or tear in one of his well-used work blankets.

The one weakness of the mare was her sparse mane and tail. The rat tail trait was usually bred away. But what she lacked in fullness of hair she more than made up for in friendliness, reminding Joe of the horse he had examined earlier, Muster, who had also shown eagerness to communicate. This one—Joe checked the nearby poster—was named Kola. Her reaching muzzle and soft eyes appealed to him. Joe was feeling as relaxed as Kola when he acknowledged further data from the poster. Kola hailed from the capture site of Harney, Oregon.

Today's northeastern Oregon was once the center of his People's country, the Niimiipuu, commonly known as the Nez Perce people. Could Kola be a descendant from the extensive Niimiipuu herds known to number in the thousands and to have been meticulously bred? It was possible; this Appaloosa could be a descendant of Appaloosas from the herd of old Chief Joseph before the land of the Niimiipuu in the Wallowas was seized by the U.S. government and distributed to white settlers.

"I'd like to put your name on her, but she'll be in the sale tomorrow, starting at $746; that includes the adoption fee, feed, and training," the voice from behind bellowed.

In good spirits, turning to face the familiar voice, Joe welcomed Dusty. "That's a lot of money for a wild horse!"

"How many times have I told you, there are no wild horses!" roared Dusty, chuckling loud enough to interrupt the arena game.

"How are you, Dusty? You're looking good! Must be the young blood you have around here. Or maybe it's that playful female you hired since my last visit. What's with you? Asking for trouble? You know cowboys aren't going to leave her alone!"

"Hey, I couldn't have kept her from this job if I'd wanted to. Haven't you heard? We have female teachers, counselors, and guards. What's to keep a young cowgirl from assisting an old cowboy training horses?"

"How do the inmates treat her?"

"With respect; she don't know how to back down."

"Glad to hear it. Hope she works out."

"She will as long as she wants it. Knows what she's doing, that's for sure. Raised rodeoing in Abbyville."

"My daughter recognized her the minute she laid eyes on her. We've watched her compete in Abbyville and at Pretty Prairie."

"Yep, Kiley goes by her initials, KD."

"Okay then, so you do have a professional working for you. I can tell she knows a lot about horses from watching her compete. My daughter wants to be just like her. I see Suanna's talking to her right now." Joe nodded toward the pair on the other side of the corral.

"Your daughter is growing like a weed! When was the last time you were here?"

"Just a year ago."

"KD's been here going on six months, but I think she's pining for the circuit. We'll see if she lasts the summer. I'm thinking she's struggling with an out date."

"Now, about this Appaloosa, how's she responding to the training? You have anyone worthwhile on her?"

"My best man, Johnny; you know him; been around here a couple three years."

"That's him playing in the arena, isn't it?" asked Joe, as he pointed with a nod. "And where did this game come from? What do you call it?"

"Slow down partner, have you been putting more than cream in your coffee? One question at a time. Yeah, that's Johnny on Trigger. The game just kind of got started a few months ago when a horse was nuzzling the ball around a pen, and no, it has no name. I've asked."

"It's got to have a name. You guys sit around, look at one another and say, 'Hey, you want to play that game, the one with the soccer ball?' Then the other fellow politely responds 'Yeah, the one where you score a goal by throwing the ball in the barrel. Yeah, I'd like to play.'"

"HEY GUYS!" yelled Dusty in his booming voice. The horse players stopped. "What do you call the game you're playing? What's the name of it?"

The response was unrehearsed. Every last one of them looked at Dusty like he was asking them to confess to a felony crime. They raised their shoulders, rolled their eyes, and snarled with upturned lips. "We don't call it nothin'," one cowboy answered.

"There you have it, Joe." Dusty shrugged.

Moving on to business, Joe asked, "Do you think this Appaloosa will be purchased early tomorrow?"

"You want her?"

"I don't need her."

"Yeah, but you want her. She may be available for you. Most buyers want a full mane and tail. Of course you know how it is; all it takes is two people wanting the same horse."

"Right."

"We'll know tomorrow. Joe, I'll introduce you to KD later, but if you can take a few minutes I'd like you to meet my newest trainee. His name is Shade, David Shade. He's from Oklahoma, claims to be Cherokee, doing time out of Coffeyville. He's black, African American. I want you to tell me what you think of him."

"How come?"

"I just want you to meet him and tell me what you think."

"Sure, I'll meet him."

"He'll be out in a minute; on the crew in the barn getting ready to feed. About to close down this horse-and-pony show and get ready for tomorrow's sale."

"We'll be back tomorrow."

"Here comes Shade."

Approaching from the barn was a hay wagon being pulled by a gently sputtering four-wheeler with three young men walking alongside it. One was black and bearded with braided hair. Like the others, he wore the standard prison blues but no ball cap.

Just then, Joe smelled onions.

As the men came abreast of Dusty and Joe, the former raised his head like a horse, signaling Shade out with his eyes, calling him over with his chin, a twitch, and a nod. "Shade, got someone for you to meet; claims he's Indian."

Joe darted a look at Dusty; he saw nothing but poker face, then returned his attention to Shade. The inmate's stone-like features matched his laminated photo ID clipped to his shirt pocket. "Good to meet you, Mr. Shade. My name's Joe Morningcloud."

"I'm David Shade," he said without visible emotion, every muscle of his mouth remaining neutral.

"I'll talk to you later," advised Dusty, then turned and walked toward KD and Suanna. KD had dismounted and was visiting with Suanna through the fence. When he heard KD giving the young girl advice, he stopped and decided not to interrupt. To their right, he noticed a family taking photos of Dancer, a high-strung two-year-old. He walked in that direction, knowing Suanna was in good hands.

•

"Yeah," said KD, "there's a big difference between Junior Rodeo and Junior High School Rodeo. It gets more competitive. As far as glasses, I wore them the first couple of years, but now I wear contacts. Did you know that?"

"No, I had no idea," said Suanna as she adjusted her prescription sunglasses.

"What you really need is an intelligent horse with good vision. The right horse can make anyone look good, regardless of the rider's eyesight. If you keep practicing, you're going to get better."

"I've got an intelligent horse," said Suanna. "Are you going to be participating in the Abbyville Rodeo?"

"I'm planning on it. Will you be there?"

"Yes. I want to enter in the barrel racing."

"I'll always like the barrels, but lately my favorite event is breakaway roping."

"KD, I want to grow up to do what you do, only in Washington, not Kansas."

"Why Washington?"

"My dad grew up there on a reservation. They have a rodeo every year. We visit."

"Oh yeah, Washington's got rodeos," KD agreed.

"KD, you've shown me that someday I can get a real job riding horses and still compete in rodeos. I can do both. It must be a dream come true for you."

"Yeah. My life's pretty amazing. Praise God!"

•

"I claim to be Nez Perce," said Joe. "You?" he asked Shade.

"I claim Cherokee Nation, but it no longer claims me," answered Shade.

"Freedmen?" asked Joe.

"Yes sir, you've heard of us?"

"An author I read, Sherman Alexie, likes to say two Indians can't have a conversation without the word sovereignty coming up, even though we can't spell it. Yeah, I know Freedmen."

"Are you and Mr. Davis joking about you claiming to be Nez Perce because you sure look Indian?"

"You know how it is, we joke about things to keep our sanity. When outsiders do it, it's not so welcome. I'm a full-blood, Nez Perce. I've lived away from my people at Nespelem fourteen years. The Nez Perce of Chief Joseph's Band is a member of the Colville Confederated Tribes Reservation in Washington. Have you heard of us?"

"No, I don't think so, but I know of the Nez Perce. I thought your reservation was in Idaho."

"The rez is. After our heroic battles in 1877, my relatives weren't allowed to return to their ancestral grounds in northeast Oregon or to the reservation established in Idaho. We were imprisoned and banished to the Indian Territory before it became Oklahoma. Several years after being exiled to *eeikish pah*, meaning the 'hot place,' we were permitted to move to the Colville Reservation, not our own. Where are your people?"

"Most of my family are in the 'hot place,' Oklahoma, around Tulsa. I'd been living in Tahlequah and working construction until I got into trouble. My capture site was Coffeyville."

"What about your people before then?" prompted Joe.

"My grandfather knew our Shade family ancestors back to the Georgia days, to 1803, but there it gets murky. The name Shade is Cherokee. Our ancestral names are lost. In 1839, the African American Shades participated in the Cherokee removal, 'the trail where we cried,' but by then my people were freedmen, not slaves. As you may know, in 2007, the Cherokee Nation voted to change the Constitution. Even though we are listed on the Dawes Rolls, the Nation declared that black descendants of Cherokee slaves with no proof of Cherokee blood were no longer citizens of the Nation. But many of us have more Indian blood in us than the ones kicking us out. This is the side of sovereignty that puzzles me."

"I'm sorry you've had something taken away from you that matters . . . that's important," said Joe. "How much does a vote change who you are?"

"Since I was little, growing up in Oklahoma, I've identified with my Indian side despite my color. It was something that made me special when I didn't feel special. When someone shut me out, I still belonged. It made me better, never worse . . .

"My parents told me to be proud of my race, to remember the Cherokees held us in slavery. I wouldn't listen to them, and they saw me more and more as troubled in the head and weak of heart . . ." Shade took a deep breath and continued, "Eventually I felt like I didn't belong anywhere—my membership had been taken away. It was inevitable. My parents and I had a shout down where my father called me racist, and I called him worse.

"I got in my car, but didn't go to my apartment and didn't care anymore. I was homeless. There was hate in my heart . . . and the rage within me began to surface. I got drunk. I was drunk and dangerous. Life didn't matter. Later, after the wreck, I learned I killed two people, a mother and her two-year-old daughter. I T-boned them—hit their car broadside. They didn't have time for a prayer . . . yet I survived.

"I don't remember, but I can't forget . . ."

Shade's face had shifted from marble to malleable clay, his hardened expression showing softer lifelines. He leaned forward, closer to Joe, and calmly asked, "Why are you here?"

"To listen. Dusty wanted me to listen."

"I didn't mean to tell you this. Somehow it just came out . . . broke loose."

"I'm glad I could be here. Is there anything else you need to tell me?"

"I'd like to be in your boots. You've voluntarily removed yourself from your Colville Confederated Tribes, while I've been forced out. I'd give anything to be welcomed back by my tribe."

"We relocated here for medical reasons and to be near my wife's family, but a bigger reason was that . . . I didn't feel worthy."

Shade laughed at his crazy world. "You don't feel worthy enough to participate in your tribe, and my tribe doesn't believe I'm worthy enough to be a part of them."

"Yeah, they call that ironic, but let's just leave it at that for now," said Joe. "We can talk more another time."

"Okay," said Shade. "Thanks for listening and for helping me."

"Well, good. You got me thinking about what's important right now in my life, so we're even. Let's talk again."

"One last thing, you wanted to know what we call the game we play with the soccer ball, when we're on our horses. We call it horseplay."

"Oh! I like it. Horseplay. That's a proper name."

"We're allowed to play sports in the yard and in the gym—baseball and basketball—but there are signs everywhere warning us, telling us, 'No Horseplay.' Sometimes, here, while we work we can have some fun. When we get a chance, we horseplay."

Snow White 8

School lunch was over. As Suanna exited the hallway door that opened onto the playground, she put on her sunhat and eyed the unoccupied swings. Just as she started running toward them in order to claim two seats, one for her and the other for her best friend Holly, she was ambushed by hate.

"Hey, Loser! Snow White!" Terri yelled at Suanna. "Where's your dwarf girlfriend?"

Suanna was alarmed by Terri's presence, but not by her insults. Sadly, she was used to them. Suanna tried to ignore Terri while visually scanning the area for allies, most notably the recess teacher who was not outside yet. She also observed Terri's nearby matching robots, a cheering gallery of two: Amanda and Tiffany.

"Loser, no one likes you except for the dwarf," Terri continued.

Suanna didn't respond, but she didn't back down, either. Although Terri was a sixth-grade student, just like Suanna, the bully was taller and thicker.

Little kids streamed out of the nearby doorway, immediately running and screaming at temporarily being set free on a beautiful spring day.

Where's Mrs. Lundy? thought Suanna. *She's usually outside by now.*

"You think you're so smart in class, but you're stupid!" said Terri. "You're stupid to think the teachers can protect you everywhere."

Suanna remained alert but silent.

"Your only friend is going to abandon you. Let's say we've come to an understanding with her."

"If you've hurt Holly, you're going to be sorry!" promised Suanna. "What have you done to her?"

"You'll find out soon enough."

"Tell me what you've done!"

"Listen, Blind Albino, you're a loser. First, you savages lost your land to civilized people. Now you've lost your last friend. Sure hope she doesn't get hurt because of you."

Suanna took a boxer's stance with her feet strategically apart; her arms were raised to chest level, each hand a balled up fist.

Terri ignored Suanna's postioning, knowing that Suanna wouldn't dare hit her. "You can't even get your color right," said Terri. "Indians are supposed to be red, but you're so white that if you weren't wearing clothes, you'd never be found in a snowstorm. Your new name is Chief Snowflake!"

In a blur, Suanna led with a left jab and followed with a solid right hook to Terri's jaw. The big girl went down to her knees while instinctively grabbing at her chin. Amanda and Tiffany gasped. They stepped forward to defend Terri, but it was over.

Students nearby on the playground stopped and stared at the fallen bully. Mrs. Lundy appeared and inquired, "What is going on? Are you hurt, Terri?"

Terri shook her head in a sideways no. Following Terri's lead, Amanda and Tiffany declined to give any details as to what had happened. But soon, younger students competed with one another to tell the teacher what they had observed: Suanna had hit Terri in the face.

Then, a teacher's aide took charge of the playground duties while Mrs. Lundy escorted Suanna and Terri to the office.

On the way to Principal Allison's office, Suanna asked Mrs. Lundy two questions.

"Do you know where Holly is?"

"I haven't seen her," the teacher replied.

"Is Officer Jennings at school today?" Suanna asked before the threesome arrived at their destination.

"Let's see," said Mrs. Lundy, "No, we had to move his classes because of playday, so that means he's scheduled to be back tomorrow."

At the office Mrs. Lundy explained to Secretary Jeanette that the teacher needed to talk to Mr. Allison. As Suanna and Terri took their seats, Jeanette agreed to watch the two separated students while they awaited court with Principal Allison. Mrs. Lundy entered his inner office and closed the door behind her.

•

Suanna thought about a lot of things while she was waiting. Her hand hurt. She knew she needed an ice pack, but figured it could wait. She was concerned about Holly being safe and she imagined the response of her parents once they learned that she had slugged Terri. Suanna also kept thinking about Officer Jennings. She wished he was with her. She liked and respected him. She knew he would be disappointed with her because she hadn't followed his classroom advice on peacefully resolving conflicts.

Officer Jennings was more than a teacher and police officer to Suanna. He was a friend, and the Lord knew she didn't have many of them. She liked how Officer Jennings was approachable and always willing to listen to her. Suanna kept reminding herself that once she talked with Officer Jennings or her father, that everything would be better than it seemed. But first she needed to participate in Mr. Allison's inquiry.

Suanna decided she would tell the truth, but she wasn't prepared to share everything. Mr. Allison didn't need to know that only her father called her Snowflake. It was his endearing name for her because she was as beautiful and unique as a snowflake. He would remind her of this whenever she complained about being different than everyone else.

After a few minutes, the principal's office door opened and Holly exited.

"Holly!" shouted Suanna, as she jumped to her feet. "Are you okay?"

"Suanna! Are you hurt?" asked Holly as the smaller girl observed Suanna cautiously resting her right hand in her left.

"I'll be okay," said Suanna. "Did Terri hurt you?"

"No, just more of her threats," replied Holly as she shot a glance at Terri, who passively rubbed her jaw.

"Suanna," said Mrs. Lundy, "Mr. Allison will see you now."

Bullying 9

From School Resource Officer Tom Jennings' point of view, his K-9 duties and the Adopt-a-School program had helped him keep his sanity when he sometimes butted heads with the police administration. He religiously visited his school one day a week, every week, during the school year when he was on day shift. Because patrol officers rotated shifts every few months, each adopted school had two officers assigned to it. That way when one cop was on nights, the other one would be available to visit classrooms during the day.

Jennings had signed up for Lincoln Elementary School because his children, Julia and Hannah, had attended it since kindergarten. Tom claimed it was a "win-win" situation. His daytime visits allowed him to see his girls more often, and both the school and the department benefited by him already knowing a lot of the students and staff.

•

Officer Jennings, while driving to Suanna's school, reviewed what he had heard about her fight. It didn't make sense to him and he wanted answers. The Suanna he knew from visiting classes was every teacher's ideal student. She'd been actively involved in class discussions; she was intelligent and on task, a person who spoke from her experience and from her heart. This could not be the same person who would deck someone! Her aggressive act represented a seismic shift comparable to ongoing earthquakes in Kansas. Something wasn't right.

Jennings planned to get to the bottom of this, and soon. He'd seek out the teacher, the principal, and Suanna. Despite his partiality, he'd be fair to the circumstances. He intended to get the rest of the story and hoped he could be part of the solution.

•

As Suanna returned from the bathroom, she spotted Officer Jennings entering the school building with Kudzu, his K-9. She wondered if he was there because of her fight or to visit a classroom. He was a regular visitor who talked about his profession, about preventing bullying and violence, being drug-free, and making good decisions.

One day while sitting at her lunch table, she learned from Jennings that he had visited Grand Coulee Dam in Washington. She, in turn, told him about her dream of living on the Colville Confederated Tribes Reservation. Ever since that day, Officer Jennings displayed continued interest in her Indian culture. He'd shown compassion about her challenge of being an Indian in a school where a majority of the students believed that her people still lived in tipis, not houses. The caring officer had also boasted to her that he had arrowheads he'd found while walking cornfields and that he'd recently watched flint arrowheads being made by a Native American in Oklahoma.

During another lunch period, Suanna told Jennings about her parents. Her mother was white, from Kansas, and her father was a full-blooded American Indian, a descendent of Chief Joseph's Band of the Nez Perce. She shared about her dad being born near the dam, just across the water from the Colville Reservation. When Jennings asked her if she visited the reservation very often, Suanna answered, "not often enough." She missed being with her cousins, hanging out at the community center, and learning Nez Perce vocabulary from real people, not apps. Suanna also recounted how on her visits to Nespelem she always left a coin on Chief Joseph's grave to honor him.

Suanna remembered that Officer Jennings had told her class that bullies sought to be in control of everything and everybody. They used people's differences as an opportunity to get what they wanted. That description sounded like Terri.

Throughout her short life, long before Officer Jennings knew her, Suanna was repeatedly a natural target of the insecure who grasped at others to pull them down to their chaotic level. She was born neither dark nor light—not bronze—but with an absence of all color. Inexplicably, she was born with albinism—most rare in nature.

Suanna had been at the school less than two years, but her biological and cultural circumstances made her story well known in and out of the teacher's lounge. Teachers consistently remarked that they had learned more about Native American traditions through her reports and projects than they had in four years of college courses. Suanna, it seemed, was a favorite of educators who had a love of learning, even as their passion for teaching was challenged by increasing demands to teach to the test.

•

"Yes," the recess-duty teacher explained to Jennings, "yesterday Suanna punched a classmate, and it was a serious punch. Suanna hit the bigger girl on the jaw; that knocked the known bully to her knees. It was either a fight or an attack, depending on how you looked at it. It occurred after lunch, near the doorway leading to the playground. There were varying details from the witnesses interviewed, of course, but surprisingly, both the sixth-grade students directly involved agreed that words had led to the physical altercation."

"What did Terri say that caused Suanna to go off?" Jennings asked the teacher.

"Terri claimed she was just joking with Suanna when Suanna hit her. According to Suanna, Terri was making fun of her albinism and her Indian culture, and Terri made threatening remarks to Holly. The comments about Suanna's lack of pigmentation had obviously been meant to hurt her and stir her up, but I didn't think she'd go so far as to hit Terri in the face. And Suanna, of all people . . . exploding!"

"Did Terri hit her back?"

"No, didn't have a chance. The fight was over before it started. Other students nearby agreed it was a full-fisted punch that knocked Terri to her knees. Now, that must have been a punch! I thought that only happened in choreographed wrestling matches. I'd have bet it was impossible from a twelve-year-old girl. Terri's a big kid, and we know she's been in a fight or two. I'm surprised Suanna would stand up to Terri. By the way, Terrible Terri seems to be okay, but the former Sweet Suanna may have broken her hand. That's what happens when you hit bone to bone. Something's gotta give."

"What happened to the girls? Was Suanna suspended? How about Terri?"

"The only consequence for Terri teasing Suanna was getting hurt. She's being viewed as the victim here rather than the bully. Suanna's the one, in my opinion, who is in serious trouble. I mean, I like her, but she never told me Terri was making fun of her, and I was on recess duty.

"Yesterday afternoon her mother was called at work and told to come pick her up. When she arrived, Suanna was in Mr. Allison's office with her hand wrapped in an ice pack. I haven't heard what was said, but Suanna was taken to the Medical Center for X-rays. She's back in school today. She got a three-day ISS rather than any out-of-school suspension time. Had it been a boy, you know he would have been home for a week."

"Maybe, but she's never been in a fight before at school, has she?" Jennings inquired.

"No, she hasn't."

"How did Terri's parents take this? Are they upset?" Jennings continued, worried that Suanna could be pulled into the criminal justice system as a criminal suspect at age twelve.

"Fortunately for Suanna, they didn't make a big deal out of it. They said, 'No problem, Terri probably got what she deserved for her big mouth.' I think Terri's fine. The only thing bruised is her ego."

•

Suanna was daydreaming when she heard, or thought she heard, Lady Bonita's squeaky leather saddle. Curious, she turned her head. It was Officer Jennings with his leather belt and holster. Then she saw his dog. "Hi, Kudzu!"

"Hello Suanna," said Jennings, "I was told I could find you here in the library. How are you?"

"Okay," she replied. "I'm glad you're here."

Kudzu was anxious, sniffing around the room for his ball so he could play. He was sticking his nose in some old, partially open, cardboard boxes when he got excited.

Officer Jennings stopped talking to Suanna, told Kudzu to sit, and looked in the box, hoping the school librarian wasn't into drugs. Instead, he spotted mouse droppings. Rolling his eyes, he turned back to Suanna. "I'm glad to see you," he said. "What happened? Why are you in this back room?"

"I got in a fight yesterday."

"It looks like it. What happened to your hand? Is it broken?"

"The doctor said it's a hairline fracture. It's wrapped up for protection."

"So, do you have time to talk with me? I'd like to learn more about what caused the fight and to see if I can be of any help."

"I've got plenty of time. Yeah, I'll talk with you, but I don't see how you can help."

Officer Jennings looked around for a chair that would hold his weight. He found a heavy-duty wooden step-stool that resembled a butcher's block. He carried it over to Suanna's table and sat down beside her so they could be at eye level.

"Now, I'm not investigating this as a crime," said Jennings, "but sometimes people are charged with battery when they hit someone else, unless it's clearly self-defense. The school wants to handle this without a police report. I'm here to see if I can understand what happened. You never know, I might have a good idea."

"If you talk to Terri, she'll tell you that she and her friends were just joking around."

"I'm not talking to her right now. I'm listening to your side of the story."

"It's not a story. I don't think you or any adult can understand why I hit her."

"Give me a try," Jennings encouraged.

"You wouldn't understand. It's just the way it is. You just can't know what it's like to be a girl that's picked on every day."

"You're right." Jennings could only agree. "I don't know what it's like to be picked on every day."

"You're a police officer. You don't get picked on, and even if you got made fun of when you were my age, you can't remember what it was like."

"Hmm . . . it was a long time ago, but I'm still called Fatso by people who are trying to get in my head."

She smiled. "I like being with my friends at school and learning new things, but I don't like rude people messing with me. How do I change that? I can't.

"Every day I come to school I get made fun of by a group of girls, and nothing ever happens to them."

"Do the teachers know you get made fun of?"

"They have to know Terri's rude because she's even rude to them! Usually when she picks on me it's either in the hallway, when the teacher's out of the room, or at recess. It happens everywhere, especially on the bus. That's the way my school day begins and the way it ends."

"Some kids get harassed and bullied on the Internet. Do you?"

"Not really."

Jennings didn't pursue his questioning about cyberbullying, but he knew that at times it was helpful in making a case.

"So your teachers don't know how bad this is on you?" asked Jennings, still reluctant to believe that the bullying could be missed by so many adults for two years. On the other hand, he'd been visiting the school and visiting with Suanna, and she'd never complained about it to him.

"They know about it, but they don't take it seriously. Only my best friend, Holly, and my parents know how much it bothers me."

"Thanks for telling me. I didn't know it was so prevalent . . . so constant. Do you ever get relief from this, to just relax or have some fun?"

"At home, and when I'm with Holly. I have the best parents. They understand me, well . . . usually. But my mom's not too happy about this fight. She's disappointed in me for hitting Terri. She doesn't know what to do with me, so I'm grounded. That includes using my phone or computer to contact her. I haven't been able to speak with Holly since my mom took me to the doctor's office yesterday."

"What about your dad? How's he handling this?"

"He and Mom don't agree on what I should do. They try to tell me how to respond to people who make fun of me, but then they each tell me something different to do. Mom always thinks I should ignore them. Dad thinks that Terri got what she deserved, that it was a hate crime; but he said it would have been better to have waited for her to touch me—then I would have been within my legal rights."

"That's interesting," commented Jennings.

"I love my mom, but my dad's the one I can talk to about anything. He always takes the time to listen and understand what I need, and lately that seems like every day after school. I'm glad he works at home."

"He's a farrier and Appaloosa horse breeder, isn't he?"

"Yeah. He does car repair, too. Mom's a geneticist."

Kudzu was getting restless, pacing by the door.

"Would you like to pet Kudzu?" offered Jennings.

"Yes! I wanted to pet him earlier, but I remembered what you said about waiting until you give the OK."

"Kudzu! Good doggie!" Suanna cooed in a soft voice as she stroked his fur. He responded affectionately, leaning against her like she was a family friend, until his inner drive to find his ball returned. Then he tried to lick Jennings' face.

"You're fortunate to have caring parents who are available. Sometimes it's difficult to know the best response to difficult situations. I don't know for sure how I would have handled Terri. I might have tried ignoring her or avoiding her. I can't imagine hitting her, especially at school."

"Believe me when I tell you, I've ignored mean comments in school since third grade, and I do try to avoid certain people. It's kind of impossible to pretend your classmates aren't around when you have to sit next to them all day."

"Yes, I'll bet that's difficult," agreed Jennings.

"I didn't know I was going to hit her until I hit her. Now, I'm told I have an anger problem. Hello? Yes, I'm angry for being made fun of! Who wouldn't? How about Terri? Does anyone notice she's my problem? Why doesn't someone fix her?"

"I'll be talking to Terri later. She's your test. We all get tested and we all have our limits."

"Now you sound like my dad. He says anyone can be pushed to their limit."

"Ten-four, that's true. But I'm thinking about you feeling good about yourself after losing control. It's difficult to feel good about yourself when you're being insulted, but it's nearly impossible to feel good about yourself when you're out of control. How do you feel about what you've done? Would you do anything differently in a similar situation if it happened tomorrow?"

"It won't happen for at least two more days because we won't see each other. I'm in this back room all day, including for lunch. My mom's dropping me off on her way to work and my dad's picking me up after school. But . . . But . . ."

"But what?"

"I know if I tell you this you'll think I deserve being punished, but . . . I'm glad I hit Terri."

"Because? Because she deserved it?" questioned Jennings.

"Because she'll think twice before picking on me again; so will her friends. My parents tell me I can't be around adults all the time to protect me—that I need to solve my own problems."

"You need to solve your own problems without creating other problems. Remember that the way you solve problems on the street doesn't always work when you're at school or a job. What do the principal and the teachers tell you to do if you're being bothered by someone?"

"To tell a teacher," Suanna said, stretching out the word *tell* as if she were exhausted.

"Have you tried that?"

"Yes, but I can't do it all the time. It just doesn't work that way. It can make things worse. When you talked about bullying to our class, you said the same thing. I was hoping you'd understand, but you adults all think alike."

"Wait a minute. So, telling a teacher doesn't work, and now hitting is your answer?"

"I'm not saying I'll do it again. I'm just saying the kids will think about what I can do to them rather than what they can do to me."

"So, you're willing to accept the consequences?"

"I'm not happy about it. My parents aren't either. But, yes, I'm accepting the punishment for hitting Terri. Being here in the media center isn't bad. Besides, after all these years, I'm glad I'm finally getting to use some of my self-defense skills. My dad's taught me how to box since I was little."

"Now, Suanna, I don't mean to argue with you, but I'm trying to give you another look at what you're saying. You've told me that you're sick and tired of being made fun of and that teachers don't, or can't, protect you all the time."

"Yep. That's what happens."

"Now you're telling me that what you call self-defense, hitting someone who verbally attacks you, is the answer?"

"You look at it like a police officer . . . or a lawyer. I look at it after being pushed around for so long. No, I didn't get hit first, but if I would have talked back to Terri she would have hit me. Can't you see it my way? I think in social studies, when we talked about Iraq, the teacher called that a preemptive strike."

"Okay. You're saying that you need to stand up for yourself because no one else does. You had to hit her to let her know to back off, that she better watch out or else it might happen again, and that you aren't going to take the verbal trash talk anymore. Plus, you're not sorry for what you did, and you're willing to accept the consequences from school and from home."

"That's right. You've got it. I may never hit her or anyone again, except my dad . . . in boxing. It's not like I'm going to go around attacking people the way Terri does."

"Is there a way for you to use your boxing skills on a sports team outside of school? You could be recognized for your talent. Then you could wear padded gloves to protect your hands and to prevent others from being injured by you.

"Tell me this, what kind of rules do you follow when you're boxing with your dad? Are you under control when you hit him? Are there rules or boundaries about getting into fights when you're not wearing gloves?"

"First off, my dad calls me 'Slugger' when we box. We have fun with real boxing gloves. He doesn't hit hard. He just keeps me from landing a blow to his body. You can tell he's enjoying himself because, when I start jabbing at him really fast and hard, he starts laughing."

"Sounds like fun for both of you."

"It is," agreed Suanna. "He boxed Golden Gloves. Have you heard of that?"

"We had a jailer who boxed Golden Gloves, but that was in his younger days before he joined the department."

"My dad boxed middle weight and almost went to the Olympics. Do you know how much he weighed?"

"I have no idea."

"He was 165 pounds. But he says he hasn't been at that weight for ten years. Do you know my dad?"

"Yes, we've met a few times at school events. I like him. I hope we'll be meeting again soon."

"What do you mean? Because of me?"

"Yeah, I'd like to visit with your parents and Mr. Allison. Has your dad been in to talk to the principal about this?"

"No, not yet."

"Is he planning on it? How about your mother?"

"My mother spoke with Mr. Allison yesterday for a few minutes. My dad's talked to Mr. Allison before, but he doesn't like the way he runs the school."

"I still think I can help, but I'm not saying I can keep people from picking on you. Sometimes things are unfair. You know that."

"I know."

"So, you've told me you're tired of people making fun of you, that the harassment is coming especially from Terri and her friends, and that they do a lot of it when teachers aren't around. What about the rest of the students?"

"I get along fine with about everyone else in class, but we're not exactly close friends or anything. Terri doesn't say stuff to me when she's by herself, but when she's with Amanda and Tiffany she gets mean and sarcastic."

"And tell me what she said to you. Wasn't she making fun of your skin color?"

"Yeah," agreed Suanna. "She called me Snow White and said that I couldn't go outside for recess in the snow because I'd be invisible if I took off my clothes. She said that if I was a real Indian I should be red, not white, and she even made fun of my big glasses. She also called Holly a dwarf and threatened to hurt her if she didn't stay away from me."

"Wow! That girl should use her creativity for good, not evil. Now, if I remember correctly, Snow White with her fair hair and snow-white skin was the most beautiful in the land."

"Officer Jennings, don't make me hit you! I hope you're not suggesting that I should take what smarty-pants Terri said as a compliment. Anyway, I don't have a wicked step-mother and I don't need to be saved by a prince."

"I was just trying to remember the fairy tale."

"I'm not part of a fairy tale," insisted Suanna. "One day when I was little, I overheard my parents talking. My mom said to my dad: 'Remember, she's a little girl with albinism, not a sacred white buffalo.'"

"Your mom sounds neat."

"We get along except when she starts telling me how I need to be a young lady! Yuck!"

"As long as I've known you, a whole two years, I've admired you for being smart, talented, and respectful. It's had nothing to do with your albinism."

"Good! I'm more than the color of my skin."

"I appreciate that wherever we talk—whether we talk at lunch or recess—we've always been able to have authentic conversations."

"I'm able to talk to adults better than kids my age because I feel safer with adults. You may not understand me, but you don't make fun of me."

"It may sound like I'm taking Terri's side, but I'm not. She has no right making fun of you. School is supposed to be a safe place for everyone, both emotionally and physically. There just has to be another way of getting Terri to stop what she's doing. And you still have no regrets for hitting her?"

"I could lie. It would probably be easier to just say I'm sorry for what I did. Is that what you want?"

"No, I'm just reviewing what you've told me. I think it's best to be clear on what's going on. If I was being made fun of all the time, I don't know what I'd do. It would be difficult to go to school."

"It is. My mom and dad are thinking about home-schooling me next year."

"Oh, really?" asked Jennings, as his voice rose in pitch.

"Yes, only Mom is gone so much with her job. She says half her work is done sitting at her computer on the Internet, so she could do that at the house. Dad's home a lot when he's not out on a farrier job. He's either in the garage repairing cars or outside training horses. I could help him."

"I just hope this school can become a safer place for you. What do you think?"

"I think I'm safer now. Terri won't be a problem anymore. I'd rather be with my friends here than with my cousins at home. But I'd like to see my friends more. Holly has a favorite Appaloosa she rides when she comes over."

Jennings stood up and returned the step-stool. Kudzu was up and sniffing the boxes again.

"Suanna, as usual this conversation seems to be filled with a little bit of everything. I've certainly enjoyed our talk. Thanks for being open. Now, I know you have work to do. I hope I'll be seeing you back in class next week."

"Thanks for stopping in to see me. Say hello to Holly for me. I still want to see your arrowheads."

"Okay, and next time we talk, will you tell me if there's some sort of guideline or creed about when or when not to use your boxing skills on others?"

"You can protect yourself."

"Okay, we'll talk about that next time."

"Bye, Officer Jennings; bye, Kudzu."

Kudzu, his mouth open and tongue out, was sniffing the air, looking for his ball. The K-9 strained forward, pulling his leash and Officer Jennings out the media-center door.

Polyphemus 10

J oe," Carl said, "Every time I've visited you in the years since graduation, I always forget how everything is so close together here. Don't you miss the open space?"

"We still have the open sky. They can't take that away," replied Joe. "But, hey, we don't drive horse trailers to go shopping."

"I've a mind to forget cashing this check," stated Carl. "The weather's getting worse."

"Just park it here. I'll stay with the truck. It'll only take you a minute. Tell them Joe Morningcloud will vouch for you. They know me. Here's a deposit slip in case they question who you are. I'm going to catch the rest of the Indian news and watch this weather develop. The dark clouds are sure building up. You go ahead. I'll be here if you need me. I'm not going anywhere."

As Carl climbed out of his extended-cab pickup, he glanced into the back seat at his godchild, Suanna. She was still wearing her sunglasses though obviously asleep, her mouth crooked, halfway open, on pause. He smiled. *Is this the first time she's been quiet since I arrived three days ago?*

Firmly grasping his check against the gusty wind, Carl headed for the customer entrance while the wind whipped his body like a flag on a tall pole. Once inside the branch bank's inner door, Carl inhaled the strong scent of fresh chocolate coffee and then observed three lines at the teller stations. It wasn't a game show, but he had to choose a window.

Selecting the teller with only one person waiting seemed like the best plan. That customer, a delicate-skinned, redheaded woman in her early thirties, however, turned to him, gave him a surprised look with her piercing gray-silver eyes, and explained she might be there for a while. "They'll be counting a large can of my coins in their machine," she said. "I'm not sure how long it will take."

"No problem," replied Carl, joining her. "I like your ball cap," he continued, admiring its Pepe Le Pew image while observing her short red hair. Carl also noticed spots of white paint decorating her sleeveless Kelly green T-shirt, reminding him he had promised his wife he'd paint the house when he returned home from his latest road trip.

"Thanks," she said, as she turned back to check on the progress at the far counter. Her teller, wearing a white blazer, was tinkering with a non-responsive machine, its lid off, body on life support. Once Jesse noticed the screwdriver in the employee's hand, the blazer resembled a lab coat; the bank teller looked like a mad scientist; and the coin machine became a robot undergoing delicate brain surgery. *Surgery could take some time*, she speculated.

Carl scanned the bank. It was small but functional. He spotted a pot of coffee and green ceramic mugs on a marble-topped table they shared with promotional bank literature ("Go Green, We Recycle Money"). Then he observed the employees. Two female tellers were helping customers in their respective lines, another at the far counter. He even counted the number of wall-mounted cameras, six that he could see, that were focused on the cash drawers and the customers . . . or would-be criminals. Then he noticed another worker at the drive-through window where the lane didn't permit larger trucks . . . or horse trailers.

•

July had survived the morning, had an early lunch in her car, took her medication, and was hoping that her growing anxiety could be held in check. But midway through her day she overheard a comment as she walked past the break room. "We went through the same thing she did and we were all back to work the next day. July's as jumpy as a scared mouse," the person said. That's when July first recognized how different she was feeling than her peers.

Only her therapist understood. Blankets were her security, sleep her sanctuary. Sure she'd been home, but every day had been incredibly tough. She still found herself getting upset when others referred to her time off as a vacation. Didn't they understand that vacations meant a time for getting away and relaxing? The only trips she'd taken on her so-called vacation were all induced by prescription medication. The drugs dulled her tension by surrounding her in a fog with no sharp corners. But still, she couldn't get the bank scene out of her head. She asked herself again, "Is this job worth it?"

July had persistent thoughts about what she should have done two months earlier as she watched an armed robbery unfold. She knew she should have pressed the hold-up alarm when she first recognized the signs of a robbery, before she was staring down the barrel of a handgun, frightened to a point of paralysis. But she just couldn't believe it was happening. In those days, a lifetime ago, she took pride in herself for never overreacting. She was no drama queen.

Even with the medication kicking in to calm her, July just couldn't get her mind off the last armed robbery—or the next one. Reaching up to check her hair, she puzzled over the best solution. She reckoned she could quit this job and start over somewhere else far removed from a cash drawer. She knew one thing for sure: something had to change—soon.

•

It was noon-thirty, but Jesse Jennings was in no hurry. Early for an appointment with her police officer husband, Tom, he would arrive any minute if he wasn't busy on an emergency assignment. They planned on sitting down with a loan officer at the bank to discuss purchasing a larger house, one big enough to include dedicated work space for her sculpture work. Jesse wanted to get back to her creative art, beyond helping her children with coloring books and pasting dried beans to poster board. She had tried making the kitchen table workable, but it was a magnet for everything else. Every time she cleared it off for herself it was time for yet another meal. She felt a lot more like a short-order cook than a professional artist.

Jesse recalled the look on Tom's face the previous week and laughed. He was still on nights and the girls were at Grandma's for a sleepover, when he returned home from working the road. Upon entering the house he followed the loud, pulsating, upbeat music until he found her beaming—wide awake—repainting Julia's bedroom.

As Jesse sang and danced with her partner, a saturated paint roller, Tom smelled the strong odor of fumes and grew concerned. He told her later: "If I didn't know you, I'd swear you were high, tweaking from speed like so many others I encounter during my nightly patrol duties."

But Jesse's high was a natural one. She was moving forward. With the bed and dresser relocated, Jesse was taking back lost ground. Their girls, Julia and Hannah, would temporarily share a bedroom.

Jesse's concern for "working space" led her to recalling her time right out of college when she lived in an artist's loft apartment. Back then she generated more income from her art. Tom agreed that they had long ago outgrown their starter house. Before the paint had dried in Jesse's bedroom studio, she and Tom decided to examine their finances and investigate a potential bank loan. Jesse suggested that a new house could be a fifteenth wedding anniversary present to one another. Tom thought of another reason to buy a new house; he wouldn't need to decide on an anniversary gift.

Jesse had already started working on a sketch of a Native American warrior that solidified out of her imagination, not photographs, in her freshly painted studio. So when the powerfully built man with full cheeks and pronounced nose walked up to her in the bank, she smiled, knowing that his presence was a sign of alignment. It was uncanny! He was a near look-alike to her unfinished drawing. Jesse tried, but found it virtually impossible to take her eyes off of him. Her sketch had come to life!

The previous night while she worked, Tom had stopped to visit and she asked him, shirtless, to turn his head to imitate her plans for a clay bust. She wanted to observe the muscle definition on his neck and shoulders. When rolls of fat materialized from his pose, they both laughed 'til they cried! What was she thinking? Due to his extra-large frame, excess weight from constant eating, and limited exercise, there was good reason for Tom's nickname, T-Bone Taz, a far cry from the imposing, majestic clay figure she wanted to sculpt.

Waiting in the bank and attempting not to stare, Jesse glanced at her can of untouched coins. There was no hurry. She could sketch him in her head. She was standing beside the real thing. Her last-minute decision to cash in the overflowing can of coins that steadily accumulated at the end of her husband's workday, had brought her face-to-face with this fascinating, striking man, a Native American. *What would happen next?* she marveled silently, hoping that anyone cashing a check must be a local Grovian. *Maybe he would at least consent to being photographed.* Her cell phone/camera was in her purse.

•

The *Native News* radio show was always a bonus to Joe's day. Call him old-fashioned, but thanks to public radio he was able to keep up with some of the tribal information from around the country without checking special links or a half-dozen apps. Rarely would he hear a report on his Colville Confederated Tribes or the Nez Perce, but he always welcomed news from his brothers in Indian country. Today he was learning about a conference being held at Carl's alma mater, Haskell Indian Nations University. Joe recalled attending Carl's graduation. It had been a long drive from Nespelem to Lawrence but it had been well worth the trip. That's where he and Elizabeth had met. Now their daughter, Suanna, was nearly thirteen-years-old.

The radio announcer continued: "Today's *Native News* takes us to Lawrence, Kansas, where we are reporting on the importance of youth leadership in the contemporary world of American Indians."

As Joe visualized the strengths of the young leaders meeting in Lawrence, hours to the north, he also watched the sky darken and traffic snarl in the bank's parking lot. Tight-faced drivers maneuvered around the lined asphalt and then exhaled as they pulled into puny parking spaces. One man with helter-skelter hair parked his beat-up Honda Accord partially on the grass by the driveway. Then with a glare on his face, he stared at Carl's horse trailer, muttering as he walked past. The only words Joe caught were "damn cowboys!"

Amused, Joe remembered his childhood when he knew he wanted to be a cowboy, but the old movies he watched kept telling him no, Indians didn't have choices. The mumbling man carried what appeared to be a folded plastic bag in his right hand while guarding his hair with the other. The stranger walked awkwardly to the front door of the Prairie Grove Bank. His body was wrong. His old legs and young face didn't fit, and his right arm seemed disconnected, limp, not swinging or helping propel the body forward through the crosswind. Joe had seen injured cowboys move like that at the Nespelem Rodeo. This bull rider, like Joe, had hit the ground one too many times.

With rhythmic breathing coming from the back seat, Joe didn't need to turn his head. Suanna was obviously more tired than she was hungry. She was sound asleep. It had been a long couple of days for her as she helped the men repair fence and then cut and haul young red cedar trees for burning. Despite her honest aches each evening, she had begged her father and "uncle" to take turns boxing with her.

It should have been simple. Just put on the gloves and protect yourself, but Suanna was never satisfied until she had challenged the men to the point where they had to use basic defensive skills developed in their youth. If mother hadn't showed up in the horse barn, the evening would have been fine. Instead, it had gotten tense when Elizabeth repeated her strong opinion that a young woman going on thirteen needed to find a non-contact sport. "Boxing is for boys and men. It's about time you begin acting like a young lady," she had insisted. "And that goes for your fingernails, too. Stop biting them!"

The words about being a lady had so infuriated Suanna that her lashing-out response was predictable. "You just don't want me to spend time with Dad! You never care about me! Like horseback riding isn't dangerous," she scoffed.

When mother and daughter argued, Joe was perplexed. He knew that Suanna was under extreme pressure during the school year with the ever-present feeling of being different than the other students.

The controversy over boxing being inappropriate behavior was especially complicated because Joe didn't agree with his wife. He had told her before: "Honey, the way we box is playing; it's not dangerous." He agreed with his precious Snowflake. "It's fun!"

·

In her dream, Suanna was at recess racing on her spotted Appaloosa and the entire fifth- and sixth-grade classes were spellbound by her agility and speed. By the time the two of them, Suanna and Lady Bonita, rounded the swing sets, their velocity caused her long dark hair to fly in the breeze. At the soccer field her bronze-like skin reflected the sun's rays, creating a golden aura around her. When she passed the ball diamond's backstop, the last leg of the course, she let out a whoop of excitement. Bonita sprinted the last fifty yards before responding to the pull of her bridle, just feet before the assembled group.

When Suanna halted in front of the students, her classmates, she was finally the center of attention in a good way—until she saw the two teachers wearing dark, wraparound sunglasses, holding long, white, wooden staffs like sentries or guards. That's when her nemesis, Terri, emerged from the space between the stern-looking teachers. Terri's grin was smirking, harsh, and disturbing, as she raised her hands up and outwards toward Suanna. One held an extra-large, oversized, shiny pair of scissors, the kind Suanna recognized from a grand-opening, ribbon-cutting ceremony. The other hand grasped Suanna's pet gerbil, Rat, by the tail. He was squirming, desperate, trying to get loose. Terri opened the blades of the scissors wider while swinging Rat closer to the sharp prongs. "No!" screamed Suanna, jumping off Bonita, prepared to fight Terri to save Rat's life.

Awakening, breathing irregularly, it took her a second to realize she was in the back seat of Uncle Carl's truck with her dad up front listening to the radio. They were in a parking lot. But where was Rat? He'd been cupped in her hands a moment earlier. And, where was Uncle Carl?

•

The police van marked "K-9 Unit" hurried through the intersection as the traffic light turned red. The uniformed officer tightly wedged behind the steering wheel texted on his cell phone while sipping from a massive soft-drink tub. Then, as the vehicle drifted left of center, the cop overcorrected, nearly sideswiping a parked truck as he licked his salty finger tips. With the smell of fries permeating the air, the vehicle shouted fast-food restaurant. Wrappers on the floor confirmed an earlier drive-through experience at the town's greasiest spoon. The trash said it all: "Hot Pockets! Fill'er Up at Fat Boy's Sandwich Shop & Gas."

Pushing the send button, Tom waited. Soon Jesse replied, and he learned that she was already at the bank. The two agreed that they would attempt to find out how much they could spend on a house, and then eat a hurried lunch, all in an hour. It could happen as long as things went smoothly. Both agreed that Gino's would be the best choice for a quick bite. They ended their communication after Tom informed Jesse that he was nearby and that the county's thunderstorm watch had been upgraded to a warning.

•

Waiting in line gave Carl too much time to fidget. He needed a smoke. It had been three long days since he had last inhaled the smoke from a cancer-causing cigarette. It had been three days since he had promised Suanna that he was done buying the nails for his own coffin. He winced, remembering how she had taken his words and examined them like she was a contract attorney.

"When you say you're not going to buy them any longer, does that mean you'd smoke one if someone offered you one for free?" she had questioned.

He must have looked like a raccoon caught in a coyote trap because both Joe and Elizabeth, sitting at the dinner table, had raised their eyebrows watching ol' Carl squirm. He'd been caught being deceitful to the one who loved him most.

But her Uncle Carl had chosen to live, not die. With his blessing, she held a ceremony before he changed his mind. After he handed over his engraved cigarette case, Suanna giggled as she snipped the last two cigarettes into small pieces. She then hurried to the bathroom to complete the service, flushing them down the swirling toilet water while slowly humming "Taps." The formality was inspiring yet sobering as Carl recalled the last time, on the reservation, when he had heard the military's final goodbye to a fallen brother. In a matter of minutes the interaction with Suanna had shifted from a silly, lighthearted ritual to a solemn affair. Like it or not, this had quickly evolved into a motivational opportunity for him.

He promised to stop. But the next day he questioned his sanity until he understood that giving up smoking wasn't just for his godchild. It was for himself and his family. He understood that Suanna's determination could give him the boost he needed to quit—this time for good.

After his promise, he took action. Rather than spending money on a nicotine patch or gum, he decided on a less complex strategy: sunflower seeds. That way when he had an urge to light one up he could, instead, chew on the seeds, keeping his hands and mouth busy. Getting into the spirit of helping her godfather, Suanna bought him tiny pretzel sticks. Once home, she individually placed half of the package into Carl's cigarette case, eating the rest. Then she returned his military memento, suggesting he carry them if he had a craving to smoke. He accepted the heartfelt gift but rejected the idea of constantly having the case with him as too vivid of a reminder of his smoking habit. It would be an invitation, not a deterrent. Instead of carrying his crushproof container in his shirt pocket, he put it in his truck's glove box.

As he continued his wait in line at the bank, Carl reached for the sunflower seeds in his shirt pocket. It was empty. He felt a movement under the collar of his shirt . . .

•

While waiting on her customers, July kept noticing a stranger scanning the bank. He had brown skin, long hair, and wore a choker. He looked to be casing the place, planning trouble. "Surely he wouldn't try anything knowing he was being recorded by half the cameras in the bank!" July thought. But, like the last time, things didn't necessarily have to make sense to her. "Desperate people do desperate things," she recalled an officer telling her.

Attempting to stop her thoughts from spiraling downward, she recognized her pattern. She was overreacting again. She'd been cautioned about this. Not every person she didn't know was a bank robber. This man, with a check in one hand, was looking around the bank to pass the time while he waited. Also, she was pretty sure he had walked from the truck and trailer parked out front. People don't rob banks driving horse trailers! she concluded, for once rationalizing her worries away instead of magnifying them. Maybe this was a sign she was getting better. She wasn't crazy.

July congratulated herself on making emotional progress as she watched a customer enter carrying a plastic bag. He proceeded directly to the employee bathroom. "Can't he read?" she muttered aloud. It was a private area with a clearly visible sign: Restroom—Employees Only. "He don't have the sense God gave a billy goat!" July concluded.

•

Jesse was thinking about her sculpture, not lunch. From texting with Tom, she could tell he was contemplating lunch, not sculpture. If only he could arrive in time, he'd appreciate the synchronicity of this powerful event! This man standing behind her had been at her easel, in her converted bedroom/studio the previous two days as a lightly sketched, two-dimensional figure. But here he had real depth. He wasn't imaginary. He was real! Jesse knew she couldn't let him get away.

"Sir, my name is Jesse Jennings and I'm an artist," she blurted out. "I'm working on a sculpture design of a Native American warrior and . . . what's so remarkable is that you and the sketch look alike. Anyhow, I'm a member of a group of artists who meet once a week and sketch or paint live models. We'd really appreciate you considering the job. It pays thirty dollars an hour through the Art Association."

"Did you say the Native American you're drawing is a warrior?" asked Carl, chuckling.

"Yes, that's right," replied Jesse. "You are Native American, aren't you?"

Smiling, Carl touched his dentalium shell choker and responded, "Yes, I'm Colville-Lakota, and my last name is Warrior." But before Carl could hear Jesse's response he was interrupted, this time by something on his shoulder . . .

"Is that a pet mouse or a gerbil?" inquired Jesse, observing a white nose and pink eyes looking out from Carl's shoulder-length hair; she was not at all surprised to be meeting this little creature in a semi-sterile commercial bank.

"I can help you over here," announced a voice from the teller's booth the next line over from Jesse and Carl.

Carl turned toward the teller, then looked back at Jesse with a shrug and a smile. He said, "I'll talk to you in a minute," then turned and stepped up to the counter. Rat retreated into his cloistered canopy. Carl placed the check before the teller and noticed more than her name tag. Up close she was stunning, with smooth dark skin, full lips, glistening teeth, and wide nose, with the whites of her eyes pure contrast to her brown irises. She wore her hair short, just long enough for it to be gathered into square-inch sections the size of caramel candy, row after row from ear to ear. So precise and orderly, it caused Carl to imagine that the bank teller was a person who would always keep her cash register or the bank's ledger balanced to the exact penny. Like him, she cared about details. She understood and respected order, especially numbers. *What was her tribe? Where was she from?* he wanted to know. Finally, he looked at her name tag. It was just one word: "July."

•

July had reached down deep, pushing herself like she and Dr. Sandoval had agreed. They had practiced how she would carry on the basic duties of her day, waiting on customers as though she were comfortable and welcoming. More than once she had resisted taking the Closed sign from beside her cash drawer and moving it to her counter window like a barricade, effectively protecting her from further contact with all customers. She stopped herself from more negative thoughts by concentrating on her breathing. She willed herself to invite the suspicious man to her register. She took the next step; she smiled.

"How may I help you?" asked July, with upturned mouth and proper eye contact.

"Sir, may I help you?" she repeated. Her voice quivered as she inquired of this foreigner with the long hair, Indian but not Choctaw, brown skin, not black or red. But he was still busy bothering Jesse, one of her regular customers. *Does he want to cash the check he's holding or visit with everyone in town?* she asked herself, and then concluded, *He's just one more man with no horse sense. God bless him.*

Carl turned to July. "Yes, thank you. I'd like to cash this check," he said.

Taking the check in one hand, she brought it closer to her face for inspection and then pursed her lips. "Do you have an account here?" she asked, knowing the answer, as her other hand below the counter, pressed the hold-up alarm.

"No, but I have a note . . ." Carl replied. He turned to look through the large bank window at his truck, searching for Joe, but noticing the growing darkness outside. He would have to show the teller Joe's account number after all. With his left hand, Carl touched the deposit slip in his pocket.

•

A disheveled man with vacant-bird-nest hair stared at himself in the bank's bathroom mirror. With dull unblinking eyes he viewed his Halloween Scream mask. One more moment of contemplation and he was ready. In one hand he held an empty, open plastic bag. In the other, he gripped a gun the color of midnight.

He exited the bathroom with no intention of hurting anyone, but he was determined to leave the bank with a bag full of cash. He needed it more than they did. The next few minutes would solve all his problems. They would cooperate!

Once centrally located, Scream cleared his voice, prepared to announce to all employees and patrons that this was a robbery. Laughing at himself, he heard the precise words dancing from his mouth: "Trick or treat, money . . . no eats!"

•

July never saw the masked man reenter the lobby. Instead, she was totally focused on her customer's left arm. His hand was out of view. He said he had a note that would explain the whole thing. Her thoughts blurred. "Just follow my directions and you won't be hurt," she heard. That's when she knew he had more than a note. He raised his hand. It was a . . .

The sound of the exploding bullet ripped the energy-charged air.

"GUN!" July screamed. "GUN! GUN! Oh my God, not again!" she pleaded. "GUN!"

•

Jesse felt the impact to her forehead. Warm liquid streamed down one brow into her eye, and then down to the crease of her nose. Confused, she asked out loud, "What happened?" She touched her face, recognizing her own blood. She tried to make sense of the unexpected blast and her facial wound. The startling sound had come from nearby. What was going on? Then she deciphered the sound, identifying it by its echoing reverberations in her head. It was like firearms practice at the city's outdoor range or when Tom target practiced with the girls behind their house. That's when she hunkered on the floor, searching the bank for the shooter she knew was there. She yearned for Tom to hold her close, to stop the bleeding, to protect her from further harm. Thank God he was a police officer. He carried a gun, and he knew how to use it.

●

Suanna had searched the back seat until the answer presented itself. Rat loved sunflower seeds. Uncle Carl had a pocket full of them, and he was in the bank she knew so well. Could Carl have unknowingly taken her sweet Rat along with him?

"I'll be right back," Suanna told her dad as she grabbed her sun hat and took off her sunglasses.

"Be careful. Watch for cars," Joe replied instinctively.

She hurried from the truck, her delicate skin an inviting target for the first volley of pelting pea-size hail. Her arms and legs sprinted around the horse trailer toward the bank's dark glass door, as if it were the finish line that would earn her a blue ribbon. Suanna had only one thing on her mind: Rat.

●

As Officer Tom Jennings approached the bank, he heard the loud thunder followed by the pounding hail and then the emergency broadcast alert on the citywide radio frequency. He assumed it was an updated weather warning. Instead, it announced a silent hold-up alarm at his bank! Jesse's bank! They'd just spoken. She was there now!

Seconds later, the dispatcher continued, speaking to all listening officers, "Additional . . . shots fired, one down, armed robbery in progress."

"No!" Tom screamed as he swerved into the bank's parking lot. He never saw the little girl run in front of his vehicle. He never heard the thump of her body bouncing from the van's front bumper. He never saw her head hit the pavement.

Instead, he watched his car door open before the vehicle ever stopped. The seatbelt buzzer's sound filled his ears as he struggled to extricate his bulk from the front seat. He had to strain, pushing and pulling his excess pounds without wedging his stomach deeper into the steering wheel. He had to avoid getting his duty belt hung up on the seat belt or door frame. His bulk wasted valuable seconds.

Finally released from his vehicle, his firearm ready, a heavily perspiring Officer Jennings was blasted with ice pellets. He tried to see inside the bank through its steamy windows. He saw no people, no suspects, and no Jesse.

•

Joe heard the bullet-like hail rattle Carl's truck. He saw the pea-size, then quarter-size pellets. "Severe thunderstorm warning! High winds! Possible hail!" the radio threatened. A hailstone slipped through the partially open window like flying popcorn. The wind whipped the branches of the bank's lone tree. Joe didn't hear the squeal of braking tires or the sudden thud. But when he heard the shrill cry of a baby bird, he recognized his child. "Pee-tititi," was her call. He snapped around to see Suanna's figure come to a dead rest. Her extended arms reached toward her somersaulting hat. It rotated like a Kansas tumbleweed. Joe rushed to her motionless body, screaming, "Snowflake!"

•

Regardless of July's penetrating cry, the masked man standing motionless was the unanimous focal point. Bystanders stared, caught in a cross fire of puzzlement, recognition, and fear. All heard one black, bold, banshee-like teller repeatedly and hysterically screaming: "Gun!" The armed intruder methodically turned his hand, palm facing inwards, examining the weapon's dark, detailed features and his twitching trigger finger. Looking up, his gaze landed on a customer, a lady with a single searching eye. It was open so wide that it reminded him of a Cyclops action figure he once had as a child.

"Where's Polyphemus today?" Ghostface asked out loud, recalling how Polly had been his favorite play-friend. Then, he refocused on the Cyclops lady on the floor beside him in the bank, holding her head, blood pulsing between her fingers. She tapped a phone with her other hand. For the first time in a long time he recognized that he was confused. *How did she get hurt? Is she calling for help? Doesn't she know I mean her no harm?*

Between the Gaelic wailing of the bank teller, there were seconds of silence when the gunman gradually deciphered the words from the

Cyclops lady: "Tom! . . . Please! . . . Tom! Where are you? Be careful! He's shooting people!"

"I didn't mean for this to happen," the masked man said robotically to the short-haired Polly, Jesse Jennings, or to no one in particular. "I'm sorry. I just wanted to help a friend. I was told this was the answer," he concluded.

With that, as the video cameras would later confirm, he turned and walked out of the lobby pointing his gun at an approaching police officer entering the front door.

A cell phone rang unheard and unanswered amid the screaming.

The would-be bank robber knew what he had to do. His finger, securely on the trigger, no longer twitched.

Sirens 11

Officer Tom Jennings approached the bank's two sets of clear glass doors, knowing it was a kill zone. This was a critical incident that would not wait for backup. Without hesitation the elephantine officer advanced with the surprising speed of a smaller, light-footed man. He was a big target, but one that fired back, and he was a crack shot.

Inside the first set of doors, Jennings prepared to hear gunfire and feel heat. But as the automatic doors opened prematurely, the masked gunman appeared from behind a support pillar. He confronted Jennings with a Beretta pointed at the officer's chest, the assailant's trigger finger clawing the weapon. Trying to force his bullets out, to catch up, Officer Jennings jumped on his trigger, firing multiple times at center mass with expected lethal accuracy. He did this while backing up and falling hard to the floor, but keeping both hands on his Glock, continually engaged with the standing suspect.

Instead of the gunman dropping, he was like some deer Tom had hunted that continued standing, grazing, chewing his cud, unaware he was dead. But Jennings had no time to wait. As trained, he fired more rounds in case of hidden body armor, this time aiming at the tip of the nose of the ghostlike face.

In an instant this initial shootout was over, the deafening gunfire echoing within the bank's enclosure. As the screams subsided, there was only one smoking gun in the entryway of the bank. The masked armed robber, limp, pitched forward to the floor, blocking the inner doorway, only feet from Jennings.

The officer knew the armed robber was no longer a threat. One down, he counted, and reloaded with a new clip, yet he cautiously wondered why he couldn't locate any of his own bullet wounds.

"Am I hit? Where's my blood?" he asked himself aloud in an uncertain tone. "The scumbag couldn't have missed me. How good is this vest? Am I shot or not?"

Jennings welcomed no signs of his own demise and then diagnosed acute, sharp back pain. But he was good, he decided, ready for the next perp before he could get to Jesse.

Scanning the bank for the living, Jennings couldn't stop a memory from surfacing. In a training scenario, Range Master Mike Gale re-taped paper practice targets and recorded the number of hits to a darting bull's-eye.

Quickly, Tom recognized he had to get up and get moving. He stumbled over the suspect's body already lying in a growing pool of blood. Tom nearly fell as he burst into the bank's lobby, looking for more threatening targets to stop . . . to shoot . . . to kill. While on the move, he selfishly prayed that if only one person were left alive, it would be his lifelong partner, Jesse. At the same time, he couldn't remember the last time he had told her he loved her, and he still needed to apologize for too little listening and too much drinking.

He had to get his big butt in gear.

"POLICE! HANDS UP! EVERYONE!" Officer Jennings barked with his husky voice as he charged further into the bank. He continued to scan it for additional suspects, willing to be a target. Then he recognized his wife whose face was running red. In combat stance, his arms already extended to eye level, he froze, the barrel of his forty-caliber Glock aimed directly at the ear canal of a man kneeling beside Jesse.

"No! Tom, he's helping!" exclaimed Jesse.

"Are there others?" Tom asked, then began to remember the employees by name—KrishnaMa, Leslie, Barbara.

"I don't know!" Jesse shouted, her ears still ringing from the gunfire. "He was the only one, I think."

"HANDS UP!" Jennings yelled again as he took a quick strategic glance behind the counter where clerks were hiding. He viewed the upstairs balcony and office and eyed two customers in a corner on the main floor, noting their hands held no weapons.

"JULY! JULY! HOLD ON!" Cassie, a teller, squealed, two octaves above her normal voice.

Tom returned to Jesse and bent over her to see the extent of her injuries. The stranger helping Jesse, an American Indian with shoulder-length hair, said he thought it was only a shrapnel flesh wound; she'd been 'nicked.' The Good Samaritan said, "I shouldn't do this, but . . ." then lifted the wet, mostly dark handkerchief from her forehead to show Tom the origin of the bleeding. His wife was not dying, but Tom lost his edge in the fight. With blood dividing her face, Jesse looked like one of her sculpture busts with a post-kiln facial crack. Jesse didn't look good, but she was alive, talking, and making sense.

Jennings could hear the sirens approaching, and he knew a lot of help would soon converge on his location. He keyed the walkie-talkie's mic and announced: "Unit 3 to dispatch, I'm ten-four inside the bank. Request ten-forty-nines to this location. We have one conscious adult with a facial flesh wound; one suspect down, code blue. Unknown if further suspects. Will wait for backup before proceeding."

"Ten-four, Unit 3, backup and ambulances are en route," the dispatcher confirmed, then continued: "All units responding to Prairie Grove Branch Bank, be advised Unit 3 is inside the bank, repeat, Unit 3 is inside the bank, suspect is down, code blue; one other injured, flesh wound. Unknown if additional suspects."

"Tom, are you okay? Be careful!" cautioned Jesse.

"Honey, you'll be fine. An ambulance is on the way. I'll be right back," he promised.

"You be careful!" she commanded.

"KrishnaMa, is anyone else here—any bad guys? How about those two in the corner? Are they okay?"

"I know everyone here, no more bank robbers," replied KrishnaMa calmly, her Hindu red dot centered on her forehead. "Those two are customers. July is conscious now. I think she fainted from the excitement. She was screaming—then she just keeled over at her station. She's all right. Our branch manager, Clayton Parks, should be upstairs in his office. I haven't seen him since before the shooting. He would have told me if he'd gone to lunch."

"Additional information at Prairie Grove Branch Bank," the emergency dispatcher announced to responding units and Officer Jennings: "We have lost phone contact with the bank manager who stated he was alone in his upstairs office. We advised him to remain there until contacted by officers. Last known to be hyperventilating, ambulances en route."

Tom held his ground, but his eyes darted everywhere, scanning for any movement, especially anyone with a weapon. He took a quick inventory. He had eliminated the present employees and customers from his list of those who were potentially dangerous. The tellers had told him there were no strangers in the bank, but there were still rooms to be cleared, including the break room and bathrooms on the first floor. There could still be others outside in the parking lot. Jesse had bled profusely, but it was being controlled with direct pressure. EMTs would arrive soon. July was conscious. Upstairs, the bank manager, Parks, possibly alone, was having difficulty breathing. These were the living.

What about the sleazeball he had just shot and . . . killed? Jennings turned his head and again snatched a glimpse of the human lump on the floor.

"Not a twitch . . . no longer a threat . . . had to be dead," Jennings said staccato-like. "The scumbag was so close when I shot him, I couldn't have missed," he thought out loud, seeing the jacket's logo he had used as his target and the eerie Scream mask with sunken eyes.

Jennings waited and wondered one more time if this was a solo armed robbery. "Are there accomplices, and if so, where are they right now?" he thought, as he glanced again to the parking lot, looking for a getaway car and driver. Instead he saw movement, familiar uniforms and familiar faces, advancing, their guns drawn and ready for action.

"Unit 3 to all units approaching the bank," said Jennings into his walkie-talkie.

"Go ahead," a voice on the radio replied.

"I'm holding my position in the bank's lobby. Suspect is down on the floor, just inside the front entrance. No other suspects at this time. Have you cleared the lot?"

"Ten-four, no suspects."

The police radios squawked: "Unit 1 to dispatch, bank parking lot is clear for suspects, ten-forty-eight at north entrance, MV versus pedestrian. One child injured, unconscious."

"Ten-four, Unit 1, ten-forty-eight, one child injured, unconscious, ambulances in route."

There was no time for SWAT, but the patrol officers on the street responded strategically.

Joe Morningcloud kneeled on the pavement of the parking lot frantically trying to wake his non-responsive daughter.

Announcing his presence by radio, the first officer in the door made visual contact with Jennings and then checked the prone bloody body for a pulse. Finding none, he notified dispatch and continued into the lobby with the next officer close behind. Holding their ground, the cops questioned the employees and customers to determine their next move. Rather than evacuate the bank, they had the civilians hunker in place and searched the first floor for additional suspects. It took only seconds. There was no place else to hide.

Led by Jennings, as the entry team's point officer, the contact team flowed up the staircase in a tight diamond pattern. They passed a glass conference room that resembled an unfurnished fish bowl. Then they prepared to enter the manager's office. Pushing through, Jennings moved straight ahead as the second officer immediately turned right, riding the wall. The third team member entered the room and stopped a few feet inside. The first two officers collapsed the room, aiming at their sector. No subjects were spotted until Jennings bird-dogged the manager's outstretched hands, palms down on the carpeted floor, protruding from under his desk. The other officers also focused on this potentially dangerous red zone. The person, who had to be Parks, was indeed, mostly, out of view. *At least he is showing his hands*, Jennings thought. The uniforms yelled as they aimed their handguns at the figure on his knees, his head bowed low like a Muslim at prayer. "Clayton! It's the police! Come out!" they announced.

The manager's response, indeed, was a prayer: "Forgive me father for I have sinned."

Once the officers gave the last "all clear," the EMTs surged into the bank. They checked the bank robber for vitals because of protocol, not hope; assisted Jesse with her forehead wound; and attempted to calm July, who was in a state of high anxiety. She was pleading with officers to arrest the gun-toting, bank-robbing Indian who was kneeling beside Jesse Jennings. Upstairs, Clayton appeared clearheaded and relieved after learning his employees and customers were safe, if not sound.

Informed of the dead bank robber, bank manager Parks quietly inquired if a chaplain had been called.

As far as the officers upstairs knew, a chaplain had not been called, the FBI had not been informed, the bank robber not identified, and the medical examiner not notified. There wasn't even time to celebrate the relatively safe outcome of the response to the attempted armed robbery. There was still so much more to do.

Bullets 12

"Who is he?" Every officer wanted to know.

"No wallet or ID."

"Watch out for blood."

"It's a wig; this guy's got a shaved head."

"Oh, a Scream mask; they're everywhere."

"He looks like Odessa-Smith from the Bissonte Apartments."

"He sure does; just a second," said the officer as he lifted each sleeve of the windbreaker, looking for tattoos.

"It's him. I recognize the ink: snake and a cross."

"He's the medical examiner's son."

"Yeah. Oh, shit!"

"He's had mental problems for years."

"Where's his gun?"

•

"Are you sure it's him?" asked Carolyn on her phone.

"Yes, I'm sure," replied Kilgore. "His Honda is parked in the lot. I saw it when I arrived."

"Birthmark?"

"Yes."

"Tattoos?"

"Yes."

"Okay, I'm on my way."

"Are you sure you want to do this?"

"I must see him. I don't have a choice."

"Of course; I'll be here," said Kilgore."

"Don't move his body," Carolyn directed.

•

"Taz," said friend and fellow officer, Mike Gale, "looks like Jesse's injury isn't too bad."

"I hope so," said Tom.

"After I learned you weren't shot, I asked the Lieutenant, 'What color is the dead dirtbag?' He didn't know."

"What does it matter?" asked Tom. "He's an armed robber shooting customers inside a bank in broad daylight. Is that probable cause enough for you?"

"Sometimes over a beer and good music I almost forget your ass is white, then you say something totally off-the-wall stupid!"

"What do you mean?"

"Taz, my white friend, you forget, black lives matter."

"Yeah, ten-four, they matter," agreed Tom. "All lives matter."

"We're all happy you and Jesse are alive. But also be glad this dead guy is as white as you and not a hostile black brother that's grown tired of being racially profiled. Nowadays, if he'd been black, then the media would be all over this."

Tom still didn't care about the race or color of the shooter. He cared about his wife. "I'm hoping the worst is over and Jesse will be all right," wished Tom as he again reached toward the shooting pain in his back.

•

"We've got a problem," Detective Captain Kilgore said to his chief of police via phone. "Medical examiner's son is the dead bank robber. I called Carolyn Odessa and she insists on responding."

"Someone else can do that," said the chief.

"I can't stop her," said Kilgore. "She's on her way now."

"What about her husband, Shawn, does he know? The old coroner is usually the responder, but I suppose it would be just as bad for him."

"I only called her. I figured she'd call him."

"Too bad for them; it won't be easy. Accomplices?"

"The smoke's still settling, boss. We just identified Odessa."

"Sorry, my internal checklist."

"It's helpful. What else?"

"What about the FBI?"

"They're going to call back. KBI is on the way."

"Jennings and his wife?"

"EMTs are still checking them out. Jennings won't leave her side. I hope they'll be off to the hospital before the M.E. (medical examiner) arrives. We're stepping all over ourselves here. Hope we don't lose any evidence."

"The ten-forty-eight? The little girl?"

"Sheriff agreed to work it. No update on her condition, and I don't expect to hear anything unless it's bad."

"Do you have anyone headed to Wichita?" asked the chief.

"No, we don't even know what hospital they've gone to," replied Kilgore.

"I'll find a reserve officer to standby at the ER because I want a uniform to represent us," said the chief. "It's going to be a long shift for everyone."

"Now, if a reserve officer will do that, it would be a big help to us. We have a lot of interviews to do and we'll need to count bullets."

"I'll let you get back to work. Good luck with Carolyn. You can help her out. I know you two have worked a lot of cases together."

"Yes, we have."

•

"Hey, Tom. Good job!" said a Prairie Grove Police Department detective.

"Thanks," said Officer Jennings.

"I'm collecting the bank robber's gun for evidence. Have you got it?"

"No, I didn't stop to take it. I was looking for more shooters."

"Okay, good. I'll do more checking. Another officer might have it."

"He fell forward. Have you looked under his body yet?"

"No, we wanted to check with officers first. Thanks."

•

"Captain," said Detective Gale, "I've known Jennings since the academy. With your approval I'd like to give Tom the news on the identity of the deceased and tell him about the weapon."

"Not necessary, my job," replied Captain Kilgore.

"We're good friends and I know his family," Gale added.

"He'll want your help later. I need to get a couple of things cleared up first."

•

"Your captain and the chief are on their way here, but they're responding from Topeka," Kilgore advised Jennings. "How are you doing?"

"Sharp pain in my back," said Jennings as he reached unsuccessfully for his vertebrae, "but my main concern is my wife. EMTs are cautiously optimistic. She'll need minor surgery."

"So, what did you see when you arrived and approached the bank? How many suspects are we talking about?"

"I didn't see anyone outside. The scumbag I shot was the only perp. I'm glad I smoked his ass."

"You didn't see anyone leaving the bank when you pulled up?" questioned Kilgore.

"No. Is someone claiming there was an additional person? I'd guess I was less than a minute away when it was originally dispatched and then maybe ten, fifteen seconds between the report of shots fired and my arrival. KrishnaMa and my wife both told me they didn't see any other suspects."

"How about your entry?" asked Kilgore.

"As I was coming in, the masked guy with the Beretta was firing at me. I returned fire until he was no longer a threat. I'm glad I killed the dirtbag, but I'm concerned about what my wife's been through, being wounded, and watching me kill someone. She's had a lot to deal with today. I've got to go to the hospital with her. What's taking them so long? She should have been out of here by now."

"We'll have to figure out how she got hurt."

"The scumbag shot her."

"He didn't shoot anyone!" declared Kilgore. "You killed James Odessa, the M.E.'s son. She's on her way here to identify his body. He was probably off his meds again since he's wearing his Halloween mask, carrying his trick-or-treat bag, and a toy pistol."

"What the . . ." said Jennings as his voice trailed off, then it raised back up. "HE tried to rob this bank! HE tried to shoot me! This was an armed robbery in progress call, and HE shot my wife! What are you talking about? This is a good shoot."

"I said he didn't shoot anyone. It's a replica gun." Pointing his finger and cocking his thumb, Kilgore turned it at Jennings. "Before this is over, you'll be lucky to DJ at birthday parties."

"You're crazy! He was coming at me firing a Beretta!"

"We'll see about that," warned Kilgore. "We're going to check the bank videos here, and we'll watch your body camera later. You can turn it in as evidence when you hand over your weapon."

Jennings looked up at the ceiling, his eyes shifting, trying to understand.

"We'll search the bank, employees, and customers for a functioning gun. Oh, one more thing, were you wearing your seatbelt when you hit the little girl out in the parking lot?"

"What are you talking about? I didn't hit anyone."

"She's been flown to Wichita by Life Watch," explained Kilgore. "Critical condition."

Jennings took a breath, leveled his gaze, and with hands on his hips, said, "I'm calling my union rep to get an attorney."

The Natural You 13

Vivian heard the doorbell at 9:00 a.m. sharp, followed by banging at her front door. Thinking it was her roommate who had just left—forgetting her keys again—Vivian yanked the door open and readied a laughing smile, interrupted from toweling her long dark hair. Instead of her roommate, she found a man, muscled and mustached; his hair was so closely cropped that he looked to have just tipped his barber. With a shield and gun on his belt, and a photo ID displayed in his open wallet, he identified himself:

"I'm Detective Nick Halas, Cottonwood County Sheriff's Office, looking for Vivian Lamott."

"That's me. Is this about James O. at the bank?"

"Yes, James Odessa-Smith," said Halas, "We're following up on yesterday's events. Can we talk inside? We've got some loose ends in our investigation."

"Oh, yeah, sure." Vivian welcomed the detective into her home, catching a scent of aftershave while showing him to the living room. "I want to find out what happened to James yesterday, but first let me get my breakfast plate. Would you like some green tea or water with lemon?"

"Water would be great, thanks," Detective Halas replied as he sat down on the couch, already examining the room. Hanging from the inside center of the bay window was a dream catcher with an intricate web, enhanced by hundreds of colorful glass beads that pulled him in like gravity. Halas got up and walked toward it, close enough to examine the oval-shaped, turquoise-colored stone that had a small black feather tied to it.

Vivian, barefoot, silently returned with two glasses and a plate and said, "You like it? I made it. Took me weeks. I didn't know what I was getting into."

"Very nice. The beads draw you to it."

"Thanks." She handed Detective Halas his glass, and they sat down. "What can you tell me about yesterday? I can't believe James is dead; and I'm having trouble accepting that he'd do something so brazen, in public no less!"

"He's dead. I'll tell you what I can, but let me start by finding out how you knew James Odessa-Smith," Halas said, opening his spiral notebook.

"Yes, he's been a customer at the Coffee Co-op over the last six months, but we've known each other since grade school."

"Oh, really," said the officer, using an open-ended interview technique.

"We became friends in second grade in Miss Keller's class at Century Elementary. He was the class clown. I still remember him, first week of school, telling everyone he was going to bring naked ladies for show and tell. And the next day he did, from his mother's flower garden!" Vivian took a bite of her bagel topped with pickled herring.

"Naked ladies, the flower, that's good!" said Detective Halas. For his report he noted Vivian's deep brown eyes and estimated her height at five foot four and weight at 130 pounds.

Vivian grabbed her napkin, wiped some cream cheese off her lip, looked down and said, "I miss him already. When James broke the rules it was always out of fun, not meanness. He had a one-of-a-kind sense of humor. He got away with so much stuff! When the teachers reprimanded him, they would have to cover their mouths to keep from laughing at his antics. In sixth grade, last day of school, everyone had cleaned out their hallway lockers and returned to class except for James. Then in he walked, holding something unrecognizable to most of us girls, but the boys were cracking up. He raised it high above his head and asked, 'Did anyone lose a jock strap?' What could the teacher do? It was the last day of school, and he hadn't broken any rules. He was just having fun."

"So he wasn't really in trouble at school?" questioned the detective.

"By seventh grade he was already smoking cigarettes. I remember during a class break when I saw his books and papers piled in the hallway. The principal and teacher were searching his locker as James looked on. Mr. Wade gripped a package of Kools while James bounced on his toes and beamed at the rest of us. He was in out-of-school suspension for days or weeks, I don't recall."

"How about high school? Were you two still friends?"

"Not really. You know, our high school was so much larger that we just drifted apart. He was smart and had a lot of accelerated classes. We didn't have the same friends. But he still enjoyed being different. He was more the nonconformist than the class clown."

"In what way?" Halas encouraged.

"Well, I don't know this firsthand, but he and his friends would get high on marijuana after he had soaked the joints in embalming fluid. They called that smoking wet, even though they were dry. From what I heard back then and from what James told me recently, he'd lose his mind, become delusional when he smoked. But he was still really nice, just moody. And like I said, he was intelligent."

"Do you know his parents?"

"I knew who they were from school functions. My friends and I used to think they were his grandparents; they were so much older than our parents. But I never really knew them. They worked a lot. I remember James' mother did autopsies. We talked a lot about what it must be like to butcher bodies. James had a favorite sweatshirt he'd wear at school that said 'Coroner' in big bold letters, then below it, the statement: 'I'm here for your body.' "

"How about after high school graduation? Did he attend college?"

"We went our separate ways. At the Co-op he told me that he had a scholarship in debate. Then during his freshman year he had a couple of psychotic episodes and had to return home to get diagnosed and treatment. It was really drawn out with all the testing, waiting, and then experimenting with medications. First he was bipolar, then it was schizophrenia, then it was something else. Later he started up at the community college, but that didn't work out either."

After scribbling more notes, Halas looked up. "Miss Lamott, our department really appreciates you sharing this information with us. What about the last six months? What were the circumstances of the two of you meeting again?"

"I work as a part-time volunteer at the Coffee Co-op on Broadway. We mainly serve coffee, donuts, pie and ice cream—not exactly health food. The money we make goes into keeping the doors open so that we can practice and perform in the arts. We mostly act in short plays and read poetry, but occasionally we have a guest singer or musician. Our shows are at the Co-op. You ought to stop by; support the arts."

"What's your specialty?"

"Poetry. James and I met at Poetry Slam Night. I read one of my poems and he really liked it. Since James was often the loner and stayed in his apartment, I was lucky to reconnect with him. The Bissonte, where he stayed, gave him the privacy he usually craved, but his computer, music, and the Co-op were his windows to the world. Whenever we had a local singer that was country or western, the place was packed. James was usually there despite the crowd. James didn't imitate Willie Nelson; he was Willie Nelson. Wore a red bandanna and red tennis shoes most the time, and knew the words to all of Willie's songs.

"As old friends, James and I hit it off. He wasn't so open with others. It all depended on his mood. Often he was subdued and guarded with a blank stare, but other times he was all wound up and so excited you could barely understand him. With James you either got the manic or the depressive, not so much the in-between. You already knew he had mental illness, didn't you?"

"Yes, we're aware that he'd had incidents with hallucinations. Officers have told me about their contacts with him both on the street and in the county jail: disorderly conduct one time when he was walking down Broadway naked; trespassing and shoplifting cases; and suicide attempts. He was a semi-regular customer with law enforcement, but never for a serious crime. Do you know if he was taking his medications regularly?"

Vivian looked out the window as if she'd seen something and said, "I don't think anyone knew." Detective Halas noticed how she turned her head and broke eye contact, but she continued her response, again meeting his gaze. "This was an ongoing disagreement with his parents. Sometimes they wanted him living at home with them so they'd be better able to monitor his meds. He lived with his brother, Jonathan, for a while, but James just couldn't be that close to his family. He felt they were always trying to control him, especially his mother. In fact, they were trying to get guardianship of him, and when he found out, he got an attorney. From what he told me, it got personal in a bad way."

"You mean his parents were trying to get guardianship so they could make sure he was taking his meds?" Halas summarized.

"That's right, and to handle his money, to make financial decisions for him. That's what James told me. I know they were doing what they thought was right, but James used their attempt to help him as proof they were out to trick him, to get him put away. He wanted his freedom, but he also felt forced to lock himself in his room because he was scared of people. It was just sad to see that he had changed from the person who used to instigate play, to the person who didn't know how to play. I already miss him."

"When was the last time you saw him?" asked Detective Halas, prepared to record her response.

"Tuesday afternoon, about four o'clock, I was working when he charged in, his eyes wild, and his arms with different colors of ink all over them. The left arm, the one with the snake tattoo, was marked up so the bull snake looked like it had been cut into pieces. Its eyes were crossed out. James said they had entered his body again and were taking over. At first I didn't know whether to call 911 for help or listen to him. He opened a pill bottle half-filled with water and showed me two little crawly things that looked like tiny worms. They were swimming or moving like miniature underwater caterpillars. He said, 'I pissed them out of me! Millions of them are taking over! Help me, Vivian!' James kept scratching his arms, chest, and crotch. He wanted me to go with him right then.

"James raced back to his apartment with me trying to keep up, and he showed me more of the tiny worms in his toilet bowl. There were four or five, all live ones swimming around. They were really there. It was gross! I figured he had picked up some sort of parasite from one of our greasy spoon restaurants, most likely Fat Boy's. After I agreed to take the worms to a medical lab, James slowed down a bit. That's when he took his magnesium and zinc pills. Then we left. You know, if those worms had come out of me, I might have been acting just as crazy. I guess you're not hallucinating if the things are really there, huh?"

"What did you do next?" encouraged Halas.

"We immediately took them to the lab. There was enough help at the Co-op to cover my shift. At the lab they were really interested in the worms. Said they had never seen anything like them before; wanted a urine and stool sample from James. He fulfilled the request while I waited, and he paid with his medical card. A few of the employees, excited, were gathered around the specimens when we left. It was a party atmosphere. Man, they must get bored on the job. I ought to mail them some baking soda in a sealed envelope . . . Only kidding!" said Vivian.

"James isn't the only one who's interesting here. Maybe I need to run you NCIC (National Crime Information Center) and see what you've been up to in the criminal world or check with NSA (National Security Agency)," continued a grinning Halas, referring to her unexpected humor in light of her friend's death. "What did you do next, after the lab?"

"We returned to the Co-op, and then James walked back to his apartment. He had closed down and wanted to be left alone. I finished my shift and left."

"Were you worried about him? Did you think about calling someone?"

"I chose not to worry; otherwise, I'd worry all the time."

"You chose not to be worried? What do you mean?"

"James had a lot of problems, whether it was from his schizoaffective disorder or the medications. When I was at work, I was part of his support system. I did all I could to help him. What good would it have done for me to worry? Would that have made his life any better?" Vivian crossed her arms. "I didn't call 911 when he acted odd. They didn't have enough reason to cart him off to Larned again, and he wasn't breaking any law." Vivian's muscles tightened. "James valued the little bit of freedom he had despite his illness and his voices. He was a good person. He was just ill. When you're friends, then the illness is secondary and not so scary. He was my friend. I was never scared of him." Vivian let out a heavy sigh. "Sorry, but I'll never believe you guys had to kill him. He was sick."

Thinking about how to answer that, Halas recognized that things had shifted. Vivian was upset. Her friend was dead. He could explain about how Officer Jennings had responded to a "shots fired" call at the bank, and about the gun. But defending Jennings would look like criticism of Odessa-Smith for being ill or Vivian for being his friend.

Vivian continued, "What would you have done if you were me, Mr. Detective? Locked him up until his behavior got better? The beatings will continue until morale improves? He didn't belong in jail."

"I'm sorry if you thought I was blaming you. You were a friend helping him. I wasn't there . . . but . . . me being a cop, I'd have probably called his parents or EMS for help. That's just part of my thinking from my time on the job."

"Right, he's twenty-four years old and having a bad day, so let's take him to an expert who doesn't have enough time to help him, can't even find his case file, but will double bill. James was coping. First, he did not cut himself; we call that progress. Second, he came to me for help. He was following his personal action plan. We were friends because I didn't act like his therapist, a cop, or his controlling, emotionally abusive mother."

"From the containers we found at his apartment, the zinc, magnesium, and gingko, with store labels from The Natural You Vitamin Shop, I'd say someone was being more than a friend; they were giving him their expert advice and a supply of pills. That's where you work isn't it, Miss Lamott, The Natural You?"

"The Natural You is about nutrition, not medication. I'm not a doctor or anything, but from what I've read, a zinc deficiency can cause damage to the pineal area of the brain, especially when there are high copper levels in the body tissues. Levels of vitamin C also drop. There's also a theory that the low magnesium levels in the blood of people with active schizophrenia may be caused by the extreme amount of stress in their lives. Increasing the magnesium levels may help people with mental illness to handle their anxiety and other symptoms, including hallucinations. Ginkgo biloba is an herb that is known for helping people improve their memory by increasing brain circulation. Just eating fish a couple times a week helps. The pickled herring I eat is high in omega-3 fatty acids and in vitamins D3 and B12. Fatty acids are vital to the brain. They affect behavior and cognitive function."

"How long have you been helping James with his nutrition?"

"Not long after we got reacquainted, I started telling him about my job at The Natural You. It gave me the opportunity to help people when they were searching for ways to improve their bodies and minds. But James didn't tell me about his mental illness for another month. He was in denial. He believed that if he didn't take the drugs, then he wasn't sick."

"Did you encourage him to stop taking his prescribed medications?"

"No, I never told James to stop taking his medications, but he complained to me about the side effects of the antipsychotic drugs. We discussed that. He didn't like the feeling of being drowsy or burnt out, and he complained that the drugs caused him to gain weight even when he hardly ate. His dry mouth caught my eye right away. He was drinking a lot of water at the Co-op, but it didn't seem to help. I learned that his meds caused the dry mouth, not from meth, which is what some people thought. It's called xerostomia, and it's very painful.

"Another thing—like someone with Asperger's or autism, James had an obsessive personality. For him it was dental floss. If he wasn't flossing his teeth, he was creating art with it, usually religious symbols or biblical characters. I've saved a few of his creations made from brand-new floss if you'd like to see them. He had photographic recall of all his creative pieces and who he'd given them to."

"Some of the jailers told me that he had a couple of nicknames when he was locked up, one was 'Floss King', another one was 'Willie'," Halas recalled.

"I've never heard the 'Floss King' label but it makes sense, 'Willie' for sure," said Vivian. "Some of our customers at the Co-op greeted James with a 'hello Willie,' which always got a positive response from him. I told you there were times he really felt like Willie Nelson, not James."

Detective Halas' phone rang and after excusing himself, he answered. The call was brief. After he disconnected he asked: "Miss Lamott, would it be okay with you if another officer stopped by for a minute? She has some additional information that the investigation has uncovered. You might be able to answer a few of her questions. It will help wrap up this attempted bank robbery."

"Sure, if I can help, but I don't really see how I can be of assistance. I mean, James is dead, and from what I've heard, the bank wasn't robbed. No money was taken, right?"

"Yeah, that's correct, no money was taken, but we still want to understand his motivation."

"Good luck figuring out why James did something if he was hallucinating or delusional. What's amazing to me is that he never hurt anyone during his troubled times. That's the surprise, that even when he was out of balance and he got anxious or confused, even violent, that he wouldn't hurt others. People got scared of him because he reminded them of what could happen to them. We're all just a critical moment from being disabled or mentally ill, and we don't want to think about it. Bad things happen to other people. Meanwhile, we turn our heads and walk away."

Good Cop, Bad Cop 14

Agent Jones arrived, and Vivian met her at the door. Jones joined her detective partner in the living room.

"Miss Lamott," said Detective Halas, "FBI Agent Jones is following up on the search warrant at James' apartment at the Bissonte.

"Agent Jones, I need to tell you that Miss Lamott has been very helpful in giving us a picture of her friend James. She's shared with me a side of him we wouldn't have known since our contact with him was usually through 911 calls. Miss Lamott also volunteered that some of the vitamin pills found at his apartment were from The Natural You, where she works. James took them for nutrition, not medication."

Agent Jones took out some papers from a carrying case, then a small digital recorder from her pocket. She set it on the table, the green light already a beacon. "I hope it's okay with you for me to record our conversation. It'll help me keep everything straight; there's been so much information in the last twenty-four hours."

"Sure, go ahead," Vivian agreed.

"How close of friends were you and James?" asked Agent Jones.

"For these last six months we became reacquainted, but we only saw each other when I was working at the Coffee Co-op. We enjoyed each other's company. I'll miss him."

"Were you lovers?" continued Jones.

"What! I agreed to help Detective Halas, but this is ridiculous!"

"Nevertheless, were you lovers?"

"No, we were not lovers. Impossible. We were friends who respected one another. James was always thoughtful, except for times when he was having an episode. You could have learned from him."

"We believe you were getting more than table tips from James Odessa-Smith," charged Agent Jones. She kept attacking. "During our search of James' apartment, we found love poems from the two of you and photographs. But our most incriminating evidence is an airline ticket for next month to New York City. It's in your name along with hotel reservations made by James. Were you playing him?"

Vivian stared Agent Jones in the eye, shook her head in denial, and clenched her hands. Vivian was the first to break eye contact. When she did, Halas followed her glance to the coat rack by the door. He noticed a camouflage jacket and speculated whether Vivian or her roommate had military experience, because military experience meant possible weapons. The name tag patch was partially showing on the jacket, but he couldn't make out all the letters. The consecutive letters *R*, *U*, and *B*, sure didn't match *Lamott*.

"But living in affordable housing, a step up from the streets, how would he have the money to pay for air travel and a hotel?" asked Jones. "Miss Lamott, tell us, what part you played in yesterday's bank robbery?"

"You're dead wrong," said Vivian, staring back at Jones. "We were friends. We never wrote love poems to one another. Any photos you found were taken at the Co-op, probably at a play or a musical show. James and I made no plans to travel anywhere together. James didn't even want to leave his apartment, and you think he wanted to fly to the busiest city in the country? That doesn't make sense. Do your detective work. The only time he's ever been in my car was a trip last week to have his parasites tested at a lab. I've already told Detective Halas about that."

"We have the evidence," said Jones. "What we want to know is how much you were involved in the attempted bank robbery and possible credit card fraud."

"Not involved because I didn't know about the bank shooting until it was over," Vivian replied. "I read about it on Facebook after a friend called. I can prove it."

"If you cooperate, we can recommend the district attorney go easier on you—maybe it's all a misunderstanding. Otherwise, bank robbery is a federal crime with federal time. Odessa-Smith dead and others injured makes it much worse." Jones continued. "Prison is not a fun place to be, especially for a young woman."

"Hold on Agent Jones," said Halas. "Vivian's been cooperative with me, at least until you arrived. You don't need to threaten her. She may be telling the truth. Are you sure of the evidence?"

"You'll see the evidence soon enough. Miss Lamott, do you want to take care of this now or later, to be helpful or uncooperative? The choice is yours."

"I'm not talking to you anymore. You can leave now," said Vivian. "I'm talking to Detective Halas."

"If you'll stop making accusations, we can get somewhere here," said Halas to his partner. "Miss Lamott has denied knowing about the robbery. She may be able to prove that."

Agent Jones made no move to leave. "One thing that would help," she said, "is a look at her computer. One way or another, we'll get to see it. We're in the process of obtaining a search warrant to take it into evidence."

"James and I have sent each other e-mails and texts, but there's never been anything sexual or illegal. That's not me. I'll show you my computer. You can see all my correspondence with him. You don't need to get a search warrant. I haven't done anything wrong."

●

No photographs of James, no lover communications, nor travel plans for him and Vivian were found on her computer or phone. But a poem by Vivian was identical to one push-pinned to his wall. There were a string of one-way messages from Vivian at the Coffee Co-op to James, inviting him to visit, telling him that she was working, and how business was slow so they could talk. The most recent correspondence, sent Thursday night, was the most interesting to the plainclothes officers. It said, "Vivian, are you working this weekend? I have a surprise for you that you will like. Your friend, O."

Agent Jones asked Vivian, "Did you think your surprise was going to be a big bag full of cash for shopping on your trip to New York City?"

"I've already told you, James barely left Prairie Grove, let alone thought about traveling to major cities, especially the Big Apple. He never told me about travel plans for us."

"I never said we found tickets for both of you . . . Did either of you discuss traveling or purchasing anything expensive? And where did James usually get his money, from his parents?"

"James received a monthly SSA (Supplemental Security Income) check for his disability," explained Vivian. "Most of it paid his rent automatically from the account. Awhile back, when he fell behind on bills, he borrowed money from one of those predatory loan companies. The place was called Dash for Cash or something like that. Most of the time he refused help from his parents, but sometimes his dad did leave him money. With his emotionally abusive mother there was always a catch. With her it was always about winning, having the last word, and being in control."

"We didn't find any loan papers in his apartment, but we'll check on that," Jones said to Vivian. "Could be he got himself in quicksand and couldn't get out, but what about the trip to New York? We have a reservation in your name with your date of birth and address, and the airline ticket has been paid. That's a fact.

"Tell us how you instigated this," continued Jones. "How would he go out and rob a bank on his own without help? Is this typical of someone with schizophrenia? You're the one telling us he stayed in his apartment alone all the time. It doesn't add up that he'd attempt this without help, and you're his good friend."

"This is unreal," said Vivian. "I told you we never talked about robbing a bank or going to New York . . .

"But wait a minute! Months ago, when James was at the Co-op on a slow night, we talked about our future plans," Vivian emphasized, "our *individual* future plans. I told James about a poetry competition at poets&poetry.com. It required a one-hundred-dollar fee, and we discussed whether it was a legitimate contest. The first-place winner was guaranteed an all-expenses paid trip to New York City and an appointment with a prestigious publisher of anthologies of poetry."

"This idea may have legs," Detective Halas commented.

"Now this makes sense," said Vivian. "I think that when I lost hope in winning the competition, James picked up on my disappointment. Sometimes he really seemed out of it, but other times he just instinctively knew what others needed. He could have decided to make my wish come true by purchasing me a plane ticket even though he was usually broke. I never asked him or told him to do it. I never even suggested it. He never said a word about it. James might have done something like that for me or anyone else if he had the money. Maybe he borrowed the money or decided to rob the bank for the cash, but I still can't see him resorting to violence. It's possible that the voices in his head convinced him it was a good idea when it wasn't. Sometimes he followed their wishes. That's what I think."

"Nice and tidy," Jones responded. "Your theory conveniently gets you off the hook. But even though you deny being his accomplice, you still had a great deal of influence over him. You recommended vitamins over medication; that's right isn't it?"

"We talked about medications and their effects. That's not a crime. We did the same with vitamins. But it was always his choice."

"It was always his choice even though he was mentally ill?" questioned Jones. "When he was irrational and didn't recognize he was ill, how could he ask for help? You're one of those types who believe crazy people have civil liberties that protect them from receiving assisted treatment."

"He wasn't crazy!" interrupted Vivian. "He was a person with a mental illness."

"Same difference to me," said Jones. "In your misguided radical world, James was better off sick, free to do his own thing, rather than being forced to receive treatment so he could live a reasonably normal life. If James had been taking his doctor-prescribed medication, instead of your placebo pills, he might be alive today. Have you thought about that? Isn't that true?"

"Does this sound radical?" asked Vivian. " 'If the people let government decide what foods they eat and what medicines they take, their bodies will soon be in as sorry a state as are the souls of those who live under tyranny.' That was Thomas Jefferson.

"Agent Jones, Detective Halas, obviously this interview is over. I agreed to help you, not be berated by you. I just wanted to help. My father's a vet, MP. He's always told me to respect police officers, but don't let them push you around. He says that sometimes they forget who they work for and begin treating everyone as a suspect. My father raised me on the Constitution. His favorite Thomas Jefferson quotation is also about tyranny: 'Experience has shown, that even under the best forms of government those entrusted with power have, in time and by slow operations, perverted it into tyranny.'

"Agent Jones, you have a funny—no, irrational—way of treating people who have agreed to help you," continued Vivian. "I call it crazy. However, if you ever decide you want help with clarity and calming yourself, stop by at The Natural You. I'd recommend magnesium, catnip, and valerian for your stress. You might even benefit from aromatherapy or Qigong.

"Let me show you both out," said Vivian, standing and gesturing toward the door.

"Oh, one more thing, if you or any of your officers are suffering from PTSD, my father received valuable help from therapy. The biggest problem, he tells me, is that half the soldiers with PTSD are walking around in potential crises, but they don't recognize they have a problem. A few, certainly not the majority, are like time bombs ready to go off."

Chinese to Go 15

Carl answered the phone at the Morningcloud's house. "Hello?"

"This is Jesse Jennings calling for Carl Warrior. We met in the bank."

"Jesse, of course, how's your forehead?" asked Carl.

"I'm fine, thanks to you," she replied.

"Glad to help. How's Tom doing?"

"He's still really concerned about Suanna."

"Yeah, we all are. Too early to know much."

"Can you handle some good news?" Jesse asked.

"Try me," replied Carl.

"Rat was captured by the FBI, found in an agent's purse nibbling on a candy bar. She was one surprised cop. Fortunately the BOLO was out: 'Wanted alive, friendly gerbil, white hair, pink eyes, capture unharmed.' "

"Great news! Thanks for the favor," said Carl. "When Suanna gets conscious, this will make a huge difference to her. Rat and Suanna's horse, Lady Bonita, are her best friends. That little fella Rat is always into something. You met him, however briefly."

"Sure did. Cute. An officer told us what happened. Finding Rat in her purse was no big deal. All Agent Jones did was zip it up, presto, captured. Easiest hook up, ever. When she got to the station with one of our detectives, they put Rat in a dry aquarium used for retrieving fingerprints from property. Rat's there now, safe, and no doubt on a new diet: fast-food and cold coffee. Would you like to have someone deliver Rat to you?" asked Jesse.

"Someone has time to bring us Suanna's gerbil?" Carl inquired. "This is unbelievable, Kansas kind; beats our tribal police for door-to-door service."

"Carl, if I need to, I'll go pick up Rat and take him to you myself. I'm just really grateful for your help; so is Tom. I know the two of you talked. I'm concerned about him."

"Me too," agreed Carl. "We connected all right, but he was still overwhelmed. Next time we meet we may need to start all over. I'm doing what I can, watching the other children—Catalpa and Bud—while Joe and Elizabeth are at the hospital. If you give me an idea of when someone's going to drop off Rat, we'll make sure to be here."

"I'll call you when I know more. I just wanted you to hear the good news from me that Rat is safe, in police custody."

•

"Are you kidding?" asked Sergeant Hunter. "You're telling me our orders are to deliver a pet rat to some off-the-reservation Indian? I heard the FBI caught the rabid rodent. Let them return it; they like headlines."

"I'm telling you what the captain told me. It's a favor for Jennings and his wife," replied the night shift sergeant. "The pet, he's a gerbil, not a rat, belongs to the girl from the ten-forty-eight at the bank."

"Oh, okay then," Hunter said, calming down.

"It's in the old interview room the detectives use for storing cold cases; aquarium used for recovering latents is doubling as a rinky-dink holding cell."

"All right," said Hunter. "I'll have Schmedley get right on this."

"Figures," said the night sergeant.

"Hey, Schmedley! . . . Get in here!"

•

Officer Schmedley was still eating when he was assigned the special duty. Orders. He collected some tape and a paper bag from the nearby supply cabinet, a stapler off the desk, then grabbed his supper—Chinese carryout—to finish later. He was off to collect and hand-deliver the gerbil. Schmedley was also imagining a catchy new motto to represent the department's mission: we serve, protect, and deliver.

Upon entering the storage room, Schmedley's eyes started watering from the acrid air. *What's that smell?* he wondered. He immediately propped the door open wide.

He flicked the light switch on and saw the gerbil in the glass cubicle lying next to a Kansas Crime Stoppers coffee mug. Things weren't right, he immediately recognized. The gerbil lay on its back, not moving.

Holding his breath, Schmedley looked closer and watched for the animal's chest to fall or rise. He kept waiting for movement, but there was none, no sign of breathing, no sign of life.

"He's dead!" Schmedley announced. Sergeant Hunter would blame him, not the detectives. The captain would be furious at everyone. This was a favor to help Tom who didn't need any more stress in his life. Now, here was one more dead body. Schmedley sniffed the air and knew what had happened. The fumes killed it. Those toxic fumes from the heated Super Glue were deadly.

A memo had warned everyone to process prints outside until a ventilation fan was repaired, but no one cared. It was just another CYA memo. All of them, every single detective's IQ was dropping faster than the body weight of meth addicts on their dangerous drug diet.

Working in this sealed dungeon recovering fingerprints while inhaling cyanoacrylate fumes, was a recipe for disaster. The plain-clothes cops were seemingly unaware they were huffing glue and killing brain cells while fighting crime (or playing solitaire). Now Schmedley had a dead gerbil to return to the family of the seriously injured girl. One minute he was projecting the pleasure of delivering good news to a citizen, a moment later he felt like a police chaplain preparing a death notification. At the end of the day the department would take more flack over this, and he was the unwelcome messenger.

Schmedley picked up the aquarium and headed for the nearest exit door in order to find fresh air. At the department's outdoor break area Schmedely set down the aquarium on a lone picnic table that was hugging the building's brick wall in search of shade. Then the officer returned to the storage room to retrieve his leftover meal and the materials that he would use to transport the gerbil's body in a cardboard casket.

Feeling anxious, Schmedley sat down and opened up his bag of Chinese carryout. He looked again at the dead gerbil and considered what he would say to the Morningcloud family.

Rat suddenly scratched his belly, rolled over, and stood up. Twitching his nose, he lifted his head, staring at the police officer with the large, magnified, watering eyes, and running nose. Rat smelled food.

Schmedley dropped his jaw.

Recovering, the officer watched Rat as the gerbil returned his gaze. "Back from the dead! You gave me a scare," said Schmedley, realizing with a grin that he was again the good messenger. He reached into the glass cell and petted the furry animal before picking it up. While holding its upper body at eye level, Schmedley observed him and said: "You're not an it, are you boy?"

"Rat, let's get you something to eat." Schmedley opened his carryout containers and presented the albino gerbil a small portion of white rice and a piece of tofu with sauce.

Schmedley joined Rat as he finished his Chinese-to-go. "See if you like this bottled water," said Schmedley, as he overfilled the coffee mug.

Drinking, Rat acknowledged the gift.

"Buddy, you'll be home soon," promised Schmedley, as he cut air holes in the carryout container.

After recovery time for Rat, Schmedley placed him in the waxed cardboard box, fastened the tabs, and then put the carton in a large brown evidence bag. With a chopstick, he pierced additional air holes in the sack. Next, he sealed the top with a stapler and evidence tape. When he was done, there was zero chance of Rat escaping this temporary pet taxi. The gerbil was ready to ride.

Schmedley blew his nose, cleared his throat, and examined his symptoms, worried he was getting the flu.

The Ark 16

Life Story

James Michael Odessa-Smith, died May 26th, Prairie Grove, Kansas. He was born 25 years ago today in Prairie Grove to Carolyn Odessa and Shawn Smith.

He was a graduate of Prairie Grove High School, attended Kansas State University and Prairie Grove Community College. James was employed at Albrecht-Davis Veterinary Clinic for two years.

His parents survive along with one brother, Jonathan; Grandparents Michael "Gran" and Rose "Nanny" Smith; several aunts, uncles and cousins; his dog Xena.

Family will receive friends following the service at the church.

Memorials may be sent to The Ark Youth Ministry to support their Coming Home Pigeon Project Club or the Books of the Bible Quiz Bowl teams; Cottonwood County Humane Society; Prairie Grove Chapter of National Alliance on Mental Illness (NAMI); Rose Pedal Pushers Club. Condolences accepted at www.daviesmemorial.com.

•

It was a short life, but a long funeral service.

Colored light, like a kaleidoscope reflecting from the stained glass windows, illuminated dark-suited funeral-home attendants who handed out ceremonial programs at the entrance to the church's spacious sanctuary.

Looking out from the cover of the folded sheet, below the words "In Loving Memory" was a close-up photo of a serious looking James, wearing a white bandana neatly rolled up and centered across his forehead. His deep brown eyes, unfocused, looked past the viewer. His tats reached out in sharp detail, jumping from his sleeveless, black muscle shirt; one partially visible tattoo, an accurately detailed, docile bull snake, stretched the full-length of James' left arm. On his right shoulder was a large, three-dimensional cross displaying the letters *RIP* stencil-styled across the horizontal beam. "James Odessa-Smith" identified the photograph followed by the verse, Matthew 5:4, "Blessed are they that mourn: for they shall be comforted."

Background music played as arrivals were escorted forward. They filled the pews beginning at the third row from the front. The first two rows of the chapel were empty, reserved for the Odessa-Smith family. Center stage sat James' chrome-like casket draped with two dozen blood-red roses. Colorful tapestries, banner-like, hung from the ceiling and decreed: "God is Love," "God is Mercy," "God is Forgiveness," "Repent", "Rejoice," and "Prayer." Vases of vibrant flowers, especially peace lilies and roses, filled the wings of the worship area. Their assorted fragrances flowed, challenging the most experienced horticulturalist to isolate and identify the layers of scent.

The pulpit was empty.

In front and to the side of the sparkling coffin were wildflowers in narrow rectangular window boxes filled with colorful buffalo clover, better known as bluebonnets. They highlighted the casket's prominent place near the pulpit. The splash of blossoming purple was mimicked in the pews with scattered spots of draped color.

When the live organ music began, the congregation stood, and the Reverend Glenn Swain, his Bible and program in hand, entered the chapel. In his white sport coat, blond wavy hair, and glasses, he strode two steps ahead of Carolyn Odessa and Shawn Smith. Carolyn, eyes forward, walked in controlled measured steps, her shoulders board-like under her black sheath dress. Jonathan, their surviving son, followed, fixated by the flowers as the extended family filled the aisle and then the pews.

"Welcome everyone," greeted the pastor when he assumed his place in the pulpit. "Today's special service honors the life of one of our members, James Michael Odessa-Smith. In this time together we will share our memories of James, hear one of his favorite secular songs, and his favorite Christian melody about mercy and grace. We'll quote scripture, sing praise to God, enjoy music by the Rock Doves, and be reminded of the importance of faith and forgiveness, the cornerstone of everlasting life.

"Ecclesiastes, 3:1-8, reminds us why we are here. 'To every thing there is a season, and a time to every purpose under the heaven; A time to be born, and a time to die; . . . A time to kill, and a time to heal, . . . A time to weep, and a time to laugh; a time to mourn, and a time to dance; . . . A time to love, and a time to hate; a time of war, and a time of peace.' "

The clergyman bowed his head and continued: "Let us pray. We just ask you Lord to help us today as we recall our beloved brother James during his short time with us. We know that he is with you now, yet we still desire to hold him, fearful of letting him go. Help us today to redirect our powerful emotions of sadness, anger, and loss, so that we will be free to celebrate his life and our lives on earth without regrets. This and all things are possible because of your forgiveness. We are reminded today of our heavenly journey. In your name, Jesus Christ, our Lord. Amen."

Several echoes of "Amen" followed as the minister sat down.

Willie Nelson's distinct voice, singing his "Somebody Pick Up My Pieces," drifted out to the congregation, causing many mourners to nod to the drumbeat.

There's controversy in every church. In The Ark congregation, not everyone agreed with contemporary secular songs being played at services, but the Odessa-Smith family had requested a range of music, including secular. Even the choice of James' casket was initially controversial until it was learned that the Kansas State University Wildcats logo was not embedded on its outside but simply displayed on the inside liner. Early dramatic visions of a purple-colored college casket with sports memorabilia also dissipated once a website address, spread as quickly as a high school virus, displayed the stately alumni casket, not dissimilar to traditional models.

At the conclusion of the music, Pastor Swain stood and read from Isaiah 54:9: "For this is as the waters of Noah unto me: for as I have sworn that the waters of Noah should no more go over the earth; so have I sworn that I would not be wroth with thee, nor rebuke thee."

As Swain moved to take his seat, Jonathan rose from the front pew and proceeded to the pulpit. His reddish goatee emphasized his long face while the mop of hair piled high on his forehead mimicked a scoop of ice cream, creating an edgy, New-World flavor. As he prepared to speak, the corners of Jonathan's mouth pulled downward in synchrony with his drooping upper eyelids. Then, as if a switch were thrown, he looked up beyond his family to the crowded audience and spoke.

"We—my parents, grandparents, and I—appreciate the overwhelming support from our friends and family during this difficult time, including our NAMI support group and medical colleagues. It's still hard for us to grasp that James is gone, that he won't be showing up at the house for a welcome visit, sending us an electronic hello with entertaining attachments, or learning from someone, even in the middle of the night, that he, in one of his episodes, needs our help.

"Memories of my big brother James are many because he helped me grow up, teaching me along the way, even, at times, showing me what *not* to do! Like a deer tick's host, he was the one I attached myself to in my early childhood, sometimes to the point that he got tired of being the responsible one. According to my parents, when I got lost it was always James' fault, not mine. When I got stitches in my forehead from trying to catch the swing he jumped off, he got the blame. But we were close and the word 'brother' will always have special meaning deep in my heart. His spirit lives!

"There were times we both got into trouble," continued Jonathan. "When James was about nine and me seven, he cussed at a friend, and I repeated the choice words. Mother was in the kitchen and overheard our profane language. When she came into the living room, she was holding a bottle of Dove dish soap. Our friend was sent home with an apology before James and I extended our tongues, ready to receive a drop of liquid soap. James was soon crying, then hiccupping, then huffing, and there before the three of us, as God is my witness, my brother was blowing bubbles out his nose," Jonathan recalled. The hint of a smile tugged at a corner of his mouth. "James and I started laughing uncontrollably, and finally Mother's stern expression lightened to a smirk and then a smile. The last bubble blew out his nose, floated to the center of the living room, and popped in Mother's face! As she recovered, her hand covering her mouth, she yelled at us, 'You boys get outside, now!'

"The Ark was instrumental in our faith, spiritual growth, and even exposure to the joys of wildlife," continued Jonathan. "The stocked pond has been here ever since I can remember. James became fascinated with the church's homing pigeons and became a dedicated member of the

Coming Home Club, participating in their care, training, and competitive races. While James never became a veterinarian, he was a big help at the clinic because of his natural, compassionate way with animals. They trusted him." Grinning, Jonathan stated, "In fact he could floss a cat's teeth without getting scratched."

Upon hearing resident ducks and geese outside, Jonathan stopped, looked down, placed a hand over his mouth, and took a deep breath.

"I'm not my brother; I never will be. James helped mend injured animals, including birds, while I enjoy hunting. This, my brother held against me! One time James had a wounded dove brought to him during the hunting season, and by the following weekend James had sabotaged my shotgun shells. I was in the field for the early morning hunt; my cartridges were dry on the outside, but their gunpowder was useless. James had used water in a syringe to soak the powder. The only thing I accomplished that day was dry firing and having my hunting dog, Brittany, confirm in her mind that I was the worst, most useless, so-called hunter she had ever partnered with!

"James and I have both loved music, and many of you know his favorite musician was Willie Nelson. What he would have given for a chance to be included in a Willie Nelson concert tour, especially if he could have ridden on Honeysuckle Rose IV, the band's biodiesel tour bus. Willie would have loved my brother, as most people did. While James was never in a band, he sure looked like a roadie. I can see him now with his signature sunglasses and dark stocking cap covering his shaved head. He always wore construction boots, but never worked construction. When James flexed his arm, his bull-snake tattoo came alive, undulating, and when James vibrated his hand, the bull snake's tail mimicked the prairie rattler. In India he would have been a successful snake charmer.

"Sometimes I thought he could have chosen the path of a stand-up comedian. At one time he had the gift of gab, was quick, and witty. But the best description of James as we were growing up, was 'rebel charming'." The memory caused Jonathan to nod. He continued: "I got used to watching him rock the boat with his nonconformist attitude, and then, before getting pitched overboard, quickly recover control using his manipulative magic. He could read people exceptionally well. Actually, I'm surprised Mother ever punished James. The first time he got caught cussing may have been her last attempt; he was so much the rebel charming. His spirit lives!"

The clusters of blossoming, light-pink flowers, known as resurrection lilies, pushed toward heaven, towering a foot above their glass vase. Hearing James described as "rebel charming," caused Vivian to smile. That was the old James, the one she first met in grade school. She'd had a crush on him when the little guy told their second-grade teacher, Miss Keller, that he knew naked ladies who lived behind his house and would invite them to visit the class. To Vivian, the flowers always reminded her of her old friend.

James could easily impress people, but in time newcomers often pulled back from him. Cindy and Jeb Walker, who sat to the far right of the chapel, did both. Nine years earlier they had survived his firecracker prank and successfully interacted with him at mediation. Friendly contact between James and the couple followed, and eventually included their three children. But when James started showing up at their house unannounced and in a state of confusion, they retreated from the relationship. They were scared of his unpredictable behavior. It might have been unfair to James, but their children's safety was always their priority. James was temporarily banned from the property even though he loved them and would have never purposely hurt them. Cindy and Jeb didn't know what else to do.

"Here at the church we talk about the B.C. members who joined before The Ark was built and those who joined after its construction or A.C. Well, in our family, at least until James' death, our world was forever divided between before and after his mental illness. During his freshmen year at Manhattan he had a psychotic episode that forced him to return home. Eventually he was diagnosed with schizophrenia. The reason I mention his illness is that it was only a part of him, yet how he dealt with the disorder defined who he was. Consistently James showed me his courage by dealing with this inexplicable and unpredictable illness. Through NAMI we've learned it can happen to anyone in any family.

"None of us really knows just how much he struggled and fought the disease," continued Jonathan. "Some people thought less of him because of his schizoaffective disorder, as though he chose it, or could will his way out of it. One unnecessary but additional challenge for James was dealing with people who stigmatized him because of his mental illness.

"I've got to tell you that people with schizophrenia are more likely to be targeted than to hurt others and are more likely to harm themselves than to ever hurt other people. Even at the bank, which I'm not supposed to mention, James had no intention of injuring anyone. James didn't have a mean bone in his body before or after his illness. He never physically hurt anyone other than himself. Now, he got confused and depressed; he heard voices and had thoughts that he felt belonged to someone else. But despite these symptoms, he didn't always want to take his medication. He struggled through it and was making progress until the end. I emphasize, James still had his normal times. He wasn't crazy. Recently he was getting better. He was talking about going back to school."

Vivian sat and listened attentively. Describing James was tricky. He was both better and worse with his mental illness. How much his meds helped him was always a question to her. It was something she wanted to explain to the police officers who visited her after his death. But it didn't matter anymore; he was gone and she couldn't explain it.

"For a while we tried living together as roommates," recalled Jonathan, "but there were times we both wore down from our differences. When we were going out, it could take him an hour to leave the house because he was so sure he forgot to do something. Other times he would disappear for days at a time, causing us all to think the worst but hope for the best. Forgive me, but I just never learned to be patient or understanding enough with James. I tried. God bless his soul, and mine.

"He helped me grow up, and I wanted to help him work his way out of his predicament. Like my parents, I wanted him to take his meds and see his therapist. I wanted him well again. It was as if he was in a card game and had been dealt a bad hand. We wanted a new deck or a new deal, but he stuck with the cards he got. Most of the time he said he was good. He was clearer and more accepting about his disease than we were. I'm constantly asking myself, What more could we have done that would have made any real difference?

"Some people with heart disease have heart attacks; James had a brain disease and had brain attacks. We called them brainstorms," stated Jonathan. "Most people don't blame someone for having a heart attack, but about everyone seems to blame people for being mentally ill.

"James was never in the military, but every day he was doing battle with his disease. He was fighting it heroically. Unfortunately, sometimes he was fighting us as well because often he believed he was fine and didn't need to take his medication when we knew differently.

"When James was in a brainstorm, it was usually after a period of clear thinking, just when our family was the most hopeful for his recovery. James would try to describe his visions or voices afterwards. 'My brain went straight to heaven,' or 'My brain went straight to outer space,' he'd tell us. It was his attempt to explain this otherworld that only he could see or hear. We were outsiders and often felt that way. How we wanted to understand and help!" confessed Jonathan.

"In closing, my family appreciates your support. We need it. Even though we did everything we could to help him, when we're weak we feel like we, including 'the system,' should have done more. We blame ourselves. We blame others. But today my goal is to be strong like James would have wanted me to be, to help my parents and grandparents, and to be sure we all have a memorable goodbye to my brother. His spirit lives!"

Jonathan strode to his seat, his fist pressed against his lips.

The congregation continued worship as it sang "How Great Thou Art" from the Book of Hymns. Long before the fourth verse, the audience was alive with a musical spirit.

"What great art God creates!" proclaimed Pastor Swain when the final chord faded.

As the clergyman rose and walked toward the pulpit, he hesitated at a damp spot on the carpeted floor, looked upward to the ceiling and stared for a few seconds at the forgiveness banner. He was looking for an opening to Carolyn's heart. Here, an hour earlier, after admiring the forget-me-nots and reading the attached card, she shrieked, "HE KILLED MY SON!" threw the vase to the floor and repeatedly ripped the card into smaller and smaller shreds as the carpet absorbed the water. "HE MUST BE STOPPED!" she promised.

Settled in the pulpit, the clergyman began, "Thank you, Brother Jonathan, for your moving and memorable sharing. You have given us a fuller picture of your loved one, and we are better for hearing it. Indeed, his spirit lives!

"Brother James knew God, talked with God, lived with God. He listened. He didn't just ask God for help when he was weak. He didn't wait until the last minute to ask God's forgiveness. We as a family have lost one of our own, but now he's part of God's eternal family; he's on the salvation bus. James had bouts with evil, but did not succumb. James saw and heard things we missed. He was a messenger who fought a good fight. We lost a soldier of Christ, but we gained an angel in heaven.

"James is fine. Because he accepted Jesus Christ as his personal savior, he's in a safe, loving place. But for others gathered here, I want to share with you about coping with the feeling of not doing enough, blaming yourself, or blaming others. Some of you are angry with God; God understands. Some are unforgiving." With his left hand the minister pointed to the forgiveness banner above him and continued, "God forgives. God is love."

But Carolyn, front and center, marble-like, was not at peace. She listened but internally questioned. *If God is love, then why did he take James from me? Why was my boy stricken with a mental illness, then violently and unnecessarily killed before giving him a chance to be well, leaving us to grieve? Why?*

"Many may ask, why would God do this or let this happen?" continued Pastor Swain. "This is a human question. We know that in John 10:10, God said '. . . I am that they might have life, and that they might have it more abundantly.' James knows God as the Good Shepherd. While James was viewed by some here on earth as a nonconformist, God knows him as a good sheep, one who is saved and has found pasture and is forever part of Jesus Christ's eternal love. Praise God!

" 'And be ye kind one to another, tenderhearted, forgiving one another, even as God for Christ's sake hath forgiven you.' Ephesians 4:32.

"In Luke 17:3-4, Jesus admonished, 'Take heed to yourselves: If thy brother trespass thee, rebuke him: and if he repent, forgive him. And if he trespass against thee seven times in a day, and seven times in a day turn again to thee, saying, I repent; thou shalt forgive him.' And in Matthew 18:21-22, Peter was told by Jesus to forgive another person 'Until seventy times seven.'

"Why should we forgive?" asked the preacher. "It's necessary for our own forgiveness. Jesus said, 'And when ye stand praying, forgive, if ye have ought against any: that your Father also which is in heaven may forgive you your trespasses.' Mark 11:25."

The dark red roses elegantly draped over James' coffin were not store-bought. Carolyn had cut them from her extensive rose garden. And they were dying. The dying blood roses on James' coffin in Carolyn's church were severed—separated from their earthbound roots. Carolyn saw a fallen petal on the patch of water-stained carpet and recognized that things were all wrong. She was not feeling Christian.

Hell can freeze over before I forgive that murderin' SOB, Carolyn privately promised God. *Scripture tells me to forgive, but it also commands us not to murder. I'm not forgiving that monster, that murderin' SOB, who before God took my boy away from me. Heaven's not big enough for both James and Jennings. That fat pig will roast on a pit in hell and pay eternally for his crime. God, please, make it happen!*

"Join me in The Lord's Prayer," instructed the minister. "Our Father in Heaven, hallowed be your name . . .

"Our closing song 'Amazing Grace,' James' favorite, will now be played and sung by our own Rock Doves. Sing along in the Book of Hymns, number 92."

"Go in peace," concluded the minister after the hymn.

As the organ music began, the visitors rose. Pastor Swain walked to Carolyn and Shawn, leaned over, and spoke quietly to them. Then he exited with family in tow as they retraced their earlier steps back up the center aisle.

Captain Kilgore stood apart at the rear of the chapel and watched the crowd spill into the hallway. People pushed without touching, moved inches at a time, baby steps, their pace slowed by hearty hugs from Shawn and Jonathan. The two jointly thanked all who had attended and who gave them strength. Shawn was heard as he responded to condolences: "It's God's will . . . It's God will."

Carolyn was absent.

Meanwhile, funeral-service attendants collected decorative sprays on their respective easels and graveside flower baskets to be moved to the cemetery.

Outside, there was a church van that promoted the "Coming Home Club." It encouraged spirituality by "Flying High with Jesus," and invited attendance. "Call for a Free Ride to Church," it said, followed by the church's phone number and address. In the van were two full cages of birds on standby. One cage had white doves, the other colorful pigeons: both the city dwelling rock doves and the woodland band-tailed pigeons. They would be released at the graveside service upon completion of the minister's prayer as a final act to honor James' pigeon-caretaker role. The sounds of their flapping wings and soaring strength would be a tribute to this unique church member.

•

On a public street, a half block from The Ark's massive parking lot, in the shade of a burr oak, an ice-blue-colored PT Cruiser with tinted windows watched. Its engine and air conditioner were running. The Cruiser faced the church, giving the driver a clear view of the upcoming funeral procession. Binoculars were visible on the dashboard. A bumper sticker on the rear of the vehicle read: "FAT PEOPLE ARE HARDER TO KIDNAP."

Flint Hills Furies 17

FBI Agent Jones and Cottonwood County Sheriff's Detective Nick Halas did their due diligence. Their investigation in the attempted bank robbery by the deceased James Odessa-Smith hadn't revealed with absolute certainty any accomplices, but one person remained a person of interest: Vivian Lamott.

They confirmed her story about being a childhood friend of James and becoming reacquainted six months prior to his death. Her information about James visiting the Coffee Co-op on Broadway for shared conversations, poetry readings, and musical events, all checked out. The only time James appeared to have traveled with Vivian was a short ride to the health department when he believed he had been invaded by parasites. It turned out he hadn't been invaded by anything. The tiny worms in the toilet were drain fly larvae—a result of drain flies laying eggs in organic matter.

Captain Kilgore, a longtime legal collaborator with the medical examiner's office, had been the police department's designee who notified the parents of James' death the afternoon of the attempted bank robbery. The next day Kilgore, with a sense of urgency, had delicately asked questions of the grieving parents as he attempted to determine if there were any accomplices to the attempted bank robbery. The law enforcement interview with Carolyn and Shawn had been difficult, but the parents had readily agreed that others must have been instrumental in the crime because they couldn't imagine James, a "good boy," of ever concocting such a thing.

Neither Carolyn nor Shawn could fathom that James had planned a bank robbery. It's not that he wasn't smart enough or capable, they said, it's just not something he would ever do—on or off his meds. When Kilgore asked the parents if they knew Vivian Lamott, their muscles

tightened before replying at once, informing him that she had been a
bad influence on James. Carolyn explained how James had viewed Vivian
as a major influence in getting him to stop taking his meds. Tragically,
Carolyn claimed, the woman's so-called nutritional advice was outdated
or hocus-pocus, wishful thinking.

Kilgore helped Shawn check on the credit card purchases, apparently made by James, for the round-trip flight to New York City and the
hotel-room reservation. When Kilgore notified the parents that Vivian
Lamott was the beneficiary of the paid trip to New York City, they were
puzzled and pensive. The reservations were quickly canceled.

The parents substantiated the claim that they had attempted to get
control of James' medical and financial decisions. They also accounted
for the Honda Accord towed from the bank's parking lot. It belonged to
James, but had been parked on their property for several months. It was
not currently registered, and James had probably kept the ignition key.
Had the police located the key? Shawn asked.

Carolyn and Shawn denied ever seeing James in possession of a replica gun. "Unlike his brother, he wasn't much for guns or hunting," said
Shawn, but they had observed James wearing the Scream mask during
past Halloweens. They recommended that the investigators speak with
Jonathan about the replica gun.

Jonathan explained to the detectives that James would sometimes
wear Ghostface around their apartment when they were roommates, especially when they watched slasher films. Jonathan also recalled seeing
the replica gun in James' Bissonte apartment a few weeks prior to the
bank robbery. When Jonathan had first seen the weapon, he had been
concerned until he learned it was non-functioning. James had explained
to Jonathan that his friend, Vivian, had recently loaned it to him. Jonathan recalled how his brother had been anxious about someone breaking
into his apartment, and the toy gun had helped lower his anxiety.

One result of a catastrophe is how survivors can blame themselves
for the results. In the case of James' unfortunate death, Jonathan asked
the detectives if they thought he was to blame for not doing anything
about his brother possessing the replica gun used at the bank. Jonathan
asked, "That toy gun got him killed, didn't it?"

It was a long shot, but one piece of evidence pointed toward Vivian lying to the detectives. She had denied seeing James in person for a
period of several days prior to the attempted bank robbery, yet, the autopsy report listed the contents of James' stomach as undigested herring,

chicken, and bread. Detective Halas recalled Vivian eating a bagel with smoked herring when he interviewed her the day after the bank shooting. Of course, Vivian wasn't the only person in Prairie Grove who ate herring, and her eating preferences didn't prove James was at her house, but it was just one of those endless pieces of information that required follow up. But this lead, like others, proved unhelpful in linking Vivian to any contact with James the morning of the attempted robbery. A search of James' apartment after his death found an empty can of chicken and herring cat food in his kitchen trash can.

The autopsy also revealed that James' body had no sign of legal or illegal drugs in his system. He wasn't high and he hadn't been taking his psychotropic medication.

The owner-manager of The Natural You spoke highly of Vivian as an employee. As a salesperson she was quick to engage customers, knowledgeable of the store's products, and helpful with recommendations. "No," the manager said, "I don't believe I ever heard Vivian give medical advice to a customer."

Finally, the investigators decided to approach Vivian's father to see if he could offer another perspective on her personal history. It was obvious that Halas, a forever Marine, would take the lead in the meeting because he recalled Vivian's remark that her father had served in the military police. But the phone call from Halas to veteran Lamott was surprisingly brief. Sergeant Lamott was direct and to the point: "She's intelligent, honest, and honorable. She doesn't break the law; she follows it. If you leave your bullshit at home, and treat her right, she'll tell you anything you want to know."

Despite the fatherly advice, after learning that Vivian had given James the replica gun he used at the bank, Halas and Jones petitioned for a search warrant of Vivian's residence. They would not rely on her cooperation. In the opinion of the two crime fighters, the fact that Odessa-Smith had purchased the plane ticket and made the hotel reservation, just days before the attempted bank robbery, was too much of a coincidence. Even though the day after the bank shooting Vivian had voluntarily showed them e-mails and texts, they still wanted a thorough examination by forensic experts. The investigators planned to seize both her computer and phone in order to look for deleted or hidden communications, despite the fact that no additional incriminating evidence had been discovered on James' electronics.

•

Detective Halas and Agent Jones knocked at the front door of Vivian Lamott's house. Her roommate, Elvira Hudson, answered. "Viv," she said, as she turned her head toward the living room, "we've got visitors."

The investigators explained their purpose, produced the search warrant for the residence and electronics, and were allowed to enter.

Elvira Hudson explained she was the owner of the property and that she and Vivian shared the residence. As Hudson unfolded the papers and began carefully reading the search warrant, she added, "Let's give this an attorney's perspective."

Halas and Jones were quiet as Hudson read. Halas looked around the living room, again noticing the attractive dream catcher made by Vivian. It resonated with him. Then he spotted the coat rack. It was bare.

"Well, it's signed by a judge," said Hudson, as she handed the papers to Vivian.

"It's legal," said Jones.

"It's questionable and far reaching," replied Hudson. "I'm wondering how much this investigation is being unfairly influenced by Carolyn Odessa's blame game. Previously, she's made false allegations against my client."

"What are you going to do?" Lamott asked Halas.

"We're going to search the house for evidence of collusion between you and James Odessa-Smith as it relates to his attempted robbery of the Prairie Grove National Bank on the twenty-sixth of May. Specifically, we're looking for correspondence of any planning, including research on bank robberies and hiding assets from robberies. It also includes a search for documents in reference to planning, scheduling, or purchases for your scheduled visit to New York City. This warrant includes a search of the residence and seizure of your home computer and personal cell phone. We're also looking for any receipts or evidence documenting your purchase of the replica gun used by Odessa-Smith in his attempted bank robbery. We have officers outside prepared to aid us in the search."

"If you'd like to assist us, that would be helpful," added Jones.

"Helpful to whom?" asked Hudson.

Lamott turned to Halas and asked, "Why are you doing this? I've been cooperative with you, told you all I know, and now you force your way into our house. I showed you the e-mails and texts to James and it confirmed I didn't contact him about the bank robbery. You don't need to do this."

"Vivian," said Elvira, "you don't need to explain to them because they don't believe you."

"But, I haven't done anything wrong," Vivian replied.

"Let me give you some legal advice," Elvira said to Vivian. "You don't need to help them. I'm still questioning how the judge could have signed this. There's speculation but no probable cause."

"Are there any weapons, especially guns, in the house?" interrupted Jones.

Vivian and Elvira looked at each other with hesitation.

"Yes," said Hudson, "but there are no weapons listed on your search warrant, and the guns we legally own are locked in a secure room downstairs. Your safety's not an issue."

"We'll decide about our safety," replied Jones. "Eventually, we'll be searching that room for evidence, and we have the authority to seize the weapons until we're done with this warrant."

"Vivian," said Elvira, "Rule number one is to not argue with the police. Rule number two is to remember that this can all be thrown out in court at a later date. I recommend we stay calm and watch them closely to see if they damage anything. They'll give us a list of seized items when they've completed the search."

"Whatever you say," said Vivian.

"Speaking of guns," said Halas, "we're looking for the customer receipt for the purchase of the replica gun used by Odessa-Smith at the bank robbery. Do you have it?"

"Detective Halas," said Hudson, "I'm representing Vivian until she gets another attorney; I'd like a few minutes to talk to my client privately so that I can encourage further cooperation with you on the search warrant. Will you agree to that?"

"Go ahead."

The two women went into the bedroom and closed the door. After several minutes, they returned to the living room where the officers were waiting.

"The replica gun you're referring to may be a theatrical prop owned by the Coffee Co-op," said Vivian. "I loaned James the prop about a month ago when he was in fear of a home invasion. James and I had an understanding that he'd return the prop in the future when it was needed by our performing artists. The replica gun I loaned him had the letters *CCB* marked on it. Is that the same one you're referring to?"

Jones and Halas looked unsure. The latter said, "I believe so. We'll check."

"Now, about our safe room downstairs," said Elvira. "We're requesting you bypass that room since it holds no correspondence to James, no purchases in reference to a New York City trip, no research on bank robberies or hiding money."

Jones started shaking her head and partially smiled. "Sounds like the perfect place to hide documents. We wouldn't be doing our job or following the DA's expectations if we bypassed the room," she said. "If there's nothing to hide, then it's to your benefit to show us. In court we can be your best witnesses."

"Or our worse enemies," continued Hudson. "When you're ready to search that room, I've got the key, so there's no need for you to force it open."

The officers began their search.

•

Vivian and Elvira drank green tea, but they acted as if they'd each guzzled three consecutive cans of Red Bull. Antsy and pacing, they repeatedly looked at one another for reassurance as the officers methodically searched the house from top to bottom.

Finally, outside the safe room, Vivian inserted her key into the solid door's lock, turned the key, heard the click, and backed away. Jones opened the door, flipped the light switch on, and was stunned to see rows of shelving stretching from floor to ceiling, methodically stocked to capacity with a variety of canned goods and water bottles. In the far left corner of the room, next to a partially open closet, was a gargantuan gun safe large enough to hold a dozen long guns and forty-thousand rounds of ammo. The closet held camouflage clothing, including pants and jackets hung from hangers, while boots, belts, and walkie-talkies lined the floor below them. Above the closet, pinned to the wall and partially draping the closet, was a dark-colored nylon banner proclaiming in white print: "FLINT HILLS FURIES, PPC." On the same banner, flanked to each side of the wording, were inked drawings: on the left was a woman with snakes representing her hair and blood dripping from her eyes; to the right a coiled snake—ready to strike—cautioned, "DON'T TREAD ON ME."

Halas walked to the closet, pulled out the first jacket and checked its nametag. "RUBY" was the identifier above the breast pocket; the second uniform introduced "RITA MAE" Shoulder patches on the jackets close-ly resembled the banner's graphics. To the left, the woman with the viper hair and weeping tears of blood identified this organization—pre-viously unknown to local law enforcement or the FBI—as the "Flint Hills Furies." To the right, the coiled snake hissed the words: "Lesbian Separatists."

Battle Buddies 18

Carl and Tom were bonded from the moment Officer Jennings stuck his smoking Glock in Carl's face. At the hospital the two men resembled battle buddies; they couldn't stop talking.

"How's your wife?" asked Carl.

"Her forehead's going to be okay," said Tom, "but it's a struggle right now. Jesse's always said that she accepts how I might get hurt on the job, but now she's been injured and . . . she's watched me kill someone . . . She didn't sign up for this . . . " Then changing the subject, he asked, "How's Suanna?"

"It's wait and see."

"God, I'm sorry I hit her! Must have been my tunnel vision; I never saw her."

"She's always running somewhere. She could have run into anyone. It wasn't your fault."

"How about her parents? How are they taking this?"

"They're pretty numb," replied Carl.

"Yeah, I guess so," agreed Tom.

"What about you? How're you holding up? First shoot?"

"Yeah, ten-four. In all my years, first one."

"It's different for everyone. Just take it a day at a time. Get any sleep yet?" he asked.

"Not really. Hitting Suanna, when they told me, I couldn't believe it, made me sick, worse than the shooting, but everything's mixed together in my head . . . especially with Jesse . . . her seeing it all and getting hurt, too. I appreciate you being there for her when I wasn't."

"No problem. Wasn't much, just applied a little pressure to a wound. Seen worse. Least I could do for an artist interested in Indians. Who knows, she might be the next George Catlin."

"George Carlin?"

"Catlin. He was a painter from the nineteenth century. Pretty good."

"Yeah, she told me she was itching to get you to the studio in a buffalo robe. Old pick up line. When we first met, she invited me to an art show."

"Well, it didn't work on me. I was getting ready to let her down easy. She said your town's local art group has a weekly modeling class. I was ready to tell her it would have to be another time, that I was headed back home. Now, that's on hold."

"Yeah. Well, we're all on hold right now. Waiting."

"Army Guard, First in War, First in Peace, so I've had plenty of practice waiting. We learned to hurry and wait. How about you? Any military time?"

"No, just policing."

"You remind me of a buddy I got to know from basic training at Fort Lewis."

"Really? He was my size?"

"No, not your size, just the way you talk."

"Oh, okay, ten-four. My extra weight almost kept me out of law enforcement."

Just then, a little boy across the hospital waiting room said, "Mommy, that fat man is sitting on two chairs."

"Billy, you hush! That's not polite," his mother scolded.

"It's all right, ma'am," Jennings said.

Looking the boy in the eye, Jennings told him, "When I was your age, I was so skinny my bones poked through my skin. I got tired of other kids making fun of my weight."

"Really?" the boy asked.

"I was so skinny that my pajamas had room for only one stripe, and my pants had only one back pocket."

"Awh," said the boy.

"When I took a shower, I had to run around just to get wet."

"Come here, Billy. We can visit your Uncle Herb now." Billy and his mother left the room.

"So, you had to run around to get wet, huh?" Carl commented, with a gleam in his eye.

"It hasn't helped all that much, but I've learned the difference in how fat people and skinny people think," said Tom.

"Oh? How's that?" asked Carl.

"Skinny people split a large combination pizza with three friends. Skinny people think chocolate Easter bunnies are only for kids, and skinny people don't celebrate with a hot fudge sundae every time they lose a pound.

"My extra weight almost kept me out of law enforcement," Tom repeated.

After Carl responded, "Mm," the two buddies fell silent for a while.

It was a relief for Tom to think of anything but the bank, recalling his early days on the sheriff's office when he was hired to work the jail a lifetime ago. The agency was desperate for new hires, and while he was on the Cadets, a joint venture of the city and county, he'd been noticed as a potential recruit, in spite of his obesity. He was a quick learner who displayed self-confidence, not arrogance. And it didn't hurt that a few of the deputies, character references, were his hunting buddies who found him likeable and generous. He shared his hunting spots and proved to be a crack shot. Best yet, they appreciated his seasoned skills in butchering game.

Tom remembered some demeaning looks and derogatory comments from a few sheriff employees and prisoners during his probationary period. But he compartmentalized the comments the same way that as a jailer he helped keep certain prisoners separated. Tom proved himself ready, a team player, even saving an inmate's life during rounds one night when he pulled the suicidal man down from the hanging sheet and began CPR until the EMTs arrived. Despite his competence, maybe due to it, he grew tired of the predictable bells and buzzers, pounding and yelling, lame stories, putrid smells, and summer heat.

Eventually, Tom got out of jail. When the sheriff's office didn't have openings on patrol, he waited. He bided his time. He didn't need to study geography in preparation for patrol's written test. He already knew the township and county roads from his years of local hunting and fishing. Occasionally, when he wasn't working mandatory overtime, he did ride-alongs with patrol officers in order to learn protocol. But finally, he was passed over one too many times, and he knew it was a perception that his extra weight was a hindrance. Some people didn't understand he was better than his size. So when the police department relaxed their physical requirements, he jumped at the opportunity to get on with the city. Except for ridiculous problems getting seat belted, he shined on patrol, showing his field training officer both his observational and people skills. Jennings loved the road and, surprise, as a former broadcast DJ he was comfortable talking on the police radio.

Patrolling gave Jennings an opportunity to interact with the public and spar with his platoon of fellow officers. Many of his uniformed friends called him "Taz," remembering his late nights in radio. They had enjoyed his upbeat country music and felt an unexplained personal relationship with him from their long, solitary nights together when his husky voice was more calming than dispatch. But Jennings also earned his nickname from the quantity of his drive-through, junk-food diet, since a Tasmanian devil was known to eat voraciously. A few of the officers, also recruits from the jail, called him "*LB*," for Lunch Box, a moniker from his deputy days when he was a jailer and ate for free while on duty.

Tom felt blessed to be paid to solve crimes and catch criminals as he worked for community justice. In public he liked being in uniform and solving problems. He also learned that he relished the camaraderie. Working outside was a bonus as it gave him back some personal freedom lost to countless twelve-hour shifts behind bars. At first, new to the game, he didn't even want to leave the LEC to go home at the end of the work shift. He obsessively hung around to visit officers after his paper work was done. But he gradually appreciated real time off so he could spend time with his hobbies, his dogs, and his family.

•

A mother and her son walked past the waiting room door. The boy, maybe ten, wasn't exactly walking. He was swinging himself down the tiled hallway on crutches, one leg in a cast. She was explaining that now he wouldn't be able to play soccer.

Carl thought of his own boy, Storm. He loved all his children, but he worried about Storm. Angel, Maggie, and Albert were all engaged with life, especially through school classes and activities. Storm, however, had little use for school, constantly argued with his siblings, resisted doing his chores, and wore an attitude against parental authority. Storm presumed adults existed for the purpose of providing him the latest technology. Generally displaying dissatisfaction with life, there were exceptions: four-wheeling, basketball, and rap music. But none of his interests helped him succeed at school.

Just twelve years old, Storm preferred to hang out with boys a couple of years older than himself. This didn't sit well with Carl and Tina. Two of these other boys had already been banned from the community center for vandalizing a tribal truck by drilling a hole in its gas tank. But what, questioned Carl, could he or Tina do to prevent these unhealthy friendships? Once something happened, Carl and Tina often heard about it, but it was after the fact, too late. They wanted to prevent trouble, not respond to it. Carl had warned Storm that "you can judge a person by the friends they keep," but this had appeared to have the opposite effect than the one intended. Storm agreed that he was a reflection of his older friends, and since they were "ace" (cool), then he was too.

Carl thought about taking away Storm's four-wheeler. Somehow he needed to get his boy's attention. He shifted in his chair and his attention came back to the present. "Sure appreciate you getting Rat returned to us," he said.

"Oh, no problem. I'm still waiting to hear details. All I heard on our radio was 'the package has been delivered.' Is the gerbil okay?" asked Tom.

"Seems fine. He had himself an adventure. Catalpa and Bud were feeding him this morning."

"Now, I know them a little bit from school. They're Suanna's cousins, right?"

"Yeah. Joe and Elizabeth are taking care of them for a while. They're Joe's niece and nephew."

"How'd you get the rodent returned to you?" asked Tom.

"Well, first off, let me say that you guys go to a lot of trouble to help people. I can't see all this happening on the reservation, but we have a lot of travel time just getting to calls. We have some good tribal officers, but a couple would rather drink coffee than take a report. I know; one of them's my brother-in-law."

"Well, that's true everywhere. We have a few like that too, but they swear that over coffee and donuts they get their best leads on cases."

"My brother-in-law Billy is always looking for one lead, where, on any particular day, the fish are biting," said Carl, laughing. "But about the other night, after me and the kids got back from the hospital, I got a call from an officer saying that Suanna's gerbil was found. He told me that he'd been ordered to personally return Rat to me as soon as possible."

"Was he in uniform or plain clothes? Did you get a name?"

"Can't remember his name. He was a white guy in uniform; no rank; drove a clean, marked Charger; he was young; wore black-rimmed glasses; professional manner. When he called, I told him I wasn't going anywhere and he said he'd see me in fifteen minutes.

"He shows up carrying a brown paper bag stapled at the top, but it looks like it's been target practice at our Cultural Camp's firearms day. The bag's greasy smell was familiar. Asks me if he can come in for a minute and I say 'sure.' Says there's some paper work for me to sign, but before getting to that he wants me to be sure that the property is, in fact, ours. So he tears open the top of the bag, evidence tape and all, reaches in and pulls out a Chinese carryout container. After we go to Rat's cage in the bedroom, he opens the box and there's Rat standing up staring at both of us, his front paws gripping the little cardboard box with his nose sniffing the air. The officer asks if it's Rat. Well, of course it's Rat, I mean, how many other gerbils are running around inside banks in Prairie Grove? Then, get this, along with the carryout container, in the bottom of the bag were a pair of chopsticks and a take-out menu: Golden Dragon. I've eaten there. I'm all smiles. Of course I'm happy for Suanna to have Rat back, but right then, because of the familiar cooking smell, I start thinking of home on the rez, our Trading Post, and, dear God, fry bread and Joe-Joes!"

"What are Joe-Joes?"

"They're tater babies."

"That must have been Officer Schmedley. He's different, but gets the job done. When he's working with children in the schools, they love him.

"Suanna has told me a little about the reservation," continued Tom.

Carl leaned back and stretched his legs. "I live with my family in a little town called Nespelem. We've got about two-hundred residents, mostly Indian, but not everyone. It's near Grand Coulee Dam. Have you heard of it?"

"Yeah, I saw the dam when I was on a hunting trip, but we didn't take a tour or anything. Wish I would have checked out your Nespelem while I was nearby. We stopped at a casino for a drink."

"The Coulee Dam is one of the largest in the world. China built a massive one, displacing many locals like the Grand Coulee did with our tribe. We lost a river with abundant fishing grounds, especially at Kettle Falls, and had our graves and spiritual grounds flooded. In return we got promises, per caps, and canned pink salmon.

"Nespelem's less than two hours from Spokane. We have an elementary school, post office, gas station with a car-repair shop, a small

convenience store, a couple bars, a senior citizen center, and a cemetery—no, a couple three cemeteries. No Walmart."

"Sounds like our small towns around here. What do you do for
work?"

"I'm a CPA, a certified public accountant. I travel a lot doing independent audits on businesses, mostly American Indian. This trip, to
help Joe, I'm delivering a horse to a buyer on my way back. It makes my
trip longer, more trouble, but Joe and me, we go way back. Best friends.
Families are close too."

"But just how's the reservation different than here? Are the laws different? I've seen some special license plates in Oklahoma."

"After we signed treaties, land was reserved for us along with rights.
We're a sovereign nation inside the borders of the United States. We're
governed by our own administrative and judicial branches. Members of
our business council are elected from our four districts. Our reservation
is huge—2,300 square miles. That's 1.3 million acres. I remember being
told in grade school that it's larger than the state of Rhode Island."

"Larger than Rhode Island? Wow!"

"Yeah," said Carl, laughing, "but I guess Rhode Island isn't all that
big. Most of our reservation is wilderness, few roads, and few people."

Tom listened and encouraged Carl with a steady nod.

"Twelve Indian bands or tribes make up our Colville Confederated Tribes Reservation, so, of course, we have our cultural differences.
We've got a good museum when it's open. Tourists don't understand
that our reservation has non-natives living on it. Because there's private property within the reservation, anyone can live there. Another
thing, we don't necessarily agree on things just because we're Indians.
We see things differently, just like people in any community. That's human nature. The closer you get to something, the more you're able to
distinguish differences."

"I hear you on that, ten-four. Sometimes the public thinks police
officers are all the same. Once the public gets to know a couple officers personally, then they understand we're not all cloned from the same
tree."

"Yeah, exactly," acknowledged Carl. "You're not all fishing on the
job," he said with a grin, again referring to his sister's Billy. "Our reservation is run by an elected tribal business council, but even when the
tribal council agrees, they take a lot of heat from the public. Our people
regularly accuse council members of wrongdoing and mismanagement.

It centers around wasting money, especially for not passing on enough of the government per capita payments earned from the dam or settlement monies. People complain about the council members being well paid, but they have a lot of responsibility. I'd say there's a general lack of trust on where the money goes. Our tribes also earn money from timber rights, cattle grazing, and the casinos.

"We also have more than our share of poverty. Our unemployment is extremely high, despite work opportunities at the casinos. That's another assumption people make; they think we're all getting rich from gambling revenue. They don't understand that we're not in Las Vegas. Our casinos are located well off the urban grid and are mostly limited to slot machines. At least the casinos help with tribal employment, especially the one at Omak. It's got a hotel and a couple of restaurants now."

"I've been to an Indian casino by Kansas City. Nice place," said Tom.

"But, even with our disagreements and challenges, it's home. At home we're less likely to feel like outsiders. We live in a valley where we have hardships, but we've also got beauty, family, and friends. The tribal administrative building is top-notch; it was built after the old one burned down. And the community center isn't new, but we use it a lot, everything from basketball tournaments to sweat lodges. We have an annual Fourth of July rodeo with powwow and stick games. And the only tipis you'll find on our rez are used during our powwow in the tribal circle. We don't live in them anymore; been a while."

"I've heard stories passed down from my family that my great-great-grandmother was Indian," said Tom.

"Really?" Carl said.

"Yeah, but I've never researched it. We don't have any documentation."

"What tribe? Cherokee?" he asked, keeping a straight face.

"Man, how did you know?"

Carl sat in silence. Then, displaying a wide grin, he started laughing before his face erupted into long, loud snorts.

An elderly couple, interrupted from their magazines, looked up with similar questioning stares that wondered: What's wrong? Is he all right?

"What's so funny?" said Tom, as he waited for Carl to recover.

"Cherokee," Carl said again, holding his sides.

"Huh?" Tom said and waited.

"The way things change. People haven't always wanted to claim Indian blood."

"I'm not claiming it; I just know it's a family story."

"It's a story all right. Might even be true. Oklahoma's down the road where the Trail of Tears ended. I've heard the Indian grandmother story so many times it just struck my funny bone. We call it 'Cherokee Grandmother Syndrome.' Maybe that's how the Cherokee keep their numbers up along with the Navajo."

"You smoke?" asked Carl.

"No, but I've got other bad habits."

"I sure need one bad."

"RATTATATAT . . . RATTATATAT . . . RATTATATAT . . . KUK KUK KEEKEE-KEEKEEKEEKEEKEEKUK KUK."

"What's that?" asked Tom, startled. "Sounded like gunfire at first. What caliber?"

Carl took his phone out of his shirt pocket, looked at the screen, and pushed mute.

"When I got back from Iraq I wanted to be home, but I also missed my buddies," said Carl. "I figured being home would solve all my problems; that I could pick up where I left off, but things were different. I was different; Tina was different. I learned that I had issues related to my combat PTS that weren't going away overnight. I had nightmares. I'm telling you so you can watch for it. Whatever you're going through now, after the shoot, is normal. If you can't sleep, normal; if all you do is crash, normal. If you're anxious, worried, obsessed, understand that this may stay with you for a while, even longer. But you need to know that if the symptoms hang on then you've got to get yourself some help. Don't wait too long.

"It took me awhile, but I did. Now, I manage my stress. I can drive cross-country for a job without a paralyzing fear of IEDs or an ambush from an overpass. I can usually stop at a box store and be okay if the stores aren't congested or the lines too long. I still prefer store-bought popcorn over homemade, because of the sound. When I first got back and Tina used to pop it, it was a trigger for one of my flashbacks, too much like rounds going off up close. But with help, I've learned to handle most of my combat stressors. Now I'm okay with my pileated woodpecker ringtone, both its drumming on an old hollow tree and its song. Now I hear wildlife and think of our back country, not gunfire, not Iraq. You like it? It works for me."

"No, I won't be getting your ringtone! I've got a lot of my own sounds and images bombarding my head right now. Don't need one more. Like you said, I've been told that what I'm experiencing is normal, considering what happened was abnormal."

"Yeah, that's it, we're not crazy; we're different. After Iraq there is no normal. Maybe it's true for you too. Welcome to our world, battle buddy!"

"Did the military give you guys treatment for PTSD while you were in Iraq?"

"First off, I'd say that about every one of us had some degree of post-traumatic stress. You can't be over there for a year and not feel the stress. Some 'event' as they say can create unending drama in a guy's head. Most of our guys never got any psychological help because if we did, there wouldn't have been anybody left to fight."

"This may sound really lame, I know you've heard it before, but how was it over there? The vets don't say much. I'm just wondering how different things are from here."

Carl was silent. This was the question others often asked when they wanted to know if he had killed anyone. It was the question too risky to answer with outsiders because he never knew what response he'd get. "Did you kill anyone?" was the question he thought he heard, followed by, "What was that like?" Carl thought of the day of the ambush . . . the car that wouldn't stop at their check point . . . and the thousands of rounds he had fired at invisible snipers in the urban landscape over his eleven-month deployment. He didn't know how many people he'd killed, but he remembered enough, up close and personal. At least when he came home he was welcomed beyond a "thank you for your service."

Carl wanted to do his best to explain things to Tom, but it wasn't always easy for him. Sometimes he got mixed up about his feelings.

"I'll try to put it into words," Carl answered. "It was different for everyone. It depended on so many variables: when you were there, what part of country, the job you had. For Operation Iraqi Freedom, I was Army Guard, First Battalion, 161st Infantry Regiment. We were in country 2004 to 2005, provided security for the Green Zone in Baghdad and conducted combat operations and civil affairs reconstruction in the southeast part of the city. We were busy. Lost four good soldiers. Bless the Gold Star families for raising men who were willing to sacrifice."

"That sounds like a long time ago, but your memories are still sharp," said Tom.

"I'm a lot older, but I think the memories will live forever. And you know, I've got a lot of good memories to go with the bad. Made some lifelong friends. There's times I think about doing it again. If I had my same unit, my band of brothers, it would be one hell of a reunion. Army Guard! First in War. First in Peace."

"Really? You'd go back?"

"It's hard to explain if you weren't there, but we became family. It started at basic. We trained to be ready and willing to risk our lives for one another. It wasn't necessarily patriotism for everyone although that was certainly part of it, especially after 9/11. We became a dream team. Where else can you find that feeling but in combat? Do you have that with your officers?"

"Pretty much. I want to be back with my team. We don't all get along, we're not all best friends, but if anyone needs help then we can count on an immediate response, especially those we work with regularly. We know each other pretty well. Just by our voice inflection on the radio we know if someone needs backup or not. When we're in chases, we won't back down."

"Roger that," agreed Carl.

"But since the bank, I'm already feeling like I'm part of a dysfunctional family. Not being able to tell my side of the story to everyone, especially with the media, is tough. I know the media shouldn't matter, but it seems so distorted, so one-sided. Then a few, like Kilgore, have never wanted me on the department. They'd be happy if I'd just go away, quit, or get fired.

"A friend of mine who has been through an on-duty shooting death has cautioned me to be ready for delays. With him, the DA's office only asked for more reports, but when he finally got a hold of the attorneys, they wouldn't give him answers. Sometimes, like me, he felt like the criminal. He said waiting for them to get back to him was really difficult."

"My family is shaky," continued Tom. "Jesse and the girls aren't as close or comfortable as before the bank. The stress is hurting us."

"Yeah," agreed Carl, "when I first left, the family thing was odd. We kept in pretty close contact, but I was changing, becoming a soldier. They were becoming independent. When I returned home, out of the combat zone, it took me awhile to rediscover my identity and who everyone else had become. Tina was busy with the kids and her meetings. The kids would listen to her before they would me. We all had to get to know each other again. Like I said, it was odd. While in country I thought it would be easy; instead it was hard.

"By the way, Tom, you're in the club now."

"What club?"

"The Killer's Club."

Tom's body recoiled then waited for the second barrel.

"That's my name for it. I didn't say Murderer's Club, I said Killer's Club. You don't get voted in. You're immediately enrolled. You have a lifetime membership. People will want you to prove your credentials, for you to talk about your killing. You'll find that the people who ask can't understand, and those who understand don't need to ask. Welcome to the club, battle buddy."

"Yeah, ten-four. Some officers at the station have told me I did a good job or nice shooting, but most seem afraid to get near me, like they might catch something. I haven't really had any of them ask me about it. But the media, led by Carolyn Odessa, is keeping this alive."

"Stay strong. With Odessa you did the right thing. He was a time bomb that no one could help. He was asking for it, and you gave him what he wanted: suicide by cop."

"I know, but if I had waited for him outside . . ."

"Hey, here comes Joe and Elizabeth," said Carl.

Elizabeth and Joe looked frazzled. Joe ran a hand through his disheveled hair. They needed a shower and a change of clothes. They needed some rest. They should have rotated shifts at the hospital; that would have been the smart thing to do, but to cope they needed one another. Elizabeth's parents had helped, and the doctors had done all they could to assure that Suanna's care was handled professionally.

Joe and Elizabeth walked up to Carl and Tom. No one spoke right away. Suanna's parents had heard the inquiry, "How is she?" so often that the question was just understood without anyone asking out loud. Elizabeth and Joe had told everyone who cared that when they learned something new, anything, they would let everyone know. Until then, they were waiting like everyone else.

Elizabeth's voice sounded robotic. She automatically started at the beginning, repeating past updates. It was easier that way. It got her primed and kept her from getting lost. "So the acute SDH is a form of TBI in which the blood gathers between the dura and the arachnoid."

Joe interpreted, "SDH stands for Subdural Hematoma. TBI is Traumatic Brain Injury. Suanna had a collection of blood over the surface of the brain. They call it acute because it happened suddenly."

"Subdural hemorrhages result from shearing injuries due to various rotational or linear forces," said Elizabeth.

"Happens with high-speed impact to the skull; you see it in car wrecks and shaken babies," Joe added.

Elizabeth explained, "Due to the hematoma's size and location and Susanna's medical and neurological condition, the doctors performed surgical evacuation of the lesion via craniotomy, opening the dura and removing the blood clot, decompressing the brain."

"The doctors opened Suanna's skull," said Joe, "then sucked out the clotted blood because the increasing pressure in her brain could have killed her."

"The follow-up CT scan is monitoring for a new intracranial mass lesion or reaccumulation of the SDH," explained Elizabeth.

"The doctors are concerned that there may be some additional bleeding," added Joe. "We're not out of the woods yet."

Carl and Joe had talked about it with one another, but they didn't dare ask what the chances were of Suanna recovering, or to what degree she'd ever be herself; that was a question for another day. But Elizabeth and Joe continued talking, sounding like an iffy weather report with one predicting a forecast as partly sunny, the other as partly cloudy.

"The mortality rate of acute SDH is high and many survivors never regain previous levels of functioning," Elizabeth concluded.

"Several studies have shown that younger patients have much higher rates of success than adults," Joe translated to his liking.

Eight & Sand 19

H ow about we stop for a drink on the way home?" asked Tom.
"Just one," Carl answered. "Got to get back to Joe's to watch
the children."

"I know a place," replied Tom. "It's called Eight & Sand. The railroad
term was used to wish train crews a swift and safe journey. Notch eight is
the final and most powerful position on the locomotive's throttle. Sand
was used to prevent wheel slipping. If you like trains, you'll love this bar.
It's in Oldtown at the old passenger train station. Just follow my car."

•

Tom's mouth was dry as he tried to swallow. There she was in her new
Armour Yellow coat. Many said she was past her prime, not worth the
trouble, but Tom could see, considering her age, she was holding up
well. Despite some weathered cracks and blemishes, she still had class
and plenty of stories to tell. And no wonder, she was from good sturdy
stock. If given the opportunity, she had years of service left in her, but of
course, at a slower speed.

"See the wooden caboose!" said Tom. "The cupola gave the conductor a great view of the train. There's the entrance. Union Pacific doesn't
have cabooses in her fleet anymore, but this private one's on track; it can
move. Some of these, and the later models with steel skin, were last used
by U.P. into the 1980s when the guys with seniority lost their jobs waving at the public and having unauthorized visitors. Actually the Flashing
Rear End Device, a.k.a. FRED, a small, metal box with a flashing red
light, along with electric switches and track detectors, replaced the men
who worked out of the cabooses. The cars were doomed because they
were non-revenue—not making a profit."

"Welcome to Eight & Sand Bar," greeted the employee, outside the caboose, standing erect, wearing a crisp, vintage, dark-blue U.P. uniform, including his vest and conductor's hat.

Tom eyed the hat's badge, noting it displayed a brass U.P. logo while the brim held gold braiding. Tom thought of his shield in his wallet and instinctively touched his hip, searching for the comfort of his duty weapon, startled before recalling he wasn't carrying.

"Good to be back," replied Tom.

"If you have your Eight & Sand discount card, I'll validate it for you," the conductor said, removing his railway ticket punch from a leather case worn on his belt.

As Tom had his bar card perforated, Carl counted the five buttons on the conductor's vest. He noticed the gold chain and followed the flowing loop to the watch's pocket. When his eyes caught the chad from the ticket punch drift to the red-brick sidewalk, he saw black, leather shoes gleaming below pressed conductor pants.

How much, Carl wondered, was this man's positive image a product of the person, the uniform, or both? This tall African American oozed authority, trust, and pride. His calm demeanor would have settled down the most nerve-racked, first-time railway passenger, had he been the conductor of a moving train.

"Here's your loyalty card," said the conductor, returning it to Tom. "Just a reminder, when you get it fully punched, you've earned a free pitcher of beer."

"Enjoy your evening," said the conductor. "Watch your step up. Use the handrail," he cautioned as Tom and Carl entered the caboose.

"See these railroad artifacts?" asked Tom, waving his arms. "The lanterns and firearms tell a story of our country and western expansion. It was a wild place. In this drawing these so-called hunters, slaughtering the buffalo from the moving train, were the reason the buffalo nearly became extinct. These guys were selfish, acting like there was no tomorrow . . .

"The bar's in the lounge car, a double-decker. It's connected and has an upper observation deck; that's where we're headed . . .

"They've already found their next railcar, a dining car!" Tom said, squealing. "They'll have a restaurant by fall. This year, if they're lucky, they could even start daytime charters. If the historical society ever kicks in (they want to purchase a Pullman car—a sleeper), then they'll be able to book private overnight travel. They don't need to buy a locomotive; they can attach their cars to the end of any Amtrak. . . .

"Too bad the Sante Fe 4-8-4, steam locomotive 3768, we saw overhead on the railroad overpass doesn't run. It was built in 1938 by Baldwin Locomotive Works and taken out of service in 1953. It belongs to the Great Plains Transportation Museum across the street." After they had taken table seats in the lounge car, and ordered a first round of drinks, Tom said, "Let me show off what the computer can do. We can program it to view scenery along various train routes. The controls give us the opportunity to select any spot on the rails so that we'll see corresponding video. We can also choose any decade back to the early twentieth century. It's like time travel. Plus, we can split the screen, and while we're looking at the terrain and the stations, there's also a parallel video of our train barreling away down the tracks or climbing mountain passes. It's awesome!"

"Really?" said Carl. "Is this a bar or a museum?"

"Oh! The more recent videos allow you to choose a season and weather! I love it here!" Tom declared with a wide grin. "Have you been on a train before?"

"As a kid, but not as an adult. Our family was visiting San Francisco where my parents met. I remember the rhythm of the tracks."

"Recently," said Tom, "our family traveled on the Southwest Chief to Sante Fe. A full bedroom suite wasn't available so we had to get two roomettes. They were so small I couldn't turn around without going out in the hallway! The girls enjoyed the trip but couldn't sit still, and I couldn't keep up with them. Still, it was an adventure with beautiful country, and the food wasn't half bad. Sure beats flying where I need to purchase two seats, and pretzels are all they give me to eat with my beer."

"So, what route do you want?" asked Tom, as he prepared to enter data on the table's touch keyboard.

"How about any train that will take us over the Columbia River before 1930?"

"Comin' up, full speed ahead! By the way, the U.P. ended their passenger service in 1971 because it wasn't profitable. Amtrak was created. From here you'd have to go to Chicago or LA to get to Seattle. You're near Spokane. The Empire Builder goes there."

"Yeah, not too far from Spokane," replied Carl, thinking it was light years away from Nespelem, remembering his long commute to Gonzaga

University, after Haskell, and after Iraq. He'd lived in separate worlds.
What a journey!

●

"Another round," ordered Carl.

"One Pabst in a can and a JD on the rocks comin' up," said the
server.

"So the dirtiest job you've ever had wasn't your tour in Iraq?" asked
Tom.

"Okay," said Carl, "We always found dirt somewhere, but after a
month we got acclimated to the heat. At least it was a dry heat. As long
as we drank our twenty liters of water every day, we made it. But I still
think my summers on a hot-shot crew fighting forest fires could be pretty rank. . . ."

"Hey, Foamer," a gray-haired, heavily wrinkled customer shouted to
Tom as he and a female companion headed for a table.

Tom lifted his chin in a Kansan head nod.

The acquaintance turned in mid-stride, abandoning his partner, and
walked up to Tom asking, "How are you? Where you been?"

"Doing fine," said Tom. "This is my friend, Carl Warrior. He's from
Washington, the state, not the capitol." And to Carl he said, "This is
John Moon, a long-time buddy."

"Nice to meet you, Carl," said the stranger. "You a foamer too?"

"He's not a foamer," said Tom.

"Haven't seen you around," said John. "How's Jesse? Kudzu? The
girls?"

"We're doing pretty good, considering," said Tom. "Jesse's still putting up with me; Kudzu's been temporarily reassigned to another officer.
Guy doesn't know what he's doing. Heck, he feeds Kudzu table scraps,
which is like the number one no-no we learned in K-9 training. A ten-
thousand-dollar drug dog eating human garbage makes no sense. Hope
to get him back one of these days. You shoot any trains lately?"

"Just got back from Council Bluffs where we visited the U.P. train
museum," said John. "Have you been there? You'd like the old firearms
and the opportunity to talk to the volunteers. They're retired railroad
employees with lots of colorful stories. There's also a plaque honoring
fallen special agents from all the railroads. The museum was pretty interesting but had no trains. Call me old-fashioned, but I still think a

train museum should have trains. I've got some photos on Facebook. If you want, I'll send you a bunch. Are you at the same number?"

"Yes, partner," said Tom, "I'd appreciate that."

"Well, I see my wife staring at me. She claims we can't go anywhere without me meeting people I know and abandoning her. Gotta go."

"Good to see you, man."

"Tom, Taz, how many names do you have?" asked Carl. "I've heard LB, and now Foamer. Is that right, did he say, Foamer?"

"Yeah, ten-four, Foamer. It's a joke about me being a train fanatic, a train nerd. We met a few years ago when we were waiting at the same bridge to take photos of a steam locomotive passing through town. But he's the one who foams at the mouth about trains. I don't travel all over the country to take a photo."

"Okay, but you're fun to watch as you get excited about incoming trains. I've seen you at the hospital when you're detecting the first sound of a distant train. It's not always the horn. Is it a vibration you feel? You stop what you're doing, listen, and wait. Once it gets louder and you've identified it, you grin like a kid. You must be the only person I know who doesn't mind getting held up by a train in traffic!"

"You know the train side of me pretty well," agreed Tom. "At railroad crossings no one's ever had to tell me to look both ways before crossing the tracks. I'm always looking. But Carl, we were talking about Iraq."

"Oh, yeah—dirtiest jobs. I take it back. With forest fires everything reeked of smoke, but after the mop-up, in a few days, the dirt would dissipate. We could blow our horns and clear our pipes without the black soot showing up. In Iraq, during a dust storm, dirt or sand accompanied every meal like an unwelcome side dish.

"What was yours?"

"Huh?"

"Your dirtiest job."

"This isn't dirty like dirt," said Tom, as his eyes grew distant, "but working with decayed, bloated bodies in enclosed areas is never a favorite. With ripe bodies, especially if they've popped open, you just want to hold your breath; after handling them—even with gloves—you scrub your skin down to the bone. Seems the funeral home always sends out scrawny guys to carry the big ones. We end up helping. I still remember the guy who died in his living room lounge chair right beside the heat vent. He melted. I could smell death on me when I left my patrol car."

"Deaths are toughest when you know the person," said Carl as he looked down at his empty hands before looking up for the waiter. "A guy I knew from my first summer with the Forest Service got burnt up in a wildfire in our Okanogan County. He knew his way around a fire, but still got scorched in his aluminum shelter. His father said later that his son could have survived, could have outrun any fire, if he hadn't stopped to help his young, inexperienced crew."

"Sorry, man," said Tom, as he gave an understanding nod.

"Thirtymile Fire killed four of us, all with the last name Firefighter."

The server approached with drinks. "Cold crap in a can and JD on the rocks," he said and placed them on the table by each customer.

"Like you, his name was Tom . . . I was a rookie firefighter when he welcomed me to a training and helped me understand the life of a fire. I never saw him play football. He was quite a bit older than me, but he was a star athlete, even broke O. J. Simpson's college rushing record. He went to training camp with the Seahawks, but injured his knee. After that any pro career was over. Tom was a popular hip-hop DJ. You two would have had a lot to talk about between football and music, even though you're country. He's buried in Kittitas County, Roslyn.

"It was when I was on a hot-shot crew that I met some guys in the Washington National Guard, First in War, First in Peace. They were dropping water bombs from their CH-47 Chinook, two-thousand-gallon bucket with a four-person crew. That's when I got the idea that I could do more than set backfires and work my Pulaski, so I joined up."

"Pulaski?" asked Tom, his forehead wrinkling.

"Oh, it's a tool for digging fire line—half hoe, half axe, thirty-six-inch wooden handle. Perfect tool. Beats a shovel."

Tom nodded and the two men fell silent. Carl sipped his second beer.

Tom took a drink and listened to the sound of a recorded train's horn giving the blast of two long, one short, and one long toot, approaching a highway-grade crossing, warning pedestrians and drivers to be alert: "We're coming through." As if regressing, Tom recognized that the bar's color scheme reminded him of his childhood bedroom, U.P.'s Armour Yellow and Harbor Mist Gray with a thin band of Signal Red separating the yellow and gray. He recalled his first toy train, a Christmas present from his parents—a Lionel with an all-black steam locomotive that derailed too often from faulty track.

"My dad was a special agent for the railroad." Tom said to Carl. "When I was a kid he'd take me on short train rides. My last photo of him is the two of us in the cab of the lead engine on Father's Day when I was seven. Here, let me show you."

Tom took out his phone and found the faded photograph of a smiling little boy wearing blue bib overalls, striped engineer's hat, blue handkerchief, and work gloves. Behind the boy was Frank, his father, proud, saying, "Look at my son!" The photo showed a big man who wore nondescript jacket and jeans.

"What happened to him?" asked Carl. "Train wreck?"

"We don't know. He just disappeared during the night shift, same day this photo was taken. Mom made a missing-person report."

"You never heard anything?"

"Nothing that amounted to much. U.P. and law enforcement did what they could, but never found evidence of his death, hospitalization, or of him starting a new life anywhere else. We've never learned what happened to him."

"I can't imagine not knowing."

"Yeah, ten-four, it sucks. Part of me believes that I'll run into him some day or find him in one of our data bases. I'd like to use facial recognition programming on the state's driver license sites to see if it matches anywhere, but to do that he'd need to be a known criminal or a terrorist suspect. I've been told 'missing people may choose to be missing,' as an explanation of their privacy rights. Someday maybe we'll get access."

"How did your mom handle his disappearance? It must have been hard on her."

"She still thinks he's coming home, like one of those lost house dogs that find their way home a couple of years later, surviving a thousand mile journey. Still, every day, Mom wears a railroad pin that Dad gave her when they started dating. Old house is too big for her, but she won't budge. She's waiting—loyal, but sad. I'm sad about it too. I know he's probably dead. It's been thirty years. To our knowledge, none of his personal data has ever been used in scams or identity-theft cases. Serial number of his second generation Glock 17, with the integrated, recoil spring assembly, has never been queried in NCIC. Nothing, it's a mystery."

•

Carl studied their table's computer screen and observed the powerful Columbia River in an era before it was subdued by dams. He was light years from home. He missed his family, his food, and his reservation.

Here he was at a train bar, the Eight & Sand, drinking with a new friend, time traveling.

While drinking his beer, Carl fluctuated between hope and loss like a bipolar disorder. The print at the bar's entrance that showed buffalo hunters shooting from a moving train reminded him of chinook salmon. They once inhabited the Big River and fed his father's Colville Tribes.

Carl grew up with stories of fishing on the Columbia, especially the steady roar at Kettle Falls where sixty- and eighty-pound jumping chinook were commonly speared and caught in nets. Those were the days before the dams turned the mighty Columbia from a river into an electricity machine.

Carl knew all about how the Grand Coulee Dam had saved the world, how its electricity made the aluminum for a majority of America's World War II bomber planes. He'd heard how the Hanford Site to the south had created the plutonium to power the atomic bomb to force Japan's surrender. He knew U.S. history. The Grand Coulee Dam may have saved the free world; it just never saved the members of the Colville Confederated Tribes Reservation, despite the government's late settlement, lump-sum payment in 1996, and annual payments since.

The history of the salmon and why they were missing from the Columbia was a story rarely told. It was more than a lack of fish ladders at dams or about increasing fisheries and salmon releases. Rather than focus on the tribes losing their way of life, the history-book writers preferred to credit the dams with cheap electricity, expanded irrigation, productive farming, and transportation of goods by barge. The loss to the Indians and to everyone's environment was pretty much ignored.

"Hey Tom, you know what a chinook is?"

"You already told me the Forest Service used them in fighting fires."

"They were wingless, work horses in Iraq too. By the way, the CH-47 is called a Chinook but the CH actually designates it as a cargo helicopter. It started off ferrying supplies and troops in Vietnam, but it has several meanings. The Chinook Indians used the word first. They're from the lower Columbia River, especially around its mouth. Early white explorers called them Flathead Indians because of the way some of them bound their infant's heads with boards. A chinook's also an unseasonably warm, dry wind that blows from the west to the east through the Cascade mountain passes to our west. A chinook can dry up everything, snow and water, in a few hours. But what I really want to tell you about is why the wild salmon are missing from the Columbia . . . "

•

"Another round, Chief?" asked the waiter.

"I'm not a Chief, I'm a Warrior," replied Carl, as he unconsciously touched his choker.

"Okay, Warrior. Another round? How about you, Big Man?"

"Call me Taz," said Tom. "Yeah, last round, but add a couple dogs and a double order of cheesy fries to my tab, and bring me a bottle of ketchup—none of those miniature baby packets."

Tom turned to Carl and said, "You hungry?"

"Yeah." Carl's mouth watered. He remembered the irregular spots on their blue-green backs, the black pigment along their gum line, and the radiant colors, from red to copper to barely black. He could taste the rich flavor and firm flesh. "Smoked salmon?" Carl asked the server.

"We're a bar, not a restaurant, but we're expanding in a few months with a dining car, so hold that thought. It'll be a minute," said the waiter as he left, collecting empty bottles and glasses on his way back to the bar.

"I'm not always in the mood to be called Chief. Maybe I'm feeling it," said Carl.

"Yeah, I'm getting a little buzz too," said Tom as he rubbed his bald head, "so I might as well ask you now. You know I love football and I'm a Kansas City Chiefs fan. Does it bother you that our mascot is an Indian chief? Some people want to make a big deal about it, like it's racist, like we hate Indians."

"I've watched K.C. get demolished by my Seahawks," said Carl. "First off, you've got to admit that when your fans are all doing the tomahawk chop, it looks pretty stupid, right? But to me, P.C. is the bigger issue. That's what bothers me. At our school in Nespelem we had to change mascots. Ours wasn't politically correct. But ask Elizabeth about Indian mascots and she'll give you a mouthful. She's active on this. She sees Indian mascots as negative racial stereotyping that relates to everything from self-esteem issues to violence. When people explain that they're really honoring Indians, Elizabeth shoots back: 'It's dehumanizing. What's so honorable about being a mascot?' "

"What was your school's mascot?" asked Tom.

"In elementary school we were the Savages."

"No way!"

"Indians told other Indians to change the school mascot," explained Carl. "In Nespelem it got Indian ugly for a while with deep hard feelings. Now my kids are the Eagles, and it's no big deal to them."

"The Savages! Bet you intimidated a few opponents. Did you have a battle cry or a tomahawk chop?" asked Tom with a laugh as he moved his vertical hand up and down at the elbow, imitating the chop.

"We had fun with it, but we were targeted too, especially at away games. Nowadays the school is busy banning clothing that's gang related. That opens up all kinds of issues. My favorite is the provocative message 'Rez Power.' "

"Rez Power," repeated Tom.

"Yeah, how can you tell an Indian not to be proud of that message? That's who we are. That's where we live. I remember when we were all about Indian Power. What's the difference? So, when is Indian pride about respecting your culture, and when is it used as a sign of being a gang member? I'd like to know."

"A gang is a group of two or more people that regularly breaks the law. They identify as a group."

"So when Joe and me were growing up together and we shoplifted candy bars at the Tribal Post, we were a gang?"

"By definition, maybe yes, but in reality, no."

"Yeah, there's always a gap between the two, isn't there? But, I can see where a bunch of friends who have known each other all their lives and then get in a fight with outsiders across the river, that they're looking out for each other. It's called safety in numbers."

"Gangs are about more than self-defense, they're about crime, but they're also about identity," said Tom.

"But are there good gangs? Because we've had calls from school about Storm."

Rhizomes 20

esse hadn't known what to expect. She had never even imagined visiting a therapist. To her, therapy implied crazy people in need of help or sane people acting crazy. But Tom had been required to see a psychologist in Wichita per departmental policy, and a bank representative had contacted her at home to follow up on her injury caused by the bullet fragment. At first Jesse had nearly hung up on the caller, thinking it was another illegal, robocall, sales pitch disguised as a survey, but she soon learned the bank was offering her an opportunity to participate in a critical incident briefing with their employees. At the briefing another free offer had been made and that's how Jesse scheduled her first ever therapy appointment.

The therapist, Gina Gilmartin, LMHC, MFT, was professional and welcoming. Thankfully, Jesse's old-fashioned image of a client lying on a couch while the male therapist sat nearby asking questions, smoking a cigar, and replying "hmm" after each response, was as ancient as silent movies.

Instead, therapist and client talked outside in a private garden among a bounty of blooming, orange day lilies and purple coneflowers (in bright eye-popping colors). Jesse began her guided journey of discovery. Gina was easy, unhurried, and inviting as she asked questions and waited for answers. Jesse noticed immediately how Gina really listened. It seemed rare and was as welcome as the garden's sweet fragrance.

By the end of the session Jesse understood that therapy was not only for crazy people or people acting crazy. It was beneficial for people like her, who were simply overwhelmed. She scheduled another appointment.

•

Arriving at her second appointment, the light rain mingled with her tears. Jesse's short, layered-cut, red hair was highlighted with water droplets the color of diamonds.

As soon as Jesse entered the therapy room she spotted an abstract acrylic painting with a large red square on a black background. Closer examination revealed no date but a recognizable signature. Jesse's shoulders dropped and her knees nearly buckled.

"Gina, if you don't mind me asking, how did you acquire this painting? The artist is Valerie Popalavata, a former roommate of mine from my college days. I've lost touch with her."

"Oh, don't you just love it?"

"Yeah, but where did you get it? Was it from here or out of town?"

"My grandmother, who lives in Hutchinson, gave it to me when she downsized. She knew it was one of my favorites."

Gina motioned for Jesse to take a seat in a plush golden chair as she sat down at an angle to her client, opened a notebook, and made an entry.

"It looks like we've got company," advised Gina. "Do you like cats?"

Jesse looked toward the doorway and watched a cream-colored Ragdoll with chocolate points approach her. Once Jesse sat down, the Ragdoll meandered over and smelled Jesse's shoes before rubbing his head against her leg.

"I love cats. What's his name?"

"He's Vinnie."

Vinnie, a large, laid-back cat, meowed, evidently asking to be picked up.

Jesse bent over and obliged. He plopped in her lap, relaxed as a rag doll.

"Good Vinnie," said Jesse, as she petted the affectionate cat, tunneling her slender alabaster fingers into his long hair. Looking into his spell-binding blue eyes, she announced, "You're gorgeous."

Gina observed tears flowing from Jesse's gray eyes and said, "You've been crying."

"Guess I'm in the right place," was her subdued reply.

"Yes, you are."

"I can't do it anymore."

"You can't do what anymore?"

Jesse rubbed her wedding ring. In a voice choked with tears she said, "Everything. I can't do everything."

Gina waited.

"Our house has been stressful, but I don't know that I've felt any trauma."

"Tell me how you'd describe your relationship with Tom right now."

"What does this have to do with the bank robbery and me getting injured?" Jesse asked while looking down at Vinnie.

"The stress of the bank shooting got you here; we've discussed that and how you need to watch for triggers that may occur, like the Fourth of July fireworks. But the stress of your marriage has been going on a lot longer; it's deeper," explained the professional, both a licensed mental-health counselor and a marriage-and-family therapist.

"I married a cop, so I anticipated stress in our lives—both good and bad. I don't really think our lives are that different than other police families, though. We all have the pressure of the dangerous work, the worry, unpredictable hours, rotating shifts, and a husband trying to sleep during the day, without missing family activities. But sleep deprivation does make everything worse. A person loses his sense of humor."

"I'm sure those stressors are universal in police families, but tell me more," encouraged Gina.

"Okay, another stressor—usually the wife is responsible for working double duty with both the house and children. I love our girls, but raising them means there's little time for me in my day. At least they're both school age now."

"Tom's not helpful?"

"His job comes first. I'm at home. That's the way it is." Jesse slid her hands deeper into Vinnie's coat. The feline reciprocated with turbo-charged purring.

"You told me he's on medical leave or suspended because of the shooting," reminded Gina.

"Yes, he's on leave due to the shooting, but he's also out with a back injury. He's working with his attorney, preparing for any possible charges. He's still anxious about everything with the job, so it still takes his time, his focus. His work is our main income."

"Okay then, he's busy. Describe your marriage."

"I just don't know where to start."

"Start anywhere," encouraged Gina, "you've already said that you're raising the children."

Jesse closed her eyes, took a deep breath, and exhaled. Vinnie tensed as if he were expecting danger.

"Our marriage . . . our marriage . . . is like an iris that no longer blooms. In the beginning, after it's planted in an area of full sun, an iris grows and flourishes. Once it's rooted, it can manage pretty well on its own. It blooms every spring. It's colorful, majestic. Our marriage is like an iris that no longer blooms."

"Good. What else?"

"Currently our marriage is like the iris that doesn't receive enough daily sun. Over the years the increased shade from overhanging trees has changed the environment. The iris is alive, but it no longer blooms. The plant looks healthy but never joyous. It doesn't smile. It doesn't laugh. It looks fine. The leaves are green, undamaged, but it will no longer be invited to an Easter service to participate as a sanctuary's bouquet. No more cutting iris stems for tall glass vases, no more store-bought fancy pastel dresses, no more outrageous Sunday hats; just a busy woman watching sharp blades of iris grow."

"Jesse, you can still bloom," the counselor encouraged. "What are you doing to take care of yourself?"

"The rhizome of the iris, that's what some people call the bulb, needs to be planted near the surface so it can be exposed to sun and air. Plant the rhizome, actually a stem, too deep and it dies."

"You need sun and air?"

"Most irises do best when planted on a little mound of dirt so that they have good drainage. There's a saying that irises don't like to have their feet stand in water; they get root rot.

"Irises, just like people, require nutrients. A healthy iris uses up the nutrients, and when that happens, the source of the energy needs to be replenished. Maybe I've used up my nutrients. I can't just blame Tom for blocking the sun or drinking the water.

"Maybe, like an iris, our marriage is in a period of dormancy. Maybe it's not dead, but it's dormant . . . below the surface. After irises bloom in the spring, they rest by going into a stage similar to hibernating animals. It's their way of coping with the hot, dry, Kansas summers.

"Or maybe I need to be transplanted," Jesse reflected. "Maybe I need to find a healthier environment. If I were a rhizome, I'd plant myself on a sunny hill and spread out my roots. I'd soak up the sun and nap. I'd relish evening rain showers.

"I feel like I'm an iris, not a gardener," continued Jesse. "I feel like I'm paralyzed and I can't cut down the tree or trim its branches so that the sun can reach me. I feel like I can't transplant myself because of my weakened state. If only Tom had the time to be a caring, nurturing gardener, then I could once again be a blooming iris. But is it fair to expect him to rescue me when, it seems, he can't rescue himself?"

"Let's talk about what you can do to take care of yourself."

"There's my art . . ."

•

"When we first started dating, I felt safer being with a police officer; back then Tom was a sheriff's deputy," recalled Jesse. "He would tell me about the jail, and later, when he joined the police department, he'd tell stories about working patrol. I felt like it was a special opportunity for me to hear all the bizarre stuff going on that never hit the news. He loved to share, and I enjoyed that.

"I didn't know it at first, but he'd filter out the really bad things and not divulge those. I know he was just trying to protect me, so it makes sense, but . . . he became so extra cautious about a number of things. He still won't leave the house without a concealed sidearm. He's told me that if we're ever confronted by someone with a gun, that he'd never forgive himself if he wasn't able to protect us.

"When we go to a restaurant to eat, he needs a special table and seat so that he'll have a clear view of the front door. He doesn't like surprises. On the rare occasions when we go shopping together on his day off, he's suddenly on patrol in the store. If I can't locate him, I know he's following a suspicious shopper. Tom can't help it. He can't relax off-duty. He can't just shop.

"And any salesman who comes to our front door might as well expect a background check from Tom. Before the last magazine salesman left our property, Tom had personal information off the guy's ID, a description of his clothing, and his car's license plate number. When the salesman departed, Tom had more information on the visitor than the visitor had on Tom. And you know what's strange? This behavior no longer seems unusual to me. I'm more suspicious too. It's par for the Jennings course.

"I remember how difficult it was to find our first babysitter who wasn't family. The high-school neighbor-girl does a really good job, but before she was hired she had to convince Tom she was responsible. He warmed up to her, but he must have checked her out with the FBI to be sure she'd never been convicted of kidnapping children," Jesse said, and laughed as she remembered. "She was only fifteen when she started. I don't think she'd had enough time to get on the most wanted list.

"At night Tom will check the doors twice to be sure they're locked and that the alarm system is working. He'll get out of bed to investigate unusual noises. We had to disconnect the ice machine on the refrigerator so he could get more sleep. If Biscuit, our old house dog—she has a weak bladder—gets up in the middle of the night, then Tom's the one already awake to take her outside."

"Tom's hypervigilant," the therapist said. "It's not unusual for police officers to be suspicious of others because they deal with criminals all the time. They don't get sent on 911 calls where the caller wants to report everything is fine. It's ironic though because crime victims, especially domestic violence and rape victims, also become hypervigilant. Twenty-four-seven, they're always on alert. Hypervigilance wears a person down. It's exhausting."

"That's Tom," agreed Jesse. "When we were first married, he'd come home and tell me those three magic words: 'I love you.' But after a while it was more common to hear: 'I'm really tired.' I thought that line was forever reserved for us women when we're not in the mood for sex."

"It's worked for centuries," Gina commented. "Or, I have a headache," she added as she brought an exaggerated hand to her forehead, lowered her eyes, and rubbed her eyebrows.

In recognition, Jesse's face relaxed and showed laugh lines. "Being on a mission to help others, plus this obsessiveness, has changed him. I often feel like he's more likely to help a stranger than me. He'd voluntarily carry a citizen's laundry into a public laundromat from their car before he'd carry our dirty clothes downstairs to the wash room."

"I've seen how people who are most dedicated to their jobs can change for the worse when they believe they aren't doing enough. Sounds like you and Tom have been challenged because of his work."

"When I realized Tom was guarding us 24/7, I didn't object because I considered it part of his professional awareness. I wanted to be supportive and understanding."

"Yes," agreed Gina.

"By our fifth wedding anniversary Tom preferred to stay home, watch TV, and drink beer. He could make decisions all day, but he couldn't tell me what he wanted for supper. He still won't help choose a restaurant. He leaves things up to me, but what's weird is when I meet with him on duty, I get glimpses of the old Tom. He's energetic and funny. He's a good conversationalist. But by the time he's home a half hour, unless he's caring for Biscuit or Gravy, (or Kudzu when he had him) he's on his recliner watching TV and not blinking. I swear he takes some sort of zombie pills when he walks in the door. I'd have the house checked for radon, but Tom's the only one in this trance-like state. He's in his couch-potato zone. If, while he was watching TV, I told him I murdered both our daughters, he wouldn't react. He's stopped listening. Once I blocked the TV when he wasn't answering, and you know what he did?"

"No, what?"

"He still didn't answer me. He only cocked his head to the side, trying to see around me!"

"That would have set me off!" said the counselor, sounding human, her voice raised, like she was the one getting upset. "What'd you do?" she asked, waiting for the answer.

"I turned off the TV and went upstairs. Later, after the show, he asked me if I was feeling okay."

"Does he admit to being burned out?"

"I've told you the worst, but he's been excited about some of his extra duties. He rebounded when he became an assistant range master and when the department selected him as the first K-9 officer. When he visits the elementary school, he's calmer for about a day. The range and the K-9 duties were times he felt he was justly rewarded for his good work. When he's working he enjoys the camaraderie with his buddies, especially on hot calls. They're bonded, as the saying goes. Sadly, they're also his drinking buddies. Tom says that he trusts them, so it's easier to relax with them."

"Does Tom drink too much?"

"Yes, I think so."

"Does he admit to being burned out?" Gina asked again.

"He admits to being stressed out and working in a hostile environment, only he's not talking about the criminals. He's talking about his bosses.

"Tom's been disappointed when he hasn't been promoted, and he's had some write-ups which have hurt his chances for future advancement. Things got worse when the chief got upset with him for wearing a T-shirt protesting a policy change. Somewhere along his career, according to Tom, the administration regressed from being fair to being 'chickenshit'." As Jesse said the words she used both hands with two elongated fingers each to punctuate the air with quotation marks. "It's too bad.

"Despite his weight, they gave him opportunities. Kudzu was the best thing for Tom because both he and the dog got regular exercise during daily training. He loved being the K-9 handler and making drug busts. Biscuit is too old with arthritis to compete any longer in the agility training or to get any good exercise. Gravy is coming along, but Tom is distracted with her lately. Now, to Tom, his bosses are not administrators, they're adversaries. Something's got to change. I think he should quit. This bank shooting could be a blessing in disguise for us."

"Have you told him that you think he should quit?"

"Not exactly. I'm waiting to see what happens with the D.A.'s office and court. I know Tom's got a lot to deal with besides his back spasms. He was already grieving the loss of his K-9 duties with Kudzu, the injury to Suanna Morningcloud at the bank, my injury, and of course shooting and killing the bank robber. He's not happy about how long the death investigation is taking even though he knows these things take time. Tom thinks the D.A.'s office should have cleared him by now. They are, you guessed it, 'chickenshit'." Again Jesse made quotation marks with her fingers.

Jesse stopped talking and remembered the turmoil in the bank after Tom killed the Odessa-Smith boy, the coroner's son; she didn't want to think of his first name. She thought about how Tom, once they were home from the hospital, finally told her that the investigators at first couldn't find the gun that shot the bullet that injured her.

He told her how he had been called by a detective and asked about the empty coin can on the counter at the bank. Tom vaguely recalled a morning weeks before the bank robbery when he'd been given a deformed bullet by a downtown business owner who said he'd found it on the sidewalk. Asked to dispose of it, Tom had put it in his pocket, and later at home, without looking, tossed it into the coin can as part of his daily contribution—a handful of change. Tom eventually remembered the event and acknowledged he was responsible for unconsciously adding the bullet to the coins.

"Jesse," said Gina, "I know you and Tom have been through a lot because of your injury at the bank."

Jesse recalled to herself how she and Tom couldn't believe that the bullet that hurt her had been in their possession until the day she was injured. They deeply apologized to one another. Tom admitted to doing something really stupid, that he knew better, and that he hadn't been thinking clearly. When the businessman gave him the bullet, he had considered, just for a moment, the risk of it being unstable. He didn't know where to put it. He should have disposed of it at the firearm's range. She was sorry she hadn't communicated with Tom about cashing in the coins, like she normally did. But they both knew she was an innocent victim. While Tom meant no harm to anyone when he added the bullet to the spare coins, Tom was the guilty party. Had she asked him if he wanted her to exchange them for currency, he would have answered in the affirmative: "Yes, ten-four, we can use the money to buy us lunch."

"Sometimes," Gina said, "you can't control the world around you, but you learn to do your best."

But the most difficult part of their conversation, Jesse considered, was speculating about how things might have gone differently at the bank. If the bank teller had never removed the metal guard from the coin-counting machine, then the safety switch would have worked as designed. The twisted bullet would have never exploded to hurt her. There were so many ifs. Even without the bent bullet, Tom might still have been forced to shoot and kill Odessa-Smith.

"Tom is now the victim," added Gina. "He's shifted from being proactive, making things happen, to being the victim where things happen to him."

"Me, too," said Jesse referring to being a victim. "I've let things happen to me. Maybe I should get a recliner, start drinking, and take zombie pills, then Tom and I can watch TV together without blinking," Jesse said and gave a sad laugh.

"Let's talk about how you can make better choices," suggested Gina. "If Tom will seek counseling, then he can work on an action plan, too."

Bat-Shit Crazy 21

After they had walked out of the Eight & Sand, Carl said, "Tom, I can't get my truck to start. Can I get a ride with you back to Joe's?"

"Sure, but I've got jumper cables," replied Tom. "Maybe it's the battery."

"I'll get it tomorrow," said Carl. "No big deal."

"You out of gas?"

"No, it's got plenty of gas. Let's just go, okay?"

•

It was too late. Tom saw the colorful, flashing, epileptic-fit lights ahead, then the signage, and realized he was caught in a funnel headed for a sobriety-check lane. Friday night and the boys in blue were out spending grant money. Tom thought of checking his breath's alcohol level with his app but couldn't remember where he put the mouthpiece.

He understood that the next few minutes of his life could be a game changer. Getting popped for a DUI would end his already questionable law-enforcement career. And he knew better. He told himself that he should have stopped at two drinks.

Despite the alcohol numbing his brain, Tom had a moment of clarity: How different was he than the countless drunks he'd arrested for DUI? It was obvious to him when they had a drinking problem. Why wasn't it just as apparent to him that he had a drinking problem? His defense had always been that he'd never gotten into trouble because of his drinking. But that could change in a heartbeat.

Tom slowed. He considered a U-turn, but then he observed a chase car, a marked patrol vehicle on the side of the road, waiting for drivers who tried to avoid the check lane.

Tom grasped for numbers. How many JB's had he drunk? What time had he started? What time was it now? While they were at the Eight & Sand, his blood alcohol level (BAL) was increasing with each drink, but at the same time, due to oxidation, as time passed, his BAL would naturally decline.

Thinking out loud, Tom said: "At least being built like a beer keg works to my advantage. I can legally hold a lot of liquor."

But Tom's brain was short-circuiting; the numbers wouldn't calculate.

His tight grip on the steering wheel felt moist. Tom grabbed some tissues to mop his forehead, but the delicate paper dissolved into globs and lumps. The wet, white, loose fibers stuck on his face and resembled the residue of a seriously shedding cotton ball, or torn toilet paper used by a trembling teen after shaving with a straight razor for his first date, trying to stop the bleeding. Tom's eyes started gushing water, irritated by the scent of the tissues. He ventilated and burped cow-like, deep, long and loud, and tasted the recycled hot dogs and cheesy fries. Droplets of water slid down his perspiring face. Tom was soaked. He needed a beach towel to dry off.

The emergency lights were everywhere, overwhelming, though he should have been used to them from his years of road patrol. He felt dizzy as he drove to his demise, as if being sucked toward a swirling drain with mystic pump power. The momentum overpowered him.

Tom considered that he might have to blow, perform the nystagmus gaze test, walk the line, and do a one-legged stand. Or he could refuse the test; but of course, that had dire consequences as well.

Hell, I can't even do downward facing dog on a good day. God, this is it! What officers are out here tonight?

"Look!" Carl shouted and pointed. "There's been an accident. Someone sideswiped that sheriff's car!"

Tom leaned forward, double blinked, and stared. There was a broken side-view mirror on the road, a heavy gash down the doors of the patrol vehicle, and a mangled traffic cone caught in the civilian's front wheel well. Officers had the driver out. She was already in custody.

"I only had two beers!" she yelled. "These handcuffs are too tight! You're hurting me! STOP IT! HELP! POLICE!"

Other deputies in their fluorescent orange reflective vests directed traffic around the accident scene with illuminated plastic wands.

Tom had dodged a bullet. The deputies were busy. He was almost home free.

"Looks like no one got hurt," said Carl.

But, just then, an officer recognized Tom's ice-blue PT Cruiser, saw him behind the wheel, and motioned for him to pull to the side of the road.

"Hey, guys! It's Jennings!"

Tom pulled far off the road, hoping to be out of reach of the next drunk driver.

Deputies came over to the open front windows and patted Tom on the shoulder; some shook his hand and nodded at his passenger.

"What do you have growing on your face, retard?" the first officer asked, which caused Tom to sweep paper wads off his forehead.

"Taz, when are you coming back to work? PD's tired of doing your job!" another officer exclaimed, followed by more deputy comments.

"Our drug arrests are way down since you've been off. We could use a little help, at least from Kudzu. We need his sniffer."

"Carolyn Odessa's the one who should be on leave, not you. That witch!"

"Don't pay no attention to the paper, that rag," advised another sheriff's deputy, "they're just trying to stir things up. You didn't do anything wrong. You did your job. It could have been any of us. Lunchbox, we're pulling for you, buddy."

"I'd like to see a judge or juror make a split-second, life-and-death decision," the deputy continued. "They either call a recess to think about it or take days to come up with a verdict."

"How're you doing, Tom?" the deputy asked. "Is your back any better? How's Jesse?"

"This car smells like a bar!" declared the officer standing near Tom's window. "Where have you guys been drinking tonight? Taz, you look bat-shit crazy! We ought to get you out to walk the line!"

•

Joe waited up for Carl to get home like a worried parent. Out the window, he watched Carl get dropped off. When Carl opened the front door, Joe pounced.

"Where's your truck?" asked Joe suspiciously.

"In Wichita," replied Carl, while chewing gum.

"Why?"

"It wouldn't start."

"You mean you're drunk again!"

Carl sat down on the living room couch with a plop. "I think the ignition interlock system is messed up."

Joe continued standing. "It wouldn't start because of your blood alcohol level. You're drunk. Your eyes are bloodshot, they're watering, and you smell like a brewery. I know how an intoxilyzer works! Don't insult me."

Carl rubbed his eyes. "You know my eyes get red and puffy from the pollens you have here. Tom and I stopped for a drink. He didn't want to go home. We talked, had a couple of drinks. No big deal."

"Great! Now you're helping Tom Jennings, like he needs another problem with his court date coming up. He may lose his job over this, or worse. Stop helping others and help yourself!"

"No harm was done. He wasn't drunk, but we saw an accident. He dropped me off here so everything is fine. I'll catch a ride with you tomorrow when you go to the hospital. I'll get my truck and drive it back."

"How about you stay here and watch the kids like you promised? They were counting on you. We called, we texted, nothing! Give me your keys and I'll drive it back tomorrow. Elizabeth and I need to talk about this."

"What's wrong, Joe? I wasn't drunk. The breathalyzer control is set too low."

"I'll get your truck."

"Joe, listen . . ."

"I can't listen right now; tomorrow, when you're sober."

"Joe, I'm not drunk. You think I'm drunk even when I'm not."

"Remember, here you don't have the reservation to protect you."

"What do you mean by that?"

"How many DUIs have you had on the rez that never got reported?" asked Joe.

"A few, but I don't drink and drive anymore."

"Only because you got arrested in Grand Coulee where they follow the law."

"Misdemeanors on the rez don't need to be reported to the state. You know that. We're sovereign. What's your point? Why are you doing this? What's wrong?"

"It's a rez thing," stated Joe.

"And what do you know about the rez? You've been MIA for years. Ever since your horse accident, you never want to talk about it."

"There's no need to bring that up," warned Joe.

"But after the accident you changed. You had your own plans that didn't include us. We weren't good enough for you anymore."

"That's not true. We just relocated and started a new life. Elizabeth's from here. We still visit; you know that."

"But now we're not good enough," stated Carl.

"We can talk about this when you're sober."

"We're just a bunch of poor, drunk, lazy, ultraconservative, dirty Indians who have our own backward way of doing things. We're not good enough. Remember, you and me used to talk about it. We promised to break the cycle, to improve things. The whites saw us as lazy if we didn't have a regular job, but they wouldn't hire us. Let's see, nowadays you raise horses and you're a shade-tree mechanic. You work for a living or not? Maybe you've got yourself a hobby."

"Carl, let's not fight about this. It's not worth it. We've been friends too long."

"You started this. I'll go ahead and say it. I love Elizabeth like a sister. Remember, I was in Lawrence the day we met her. It was my graduation. I'm the one with the college degree, not you! She and Tina hit it off at the powwow. They connected then, and again later at Nespelem when you brought her out to meet the family. But after you married and moved off, you changed. Now you act like you're better than the rest of us. I get it. Money changes people. Instead of building a sweat lodge fire you start your patio grill. You used to be proud of being a full-blood. What happened to you? You marry a rich white woman and then look down at us who have to live off per caps."

"Leave Elizabeth out of this!"

"I don't think she's the direct cause of your shift, but it happened about the same time. You changed. She didn't even want to leave! Elizabeth had Tina sharing all her family stories. She was captivated. She appreciated us and where we live. She wasn't embarrassed to be among us. Heck, she married you. That's proof!"

"Okay, I changed. My leg shattered in a hundred pieces. My boxing career was over. Elizabeth nursed me back the best she could. Her parents had expert medical-care connections. I left the rez, so what?"

"And you've never returned."

"We've been back! You know we have. Suanna loves it there. Elizabeth too."

"But what about you? In spirit, you've never returned. How come?"

Joe considered Carl's question. Carl was right. In spirit, he had never returned.

I've been absent all these years because of my belief that I let my Confederated Tribes down. I've repeatedly blamed myself for my failure to become the world-class American Indian boxer I expected. I tasted the thrills of personal success in the ring, and I wanted to return that confidence to my people. First, I blamed the property owner for my catastrophic horse accident because of his buried barbed wire, and then I blamed myself for not being more careful. A million times I've asked myself if I could have done anything differently that would have prevented the horse from falling and remaining on top of me. My shattered leg shattered my dreams. It cost me my boxing career, and unfortunately, my belief in myself that I could make a difference.

Apparently, Carl never guessed the real reason. He had accused Joe of wanting to be *white* when all Joe really wanted . . . was to be *Indian*.

Social Media 22

As we gather more information about the death of #JamesOdessaSmith, our thoughts and prayers go out to his loved ones.

•

Early reports are that #JamesOdessaSmith was robbing a bank when he was shot by a police officer.

•

I've heard that customers at the bank said that #JamesOdessaSmith was shot a dozen times. Why so many? Couldn't they have shot him in the arm or the leg?

•

Thank God for officers who risk their lives responding to 911 calls that put their lives at risk. Pray for them and their families for their dedicated community service.

•

Another Brother bites the dust at the hands of the pigs. #BlackLives Matter

•

Black L-I-E-S Matter when they play the race card. He WAS committing a crime; he DID threaten a police officer; he was NOT shot in the back; he did NOT have his hands up. Sound familiar? I'm from Prairie Grove where the shooting occurred. A WHITE officer shot a WHITE criminal robbing a bank while the suspect pointed a gun at the police officer. Everything that happens is not a result of so-called racism.

•

When cops racially profile they are asking for trouble. #4Equality.

•

Muslims self-radicalize. So do Black Men after a lifetime of being disrespected, harassed, and feared.

•

#BlackLivesMatter is not saying that lives of people of other races don't matter. We're saying that Black Lives Matter too.

•

#JamesOdessaSmith was a member of our Coming Home Club in our church. He had a love of the human race and a faith in All Mighty God. RIP James.

•

If you don't respect the police, then don't expect them to respect you. When you protest and chant "What do we want? Dead Cops! When do you want them? Now!" you are asking for trouble, not solutions. #BlueLivesMatter

•

Understand that you can desire equality and safety for your children without being anti-police.

•

If you don't respect African Americans, then don't expect them to respect you. When you shoot unarmed black men, you are asking for trouble. #4Equality

•

This page is in memory of #JamesOdessaSmith. Those of you that are hijacking this memorial site should think about it and stop.

•

One in five Americans lives with a mental illness. To find out more, visit NAMI, that's the National Alliance on Mental Illness. There is free educational support.

•

#JamesOdessaSmith was a fantastic human being! He had a mental illness and was probably off his meds or he would have never robbed a bank! James, see you in Heaven!

•

Tribal warfare starts with tribal affiliation: Red, White, Brown, Black, Blue (cops), & Green ($). Until we join together, tribal warfare will continue. Right now it's circle the wagons, fighting real and perceived enemies.

•

Hate speech and anti-police speech have consequences because both create an environment where the desperate and deranged do desperate things. This cycle of reaction and distrust continues between cultures.

When and how does it stop?

•

Police officers often don't know who is mentally ill and who is not mentally ill when they respond to emergency calls for help.

•

#JamesOdessaSmith is another example of police officers shooting first and asking questions later. I know because my brother was shot and killed for DWB. #BlackLivesMatter.

•

Sorry for your personal loss. Black Lives do Matter but so do lives of People with Mental Illness. MIs are 16 times more likely to be killed by police.

•

I'm so sick of this. What's the point of giving cops Tasers if they don't use them?

•

Cops don't use their Tasers when someone has a gun.

•

Cops are too quick to treat people as criminals.

•

Don't rob a bank and you won't get shot.

•

James will be missed by the customers and staff at our veterinary clinic. He had a special connection with the ailing animals. RIP.

•

Criminals are quick to claim they are being profiled so that they have an easier chance of escaping justice. It's called playing the Race card.

•

Cops do profile. They play judge, jury and executioner. They are cowards! Stand up for justice!

•

No Peace, No Justice.

•

#BlackLivesMatter A violent system will meet a violent demise.

•

If people, especially police, were respectful of people of color, then there would be more trust by people in the community.

•

Every profession has some bad apples. When people say all police officers are bad, then they are biased and can't see the good.

•

When cops see every person of color as a potential criminal before they see them as a human being, then there can be no peace or justice. Yes, every profession employs caught and un-caught criminals, but not every profession has the license to kill people. Big difference.

•

A problem with the USA is that our foundation as a country is based on two sins: stealing land from the Indians and slavery. We see the results of those sins every day while we waste time and energy focusing on trying to figure out if cops need better training, better people, or better cameras. It's a social issue, not only a policing issue.

•

Cops are not psychiatrists. They respond to all kinds of people including those who are mentally ill who are not in touch with reality. They can't cure people. They can't do everything. MI is a social problem.

•

#JamesOdessaSmith was a kind and considerate person who had no enemies except for the police who murdered him.

•

He wanted to die and he got his wish. Suicide by Cop.

•

The cop that killed him is a BIG FAT SLOB who should have never been hired!

•

Suicide by Cop is real but crazy. Besides the trauma of the shooting, officers have to deal with those that second guess them without understanding. This includes the media and protestors.

•

Where is the video? If the police won't show a video, then the police are guilty.

•

Yes, let's see the video. The officer may have a personal video and the bank should have more videos. This should be easy to figure out why #JamesOdessaSmith was killed.

•

#JamesOdessaSmith, your life will not be forgotten.

•

The government continues to incarcerate people with mental illness instead of providing them medical services. This approach guarantees more future heartache and unnecessary deaths while money is thrown away.

•

In the 1950s there were a half million beds in psychiatric institutions. Today there are only 40,000 and the population has doubled. When the government cut the institutional care, they promised the savings would go to community supports for mental illness. Didn't happen. More of the same: broken political promises. Who got the money?

•

Our sheriff deputies are trained in CIT. More cops need to take the Crisis Intervention Team training. Officers receive special training in working with people who are mentally ill. They learn to use de-escalation techniques which are useful in dealing with all citizens.

•

Our son has been diagnosed as having schizophrenia. My husband and I took a free educational NAMI course called Family-to-Family that saved us by helping us learn how to cope and problem-solve with our son. We have so many resources now that we didn't even know about before this course! Go NAMI!

•

The officer deserves a medal of honor for risking his life to protect others during an armed robbery.

•

The FAT A** deserves to be fired and charged with murder! He shot a mentally ill person carrying a toy pistol.

•

How many people could decide in a split-second if a gun pointed at them was a real gun or a replica gun? The officer was sent to the bank to protect other people's lives. He did his job.

•

When you point a replica gun at a police officer, you are dead.

•

I knew #JamesOdessa-Smith since he was in grade school. He was a funny and kind classmate that had a joy for life. He cared for others. RIP

•

Why didn't Officer Jennings send in his K-9 dog to subdue the bank robber?

•

He didn't have his K-9 with him.

•

Is it true that the Cottonwood County Medical Examiner is the one who pronounced her son dead?

•

The bank robber was shot and killed by a Prairie Grove police officer. #JamesOdessa-Smith was the son of the Cottonwood County Medical Examiner but I've heard that she knew her son was dead before she arrived at the bank because the police had called her.

•

Man, that would be the worst thing to have to do, see your own son dead while you were doing your job.

•

The dead bank robber's father also works in the medical examiner's office. He used to be the coroner before the state changed the system to where the medical examiner had to be a pathologist.

•

Why was the officer suspended for doing his job?

•

When there is a police shooting in the line of duty, they typically suspend the officer with pay until the investigation finds if the lethal force that was used followed policy and procedure.

•

Why do cops get "paid time off" for murdering people? Other people get locked up!

•

I heard the officer was injured during the bank robbery. How do you get injured by a toy gun?

•

Thanks to the Rock Doves for sending James off at his funeral service with the music he enjoyed in his too short life. RIP

The Ax 23

've been axed!" Jennings told his attorney over the phone.

"Wait a minute," María Sanchez replied, grabbing her note pad.

"They fired me," Jennings stated. "Remember me telling you the other day, things couldn't get any worse? Well, they just did."

"When did this happen? What did they give as reasons for your termination? Do you have paperwork with you?" asked attorney Sanchez.

Jennings explained it had just happened. Fired. He was currently sitting in his truck outside the law enforcement center. He'd been called at home by his captain and told to meet at the chief's office. On the drive to work he started to hope, started to believe there would be no prosecution, that the case was being dropped. Instead, at the brief sit-down, the chief, flanked by Patrol Captain McArdle, and Detective Captain Kilgore, gave him the worst possible news. Sergeant Garcia, apparently his last supervisor, was there too, but he was a silent observer.

"I've got the paperwork with me if you can see me today," Jennings told her. "They reviewed my personnel file, well, the recent write-ups, not the attaboys. They reminded me that my not reporting a ten-forty-seven—that's a non-injury accident—about a week before the bank shooting, was the precursor to this outcome. That so-called fender bender was what caused me to get a letter in my file warning me about no more screw ups, or else."

"Okay, we'll meet about this, but did they say whether any of your actions at the bank was a reason for your termination?"

"Yes, there's a list; they said my response entering the bank on my own, without backup, warranted my dismissal due to my errors in following protocol. At every active-shooter training I've been at, the trainers tell us we should have three officers team up before entering a hot zone, but then they always follow up by telling us that if people were getting shot, they wouldn't wait; they'd go in alone. The bosses are selling me down a shark-infested river. They're also blaming me for hitting Suanna Morningcloud. You told me we had a solid case to win this."

"We do," said Sanchez. "We absolutely do. We have the best legal precedence—Supreme Court decisions. *Graham versus Connor* will support that your actions were in self-defense, that you engaged the suspect who posed an immediate threat, and that you appropriately fired until the threat was neutralized. You had *objective reasonableness*. If this case ever gets to criminal court, we'll have the jurors listen to the radio recording between dispatch and police; we'll show them the bank videos and, best of all, the replica gun. They'll see how you had to make a difficult, split-second decision. Between the video, the witnesses, and your testimony, there's every reason to believe that the only thing you're guilty of doing is the job you were sworn to do: protecting the citizens of our community. That's what you did. You should be cleared . . ."

"Should be cleared . . ." Jennings echoed, still looking for certainty in an uncertain world. "But what about my job?" he asked.

"The criminal charges against you, the most serious, may be the least complicated part of this. When it comes to being fired from the police department, we're talking about a citywide workplace environment that's prone to favoritism. It exists in every business."

"If the boss wants to get rid of me, he'll find a way to get rid of me. Is that what you mean?"

"Pretty much," agreed Sanchez. "It's impossible to treat all employees the same, especially when there are multiple supervisors. I mean, unlike criminal law, I think more often than not the employee can be right, but we can't prove the employer is wrong. The employer is the big dog in the fight. The employer carries more weight and makes the rules."

"Do you have the experience in this? I know you're well recommended on the criminal docket but what about on the civil side?"

"It's not my expertise, but I've worked plenty of cases. I'm not as current on all the civil updates, the case law, but I'll take a look. I can recommend another attorney if you want. Will your FOP lodge support you on this, too?"

"I haven't even asked, but I expect their help. You were my first call."

"You come by this afternoon; I'll get you in. Yeah, it's horrible timing because the publicity can hurt our criminal case, if there is one, but we can get through this. If the city has overstepped its authority, then you'll be exonerated. Let me see if we can appeal this; there's always arbitration, or the city council, but you know this all takes time."

"Yeah, ten-four, I know—and money. Call me crazy, but despite the shooting, this job means a lot to me. I'm fighting to keep it. I'm not ready to have someone else tell me I'm done, or wrong about the shooting. I'm a warrior, not a sheep. You know he forced me to kill him. I was there to save lives, including Jesse's. I want my career. If I leave, I want it to be my decision, not theirs."

"We'll work on that. Remember, he forced you to *stop* him, not kill him. Now, how's your back feeling?"

"The same, Doc has me on pain pills right now and limited activity. I was just telling someone yesterday that at least I'm getting paid while I'm off. But, with me on medical leave and getting fired, what happens now? I got hurt on duty."

"We'll talk. How's your wife feeling?"

"She's doing better, but she sure doesn't need to hear this."

"You haven't told her yet?"

"No, I called you first."

"Okay, I'll see you right after lunch—1:00 p.m. Bring with you all written departmental communications about this. I want to see every scrap of paper in your personnel file. I've already got the policy and procedure downloaded."

"Some of my communication is on my work e-mail and my phone," advised Jennings.

"Bring what you have," said the attorney.

"Okay, thanks for seeing me on such short notice. See you at one."

"Go tell Jesse what happened. Tom, she needs to know as soon as possible, and she needs to hear it from you. Give her my best."

•

"Okay, Tom, we'll review these reprimands in chronological order," said Sanchez as she examined a page from her open file folder. "How many years have you been on?"

"Thirteen," answered Jennings.

"Looks like you've had about nine or ten reprimands during that time."

"I believe that number's high. Some of the punishments have been reduced or decisions overturned after I appealed them."

"We'll go through each one that's listed here."

"How about my years as assistant range master with firearms and being the department's K-9 handler? How about all my attaboys, all the good stuff? Don't they count? There's a ton of them."

"Attaboys help for your annual evaluations, but one written reprimand or suspension about cancels out all the positives. The citizens can love you, but if a supervisor writes you up, then that's it, unless you get it overturned on an appeal."

"Here's an off-duty vehicle stop," said Sanchez, digging into the file. "You made a traffic stop while in civilian clothes and driving your personal vehicle. Is that right?"

"Yes ma'am, but that happened while I was waiting on the academy. Rookie mistake. The driver and passenger were sharing a pipe—using illegal drugs. I messed up on that. I wasn't aware it was against policy. I thought I was doing my job. That was done at a time when I believed there was a war on drugs. I hadn't learned yet to ignore misdemeanors. I was nearly fired before I got my uniform."

"Improper use of MDT?"

"Ten-four, mobile data terminal."

"Officers heckling one another over results of Dallas-Raiders game," read Sanchez. "Patrol division previously warned about use of MDTs for official business only," she continued.

"What can I say? The supervisor was a Raiders fan. He was a poor loser with no sense of humor."

"It looks like you weren't even the one commenting," surmised Sanchez.

"Precisely, I was aware of the messages, but I didn't send any. If it had been a Chiefs-Raiders game, I would have probably jumped in with a 'Go Chiefs,' but I did stay out of it, or so I thought."

"You were suspended for three days and then it was reduced to a written reprimand, is that correct?"

"On appeal, right. I just wanted to stay out of it, but I was reprimanded for not reporting the misuse of an MDT."

"Well, okay then . . . Here's another one," said Sanchez as she turned the page. "Not pulling a warrant from NCIC after an arrest."

"This is about Kilgore hating my guts. He always has. Day one, on probation, he warned me he had six months to find reasons to get rid of me. He told me I could find myself back in the jail working for SO. Personally, I think he's got a phobia about fat people, but I can't prove it. Any chance of an obese bias defense? He may have cacomorphobia."

"Caco . . . What did you say?"

"Cacomorphobia, a fear of fat people," explained Jennings.

"Let's get back to the warrant not being pulled. Is that a big deal?"

"It's a big deal. No officer wants to be going ten-fifteen on a warrant when the subject's already been arrested on it. If we got sued, that could get expensive for the department."

"Okay," said Sanchez.

Jennings took a breath, already feeling winded, like he was under cross examination. "I've talked with other officers who were not written up the first time they forgot to have a warrant cleared from NCIC. On this one, I actually thought I'd taken care of it, but I didn't have a paper trail to prove it. Without any documentation, I wasn't going to fight Kilgore."

"Next. Not responding to dispatch after they checked via emergency radio communications over a thirty-three minute period."

"Ten-four, a.k.a., sleeping on duty. Me and Kudzu had been called out a lot on traffic stops to search for drugs. I had court that day, and then I had to work back-to-back shifts. I helped out the department when they called; then they screwed me for being exhausted."

"You might have a point on that," said Sanchez, "about working forced, double shifts, but let's wait and see for right now. What about this? You were written up about missing a deadline for losing weight? I never heard about this."

"It was overturned. I didn't think it mattered. FOP supported me on it."

"Since this was overturned, it shouldn't even be in your personnel file. Do you know if it was removed from the city's original file?"

"I don't know," answered Jennings. "I've had a couple other incidents thrown out or the punishment reduced. I should have appealed the write-up for not clearing the warrant from NCIC. I've since learned how important it is for the department to be consistent in evaluations and reprimands. This reprimand was overturned because the department hired me overweight, and then a couple of years later, with a new chief, ordered me to lose fifty pounds in six months. They hired me supersized then didn't like me jumbo-sized. But, if the department required everyone to be in top shape, then they'd risk losing a few of their oldies but goodies. If we all had to complete the mile-and-a-half run in the required time, the department would need the jail's transport van following us around in order to scoop up our sorry asses off the pavement. I wouldn't be the only one dropping."

"You've got the right approach on this. The administration can't be selective about punishment. If we can show you've been singled out on reprimands, or marked down unfairly on evaluations, this can help our case.

"But," continued Sanchez, "on this one you handcuffed a neighbor for throwing a rock at your dog. Have any other officers done this and not been suspended?"

"Yeah, I mean no . . . but it wasn't my dog. They suspended me for protecting the department's K-9, not my personal pooch. Kudzu is the same K-9 who protects officers; he's the same K-9 that a community group purchased and had trained for the cost of $10,000. He protects us; we should protect him. He's part of the thin blue line."

"On point, but handcuffed?"

"I needed to get this guy's attention. When K-9s are injured or killed in the line of duty, suspects are arrested and criminally charged. I saw it as the same thing as assaulting an officer."

"Yes, but this says you were off-duty, walking the dog when he crapped on your neighbor's lawn."

"When I'm caring for Kudzu, I'm paid extra, so wouldn't I be on duty?"

"We'll save that argument for court. Here's an evaluation where your attendance is below standard. It also calls attention to you often missing your first scheduled work day after being off."

"Yeah, ten-four, but I wouldn't say often. It happens. When I show up to work sick, then they tell me to go home. I've got plenty of sick time on the books, so I can't be doing too badly. It's earned sick leave."

"Okay," said Sanchez, "Help me understand this one. Captain Kilgore wrote you up for arriving at a crime scene when you weren't requested."

"So, I'm unreliable if I'm called at home after my shift or on days off when I can't respond because I've been drinking. Then, when I show up at a scene because I'm on duty, I need to make sure Kudzu doesn't help the department before being specially invited by the supervisor. But, my fault—handler's error—for allowing Kudzu out of the van before I had orders. He didn't know better. He thought he was working, looking for his toy."

"Did he piss on some evidence or shit on the crime scene?" asked Sanchez, in an attempt at humor, out of character for the attorney.

Jennings smiled. "Actually, he was alerting to drugs or something unusual where the ground had been disturbed. But Kilgore ordered me and Kudzu back in the van. I got the hell out of there, but I still got written up: 'Disturbing an active crime scene.' More Kilgore bullshit.

"Found out later that Captain Kilgore 'discovered' a handgun and drugs hidden at that same spot. Kilgore supposedly used his metal detector he keeps in the trunk of his car to find the evidence, but I know what really happened. He's never wanted my help. When I've been called out, he makes sure to have someone else make the request. Fat phobia."

Sanchez ignored Jennings' plea for a fat phobia defense. Instead she kept digging into his personnel file. "Oh, here's one we'll have to discuss if your case goes to court. This is why your chief doesn't appreciate it when the media learns about officers who are not politically correct. Ask yourself, how many perspective jurors would understand this cop humor? What were you thinking, Tom?"

"Which one?"

"T-shirts."

"Yeah, ten-four, I've still got a few left if you'd like some. How about I bring you one and you take twenty bucks off my bill? I'll leave it with your receptionist. Medium or large?"

"I can still see the headline in the *News*," recalled Sanchez. " 'Smoke 'Em, Don't Choke 'Em: FOP T-shirts for sale!' You and every officer in today's social media world should know better than to do anything even resembling this! You're all smarter than this. It's already tainted the FOP and the department. And it will hurt you again. You've got to know you can always be googled."

"I thought it was okay since I was off-duty, and it was to raise money for the FOP," Jennings whined.

"Don't even try that with me," cautioned Sanchez. "You raised the chief's blood pressure, and you know that was the reason you guys did it. The FOP might as well have been selling shirts outside the *News*. You need to be honest with me."

"We voted for the 'Smoke 'Em, Don't Choke 'Em,' choice, but it could have been worse."

"I don't see how. This can really hurt us if we go to court. This was bad judgment from you and the FOP. I'd expect your profession to be more professional."

"It could have been worse," Jennings repeated. "Under the category of 'things felony suspects should never say when confronting police,' we considered a couple other responses. One was, 'You're too big a pussy to shoot me.' The other said, 'That uniform makes your ass look really big.'

"Well, the chief banned the use of carotid holds," Jennings continued. "We saw it as him caving in to the media. We felt like he was taking away a practical combat response to criminal assaults. A scumbag tries to take an officer's gun and, so, he's choked, I mean restrained."

"You agreed to eliminate 'scumbag' from your vocabulary."

"Sorry—perp."

"But why did the chief single you out rather than the organization?"

"He wasn't happy with any of us. I found the idea online, out of Vancouver, from decades ago. Unlucky for me, the chief was in the LEC on a Saturday night; caught me going into the locker room wearing the Smoke 'Em shirt. Ordered me to take if off and keep it off whenever I was on city property, or for as long as I was employed by PD. Again, no sense of humor."

"Your cop humor cost you your job," concluded Sanchez.

"After that I was a marked man. The next week the K-9 program was temporarily suspended. Then an e-mail was sent out to see if other officers were interested in getting trained as a handler."

"You did it to yourself."

"Harsh."

"A sense of humor is what makes you laugh. Being funny is what makes others laugh."

Jennings nodded and looked down.

"We've got more to cover. I need to understand this incident about not reporting an accident. On paper this appears to be what caused the administration to put you on notice for potentially losing your job. This event was the administration's last warning to you."

"Yeah, ten-four," agreed Jennings "After the T-shirts, I couldn't lay low enough. I was on their radar."

"You were on duty, stopped at a traffic light, and bumped the car in front of you. And the driver of the car just happened to be our honorable mayor. Small world."

"Yeah, that's right. I was in one of the car pool cars, not the K-9 van."

"And you said there was no damage, so no need for a report?"

"My point. No injury and no damage to either vehicle means no report. Heck, sometimes we have drivers plead with us to make a report and we don't. There's nothing there. It's not a reportable accident."

"Tell me more on this incident."

"After the tap, I put on my emergency lights, we pull over, and the mayor and I talk for a couple of minutes. I apologize to him. He says no harm, no damage, and no need for a report, forget about it. He notices Kudzu's not in the car, and he asks me if he's sick. I just tell him he's not with me that day. I don't tell him why. Then the mayor tells me he's got to get to a city council meeting, jumps back in his car and leaves—without using his turn signal."

"Okay, then what?"

"I guess a couple days later the mayor sees the chief and mentions that he ran into me recently, or I ran into him. That causes the chief to ask my patrol captain what he knows about it; then my captain calls me into his office. I'm grilled about why I didn't report an accident and if I was wearing my seatbelt."

"Go on; this is getting good," encouraged Sanchez.

"First off, he tells me that I should have immediately contacted my supervisor because these are the things that the administration needs to know about, that bad news travels fast. He tells me that this is another example of my poor decision making; that I don't see the big picture. Then, as if to prove his point, I admit to my captain I wasn't wearing my seatbelt. But it's a good thing I'm honest because I learned that when I tapped the mayor's car the driver next to me saw I didn't have it on."

"Go ahead. I know there's more."

"So when I slammed on my brakes, my drink spilled on my radio, the police radio. I cleaned it up, but the next shift complained about a radio problem and the radio technician eventually examined it. That's how I got reprimanded for tapping the rear bumper of the mayor's car even though it caused no damage and no injuries. Like I keep saying, it was not a reportable accident."

"Hmm . . . but the radio was damaged," Sanchez countered.

"It was fixed in a few minutes after cleaning, but that's how I got put on notice that the next screw-up would cost me my job."

And you weren't wearing your seatbelt."

"One more thing," Jennings continued. "The bosses were about done with me when Kilgore had a couple of questions for me. Even though I'd previously been asked about it by my captain, he wanted to know if I had purchased and sent flowers to the funeral service of James Odessa-Smith, including a card addressed to Carolyn Odessa.

"I told him no, just like I'd already told Captain McArdle. Then he asked why, on the day of Odessa-Smith's funeral, I was parked along the funeral route to the cemetery.

"I just told him I was going through an emotional process of dealing with the shoot and that I hadn't bothered anyone, especially the Odessa-Smith family. I also told him that after hearing about the Odessa-Smith supporters, I was curious if there was going to be a demonstration by agitators outside the church."

"Yes," Sanchez commented, "I wonder where he's going with this."

"I already told you about the stalking order that Carolyn Odessa attempted to file on me. Since it was denied by the judge, I was never ordered to PFA (Protection From Abuse) court. But I learned from a civil process server that her allegations included how I was harassing her by sending flowers and a card, and that I had stalked her around town.

"Her attempt to get the protection order against me wasn't mentioned in my termination letter, so I don't know why Kilgore was asking me about this. Personally, I know Kilgore's a lot closer to Odessa than he is to me, so he may have been helping her railroad me."

"That would be hard to prove."

"Anyways, I'm following your advice; I haven't had any contact with Carolyn Odessa or her husband."

"Good for you. Be smart. Stay strong."

"With all her Facebook activity talking about me killing her son, and the criminal justice system being unfair to people with mental illness, can you get the judge to stop her from ranting online about me being guilty of murder?"

"Remember what I said," reminded Sanchez. "The medical examiner is an authority on autopsy reports. Any time a person is killed intentionally, even if they're robbing a bank, the wording in the report and on the death certificate specifies that the victim died of homicide. James Odessa-Smith was a homicide. The State's Attorney Office or a jury will decide if his death was justifiable. Right now, Carolyn Odessa has the First Amendment, freedom of speech, on her side. But I've tried to get the courts and the city to put a gag on her inflammatory posts if they want to have a trial in Cottonwood County.

"Part of my job is to understand that people in our country, including Carolyn Odessa, have the right to their free hate speech," concluded

Sanchez. "How much she can continue to do this and stay employed may be another question to explore, but I don't think it will change our plans in your case."

"María, I know some people think I should apologize to the Odessas, but for what? Maybe they should apologize to me."

The Greys 24

In Suanna's dream the greys were everywhere.

The open doorway of her thatched hut welcomed the birds to come and go as they wished. They could always count on fresh water, conversation, and mirrors. Suhaila, known locally as "The Princess of Parrots," or "Bird Whisperer," was clearly their dedicated friend, confidant, and protector.

Living in the shadow of the Minziro Forest Reserve, there were other delightful birds to admire outside, especially the great blue turacos and blue swallows, plus hundreds of varieties of butterflies. Her favorite was the gold-banded forester. Though partial to the color blue, Suhaila's dearest bird was easily the African grey parrot. Most people recognized the greys as intelligent, quick learners at mimicking Haya or Kiswahili vocabulary, but Suhaila understood how their linguistic skills permitted them to engage in real conversation. People swore that the wild greys would say her name, "Suuu-AY-la!" with the greatest excitement whenever they approached her, while ignoring others nearby, even her children.

The children were off to school, a considerable time-consuming walk, even when they didn't dawdle to examine wildlife tracks or to pick a treat off the trees near the dirt path. In fact, a neighbor had recently complained to Julius, father of the children, about their ongoing care-free consumption from his *baobab* tree. He said he regarded it as theft. It wasn't their tree and it wasn't their fruit. "Why didn't they eat bananas or plantains off their own trees?" he asked. And how would Suhaila like it if he and his family ate grey parrot twice a day, especially the plump ones with tender flesh that squawked her Kiswahili name? He could make it happen.

At school the children received lessons about their personal safety. A poster hanging at the school's entrance warned the children to beware of strangers and abductions. But Neema, the oldest child, already twelve, had regularly heard the stranger-danger talk from her parents. Not only were the children warned to be cautious because of their youth, but Neema and her nine-year-old sister, Mahalia, each carried additional risk due to their skin condition.

The sisters' albinism was more than an inconvenience to them from severely sunburned blisters and visual impairment. They had experienced other children being cruel to them because of their lack of pigment. In a crowd or in a classroom they always stood out and had to explain that they were black, even though they looked white. And, no, their mother did not get pregnant twice from sleeping with white men! It was tempting for the girls to pass along a myth that could help guard them from ongoing bullying; some people believed that the cause of a newborn baby with albinism was due to one of the parents having once made fun of a PWA, a person with albinism. This was an example of African karma.

Occasionally the girls heard the derogatory word *"Zeru! Zeru!"* either whispered or loudly cursed at them. Its Kiswahili meaning, ghost-like creature, was an example of ongoing prejudice. To some, most often adults, they were not human but ghostly; they didn't die but disappeared; and because of that they were ostracized, mocked, and feared. Muslims sometimes called them *"nguruwe,"* meaning pig. But, while some people despised them, at other times strangers would ask to shake their hand for good luck. Neema recalled the previous year when she was only eleven; a sickly old man offered her money to have sex with him so he could be cured from his AIDS. Clearly, it wasn't easy being a child with albinism, especially in the backcountry of rural Misenyi District. One minute she was hidden inside the house for her own protection, but the next thing she knew her parents were ordering her outside to go do chores or run errands. Always, as an afterthought, her mother added: "Take Mahalia and Abasi with you."

Despite their youthful ages, the girls already knew that evil witch-doctors, not the modern healers they relied on, encouraged albino mutilation or murder in order to obtain blood or body parts. This magical ritual or sacrifice was known as muti medicine. It was gruesome just thinking about the stories of targeted children. Neema and Mahalia had heard of albino girls and boys disappearing without a trace and other reports where witnesses had seen the abductions. Rarely were the lost children found alive, but sometimes the bodies were discovered missing arms, legs, or heads.

"Why did such a cruel world exist?" Neema asked her parents. She learned of a region of violence that had erupted from outside her country, when a thousand bodies a day flowed down the Kagera River on their way to Lake Victoria. Before she was born, Hutu extremists massacred Tutsis as a part of ethnic cleansing. If the Rwanda genocide could number 800,000 people, then it made sense that the few like her, especially children, were expendable, powerless. Who would ever stand up for people like her?

Neema had also seen war memorials from the War of Kagera when Idi Amin ordered his Ugandan troops to invade her tribe's territory. But in her young life near her home she also knew firsthand about hardships of family and friends, the turmoil caused when parents died of malaria or AIDS, leaving orphans in her surrounding community. To be sure, life was unpredictable. Neema's father said people outside their influence were caught up in the forces of greed, poverty, and politics. But Neema simplified it: "How much is my world a result of God's wishes, and how much is it from witchdoctor curses?"

Neema recalled one village boy who had survived his bloody castration at the hands of a neighbor, not some dangerous stranger. Her father said the savagery was due to superstitious beliefs that were not true. People craved health and wealth and would pay witchdoctors for magic potions to try to influence malicious spirits. Mother explained it differently: "The people who were lazy and greedy were competing with others who were sick, selfish, or stupid."

Fortunately, the children had been assured that their safety was nearly guaranteed by staying together and not speaking to strangers. Then there was the everyday command for the girls to be responsible for the security of their brother Abasi, just seven, by having him always walk between his sisters and to remember to always hold hands with one of them when they were in a crowd. As the older siblings, the girls were reminded that they were Tanzanian warriors, each a human shield for protecting their youngest, the most vulnerable, from danger.

"Please, Neema, just one fruit. I'm hungry," begged Mahalia as she slowed on their walk to school.

"We've been warned to stay away from his tree; you know that," replied Neema.

"The tree is full and one will not be missed," promised the younger sister, already stopped and gazing up for a pod within her reach.

Abasi released his grip on Mahalia's hand and looked to the ground, scanning, beginning a visual search below the leafy tree limbs which in other seasons looked like giant snarly roots.

Neema glanced ahead up the path, then back toward their fresh footprints. Seeing no one in the vicinity, she said, "I like their grapefruit taste."

Mahalia walked under the *baobab* that her parents called the "tree of life." "Help me up," she said, "I like the pods because they taste like pears. Neema, will you lift me, please?"

Neema locked her hands together like an adjustable step and supported her extended arms against her body. Mahalia climbed up and, with the shifting weight, Neema tried to steady herself.

Bent over, Abasi picked up a rotten pod and competed with intoxicated insects. Instead of discarding it, he licked the dripping liquid and smelled his hand. "I love vanilla," he smiled. "What could taste better than vanilla?"

"Neema!" yelled Mahalia, as they laughed, off balance, collapsing together to the ground with Neema's wide-brimmed hat flying off her head.

"YOU CRIMINALS!" screamed the neighbor, rushing toward them and his *baobab* fruit while brandishing a machete.

Abasi dropped his treat as the girls hurried to their feet. Hastily, all three raced for the path as their un-neighborly neighbor continued yelling: "THIS IS THE LAST TIME YOU'LL STEAL FROM ME!"

The children were a blur in the bush as they kicked up dirt in their eagerness to escape. Seconds later, Neema turned to see her younger siblings falling farther behind. Neema slowed long enough to allow them to catch up and pass her while she surveyed the predator's path behind them. Out of breath, she realized that the man was nowhere to be seen. He had not followed.

The remainder of the hurried walk to school was one of silence from the children and steady glances over their shoulders to the trail behind. Instead of talking, they listened for unusual noises but heard only the birdsongs and howling monkeys—both the black-and-white colobuses and the red-tails.

•

"Welcome, children. You're on time; congratulations," said a volunteer at the school's entrance. "Later today, we have a guest visiting for an assembly and to share lunch with us. Be on your best behavior."

•

Neema, Mahalia, and Abasi were walking home after school. Mahalia held Abasi's hand. The girls had already discussed whether to take a less-direct route in order to avoid their upset neighbor.

"Neema," said Mahalia, "I saw you talking to the visitor at school today, before the assembly. What did you talk about?"

"Her name is Mrs. Kilanguva. She asked what kind of books I like to read and what food is my favorite."

"Why was she asking, and what did you say?" inquired Mahalia.

"Don't you ever listen? Our headmaster told us that she lives in the United States, but she was born here in our country. She's Tanzanian! She's planning on sending books and expanding our lunch program."

"Yes, she did talk about that. So, what did you tell her about her questions? Did you tell her of the *baobab* fruit?"

"When I told her *maandazi* was my favorite food, she laughed and told me it's her favorite treat between meals. But when I told her I had trouble reading the small letters, she promised to send books with large print. She said they were common in the United States."

"Yes, books for us to read more easily," said Mahalia.

"She also told me that she wants to be sure our school has a computer for student use so we can read our assignments with ease," said Neema. "She said it will enlarge the print like magic. In the United States old people with poor vision use it to read newspapers."

"Our headmaster has a computer in the office; I've seen it," said Mahalia.

"Her first name is Farida, and she wrote down my name when we talked," added Neema. "She was born in Dar es Salaam and graduated from college twice."

"My favorite was when she got up and danced with us," said Mahalia.

"Yes, she was very good. I told her about mother's greys and father's work in the forest reserve. I invited her to visit. She said she didn't think she'd be able to stop by this trip but maybe the next time. Farida told me African grey parrots are as smart as chimpanzees and small children! And she cares about the forest reserve losing buffalo and rhino to poachers and about its deforestation by illegal logging. She's really nice and smart!"

"It would be something to have her visit us at our home, but why would she do that?" asked Mahalia? "She doesn't know us."

"Because she likes me; that's why. It wasn't about being albino. She didn't ask about that. That was a nice change. You know how outsiders get."

"Yeah. My eyes are not red!"

Abasi refused to hold hands with Mahalia any longer, reminding her that the rule only applied in a crowd. He brandished a stick like a machete one minute, and the next, dragged it behind him like it was a heavy weight, marking his trail.

"My machete will protect us from our bad neighbor," Abasi commented.

"Look!" said Neema, "a baby hyrax. It must have fallen." Without hesitation, she picked it up and held it like a baby, examined it for injuries, and then bent her head upwards, searching the trees overhead. A cardinal woodpecker with his red cap, hanging upside down near a tree cavity, stared down at her and then gave a contact call to his mate.

"We'll take him home," said Neema. "Mother can help him."

Mahalia and Abasi gathered around Neema. "Let me see too," said Abasi, stretching his neck.

Neema knelt down so her siblings could observe the young tree hyrax.

"I don't see an injury," said Neema. "Let's count his toes to be sure they're all here: one, two, three, four in the front . . . and . . . one, two, three on the back feet."

"*Jambo*, hello," greeted a tall stranger, wearing khaki pants and a green shirt, blocking the trail, holding a partially folded coffee bean sack in one hand.

Neema observed part of a net hanging out of the sack and wondered what he wanted.

"*Habari?* How are you?" he continued.

Neema and her siblings straightened up but said nothing.

"*Habari*," he repeated, no longer a question.

Neema narrowed her eyes and gave a forced smile. "*Mzuri*," she replied, although she felt anything but fine.

"We've been waiting for you so we can shake your hand and be brought good luck for finding gold."

Hearing the word *we*, Neema knew another person was behind her on the path they had just walked. She glanced over her shoulder and confirmed a shorter man she did not recognize. He was carrying the same, familiar, empty sixty-kilogram coffee bag. Even though the man had claimed that he and his cohort were searching for gold, Neema wondered if they were actually stealing animals—birds, butterflies—or even ivory from the forest's floor.

"Our parents don't allow us to talk to strangers," Neema replied. "We must go. They'll be worried."

"How long will it take to shake our hands?" the stranger asked. "We aren't like those who think you're cursed. Don't be rude to us. Won't you help us by sharing your magic?"

"Mahalia, take Abasi home," ordered Neema in a flat tone of voice, "I will follow. Go now."

"Don't be greedy," said the short man as he grabbed Mahalia before she got away.

Mahalia moaned and whimpered and gasped for air.

Neema leaned forward and screamed: "LET HER GO! She hasn't done anything wrong! RUN ABASI! GET HELP! RUN NOW!"

Abasi dropped his stick and ran.

When Neema was grabbed, her baby tree hyrax fell to the ground, squeaking and whistling with his voice rising to a piglike squeal. His nocturnal family awakened immediately. Alerted by his cries of crisis, they responded from the tree tops with their very distinctive call, a growl culminating in a child's bloodcurdling scream.

Neema and Mahalia struggled to break free. Their shrieks competed with the forest animals, creating pandemonium. Grey parrots suddenly arrived and began swift attacks upon the men.

The attacker restraining Neema, the taller one, suddenly produced a machete and feverishly clubbed her head. Blood erupted. "MUTI MAGIC!" he yelled. He again swung his weapon and Neema attempted to stop the blow. Defensively, she raised her hand to block his assault. Part of her hand disappeared. Severed fingers fell to the ground. Neema ran into the forest screaming and dripping blood. Her attacker raced after her, then slowed. A storm of grey and red engulfed him as African greys, flapped their wings, raised their shrill voices in a crescendo of alarmed anger, and slashed the armed aggressor with their beaks. The man blindly batted his weapon at the greys as they continued to bite, even claw, his face.

Neema's attacker yelled at his partner to help him, but the second man was also being steadily pummeled from the air. This man picked up Mahalia and draped her over his shoulder. He hurried away, his head down, trying to disappear, to escape farther into the forest.

The first attacker, despite being overwhelmed by the birds amongst their squawks and shrieks, felt a sharp sting on his ankle. He looked down and saw a rhinoceros viper retreating into the underbrush. Recognizing his worsening dilemma, he yelled for help.

"JOSEPH, COME BACK! I've been bitten by a rhino viper! He got me on my ankle. COME BACK! HELP!"

•

Suhaila was alarmed by the noise. She knew something was seriously wrong. She hurried outside and breathed deeply but didn't smell smoke. Nor did she hear chainsaws, gunfire, or stampeding animals.

"My greys!" Suhaila said.

There was a commotion with numerous birds approaching, talking at once like excited children. Yes, birds speaking at one time, making it difficult to decipher their words. As they landed, she looked into their yellow eyes and listened.

"GET HELP!" one shouted.

"RUN NOW!" another cried.

"A-BA-SI RUN!" the last proclaimed in four syllables.

Suhaila grabbed her machete and raced to the path leading toward school, already searching ahead for her children. A small flock of greys at her eye level led the way.

"GET HELP!"

"RUN NOW!"

"A-BA-SI RUN!"

•

"What's wrong?" asked the teacher as children surged into the school, surrounding Abasi.

He breathed deeply, out of breath, his mouth opened but it only swallowed words. His eyes were enormous, his body soaked with perspiration. "My sisters . . ." he exhaled.

"Are they hurt?" asked the adult.

"Strangers . . . in the forest . . . on our way home. Help us, please," Abasi begged.

•

Along the trail Suhaila saw a single grey feather, then more, and finally clumps of color: grey wing feathers and red tail feathers. The dead and struggling bodies of the greys were next. Some were attempting to fly, trying to escape the deadly forest floor. Those dying refused to squeak or squawk. They knew that their cries would only attract predators.

But seeing Suhaila gave them hope.

"Suuu-AY-la! Suuu-AY-la!" they began, looking to her for an opportunity to be comforted. "Suuu-AY-la!"

"MU-TI MAGIC!" an injured grey yelled.

"RHI-NO VIPER!" another cried out.

"MA-HAL-YA! Ma-hal-ya!" still another shrieked, the second time more weakly.

Suhaila cried out for her children: "NEEMA! MAHALYA! ABASI! WHERE ARE YOU?"

That's when Suhaila saw the form on the ground, thirty meters off the path. She ran to the spot, to the grey school clothing, to her daughter. Recognizing Neema's bloody face, Suhaila was shocked further by the blood oozing from her daughter's mutilated hand, a rusty red stump on the damp forest floor.

Superheroes and Arch Villains 25

I know it's not the same thing," Mike Gale said, as he leveled his sight and slowly pulled the trigger, "but we both killed someone in the line of duty. It's something we've talked about since the academy. It was always out there. We prepared for this."

"Yeah," said Tom, as he fired rounds at the steel dueling-tree target, "remember the instructor who didn't really hypnotize us, but gave us suggestions about surviving a gun fight?"

"Peters, Bill Peters," said Mike.

"Yeah, ten-four. He was a character all right, old school."

Both men holstered their weapons.

"He told stories about walking the beat in Kansas City," said Mike. "I still recall his banana story. Once you accept the first gift from a person, no matter how inexpensive it is, then you're on your way to being compromised. A prostitute's a prostitute, no matter the price."

"Well," said Tom, "I've taken a few free cups of coffee, but I never felt like it compromised me. There's such a thing as being polite without selling your soul."

"Speaking of your soul, I just want to remind you to keep the faith," advised Mike. "You're not in this alone. Don't let a few people, especially Carolyn Odessa or the liberal media, pull you down. You're stronger than this. God is with you."

"Mike, I appreciate you helping me through this. I'm feeling pretty isolated from the other guys right now. Sitting around the house instead of pulling a shift is a big change to my routine, although I've had some quality time with our girls. Singing is our specialty. We've got some nice video we've sent to family and friends, but I'm not permitting them to post any online. If my back was better, I'd be dancing with them too."

"Taz, I'll keep reminding you, you were the one who didn't hesitate, who put yourself in harm's way. Under deadly circumstances you stepped up. Your actions were extraordinary even though you see it as just doing your job."

"Yeah, ten-four. Thanks again, but for me there's a disconnect. I believed I was just doing my job and all was good, then I got fired for doing my duty. So, there're things I'm still trying to work out. At least Jesse's healing. If Suanna will just get better, I think I'll be okay. Like I said, I can live with the shoot."

After Tom and Mike reset the hinged plates on the steel dueling tree, they returned to the firing line, reloaded, and adjusted their earmuffs. With two simultaneous nods, firing commenced. Bullets pinged and steel targets swung back and forth, back and forth. Two friends with peaceful intentions, members in a killer's club, dueled for life.

"Yeah, we both shot and killed someone, but that's where the similarities end," Tom continued. "No, wait, we both got recognized too, only you got a commendation and I got fired and publicly crucified online," he grumbled sarcastically.

"This isn't over. Sorry you have to go through so much bullshit on a good shoot. It's not right. Those protestors are being led around by their tweets. They don't know what they're talking about. Wait until they need emergency help. Who will they call then? A bank robber having an out-of-body experience?"

"Yeah, ridiculous," agreed Tom. "How can I be the bad guy in this?"

"It's like the stories of Vietnam vets when they came home and were called baby killers. Some of those veterans were warned about wearing their uniforms in public places. It's all so screwy. It's the same thing, dedicated people being judged by outsiders."

"So our soldiers who served in Iraq and Afghanistan are publicly thanked in airports, while police officers are accused of being racist murderers. Wow, the world's spinning out of control," concluded Mike.

"And with less support and trust from our communities, it will be harder to find dedicated people to risk putting their lives on the line as police officers. But Bro, tell me again about the time you were dispatched on Odessa-Smith."

"The arrest? You want to hear that again?"

"I was just thinking that he could have been shot a couple different times by other officers before the day I plugged him. He'd been asking for it."

"Yeah, I guess he was on borrowed time. He'd dodged a bullet or two."

"So?" said Tom.

"So, what?" asked Mike.

"Are you going to tell me about him charging you?"

"Okay."

"Thanks, but tell all of it."

"He was trippin' when we booked him in, delusional. Never knew if it was too many drugs or him being off his meds. He thought he was the one and only—Willie Nelson."

"How long ago was that?"

"Oh, it's been about five years now. He went to the county jail, so he was at least eighteen."

"It was a traffic stop, wasn't it?"

"Sort of, sent on a noise complaint, white male parked in a vehicle up in Richmond Heights. Sure enough, when I'm a block away, the cottonwood leaves are a'shakin'. I call it in, park behind the pickup, and get out. As my feet touch the ground, the truck pulls up two car lengths and stops. He's got my attention. I should have got back in my vehicle, but instead I request backup and go ahead and continue my approach. This time the truck kind of lurches forward another car length, stops, engine dies, but the music is still blaring. I've got my holster unsnapped, grippin' my Glock, and I hear this hysterical laughter above the sound of really loud music and singing; only I'm not laughing."

"Was he buzzed?"

"Like I said, I never found out for sure. I ordered him to show me his hands, to put them out the window. No response, nothing. Right away, in less than a minute, Hendricks arrives as backup. The truck's got expired tags, but it hasn't been reported stolen. Because this thing is so unusual—weird—we treat it as a felony stop. With both our units parked behind him, our weapons drawn, I get on the loud speaker and tell him to shut off the music."

"Did he get out on his own?" Tom encouraged even though he knew the answer.

"Not until the song was over. Instead of putting his hands out the window like we ordered, he opens the door, jumps out and comes charging at us with his hands up—empty—and with the biggest shit-ass grin I've ever seen! We nearly shot him. It was all a game to him, like we were playing cops and robbers. Like we were kids with toy guns and nobody would get hurt. Like it was all a game . . . pretend . . . not real life. If we hadn't seen his hands, he was a goner."

"What'd you do?"

"We could see he wasn't holding anything. The screwball was smiling! He stopped about ten feet from us and asked us—I said, asked us—what the problem was! Fortunately, he cooperated; he even let us handcuff him while we checked out his story."

"What were the charges?"

"First off was the noise ordinance; I'd heard it well over fifty feet away. Then, because I'd seen him driving, I had him for the expired tags and no proof of insurance. Hendricks saw marijuana seeds on the floorboard and then found a roach in the ashtray, so we charged him with possession of marijuana too. But the most unusual charge was that of his identity. He didn't have a driver's license or any other ID. Even though we figured we probably had his real name and address from the old license registration, he wouldn't admit to being James Odessa-Smith."

"He said his name was Willie Nelson!" interjected Tom, who helped tell the story like a child at bedtime.

"Yep, at the car stop and on the way to jail, even at the book-in counter—'Willie Nelson'. Even knew the real Willie Nelson's middle name. I still remember him telling the jailer he was born in Abbott, Texas, and that he had no history of mental illness. The date of birth he gave us checked out with the real Willie Nelson. We confirmed it later."

"You brought him to jail even though he was acting crazy?" asked Tom, again knowing the answer, but looking for the reasoning behind it.

"Yeah, like I said, where else? You know if we'd taken him to the ER they would have made us wait for hours and then released him. Was he a danger to himself or others? Well, he almost got shot and killed, but he didn't threaten to harm anyone."

"It never went to court," recalled Tom.

"Right, plea bargained. I think he paid a fine for no insurance and got probation on the possession of marijuana. The false name charge was dropped. Of course, the court costs and attorney fees were the real penalty."

"Yeah, ten-four, no doubt paid by his parents."

"Probably. Like I said, he surprised the hell out of me. I almost shot him. Outside the wire he would have been dead. Something else I thought of later, the loud music he was playing wasn't heavy metal or rap. It was a country western song sung by Patsy Cline. You've heard it, 'Crazy'. Only remember, she didn't write it. Willie Nelson did."

"That's right," agreed Tom.

"One more thing that was odd. At his arrest and book in, his eye color was light brown, no doubt about it. I saw them. The DL we found later for James Odessa-Smith didn't match up. It stated his were blue. Now, one could argue that errors happen every day and that maybe there was a mix up at the DMV. But the reason I mention this is that one of SO's jailers, Jordan, swears that upon Odessa's release, his eyes were blue and he still wasn't wearing contacts!"

"No contacts?"

"No," replied Mike. "They checked at book in and at his release."

"How did they explain that?"

"They never did, but later on we learned that Willie Nelson's eyes were light brown."

"Hmm."

"A few years back Odessa-Smith was sent to Larned State Hospital," said Tom.

"Yeah, they tried to fix him. Guess he was okay for a while, took his meds."

"This was after the call when he tried to kill himself."

"Oh, yeah, our new officers don't believe us when we tell them what he did."

"Go on," said Tom. "I want to hear this again."

"The call came in as an MI (person with mental illness) involved in a disturbance at the Clusters. At least we had a warning what we were getting into. It was called in first by the landlord who was concerned about the damage to his property. He wanted the 'maniac' arrested before other tenants were hurt. Then Odessa-Smith's parents showed up to help. They called, too."

"They knew back then he wasn't right," said Tom. "When he was a young teenager, before his mental illness, I worked my first case with him. Razer could have shot him too."

"Yeah, his parents emphasized to dispatch that he had no access to guns, but he was smashing things up with a ball-peen hammer. When they tried to intervene, Odessa-Smith chased them out of the apartment, so they called us."

"That surprised me," said Tom. "I figured the medical examiner could get anyone to obey her command."

"The parents had heard him tearing things up. They opened the door with an extra key and tried to get him to calm down, but he ran them out. He was telling them he couldn't find Willie—that Willie wouldn't come out and play.

"When our first officer arrived at the scene, he met briefly with the parents. They told him about their son's mental illness, but said they'd never seen him so violent and out of control. The parents assured us that James didn't have access to any firearms, but we couldn't be so sure of that. The hammer was dangerous enough. We just needed to be extra cautious with this subject. A decision was made to keep his parents out of it. They wanted our help, but wanted to tell us how to do our job. We didn't have a lot of options."

"I can't remember our uniforms ever calming him down," said Tom.

"We could hear Odessa-Smith screaming inside his apartment. We considered surprising him since we had an extra key or talking to him through the closed door. But, to start with, we decided to try and sneak a look with a miniature camera. What the officer saw shocked us to the core. Our veteran officers hadn't seen anything like it in their entire careers.

"Odessa-Smith was lying on the floor, holding a single bullet in one hand, centered on his forehead with its tip dug into his skin. It was bleeding pretty good. He was repeatedly striking it with his hammer, yelling 'Die, devil die!' We charged into the apartment, yelling for him to put his weapon down. About the same time we tased him. We had him handcuffed before he knew what happened. It went down really fast. With him being so speeded up and all, I wasn't sure if only one tase would do the trick, but it was enough.

"That bullet was a live round—a thirty-eight caliber. Makes you wonder and be thankful. If he had a bullet, he could have had a gun too."

"Yeah, ten-four, a real one," added Tom.

"Hey, here comes Jesse and the girls."

"Looks like liquid refreshments, but don't count on beer, sorry," said Tom.

"I hope you're joking. You know guns and alcohol don't mix," commented Mike.

"Yeah, pretty much."

"It's been awhile since I've seen the cuties. How are they?"

"They're still kids. Thank God for that. I kill a man and get fired, but you know what they're still talking about?"

"What's that?"

"They missed the ComicCon celebration last month in Hutchinson."

"Good for them! Leave it to children to give us some perspective," said Mike, with a laugh. "You know, it's pretty cool that Hutchinson's city council renames their town "Smallville" every year to support the event."

"Hello, cowboys!" said Jesse as she arrived at the shooting station. "How are you, Mike?" she asked as she gave him a hug. "Thanks for being here."

"Doing fine, Jesse," replied Mike, "as long as Tom keeps letting the range master beat him on the dueling tree."

"That'll be the day," said Tom. "We're not done yet," he promised.

Hannah and Julia handed each man a glass of iced tea.

"Thank you, darling," Mike said to Hannah. "Both you girls are growing up and looking prettier every day. What have you been doing this summer?"

"Swimming," replied Julia.

"Art classes," offered Hannah.

"Is your mom teaching you art?" asked Mike.

"No, we do it at the community center by the swimming pool," explained Hannah.

"Have you been in any parades lately?" asked Mike.

"No," the girls answered, their eyes narrowed.

"Next month I'll be driving one of our police cars downtown in the Emancipation Proclamation parade. I've been ordered to find some superheroes to accompany me."

"Are you saying you're looking for superheroes to ride with you in the parade?" clarified Jesse.

"Yep, that's right," said Mike.

Turning back to the girls Mike continued, "Do you know any?"

"Girls," stated Jesse, "tell Mike about the costumes you've been working on."

"I'm Wonder Woman!" said Julia.

"I'm Poison Ivy, and I have a costume that's covered with leaves! It has a bracelet, a necklace, and a crown. The stockings have leaves painted on them too!" shared Hannah.

"Can Mom go with us?" asked Julia. "She dresses up as The Joker with green hair!"

"Actually, I should have talked to your parents about this before I mentioned it to you," remarked Mike. He sheepishly looked at Jesse and Tom, while exaggerating the gritting of his teeth.

"I think it's a great idea," said Jesse. "What do you think, Tom?"

"Well, let's think about it. We've got a little time. In parades, usually the passengers are family members of the officers. We don't qualify. I'm not a city employee any longer."

"Awh, Dad. We already missed ComicCon in Smallville," complained Hannah.

"We'll talk about it, girls," encouraged Jesse. "There's time. It's the first weekend in August."

"So, the captain has you doing parades now? I was wondering who would take my place," commented Tom.

"No one can take your place, Taz. And no one can attract a crowd like Kudzu," remarked Mike.

"That's for sure. When I was in parades, the children were saying hello to Kudzu, not me. I was just the driver. Sure miss that K-9."

"I don't think I'm the official parade guy," said Mike, "it's just that the chief knows I'm a regular at the NAACP meetings. I'm a familiar face in the community—a familiar black face."

"Well, okay, you're a bonus this year, but I've been in the parade several times without feeling like I was the wrong color. The crowd's always friendly, welcoming. You going to the park afterwards for the picnic?"

"Yeah, the barbeque and watermelon always hit the spot," recalled Mike. He winked as he rubbed his stomach in a circular motion.

"I'm getting hungry thinking about it," said Tom, as his stomach growled.

"Why don't you attend? There are a lot of people who wish you well and ask about you. Don't be a recluse."

"Maybe I will. Right now I'm feeling like I'm on self-imposed house arrest."

"Can we go to the picnic too?" asked Julia.

"Your mom and I will talk about it," said Tom.

"That's what you always say," complained Hannah.

Jesse talked to Tom privately and then waited.

Tom turned to the girls and asked, "Who wants to target practice?"

Hannah screamed, "I DO!"

Julia yelled, "ME, ME, ME!"

"Girls, you get your earmuffs and safety goggles, and I'll get your twenty-twos," ordered Tom. "Meet me here in five minutes."

"I'll stay and talk with Mike until you get back," said Jesse.

Rabbit Chief 26

Joe popped his knuckles and stared out the hospital window. Day after day, Suanna was stable, but never better. He said, "I'm willing to accept injustices when they occur to me, but this seems so wrong. Suanna is just a child. What kind of God would do this?"

Elizabeth was silent, but she knew his answer—a vengeful God.

"What kind of God would do this to our innocent girl?" Joe asked. "When she was born with albinism, I accepted her as a gift from God. So, why would he give her to us and then turn around and take her back?"

Elizabeth offered no reply. She felt distant—removed from everyone. She wondered again why she had ever agreed with Joe to welcome more children into their lives when Suanna was more than enough. Elizabeth knew that she had only so much to give before it felt like others were sapping her life blood. The unconditional love that Catalpa and Bud needed was beyond her capacity to give.

Turning toward the bed, Joe leaned over and kissed Suanna on her cheek, a portion not obstructed by her respirator or feeding tube. He walked to the open door, hesitated, and vanished.

Elizabeth bowed her head and prayed for her sanity and for Suanna's full recovery.

•

The trip home for Joe was a blur of memories and conversation.

As a child, from his bedroom window in Nespelem, he could look up the hill, across the dusty road to the north, beyond the wire fence, and see the white granite memorial marking Chief Joseph's grave. On windy days he could hear the prayer bells tied to the rugged, weather-beaten, solitary elm.

Often, sitting beneath the sparse shade of the stunted tree was Joe's grandfather, Charlie, a quiet man who did quiet things. In good weather Grandfather's daily routine was to stop at the cemetery, move on to fishing at the nearby creek, and when the fish weren't biting, stop out front at Casey's town store for a game of chess. The old man, never caught without his trademark sheath knife, whittled anywhere outdoors, especially on the crowded front porch that he shared with high stacks of winter firewood.

"Forgive me, Snowflake!" Joe said out loud. "I'm sorry I didn't give you the rabbit doll and sacred pouch at your birth as Grandfather wished.

"Grandfather Morningcloud, the one called Big Face, was your great-grandfather. He made you a special gift that resembled Chief Joseph wearing his headdress and buckskin shirt. Only this doll, as a portion of his headdress, has rabbit ears standing up, erect. At first glance he looks human, traditional, wearing regalia, but a second look reveals his ears a good inch longer than the sculpted row of feathers. This is Rabbit Chief Joseph.

"Big Face made him for you while you were the size of a grasshopper. I'm on my way now to retrieve your rabbit doll. I've kept him from you when he could have been your protector.

"Grandfather was an elder who practiced our ancient ways. He told me very little about making you the doll or the leather pouch, but he whittled the totem out of cedar he saved for special occasions. The pouch that is tied around Rabbit Chief Joseph's neck must be a sacred bundle that was meant especially for you. I've prevented you from having what is deservedly yours."

Joe remembered how weeks earlier, Suanna, while helping clear pasture, had wished for another visit to Nespelem to see relatives. She had said that whenever she smelled cedar trees she thought of the Colville Tribes Reservation. When she added, "Dad, I want to learn more about my people," he felt he had failed her. "When can we visit again?" she begged.

"This sculpted doll has to be sacred cedar from the original longhouse, the weathered, sagging shelter down by the river, between town and the agency. This is where Chief Joseph and his band of Nez Perce lived for several seasons when they were forced to stay on the Colville. The band preferred their tipis, not houses, and their lifestyle of raising horses, not farming. Back then, when a Nez Perce built a house, it was interpreted by some outsiders as a sign of contentment, that they were satisfied on the reservation and weren't planning on returning to their Wallowa Valley. Building a house was giving up, admitting defeat, accepting the illegal and forced removal of the Niimiipuu. The first longhouse, a safe place for ceremony and worship, was a group of connected tipis, before the cedar log structure was finally built in 1911, after Chief Joseph's death in 1904.

"Grandfather was a talented wood carver who whittled more than he talked. I remember watching him on his porch when he'd create an animal or person and other times when he'd eventually convert a log or stick into nothingness. He'd be sitting there in his homemade rocking chair with his knife in his right hand working away; after a bit, his left hand was open and free, holding nothing, as if he had performed magic. At his feet sat a pile of wood shavings. When I'd first see him working on a shape, I'd ask him what he was making, and he'd always reply, 'Depends on what I find inside.' I guess sometimes he never found anything. But even when he didn't discover anything, he was helping us. Whenever my brothers or me were making fire in the cook stove, we always knew where to find a bucket full of shavings to start it. We hurried to his porch and were usually rewarded."

Again, Joe asked himself why he hadn't given the doll to Suanna at her birth or while she was growing up. This was a question he had never fully answered, one he had avoided.

"Grandfather's dedicated gift to you had to be about rabbits being timid, scared, and fearful. I felt differently. But now that you're in the hospital, this is an opportunity for you to regain strength for your journey. With the help of Rabbit Chief Joseph, you can reenter our world. I'm going to take him and his hallowed bundle to you to help you recover. He's in my old trunk at home. I'll be back with your sacred medicine."

•

After Joe's truck, like a good horse, carried him home, he hurried inside, barely aware of his trance-like trip from Wichita. His mission was to return as soon as possible with Suanna's rabbit totem.

Carl's truck was gone. A note on the kitchen table, highlighted by the overhead stained-glass light, revealed that Carl and the children were at the downtown water park as one last treat together before the three of them headed back home to Washington the next morning.

Joe was glad to have a vacant house. It would be easier to access the guest bedroom where the siblings had stayed for several months.

At seven and five years old, Catalpa and Bud, were his niece and nephew, children of his oldest brother, Sam, and Sam's wife, Alice. Once loving parents, Sam and Alice had self-imploded due to their substance abuse and addiction. Officially absentee parents, they neglected the children. Sam remained reachable due to his incarceration in Walla Walla Penitentiary. Alice surfaced around the state of Washington for short periods of time and then disappeared as suddenly as a fishing bobber in dark water on a calm night. Sam and Alice had finally authorized Joe and Elizabeth to raise their children, at least temporarily.

As Joe entered the newcomers' room, he checked Suanna's gerbil cage to be sure Rat hadn't escaped again. He spotted the gerbil under store-bought scented shavings and chewed cardboard. Then Joe eyed the bedroom closet. Its doors were blocked by the beds of Cat and Bud, pushed together again during the night. Joe nudged Bud's bed away from the wall and slid the closet door open. The shiny, black-and-silver trunk occupied a substantial amount of floor space. An undone clasp revealed that the storage footlocker had been disturbed. One of its three latches, like a coyote trap ready to snap, was in the open position.

Joe wondered if someone had actually opened it to look inside, or if the latch had merely been tossed about in some sort of playful game. On the floor was Joe's answer. Due to its contrast with the white tile, a tiny black speck caught his eye. It was a bead—no doubt his Indian bead. Someone had been into his personal belongings, items he packed away to forget. Long ago he could have thrown them out, burned, or buried them, or handed them over to others at a giveaway. But he was glad he hadn't.

Joe slid the trunk out of the closet, placed it on Catalpa's bed, and sat beside it. He didn't care if his powwow shirt or leggings were missing. He didn't care about headbands or worn-out, duct-taped moccasins. He wanted one thing for Suanna—Rabbit Chief Joseph—with the special package worn around his neck. He knew it just had to be a medicine pouch that held powerful healing inside.

Under an assortment of dancing regalia he located his old moccasins and checked inside each one. Nothing. He dumped the trunk's entire contents on the bed. One by one he replaced them into the repository: his old moccasins, his beaded buckskin shirt and leggings, a porcupine breastplate . . . With the larger items back in the footlocker Joe rubbed his stiff neck and recognized his dry mouth. He gradually accepted the inevitable, that the rabbit doll was gone—missing. But his momentum completed the act. He individually picked up the turtle rattles, the braided sweet grass that had nearly lost its fragrance (he held it close to his nostrils and inhaled deeply), and finally a smoking pipe. He placed each smaller object on top of the leather outfit in the receptacle. "How could this be happening?" Joe asked. "No one in this house would disturb my trunk."

But someone had been in his storage chest. Joe had to decide his next step in finding Rabbit Chief Joseph so that Suanna could recover. He needed to locate the spiritual offering. He'd check with Elizabeth. Suanna would have never opened the trunk; with the exception of the Indian doll and its medicine pouch, she had seen it all before and had agreed to look at what she called his "powwow stuff" only when they were together. Joe began to wonder if Cat and Bud had taken his property. Joe took a deep breath and exhaled. The newcomers were troubled; this was another sign.

Before going to search the room and house, Joe replaced the trunk and retrieved the black bead with his thumb and index finger. Then he placed it in the center of his cupped hand. He heard the back screen door clang shut followed by the familiar voices of Carl, Catalpa, and Bud. Carl and the young children entered the kitchen laughing, sounding like one happy family. From the hallway, Joe observed each with a beach towel draped around the neck, highlighting their wet hair and brown native skin. Carl's clothing was dry compared to the children's wet shorts and T-shirts. They'd returned home directly from the water park.

"Uncle Carl," said Bud, "My favorite part was when I shot you with the water gun while you were reading the paper!"

"That wasn't my favorite," said Carl. "I liked when Catalpa walked through the hidden sprinklers and kept getting surprised when she'd be blasted. Cat, your face was so funny, and you'd yell like you hadn't thought you'd get soaked!"

"I like surprises, but I don't," commented Catalpa. Maize, their yellow house cat, spotted her and darted away.

"Oh, Joe, I didn't see you there," said Carl. "I thought you were in Wichita."

"I was. Car's on the side of the house. Elizabeth's with Suanna," Joe explained.

Noting Joe's down-turned open mouth and unblinking eyes, Carl asked, "Has Suanna turned worse?"

"She's the same, but that's not okay, not anymore. Everyone, have a seat at the table. I need to talk to you," directed Joe, making sure that the children did not sit across from one another.

No one was laughing as they sat down and got settled, despite the squeaking of the children's wet shorts. Joe grabbed a crisp, white napkin, placed it in the middle of the table, and positioned the bead at the napkin's center. He pulled his hand away, as though it had been guarding a candle's fragile flame from a draft. He kept his eyes on Catalpa and Bud, saying nothing.

Carl followed Joe's lead. He quietly observed the children. They were still, staring at the tiny, black bead until Bud asked, "What's that?"

"You tell me," replied Joe.

Bud looked at his sister for help. She continued gazing at the napkin. Finally, Bud said, "It's a bead."

"Where did it come from?" asked Joe.

"Don't you know?" replied Bud.

Joe paused.

While Cat was outwardly calm, Bud began squirming in his chair. "I need to go to the bathroom," Bud said.

"You're not going anywhere," stated Joe.

Carl turned his head to Joe with lips tightened like a bow, nostrils open, while searching Joe's eyes.

Bud began to sniffle and then cry. He said, "It's an Indian bead. It might be from the trunk."

Cat's upper body snapped toward Bud to confront him. Baring her teeth, she snarled, "Shut up! You little snitch!"

Her shrill, angry voice startled Bud, who quit crying for a moment and then burst out, "I have to pee-pee, now!" As he got up from the kitchen chair, a yellow puddle formed at his feet. He grabbed his crotch and pressed hard, running to the bathroom, sobbing. Carl followed.

With lowered eyebrows and compressed lips, Joe stared at Catalpa and said, "Don't you ever yell at your brother like that again! Understand?"

"You're not my father! You can't tell me what to do!" declared Cat.

"No, I'm not your father. I'm helping take care of you because he's in prison."

Cat folded her arms, pressed her lips tight, and closed her eyes.

"Suanna's not getting better," stated Joe. "I think she can improve if I take her a sacred Nez Perce offering, a medicine bag. Only I can't find it. It's a buckskin pouch around the neck of a wooden Indian rabbit doll. The doll and pouch were in my trunk that I keep in the closet in your bedroom. You've been in it."

"I haven't seen any doll."

"The bundle can help save Suanna's life."

"I don't know what you're talking about," Cat replied in a single breath.

"Catalpa Morningcloud, you sit here and don't move until I tell you to get up. We're searching your bedroom and talking to Bud."

Cat remained still and mute.

Joe stopped by the bathroom to talk to Carl. They agreed to meet in Bud's bedroom after cleaning up the dining room floor and having Bud change into dry clothes. Joe explained that Catalpa had clammed up and was denying any knowledge about the Indian rabbit doll or the bundle. "She lies about everything," he said.

Before searching the bedroom, Joe was hoping that Bud could answer some questions. He was surprised by how hard the little boy fought to keep his secret. Despite Joe's calm approach of explaining how the Indian rabbit doll could save Suanna's life, Bud clammed up, too. He trembled slightly, apparently concerned for his own well-being. Cat was Bud's closest and most dependable kin. If he lost her, then he was lost. This was about his survival.

But soon, Bud was helpful.

"Bud, who got in my trunk?" asked Joe.

"Suanna opened it," answered Bud.

"You're saying that this was Suanna's idea?" asked Joe.

"Yes, we didn't know what was in the trunk until she told us. She was sorta' bragging."

"Hmm," Joe responded. "And when did you all do this?"

"It was just a couple of days before she got hurt."

"Okay," said Joe. "Where's the Indian rabbit doll right now?"

"He's by the tree house. I'll show you."

Carl remained inside guarding the prisoner under house arrest.

Bud led the way outside. Joe looked up and observed the weathered boards, two-by-fours, marking the skyward path up the cottonwood to the tree house. He and Suanna had built it together four years earlier when she was eight. It seemed a lifetime ago.

In the shade of the tree Bud bent over and retrieved a half-buried rabbit doll from a mole hole. Joe exhaled but not from relief. Doubt was creeping on hope. There was no sacred pouch.

"Bud, where's the little bag that was around his neck?" asked Joe.

"There wasn't none," was his brief reply.

Joe believed Bud was telling the truth, but asked again: "Are you sure?"

"Yes, Uncle Joe. When Suanna opened the trunk, she showed us everything inside. She pulled Indian Rabbit out of a big moccasin. I like him now. We're friends."

"He's a good rabbit chief," said Joe.

"Are you mad that I played with him? Suanna said I could."

"No, I'm not mad about that. I'm sorry I yelled at you inside. But I need to find the pouch. I'll check the moccasins again. Maybe the pouch is down in the toes. I've got to ask Cat for help to see what she remembers."

"She's mad at me," said Bud as he bit down on his lower lip. "I hate it when she's mad at me."

"Yeah, it doesn't feel good. But the sooner we find the pouch, the sooner I can take it to Suanna so she can get well."

"You're taking Indian Rabbit away?" Bud asked with a frown.

"Yes, for a while. I want to take him to Suanna along with his pouch. I've got to find it."

"Suanna needs the Indian rabbit to get well?"

"I think so."

"All right."

"Together we can take her Rabbit Chief. You can give him to her if you want. How would you like that, Bud?"

"Okay."

"We need to go inside, but first let's clean up Rabbit Chief. Bud, wash him off at the pump while I check on the horses. Stay outside. I'll call you from the back door when I'm ready for you."

"Let's get you cleaned up," Bud said to his newest, "bestest" friend, one who never broke promises.

Joe's mouth turned up as he watched little Bud walk toward the pump. Joe moved to the corral by the barn to check on Lady Bonita, Suanna's spotted Appaloosa. While petting her he said, "How you doin, girl? Yeah, we're all missin' Suanna. She'll be home soon. You'll see. Rest up while you can, you'll be barrel racing and roping soon enough. You know Snowflake wants to be just like rodeo champion K.D. Denton. We're counting on you to help her along."

While Joe talked to Lady Bonita, he heard a movement in the stable. Seconds later he heard it again, and thought it was the fluttering of a nesting bird. Curious, he quietly walked toward the barn and found their fighting rooster, Hubcap Houdini, pecking a white ribbon tied to some jingle bells. Hubcap was fascinated with the sound; he looked like he was ready to swallow the bells one by one. Joe intruded, and Hubcap clucked, scratching his claws in the dirt and flapping his wings as a warning sign. Joe ignored him and grabbed the ribbon to have a closer look.

The end of the ribbon nearest the ground had three clusters of bells tied to it while the other end was looped over Lady Bonita's saddle, the western outfit resting on top of a saddle horn. Joe hadn't seen the ribbon before, but he shook it sharply. The bells were familiar. When he spotted the spent ammo casing attached to one cluster, it gave him absolute confirmation; the bells were part of his regalia that he stored in his memory chest.

Joe questioned what else was missing. He couldn't imagine that Catalpa would have ever accepted being left out of the souvenir grab bag, especially since Bud had received a respectable prize of the Indian rabbit doll. She would have insisted on having a right to all valuable plunder. If she had taken his pouch, where would she have hidden it?

Joe returned to the trunk and searched it more carefully, this time looking for the lone, small, sacred bag among his regalia, but the results were unchanged. To save time, Joe asked Carl to continue the search in Catalpa and Bud's room while he examined Suanna's. This left the children unattended—Bud outside and Cat still isolated at the dining room table.

During Carl's search he discovered a lot of hidden food around their room, especially in the pillowcases. "Joe, I think the kids are planning on running away, maybe back to the rez or to find their parents; this must be food for the trip. Why so much hidden food? They're like squirrels saving up for a long winter."

"Exactly," said Joe, "they don't know when there will be a drought or a freeze, or when they will be sent away. They've learned the food can stop at any time so they store it to prepare for the hard times ahead. Me and Elizabeth have talked to them about this. It's not uncommon in foster care."

Joe tried to search quickly, but got slowed by photographs and memories.

When both men (best friends for life despite their disagreement about Carl's drinking and Joe's tribal loyalties) completed the search, they met where it all started—the trunk. Joe opened it a third time. Then, on the floor by Catalpa's sneakers, Joe picked up a piece of straw that was less than an inch long. It may have entered the house stuck in the tread of one of her shoes, or caught a ride on a sock or in her shoulder-length dark hair. Joe took the yellow stem and carefully closed the lid on it so that when it was opened the next time the straw would drop to the bed. Finally, he latched the three clasps and left the trunk in easy reach of the accused.

"Carl," Joe said loudly, "let me show you what I found in Suanna's room." As they walked down the hallway, they observed Catalpa invisibly bound to her chair.

"Stay out of your room. Leave the trunk alone. Don't mess with it. We'll be right back," Joe ordered Catalpa.

Inside Suanna's room, this time with the door shut, Joe whispered to Carl. "Catalpa has the pouch or something else of mine. She's no innocent observer in this. I want to see if she makes a move to replace anything in the trunk. I've given her opportunity, and I've dared her to take the risk. She can't help herself."

"Let's go, that's all the time she gets," said Joe. The two again walked past Cat to the bedroom's trunk and immediately spotted the straw on the bed. "Yeah!" they celebrated quietly, nodding, eyes aglow, eager. The men opened the trunk like treasure hunters with gold fever, however, there was no bundle. Instead, inside a moccasin Joe found an old rawhide necklace. Holding it, the leather felt cool and damp, and Joe knew. Catalpa had been wearing it under her T-shirt while sitting directly across from him at the kitchen table. Her long wet hair was covering it while she crossed her arms in denial, in cold-blooded defiance. The nerve! The blood in her veins was ice water. What could they do with her? She was only seven!

After Joe and Carl left the room, Rat, safely in his cage, came out of his hiding place chewing paper, cardboard, and what appeared to be little pieces of leather cloth.

Postpartum Depression and PTSD 27

After twelve years Elizabeth's postpartum depression had returned. Totally unsuspecting, she was again overwhelmed by it all, the erratic sleep, mood swings, and again that feeling that she'd made a mistake becoming a mother. Well, at least this time there wasn't the difficulty in breast feeding.

It didn't make sense. She'd done the research and couldn't find a similar case. If she hadn't been so smothered in sadness, she'd have kept notes for her own scientific research and article submission. How would she title it? "Postpartum Flashbacks: A Study," "The Psycho in Psychogenic Shock," or maybe market a novel with additional alliteration, *The Mad Monster Mother Returns*. And that's how she felt.

The long days of waiting for Suanna to show the slightest sign of progress were anxiety-filled and heart-wrenching. One moment Elizabeth prayed for Suanna's full recovery with the faith of Saint Mother Teresa and an instant later considered the consequences of an unplugged respirator machine—like a modern Medea, the murderous mother of Greek Mythology. She couldn't take it any longer. She wasn't a loving mother. She was a fraud.

•

Suanna's birth was normal, yet that was only the beginning of a period of turmoil as her mother searched for answers. Elizabeth was assured by her parents, both medical professionals, that the first few weeks after pregnancy were known as the "postpartum blues" with symptoms of tearfulness, irritation, and restlessness. That described her, but why was she crying more than the baby?

She knew something was wrong, but she didn't want to admit to being weak. She'd always wanted children and had expected she'd be a great parent. But she was increasingly questioning her fitness, her wiring for motherhood. System overload was causing a short circuit, and she worried she was on her way to a full-blown meltdown. She acknowledged that she wouldn't be accepting any awards for best parent of the year as long as she was content to stay in bed one floor removed from her baby. Another somber sign she recognized was that instead of referring to her newborn as "baby-girl," or "cutie-pie," she spoke of the infant as "it."

According to medical studies and charts, Elizabeth was not a candidate for anything worse than a temporary case of those baby blues. The pregnancy was planned. She had no mood disorder before the pregnancy; no close family member with mental illness; no alcohol or drug abuse; and she didn't smoke. She had plenty of support from her family—including her husband. No financial problems. But the fact that Suanna was born with albinism was a shocker, and there was additional stress in Elizabeth's life because of her husband's severe physical injury that could permanently derail his once-promising boxing career. Fortunately, despite his slow and limited recovery, Joe stepped up, euphoric in being Mr. Mom. He was Suanna's dependable caregiver while Elizabeth was absent in body and spirit. Joe was also Elizabeth's amateur psychiatrist without an inkling of a diagnosis.

•

For years Joe had tried to help his oldest brother who was always chasing drugs. Before marijuana was legalized in the state of Washington, Sam had been captured on Owhi Lake in Okanogan County with marijuana estimated to be worth a street value of half a million dollars, yet he was always broke. After Sam was incarcerated in The Walls, Joe and Elizabeth shared a desire to help Sam's children, Catalpa and Rosebud. The children had refused to leave Indian country and had lived with Joe's mother, Nina Waters, in Nespelem, until she required surgery and the children were forced to move. Joe and Elizabeth agreed to a trial period with the children. Joe's niece and nephew would live with them outside Prairie Grove.

Suanna, excited, helped prepare the guest room to welcome them. The planned arrangement took the burden off Grandma; it gave everyone an opportunity to learn if a change in location could benefit the young children; and it gave Suanna increased contact with her Indian relatives.

After Suanna was nearly killed in the car accident at the bank, Elizabeth and Joe became fixtures at the hospital. They were her parents, obsessed with her survival. Thanks to Carl's visit to Prairie Grove, he became the adult whom Catalpa and Bud relied on for companionship and supervision. In addition to Suanna's medical emergency, Catalpa's theft of the rabbit totem's medicine pouch and continued lying to Joe sealed the deal. The trial period was over—a failure. Like a perfect storm, Carl's drinking and confrontation with Joe brought things to a head. The three road warriors would return to the reservation where additional family members had agreed to help Catalpa and Bud so that the foster care system wouldn't seize, scold, and store the children.

Hindsight proved the effort untimely and fruitless. Elizabeth and Joe had imagined they could help mend the broken children by offering a healthy diet, a clean house, patience, and love. Instead, they learned that the two newcomers displayed resistance to—and a lack of appreciation of—what they perceived as an alien environment. They acted as if they were two Indian children who had been kidnapped, placed in a boarding school, and had their hair forcibly cut while being forbidden to speak their native languages. It may have felt that way to the youngsters because Catalpa and Bud were homesick for their parents and their friends on their sometimes desert-like, and sometimes frozen, Colville Confederated Tribes Reservation. When the children heard they were returning home to Nespelem, they gathered their stash of hidden food into personal pillowcases in preparation for the road trip. Until they departed, Catalpa became a broken horse at Carl's side, with Bud trailing close behind. They were afraid of being forgotten.

•

Carl should have been in a hurry to get home and deal with the latest episode with Storm who had been caught huffing gasoline, but he wasn't sure how to approach his son. Carl tried to learn about Storm's destructive reasoning through Catalpa. He asked her if she had ever seen his son huffing while she and Storm were out four-wheeling, but Catalpa replied innocently, "What's huffing?" He wanted to believe her—but then he reminded himself of her theatrical lying to Joe.

•

Once the Appaloosa filly was loaded, the three cross-country travelers buckled up their respective seat belts. Carl set the trip odometer and blew into the mouthpiece of the interlock system to start the ignition. With no alcohol in his blood, the truck started immediately.

"Carl, thanks for hauling the horse," said Joe. "Tell Mom we'll visit once Suanna's better."

"Thanks for visiting and helping," added Elizabeth. "You kids listen to Carl so he can drive safely."

As Carl shifted his truck to drive, he said, "I'll keep Suanna in my prayers."

"Love to Tina!" shouted Elizabeth.

Catalpa and Bud waved goodbye, but didn't speak. They were being sent off again to live somewhere with someone else.

They pulled out of the driveway. The odyssey had begun.

Carl handed Catalpa a road-map guide and instructed, "Here's a map; you're our navigator."

"Bud, I need your help too," Carl continued. "Watch for police cars so we can be sure and wave at the friendly officers."

Catalpa thumbed through the atlas of state maps and asked, "Can we stop at the Nez Perce reservation in Idaho? It's on the way home."

Carl didn't commit to stopping anywhere, but he considered the possibilities of multiple excursions. It was a long trip, especially with kids and a horse. Catalpa's search for blood relatives caused Carl to think of his own Oglala people on the Pine Ridge reservation in South Dakota. Since they'd be in the vicinity, they could stop for gas and a meal. If he didn't have Joe's horse, and if Tina wasn't so anxious about him getting home quickly, he'd be taking his own sweet time. He even considered visiting the location of the former Oceti Sakowm camp and water protectors' sacred fire. It sat at the mouth of the Cannon Ball River, where the Dakota Access Pipeline struggle erupted after the Army Corps of Engineers and Dakota Access violated native rights.

As Carl checked his side-view mirror and observed his attached horse trailer, he again questioned the reasoning behind the sale of his live cargo. "I still don't know why someone from Montana, a neighboring state to Idaho, would buy a horse from here in Kansas! Idaho's got the best Appaloosas and potatoes in the world."

Not to be left out of the travel conversation, Bud announced to Carl, "I want to go see the Grand Canyon."

"That's not even close to the way we're going on this trip," said Carl. "Let's go there another time."

Carl knew he had the luxury of a couple hundred miles before exiting the interstate for any side trips. He sure didn't want to be irresponsible and let Joe down again, and he didn't want to disappoint Tina, who was a saint for raising their four children. She needed Carl's assistance and was putting their son, Storm, into his custody once he returned home. *To say the least*, Carl thought, *life is interesting.* But it was also complicated, and that's when, for the third time that morning, he felt a craving. *I need a cigarette . . . and a drink.*

Ignoring those cravings, Carl asked the children, "What else do you have in those pillowcases?"

Catalpa offered him beer nuts and cheese curls. Bud pulled down a paper candy wrapper and said, "Here's a Life Saver."

"When we get home, I can't wait to have some Ramen Noodles," declared Catalpa.

"Will Grandma be able to make her chocolate chip cookies for us?" asked Bud.

Carl's eyes glazed over, his driving questionable, as he imagined the satisfying taste of fry bread. "Yes!" he said. He savored the salty batter, deep-fried in oil, topped with powdered sugar and sweet honey.

Nothing but the Truth 28

It was an old courthouse with old structural cracks. Some had been there before the fracking, before the Ogallala aquifer's commercial contamination by salt-water disposal, before the seismic shifts, and before earthquake insurance was seriously considered as an umbrella policy. The country wanted cheap energy, freedom from energy blackmail; the county liked the tax bump; and the people allowed Oklahoma City to know best. But Tom knew that canaries were once kept in southeast Kansas coal mines for good reason—to warn the miners of deadly gas leaks. Earthquakes in Kansas were modern-day canaries. From a fifth-floor courthouse window he watched the courthouse pigeons. What was the chance of the birds being an early warning system to county employees and the visiting public prior to a building collapse? No chance. The pigeons, doves to some, lived on the roof of the courthouse and found crevices in pipes to build their nests and raise their squibs. They had their own priorities.

Tom felt the vibration before the pigeons did, or maybe like him, they were accustomed to it. No need to be alarmed. The Burlington Northern Santa Fe, a.k.a. BNSF, was coming through town. Tom moved to a nearby window for a better view of the tracks and observed the local lazy automobiles. While waiting for the locomotives to take center stage, he viewed the spacious streak of distant clouds to the southwest. Beyond the water tower, the sky, like a canvas, displayed a giant white X—vapor trails from plane exhaust.

He heard the train's wayside horn blow, following the General Code of Operating Rules, its standard loud greeting at all public crossings: long, long, short, long.

A lawnmower started up. Again, Tom looked away from the train tracks. He saw a work-release inmate in his blues and red ball cap pushing the gas-powered mower. Noticing the man's beard and braided hair, Tom was surprised that regulations allowed for this dress-code grooming diversity, but the grass was dark green and the flower beds bright.

The automatic warning bells began their clanging. He focused on the grade crossing as the activated lights flashed. Suddenly a car bolted forward into the dead zone. The auto appeared to have been goosed; it surged across the tracks as the crossing gates lowered.

•

"Let the record show we are beginning the afternoon session of the Cottonwood County Grand Jury: *State of Kansas v Thomas Jennings*," stated the Cottonwood County district attorney. "Jurors," he continued, "a reminder that things you may have heard in the media are not evidence; they're stories. Now, you've already listened to the interview recording between former Officer Jennings, Detective Halas of the Cottonwood County Sheriff's Office, and FBI Agent Jones. You've also had the opportunity to hear Sergeant Garcia's report of the police department's emergency response to the bank alarm. And you've seen the videotapes from the bank's cameras and the body camera worn by Officer Jennings. This morning you will hear the recollections of Thomas Jennings as the first police officer on the scene of the attempted bank robbery. We all know why he's here, so let's get on with it.

"Please, ask Mr. Jennings to enter now."

Tom Jennings was duly sworn to testify to the truth, the whole truth, and nothing but the truth in the case aforesaid.

"Please state your name and rank and where you are employed," began the district attorney.

"Tom Jennings; I'm currently unemployed."

"On the twenty-sixth of May, this year, were you employed by the Prairie Grove Police Department as a patrol officer?"

"Yes, ten-four, I was."

"Please tell the grand jury the date you severed your employment with the city of Prairie Grove and the circumstances of your departure."

"On the third of July, while I was on medical leave from the Prairie Grove Police Department, I was terminated. I'm appealing my firing as unjustified, based on unequal enforcement of the department's policy and procedure and violation of the First Amendment's right to freedom of speech, including rights of a Fraternal Order of the Police representative and off-duty statements about workplace safety on matters of public concern."

The district attorney continued, "At this time let me again remind the jury that your responsibility is to determine if former officer Tom Jennings committed a criminal act on the day of the attempted bank robbery and shooting. The focus remains on the actions of Officer Jennings and the shooting and killing of James Odessa-Smith. Here is the question to keep in mind: Was the response of Officer Jennings a legitimate law enforcement reaction to the emergency dispatch assignment of the bank alarm and confrontation with Mr. James Odessa-Smith? This jury is not asked to determine if the employment termination of Officer Jennings was proper or improper. That may be decided at a later date by another court during civil proceedings.

"Now, back to you, Mr. Jennings, are you here voluntarily?"

"Yes."

"So, you want to be here and tell the jurors in your own words what occurred on the twenty-sixth of May, this year?"

"That's correct, yes."

"On the day in question were you a state-certified law-enforcement officer?"

"Yes, sir."

"And on this date, what hours or shift were you working?"

"I was working the day shift from 6:00 a.m. to 6:00 p.m."

"Prior to your response to the bank, what were you doing regarding calls for service? Was it a typical day?"

"It took place on a Friday. I remember I had an assignment of a disturbance in progress where a tenant was refusing to leave from his apartment after being served eviction papers. Sergeant Garcia backed me up. When we cleared that call, I was actually on my way to the Prairie Grove National Bank to meet my wife for a business appointment. The weather was still changing, the sky getting darker, and the hail beginning."

"You were on your way to the Prairie Grove Bank on Broadway Street?"

"No, I was headed to its branch bank on Schlimpert."

"Okay. At 2601 Schlimpert, in Prairie Grove, Cottonwood County, Kansas, is that correct?"

"Yes, sir, ten-four."

"And, when you were en route to the bank, what were you wearing?"

"I was in my summer departmental uniform, brown in color, with short sleeves and long pants. I was also wearing my duty belt that held my duty firearm and other equipment."

"Were there departmental patches on your uniform?"

"Yes, each sleeve identified me as an officer with the Prairie Grove Police Department. I also wore my police shield and name tag above my left shirt pocket."

"You mentioned you were wearing your duty belt. Please explain what items you carry on your belt, with particular attention to your firearm and any other weapons available to you."

"The duty weapon I carried was a Glock, Model 19, forty-caliber. It holds fifteen bullets or rounds in each of the three clips or magazines. My Glock, with a total of sixteen bullets, was carried in a Blackhawk holster. Besides the Glock and extra magazines, the duty holster carried my Taser, expandable baton, handcuffs, walkie-talkie, flashlight, and latex gloves."

"You said you had sixteen bullets loaded or available in your weapon?"

"Yes, sir; I had a total of sixteen bullets. With that model, while on duty we are trained to carry sixteen rounds; that's one in the chamber, ready to fire, and fifteen more in the attached magazine."

"I see, thank you. Now, describe to the court the vehicle you were driving at that time."

"I was still driving the department's black and white Chevrolet Tahoe that was set up to carry the department's canine. It was fully marked or identifiable with police decals on the sides, rear, and front, and also departmental shields on each door. Then there was an emergency-light bar attached to the top of the vehicle."

"And tell us what happened next," the district attorney continued.

"I was about a minute away from the bank when emergency dispatch advised all listening officers of a silent bank alarm at the branch bank's location. Shortly after that, maybe ten seconds or so, dispatch followed up and said that there had been shots fired and one person was down or injured inside the bank."

"What was your response?"

"I figured I had to be the closest officer. I advised dispatch I was nearly there, and I knew I had to immediately act to counter the deadly threat to others in the bank."

"What did you do next, upon your arrival?"

"I pulled my patrol van directly in front of the bank while attempting to see the suspect or suspects inside the bank. I believe I called in my arrival, that I was ten-twenty-three, which is the ten-code used to inform dispatch that I had arrived at the scene. I did this while exiting my vehicle and approaching the front glass doors. Due to the thunderstorm and hail, the glass doors and windows offered me no useful images of anyone inside the bank."

"Did you have any trouble getting out of your vehicle or into the bank?"

"For a moment my walkie on my duty belt got hung up on the seatbelt, then I continued to the bank's front entrance," explained Jennings.

"What happened next?"

"The entrance has a double set of doors where you open the first door manually with your hand; the second set of doors, they open automatically once you step closer to them. Upon entering the bank's outer door, really even before that, my focus was trying to locate the suspect or suspects. I detected people or bodies on the floor during the time I was scanning the bank's entrance and lobby. Suddenly—and this all happened really fast—the suspect, wearing a mask, appeared from behind a pillar walking quickly toward me with a handgun held in his right hand, out in front, pointed directly at me." Jennings cleared his throat and said, "I fired a series of shots attempting to stop the threat."

"You said that the suspect was walking quickly toward you with a gun pointed at you, and you fired to stop the threat? Is that correct?"

"Yes, ten-four."

"Were there any words exchanged? Did you identify yourself as the police or tell him to drop his weapon?"

"Well, neither one of us said anything that I recall. We were just suddenly upon each other. I'd estimate our distance was not more than fifteen feet when I became aware we were on a collision course, so I engaged in gunfire."

"Do you recall how many times you fired your weapon?"

"No, not exactly," answered Tom, as visible sweat appeared on his forehead. "I know that I fired a series of shots at his center mass. He continued toward me and I kept firing. When he was just feet away, I was backing up and firing at his head in case he was wearing body armor over his chest. My last shots were fired as he fell forward, almost touching me. For a split-second I wondered if my gun was shooting blanks because he wasn't slowing down."

"Were you injured during the confrontation?"

"Yes, but at the time my mind was telling me contradictory things that didn't make sense."

"Please explain what you felt was contradictory," the district attorney stated.

"Well, one belief I had at the time was that I must be shot since he was just as close to me as I was to him. I mean, he couldn't have missed. When I fell to the floor, I injured my back on the metal frame of a sign holder that was near the entrance. When I attempted to take an inventory of my injuries, before confronting additional suspects, I thought I had somehow been shot in my back. This didn't compute. Then, even before I got up off the floor, I remembered some training where the instructor reminded us to have a warrior attitude, a belief that if we knew we were injured then we were alive and would survive. We needed to press on and stay alert."

"What else, if anything, do you remember from this initial encounter, shooting at the suspect?"

Jennings hesitated.

Okay, I'm not going to say this out loud, Tom thought, *but right now, as we talk about this, I can smell chocolate gunpowder, yeah, chocolate gunpowder. When I walked into the bank and fired my weapon, the chocolate coffee's aroma and my gunpowder somehow got mixed together in my senses.*

"Mr. Jennings? Would you like for me to repeat the question?" asked the district attorney.

"No, sir, sorry. I remember the smoke and the smell of the gunpowder more than I do any loud gunfire. The gunfire sounded like popping in the distance. I also recall that the suspect's gun didn't have any kick or recoil to it even though I watched his index finger repeatedly pulling the trigger. I also knew that after I finally fired some head shots, aiming at his nose, that there was no way he could survive that impact. I was firing a forty-caliber at close range. They were head shots, and I saw them hit and enter the mask he was wearing."

"Anything else?" asked the district attorney.

"Not immediately, but a little later I realized I had blood on the front of my shirt which also made me think I'd been shot, but it turned out it was the suspect's blood. He was that close to me when he fell forward."

Yeah, I'm not sharing everything I remember, thought Tom. *I'll never forget the blood and my wet pants. By God, I wasn't shot, but I was leaking bodily fluids. Fortunately, the blood was his, but my pants . . . damn! I had pissed my pants!*

"Before shooting the suspect, did you say anything to him or identify yourself as a police officer?" the district attorney continued, repeating himself.

"Not that I recall," answered Jennings, his body rigid. "I had a gun pointed at me, and I fired my weapon to stop the threat."

"Did the suspect say anything?"

"Not that I recall as far as any words. After I stopped him with the head shots, he did make kind of a grunting noise as he fell to the floor."

"Did you think he was dead?"

In disbelief, this question caused Tom Jennings to again internally reflect on his lethal shoot. He folded his arms across his chest.

I knew he was dead because I blew his brains out, is what I feel like telling you, but I can't say that because it's not even close to being politically correct. Would it help if I told you that despite his mask, his brain matter was on me and the floor or that it took me a second to recognize what it was? Instead, I'll translate my answer for the court.

"Like I said earlier," Jennings answered out loud, "I knew many of my shots had to hit their target, and I saw a couple of my bullets go into the suspect's mask—into his face."

Again Tom remembered. His memory flashed. It was like a paper target at the firearms range, only in the bank his bullet holes perforated the white plastic mask, emphasizing the contrast of light and dark, life and death.

"Once he fell, I knew he was dead," Jennings told the district attorney and the grand jury members. "I automatically reloaded while scanning the bank for additional suspects."

"So, the reason you kept firing at the suspect was because he kept advancing on you with his weapon drawn? Is that correct?"

"Yes, sir, ten-four."

"When you fired your duty weapon at the suspect, did you know his identity?"

"No, sir. He was wearing a Halloween mask over his face, a mask made famous from the Scream slasher movies. The mask had a dark hoodie attached, covering the rest of his head. Later, the detectives determined he was wearing a brown wig under the hoodie. Besides that, he wore a dark T-shirt, a windbreaker, and blue jeans. It was later on, after we'd cleared the bank, that I learned the identity of the deceased suspect."

"At any time did you contact emergency dispatch and request an ambulance for the suspect?"

"Yes, even though I knew an ambulance would be en route for the original call, I advised dispatch of additional injuries inside the bank, including the bank robbery suspect."

"What radio did you use to contact emergency dispatch?"

"I used my departmental police radio that I've always called a walkie-talkie. The radio is held on my duty belt, but I have the microphone for it attached to my shirt. It wasn't until I was trying to contact dispatch with an update on injuries that I realized my radio was on the wrong channel, a channel we use for training. Once I switched it back to the correct channel, we were able to communicate, and the dispatcher repeated back my update. I believe the walkie's switch got reset when I was getting out of my patrol vehicle, just before entering the bank."

"I understand that once the suspect was stopped and collapsed to the floor, that you continued to be concerned about additional suspects in the bank, but did you ever take the time to check the suspect for signs of life or to administer CPR?"

Maybe I should say this out loud, too. I'm not painting a clear enough picture for you. I don't want my self-confidence to sound like arrogance. I was cautioned about that. I compete, or did compete, across the state and into Oklahoma on the department's firearm competition team. I regularly score nearly perfect targets at the range during our qualification shoots and at the training scenarios. I'm a deer hunter, who does his duty, who gets his limit every year so that the state and county roads will be safer for drivers, especially during the rut season. I put enough lead into Ghostface that he would have set off Kilgore's metal detector from twenty feet. There was no need to check his pulse because that would have been a waste of valuable time. Notifying the medical examiner's office to send out a body bag would have been more productive. Jennings stopped thinking, exhaled a noisy breath, and answered the question.

"No, my concern was the possibility of additional suspects, my safety, and the safety of the employees and customers."

"Were you aware of anyone else checking the suspect for signs of life, say paramedics, once they arrived?"

"No, not that I recall."

"Now, for a minute, I'm going back to after the suspect collapsed to the floor. What did you do next?"

"I saw my wife, Jesse, on the floor with a head injury, and I saw a guy, a Native American, helping her, only at first I wasn't sure if he was an additional suspect."

"Go on," encouraged the district attorney.

Jennings felt his heartbeat pounding.

"I kept yelling 'Police' and 'Hands Up'—for everyone in the bank to raise their hands and to keep them up. I checked behind the teller counter and saw only bank employees. I asked if there were additional suspects. Employees told me that besides the customers in the lobby, there were no additional people in the bank except for the manager, Clayton Parks, who was last seen in his upstairs office. At about the same time, officers from outside were entering the bank to assist me. Dispatch was informing us that the bank manager had been on the phone talking with them, but that they had lost contact with him. They also said he might be having a medical emergency."

"And what happened next?"

"We decided to keep the bank employees and customers in place while we searched the bathrooms and two rooms upstairs. We assessed the risks, weighing the potential medical needs versus safety. It took us only a minute to be sure the bank was clear of additional suspects. It's a small area and the offices upstairs have glass walls, so they were especially easy to clear. By not evacuating, it allowed EMS to enter and assist those who were injured. Turned out the bank manager had low blood sugar and a bank teller had an anxiety attack, and my wife, Jesse, had been injured in the forehead with a piece of embedded metal from a bullet. Fortunately, her physical injury wasn't more severe."

"Earlier we established that your wife's injury was not fired by the suspect, James Odessa-Smith," said the district attorney, "that it was the result of the bank's malfunctioning coin-counting machine. I'm going to return to your wife in a moment, but first I'd like to review your arrival and entry into the bank. You said that when you arrived you immediately approached the front entrance. Is that correct?"

"Yes, ten-four."

"Did you consider waiting for additional officers so that you could enter as a team?"

Jennings felt a thickness in his throat.

Here we go again. Monday-morning media quarterbacking. Someday an officer will wait outside while people are being killed and I guarantee you, that officer will be crucified as a coward. But I know the DA's only doing his job. He's giving me my opportunity to clarify things for the jury.

"In law-enforcement training there are two major types of responses to suspects with a gun," explained Jennings. "If they're not shooting people, then we have time to set up a safe perimeter and attempt to make contact with the perpetrator. But when we have an active shooter situation, then we're trained to run toward the gunfire in order to save lives. At the time, I believed it was my duty to stop the threat as soon as possible. That meant entering the bank immediately, being a target, and not waiting for backup or an emergency response team."

"Thank you for your prior service, Mr. Jennings. Now, can you tell us what you were thinking or what you said once the bank was secure and you realized all the bank employees and customers were safe? Do you recall?"

"After I learned that my wife was alive and that her wound wasn't deeper or more severe, I was feeling some relief, but I was still worried. I was excited and relieved, happy to be alive, and to have my wife alive, but I was worried about her. It wasn't happiness that I had killed someone; it was relief that I had survived a deadly encounter with only a back injury."

"Do you remember saying anything to another officer about shooting the suspect?"

Jennings felt his cheeks burning.

"Yes, I recall saying something like, 'I had to shoot the scumbag. I'm glad he's dead.' "

"Anything else?" asked the district attorney.

"At the time, I thought he was trying to kill people, including me, so that's why I used the word 'scumbag'. It was said when I thought it was me versus him. I was relieved when I said it even though I didn't know who I'd shot. It wasn't an insult about James Odessa-Smith as a person. I hardly knew him. I was just venting out loud due to my stress."

Tom considered why some criminals were scumbags and others weren't.

I've had time to think about this. By Odessa-Smith wearing a mask, especially a Scream mask, he was easier to shoot. At the time he wasn't human. Carl has told me that when I called Odessa-Smith a scumbag it was a protective layer insulating me from recognizing that I'd taken a real person's life, that in the military they have all kinds of derogatory names for the enemy. But the DA should know that if I was in the same situation today, the perp would be just as dead with just as many entrance wounds.

The district attorney continued, "If you didn't know the identity of the bank robber when you shot him, then how would you have known he suffered from a mental illness?"

"Exactly. Only after I learned who he was, did I know I was dealing with a person who was mentally ill."

"At what point in the investigation, after the shooting, did you learn that the gun pointed at you by Mr. Odessa-Smith was a replica gun and did not have the ability to fire bullets?" the district attorney inquired.

Tom, turn your filter on. It's filter time. Take a second here. At the time I was feeling alive, that I'd done good, but then this replica gun caused me to have a bad feeling in my gut. I'd done right, but I felt wrong. Rather than being proud of doing my job, I was pissed off and angry about being tricked and used by a crazy coward. My aliveness was sucked dry the moment I learned that gun wasn't real. And then I was sick again when I discovered Suanna Morningcloud was hurt. I'd already pissed my pants; then I nearly threw up.

"While I was still at the crime scene, I learned about the gun. At first the officers couldn't locate the weapon, so they asked me what I'd seen. I told them I thought it was a semi-auto Beretta. Eventually the gun was located under the suspect's body. When the officers examined it, they discovered it was a replica gun."

"It's standard procedure in shootings by officers to have the officer give a cursory interview. This is a brief interview to investigating officers so they will know what and where to look for evidence. Did you give a cursory interview while at the scene?"

"Yes, it was brief because I was concerned about my wife's injury and then concerned again when I learned there had been a ten-forty-eight out front. A child was injured by my patrol vehicle when I arrived."

"Who interviewed you?"

"Detective Captain Kilgore asked me questions."

"What did you tell him?" the district attorney inquired.

"I told him that I had to shoot the suspect because he was charging at me with a gun, that I was concerned about the safety of everyone in the bank. He asked me if I knew how many shots I'd fired, and I told him I wasn't sure, that I thought I'd fired a series of shots that might total nine or ten rounds. I told him I had reloaded before the first clip was empty in case we encountered additional suspects. Again, I explained that I didn't stop shooting until the threat was stopped. He asked about my well-being, both my back injury and how I was doing. This is when I told him I had to shoot the suspect and when I called him a scumbag. I insisted to him that I be allowed to accompany my wife to the hospital, and that I could be examined there too.

"I also told Captain Kilgore that our children were at a neighbor's house and that I was concerned they would hear about this and be worried. My wife was supposed to pick up the kids. And I told him I needed to call an attorney, that I had my FOP membership card in my wallet with an emergency phone number. I called for the attorney when I was still in the bank, after the detectives arrived."

"Who investigated this shooting?"

"The attempted bank robbery and shooting was investigated by the Prairie Grove Police Department, Cottonwood County Sheriff's Office, KBI, and the FBI. They worked together. Since the day I was suspended for the use of force, I've had very limited contact with the investigation. Pretty much everyone has been told to not talk to me or one another about the shooting."

"At what point did you turn over your duty weapon and uniform to investigating officers?"

"Since I was going to be at the hospital for an undetermined amount of time, Sheriff's Detective Nick Halas met me there. After my attorney arrived from Wichita, Detective Halas took photographs and collected evidence, including a drug test, my duty weapon, extra ammo clips, body camera, and my uniform. Detective Mike Gale, a friend, brought me my civilian clothes from the PD locker room."

"After your examination by the doctor at the hospital, what were you told was the diagnosis?"

"X-rays revealed there were no broken bones. The doctor prescribed me pain killers for pulled muscles."

"Have you ever been involved in any other incidents where you needed to use deadly force?"

"This was my first use of deadly force. There were other times in my thirteen years on the department that I needed to use force, including my Taser."

Jennings' mouth was dry and energy spent.

"Members of the grand jury, this is your opportunity to ask the defendant questions," stated the district attorney.

One female juror raised her hand and was acknowledged by the district attorney. "Would it have been appropriate to use your K-9 in your response to the reported bank robbery?" she asked.

"I didn't have the department's K-9 with me that day," Jennings answered,

"Did you videotape a recording of your arrival from your car's dash camera?" another juror inquired, "because we didn't see it."

"No. The recording starts when it's manually turned on and whenever we turn on our emergency lights. Since I was so close to the bank, I didn't turn on the lights, and I didn't consider turning on the camera manually."

Another question followed. "While you were shooting at the suspect, did you consider that one of your bullets might injure someone else in the bank?"

Here we go again.

"From what I'd heard from emergency dispatch," said Jennings, "I considered that people might be getting killed in the bank by bank robbers. I decided to take the risk, to enter the bank so that the suspect would focus on me. When he approached me with his weapon drawn, I made every effort to make all my shots count so that bystanders wouldn't be hurt."

Hell, at that close range, I was surprised I threw any shots off target. Guess it was the stress; my heart was pumping.

"Mr. Jennings, is there anything else that you'd like to tell us that has not been asked? Anything that can help the jurors get a clearer picture of this incident?" asked the district attorney, preparing to end his questioning.

"The Constitution guarantees the accused a trial before a jury of his peers. Well, I wasn't expecting a jury made up of police officers or ex-police officers, but I'm still hoping that the court will allow the jurors an opportunity to walk in my shoes. I'm glad there's video of the shooting that shows how quickly I had to make my decision to use deadly force.

"My police-officer training included practice on the shoot-don't-shoot interactive simulator. I wonder if it's available for the jury's use at the Kansas Law Enforcement Training Center, near Yoder. If it is, I believe that it can assist the jury in getting a clearer picture of my response to the conditions of an encounter with an active shooter.

"Another thing that I feel would be of benefit to the jury, is to consider the term used when a suicidal person forces a police officer to respond with lethal force. I know that the medical examiner's office classified this as a homicide, which is pretty typical because one person was purposefully killed by another. But there are experts who can inform you of other options regarding classification. Different jurisdictions do it different ways. I consider Mr. Odessa-Smith's death as a suicide by proxy, more commonly known as 'suicide by cop.' If the medical examiner's office had classified this as a suicide, then we might not be here today.

"I stopped, neutralized . . . no, I killed Mr. Odessa-Smith, but he forced me to shoot him. He wanted to die, and when he raised his replica gun at me and pulled the trigger, he knew I had to use deadly force. He committed suicide—only he used me to do it. He didn't overdose from pills or hang himself, but he made a decision to die. He forced me, a police officer, to be the tool of his death . . . but I didn't murder him."

"And, if the suspect had left the bank without being challenged?" asked the district attorney.

"Under the circumstances the suspect was a deadly threat," said Jennings. "If he had left the bank and driven away, his vehicle could have been a deadly weapon against other officers confronting him, or the public could have been hurt. Or, another officer would have had to shoot him when threatened by the same handgun. Police officers shouldn't have to wait until a bullet is fired at them to defend themselves and others."

"As a police officer, was it your duty to engage the suspect and not allow him to leave the scene?" the district attorney concluded.

"Yes, sir, ten-four."

Forget-Me-Nots 29

"Hello, this is Tom Jennings trying to reach Shawn Smith. Do I have the correct number?"

"Yes, this is Shawn Smith. How may I help you?"

"Well, I know you and your wife have gone through a lot since James' death . . ."

"Yes . . . we have . . . go on."

"I was told by my attorney to not initiate any contact with you until this had been to court," said Jennings.

"Yes, sounds like familiar legal advice," said Smith.

"Now that it's been to the grand jury and I've had more time to think about your tragedy, I just wanted to tell you I'm sorry for your loss."

"Well, this is a surprise. Thank you for calling."

"Do you have a couple minutes? Can you talk any longer?" asked Tom, feeling like he wasn't done.

"Hold on a second," said Shawn, as he moved to a window looking out at the flower garden and observed Carolyn in her sun hat and gloves.

"Yes, I'm back; the reception's better here," continued Shawn.

"Now that I've had time to think about James' death, not my wife's injury, I've become more aware of how his loss must affect your family. I'm sorry your son had to die."

"Yes, nice of you to show your concern. Over the last few years, since his mood swings and hallucinations, we felt like we were losing him a little bit at a time."

"If I had to do it over again, if I'd only known it was him in a personal crisis with a replica gun, I'd take my bullets back."

"Well, that's good of you," said Smith warmly.

"I know your wife blames me, and I know there's nothing I can do to change things."

"You're right about that, and I recommend you leave her out of this. She hasn't taken his death well. If you still read the newspaper or social media, you know what I'm talking about."

"Yes, I've seen some of it. I don't expect to change her just because of a phone call," agreed Jennings.

"Good, because you won't. In fact, around here things can always get worse, long before they get better. I wish I could tell you that the attacks on you will stop, but don't count on it. Once Carolyn gets a thing in her head . . ."

"If I lost one of my two girls, there's no telling what I'd be like," said Tom, thinking of his big babies, Julia and Hannah.

"Yes, I guess that's the truth. You never know until it happens to you."

"Well, I appreciate you talking with me."

"Now that you've called, I've got something to tell you."

"Pretty bird! Nice bird!" squawked the Amazon parrot as his eyes flashed and his tail flared.

Shawn ignored him, but with a swoop, Paco landed on Shawn's shoulder.

"Hello?" said Tom into his phone.

"Ow! Damn bird!" yelled Shawn after Paco bit his ear lobe, causing Shawn to drop his phone while fighting off the vicious attack.

"Let go! Get away!" yelled Shawn.

"Pretty bird! Nice bird!" the parrot continued speaking as it flew back across the room, landing on top of its cage.

"Hello? . . . Hello?" said Tom.

"Hello," said Shawn. "Sorry . . . I'm back."

"Are you okay? What happened?"

"Oh, just another attack by a passive-aggressive parrot that hates my guts and loves to bite me when I'm not looking."

"Should we hang up?"

"No, now I've got something to share with you. I know you were officially accused by Carolyn of harassment by sending her flowers and an inappropriate card."

"Yes, I was questioned about it by my supervisor. I didn't know anything about it."

"I'm sure you didn't. It was all a set up by Carolyn. She did the whole thing without my knowledge: the forget-me-nots, the card, the message. With her it's about being in control, and being the martyr helps her reel people in. Believe me, you can't win. It was her way of hurting you by making it appear that you were the one acting bizarre. Like I said, it's her way."

"Really?" Tom responded, letting the idea sink in that Carolyn Odessa had manufactured evidence against him.

"Yes, really. I wanted you to know who was responsible. I'd rather you didn't involve the police in this, but do what you must. I'd hate for Carolyn to lose her job over this. If it got out she'd made a false police report . . . Since you called and apologized, I just had to tell you. It sounds like you understand how difficult this is on us."

"Thanks so much for telling me. I couldn't figure out who would do a thing like that."

"She's excellent at autopsies. I'd hate for her to lose her career."

"Yes, I guess she's good," said Tom, remembering some past death cases but also thinking about his own termination from the police department.

Shawn looked out at the garden again, but he didn't see Carolyn. Suddenly, he had a sinking feeling. Turning slowly to the doorway, he saw her standing there, wide-eyed. She was still wearing her blue sun hat and her leather garden gloves. In one hand she held freshly cut blood-red roses, still in summer bloom. In the other hand, she held her rose-stem cutting knife.

"Well, nice talking to you. Thank you for calling. I've got to go now," said Shawn as he steadied his phone and pushed the disconnect screen.

"Who were you talking to?" asked Carolyn.

"How long were you listening?"

"Long enough to know that you're betraying our family secrets."

"It was Tom Jennings."

"Jennings!" she howled, "That cold-blooded murderer!"

"Yes, he called and apologized."

"He's a murderer!" she continued in a guttural roar.

"He's not a murderer. He thought James had a real gun. He was protecting others."

"You told him something you shouldn't have, didn't you?"

Shawn studied Carolyn. He looked into her dark, deep-set, penetrating eyes and recognized that she knew what he had done.

"You told him about the flowers and the card," she accused.

"Yes, I did," admitted Shawn.

"You had no right! This is your fault! You've betrayed me, and you'll regret it. You're useless. You let James get off his meds, and now you've sided with his murderer. Why have you done this to me?"

"I'm tired of protecting you. You've held a grudge against Jennings since the night he helped arrest James for those fireworks. I'm not taking anyone's side; I just want this to be over."

"This will never be over, not now!" roared Carolyn as she dumped the flowers on the table. "You're done! You're history. You're fired as my office boy. I won't work with anyone who's not loyal to me. We're better off without you.

"Your ear is bleeding," she added. "Don't get blood on the carpet."

"That damn parrot."

Carolyn still gripped her rose-stem knife. She raised it in her closed fist and pointed it at Shawn, taking measured steps toward him. "You've not only betrayed me; you've betrayed James."

"What are you talking about?" asked Shawn as he rubbed his forehead.

"You minimized his death, just like the grand jury did. They were as incompetent as the police."

"I would never minimize his death! He meant everything to me."

"Now everyone will say it was James' fault, not Jennings', or they'll blame me, that I'm a bad mother."

"Actually, betrayal is what you've been doing to me with your long-time affair."

"What do you know about anything?" Carolyn snorted.

"I've focused my energy on our boys and my work, while you've had your affair with a married man—one who supposedly enforces laws and protects our community."

"Don't bother blaming anyone but yourself."

"Oh, I'm to blame for your affair?" asked Shawn as his voice escalated.

"It's really pretty simple. You haven't always been what I needed. Don't take it personally."

"I thought staying together would somehow be better for the boys, especially James, but that hasn't helped anyone."

Carolyn looked at Shawn without blinking. "It sure didn't help James. I'm taking these flowers to his grave. You . . . you pack your bags. When I get back, I want you gone. I'm done with you, but I'm not done with your friend, Jennings."

Moon Children 30

I n Suanna's dream, the tropical breeze fanned her in her hammock until she fell asleep.

•

On the moon-filled night the light gradually dimmed and villagers cried out, "The Sky Dragon is eating the moon!" They hurried to their huts to hide, following the orders of the town council to never gaze at the moon as it was being attacked. Yes, Sky Dragon had returned and was again attempting to destroy their world. As it grew darker, Sipu Nono and people like her, moon children, responded to do battle. It was up to the ghostly white-skinned, white and golden-haired, *ni mimmikana* (or *ipekwa*) to guard their community islands and coastal villages from the end of the world. Since the few moon children of the Tule People were believed to be closer to the spiritual world, it became their duty to protect the others—their brown-skinned brothers and sisters—during times of eclipses when the dragon attempted to devour the moon.

The moon children shouted prayers to the Great Spirit and shot their arrows skyward. And their aim never failed. While the arrows they released toward the moon always fell from the sky, often in the waters just off their islands, the soul of the arrows hit their mark. The dragon was repelled or killed so that the moon could survive. And who could doubt the power of the moon children to engage evil spirits? The proof was in the return of the night's glow. It was a moon-filled night.

Breathing deeply, her hammock swinging, Sipu Nono opened her oriental eyes knowing this night would be a rare opportunity for her to fight for her people. Sipu would wear her special *mola* blouse, redden her cheeks with *makepa* paint—representing the life-giving blood of the Earth Mother—and have a fresh witch mark painted on her forehead as additional protection from evil spirits. But first she must run and tell her best friend Claudia of her dream and alert Chief Nele Kantule of her premonition. This news would likely cause havoc to Claudia's planned *inna* feast beginning the next day, but what choice did she have? It was her duty.

The *inna* was the tribe's traditional coming-out ceremony honoring a young woman and formally introducing her to the community, including the fact that she was now eligible for marriage. Throughout a young woman's life she was honored and blessed at a puberty ceremony, haircutting ceremony, coming-out party (or *inna*)—all in preparation for her parentally pre-planned marriage.

For years Claudia's family, not wealthy, had been building resources for her *inna* and actively preparing in recent months with their friends and extended family. Friends, neighbors, and local dignitaries had been invited. The *chicha*, a maize/sugar-cane beer, was fermented. Fourteen jars, each covered with banana leaves and tied at the top with a reed, awaited the participants in the *inna neka*, the drinking hall. Big game had been hunted and cleaned, the cooking fires prepared. Any news of powerful foreign spirits planning to disrupt Claudia's sacred service could delay, possibly destroy these preparations. The waste of the family's life savings would be crushing, but worse yet it would be viewed as a sign that indomitable evil spirits were instigating a fight with the family. The public acknowledgement of Claudia's readiness for marriage, availability to a suitor, and willingness to procreate for the good of the Tule people, were at risk. What family, what unmarried man, would be willing to invite this kind of otherworld trouble?

Claudia was already nervous. The wait was killing her. She was relieved to see her best friend Sipu, also twelve years old, enter the family hut.

"Sipu! Thank you for coming!" said Claudia.

"You already look beautiful!" said Sipu, admiring Claudia's short hair and her new coin necklaces, and commenting on the black beauty line painted down her nose. "How are you? Your *inna's* almost here!"

"It all begins at noon tomorrow with the mind-numbing *chicha*," said Claudia. "All this ceremony, for what? In three days most everyone will be sick in their hammocks or passed out on the ground feeling like they've been poisoned! How many will even remember it? But, at least it will be over."

"Enjoy it!" said Sipu. "You're fortunate. You'll be one step closer to having a boy, I mean a man, in your house. Then, Earth Mother willing, nine months later a little fisherman or a water carrier will arrive."

"Stop it!" said Claudia. "You know I'm in no hurry for marriage. I just want to have a choice of which boy I marry. I'll never be out of mother's house!"

"I know!" said Sipu.

"Will you visit me often at the reception tent? You can help me endure meeting so many people, and you can see what it's like. Your *inna's* getting closer."

"Well, don't forget one little thing that's been delayed by Earth Mother," reminded Sipu. "You know how my parents are still waiting for me to tell them that I'm mature, that I've reached my moon time. So, you're a bit ahead of me in ceremonies."

"Yeah, my parents have constantly talked about this *inna*, but mostly it's about the enormous cost to feed everyone and get them drunk. Having all boys and one girl, they've been spared the expense of more *innas*, but they remind us that one day they'll lose my brothers' help and income when they marry and move out. My parents are counting on me."

"You know I don't expect to ever get married," said Sipu, "I can live with that. I'm not attractive to others. I am who I am, an albino, just because one of my parents gazed at the moon too long while my mother was pregnant. But someday, if it happens, I want a husband I can love and a mother-in-law I don't hate!"

"Don't give up. Once you have your *inna*, you never know how soon the marriage will happen. Times change."

"Yeah, but what choice do we really have? Remember Nus Maria?" asked Sipu. "By the end of her drunken *inna* feast her parents were already talking to the parents of the boys they considered hard workers. They didn't waste time. I think her parents were more concerned about coconuts than how the two would get along."

"Sipu, we've got to stop this! One step at a time; don't talk about marriage. I just want to survive the next three days."

Sipu scratched an infected mosquito bite on her arm. "So," she said, "do you want to know why I'm visiting you? Aren't you curious?"

"Since when do you need a reason?" asked Claudia.

"I had a dream this morning."

"Sipu, I'm only listening to good dreams. Any others will have to wait until after my *inna*."

"I'm telling you first, then Chief Kantule."

"No!" Claudia cried out. "Don't do this to me now."

"You know what I've told you before; it's a gift and a curse. I can't help it."

"Just leave," pleaded Claudia. "Go home. Have another dream. Don't tell anyone."

"Okay, if you want I'll leave without telling you, but next I'm off to see Chief Kantule."

"Don't!" Claudia begged, "Leave well enough alone. We've been planning this forever, and now you're going to ruin it. I know you!"

"I trust Chief Kantule to do the right thing. He's saved my life and the lives of many moon children."

"Yeah, but his right thing may not be my family's right thing, or my right thing. We're part of this village, but once you tell the chief about your dream he may not care about my *inna*. My parents will never forgive you. Sipu, I will never speak to you if you delay my ceremony! We can't afford to reschedule this. It could take years! The *chicha*, the food, the officials, they cost a fortune. We've already paid. We can't do this again, Sipu. If you ruin this for me, I won't be your friend ever again. Please don't wreck this for me! Don't let your jealousy ruin our friendship. Just because you haven't had a moon time doesn't mean I should wait for you!"

Sipu pursed her protruding lips and left the hut. She was jealous, but her dream was real, and without Chief Kantule, more albinos would be shunned by the community or buried in the sand under the birthing hammocks. She didn't have a choice. She had to tell him.

•

"Chief Kantule, do you have time to talk to me?" asked Sipu.

"Certainly, my child. I figured you'd be helping your friend Claudia."

"She doesn't think I'm helping her right now. I stopped to talk to her about a dream I had, but she doesn't want to hear it because she doesn't want me ruining her *inna*. I reminded her that you will help make the *inna* safer, and that without you as chief I might be living in the jungle with my family."

"I know we've talked about this before, that some chiefs before me feared your whiteness because it reminded them and others of the first days of the big ships: forced labor, diseases of the white man, and near extermination. They were blind to your spirituality and closeness to God.

Without you helping me today as my *absogedi*, I could make a mistake in diagnosing causes of illness. You absolutely make a difference with your magic songs. Despite your youth and my age, we're a productive team."

"Thank you, Chief Kantule. You always make me feel special, not an outcast. My parents, they've told me stories about how you saved the Guna people by sending some moon children to the United States to visit, so that its people could see that the Tule nation had people that looked like the whites among them. Is that true?"

"Yes," answered the chief. "Nearly twenty years ago a man named Richard Marsh helped protect us from being destroyed by the black Panamanian police. It was our revolution. There were atrocities, but we would not kneel. Even today we have challenges. But you didn't come here for another history lesson from an old man. Sipu, my *absogedi*, how may I help you?"

"Chief Kantule, these dreams are so real."

"You continue to help the Tule people with your guidance against evil spirits. Now tell me of your dream."

"In the night's sky I saw an enormous tree that filled the sky from its roots on the mainland. The Sky Dragon climbed it to attack the moon. Our people were in fear and I was shooting arrows into the sky, but they were missing their mark while the dragon kept eating the moon. I couldn't stop him. The dragon devouring the moon is coming soon! Tonight, I think."

"Have you told anyone besides Claudia?"

"No, only Claudia, not even my parents."

"Let me consult on this. The attack on the moon is not expected. We'll need a gathering and chanting. Many of the *unchus* are already in place for the *inna*. There's a good quantity of *saptur* juice. Together we can handle this. Your parents will be proud of you for your contribution."

•

Chief Nele Kantule checked in with medicine man Upikinya to see what evil spirits were attempting to steal souls and take them below to a subterranean level of the earth. He visited Claudia's parents to warn them of the impending night attack so that they could be on guard, especially at the meeting hall where the *chicha* was nearly ready.

Every Guna understood that an attack on an *inna* was an attack on Earth Mother. Every *inna* was a celebration of the miracle of reproduction, specifically the young girl's maturation, but attending and participating was also a prerequisite to heaven. All Gunas knew that if they didn't get drunk at the *inna* fests then they could not enter the afterlife. No *chicha*, no ceremony; no ceremony, no *chicha*, no salvation. At the *innas* their spiritual rebirth required a death-like drunkenness or unconsciousness.

Chief Kantule explained the crucial circumstances to the *chicha* taster and his assistant, and they quickly agreed to the chief's desire to immediately start burning the cocoa bean incense. By filling the *inna* hall with smoke, it would prevent the evil spirits of disease or *poni* devils from injuring or killing the participants. The *inna* would not be postponed.

The chief spoke to the gatherers of the *saptur* fruits, and with the approval of the *inna* hosts, moon children were to be permitted to renew their witch marks with the dark juice to help fight the Sky Dragon in case he appeared, thereby protecting the last-minute preparations for the *inna* ceremony and feast. It was Guna teamwork at its best.

•

Sipu returned home, complained of a stomachache, and told her parents of Chief Kantule's increased concern for security at the *inna*. She wanted to rest, but found that impossible. Instead, she continued carving her *inna* gift for Claudia. The medicine idol, an *uchu*, was nearly done. This one, called Kalele, was made from hot pepper wood. He was about eight inches high, including his removable hat that would hold incense. His purpose was to cure sickness by rushing down underneath the earth's surface to find cities of evil spirits and confront them with the hot pepper smoke. When the devils fell down choking, he would demand information from them about a particular stolen spirit. After the guilty devil confessed and surrendered the spirit, the Hot Pepper Man would guide the spirit to the surface where it was reunited with the patient, all under the guidance of the medicine man or medicine woman.

Sipu valued Claudia more than anyone else and wanted her protected from all diseases. Once Sipu completed carving the devil-chasing *uchu*, she would paint it so that it would be available to Claudia in case of emergency. She expected Claudia to tie it to her hammock to be used as preventive medicine.

•

Claudia's entire body was ceremoniously darkened with *saptur* juice by her grandmother.

A heavy gathering of clouds blocked the moon for several minutes, creating a stir from the villagers, but there was no lunar eclipse.

The feast was protected, the *poni* devils scared off by Sipu's warning dream.

The yucca roots, plantains, bananas, smoked fish, tarpon, iguanas, rabbits, deer, and *agoutis* were plenty.

The *chicha* tasted perfect.

Claudia received greetings and gifts at her reception tent, but gradually felt ignored at her own party.

Sipu, with her witch mark on her white-skinned forehead, wore her favorite *mola*, her mother's best work. It depicted her value to the Gunas as a protector. In the center the moon child, with bow and arrow, was fighting a jaguar. On the border of the *mola* were swastikas representing Earth Mother's tree of life, birth, and immortality.

Sipu wore her red-dyed head kerchief; her heavy, gold nose ring; and saucer-sized, matching, pierced earrings. She was draped with necklaces over her loose blouse. Most of the necklaces were beaded, but others included wild animal teeth and old coins. Her arms and legs were wrapped with orange-and-yellow-beaded rings that created another abstract design. Barefoot, she wore a wraparound knee-length skirt, or sarong, just a straight piece of fabric with the two loose ends tucked in.

Whether it was the excitement or total exhaustion, Sipu felt her head spin and lost her balance like a drunk on *chicha*. Hopefully, it wasn't a return of the malaria with its fever and cramping. The long day and long night had caught up with her. She cautiously returned home to her family's hut and her welcoming hammock.

•

Waking up during the night, Sipu overheard her parents talking. She learned that at the *inna* they had been approached by other parents who commended them for having a special daughter, one who was clairvoyant and in touch with the spiritual world. "She will make a valuable bride someday," they predicted.

Sipu scratched her arm.

"They were feeling the *chicha*," her father continued, "but I was so proud when they said Sipu will make a valuable bride to some hard working boy someday."

Sipu felt heat in her abdomen.

"Yes," replied her mother, "I feel hope, but should we tell her or keep this a secret?"

For a moment Sipu felt like she had to pee, then she detected wetness on the inside of her thigh. She presumed she was really sick.

"Let's leave this alone for now," said her father, "in case it was the *chicha* talking. She still waits for her moon time."

Sipu asked herself, "Is this it? Is this what it's like, what I've been waiting for?" With her fingers Sipu touched a spot of her blood and in the moonlight strained to see its color. "Finally!"

With her index finger she began at her forehead and painted a blunt, vertical, beauty nose line down to its peak. Exhausting her Earth Mother's paint, Sipu slowly and lightly made colorless circles at the tip of her nose. Finally, she touched her finger to the tip of her tongue, tasting the stained blood. As she closed her eyes, she relaxed her mouth and smiled.

Brain Guppies 31

Suanna, half asleep, tried to scratch her mosquito bite. Instead, she felt a rubber tube. Her stomach ached and she rubbed it slowly. She smelled cocoa beans and patted above her lips, searching for her gold nose ring. Instead, she felt an obstruction and pulled it away. She thought of her friend Claudia, the *inna* ceremony, and reached down to touch the wetness inside her thigh. On one finger she collected the blood from her menstrual period and painted a red nose line on her milky-white albino face.

Suanna's eyes were blinking herself awake when her mother entered the room, looked down at the blood on Suanna's nose, and screamed, "NURSE! NURSE!" as she reached down for the call button and Suanna's hand.

Suanna reeled from the cosmic shock, but had no place to hide. She fully opened her eyes, saw that her fingernails had grown and were colored. At first she believed the coloring was makepa paint representing the life-giving blood of the Earth Mother. Confused that her nails were no longer bitten down to her skin, and surprised that they had been painted with red fingernail polish, she was between worlds. Then she understood her mother had been busy while she slept.

"Mother!" Suanna protested in a slow, raspy voice. "I told you I'm not painting my nails! And red is old-fashioned!"

"NURSE!" yelled Elizabeth, "In here! Room 315!"

"Suanna!" said Elizabeth, "I've been waiting for you!"

"And, I'm not getting married, either!" declared Suanna. "So there!"

While Suanna stumbled out of her dream, she was tugged back for a heartbeat, wondering if her absence would cause undue harm to her Guna community. In one last desperate attempt to warn others, she attempted to yell, "The Sky Dragon is eating the moon!" Instead, her words escaped as a loud whisper.

Elizabeth kept one hand holding her daughter's fingers while the nurse examined Suanna. Elizabeth called Joe on her phone. Suanna, who was becoming alert enough to be assertive, instructed the nurse to not disturb her ceremonious nose line. It was sacred medicine.

"Where's Rat?" Suanna asked. "Where are Uncle Carl, and Dad? What happened? Where am I? Are we in the past or in the future?" she questioned as she saw a medicine idol, the *uchu*, beside her hospital bed. It was in the form of Rabbit Chief. It had protected her from the evil spirits that were attempting to steal souls. She relaxed.

•

Suanna's doctor finally arrived and examined her patient. For weeks the extent of Suanna's physical activity had been her breathing. Nurses had checked, adjusted, and cleaned her, monitored bags, and compared computer data. Now she answered the doctor's questions and, whenever the physician paused, made her own inquiries. Suanna's voice was scratchy, but her speech and cognition were fine.

Elizabeth explained to Suanna about the car accident at the bank and about their weeks-long stay in the hospital. Carl, Catalpa, and Bud had returned to Nespelem. Her dad was on his way from Prairie Grove and would hopefully avoid a speeding ticket, or worse. Elizabeth finally had to tell him to get off the phone and drive safely. They'd see him when he arrived. "Be careful, drive safely," she repeated to him like a voice-over on a TV public service announcement.

Prior to Joe's arrival, Elizabeth and Suanna spent moments alone in the room. "You've had your period," whispered Elizabeth.

"I know already," said Suanna. "I dreamed it."

"My child," said Elizabeth, "you're going to be fine now, and I'm back too."

•

Joe burst into the room, his mouth open wide in a smile and his eyes rapidly blinking. Feeling breathless and lightheaded, he rushed to hold her.

"Oh! My Snowflake! You're awake!"

•

Rat tunneled into Suanna's sheets and explored the bed. Joe had some-how had the clarity to collect the gerbil before his mad dash to the city.

Elizabeth and Joe overflowed with gratitude, alternating with brief jolts of doubt and worry about whether their grueling experience was re-ally over. They thanked the hospital staff and the doctors after they were told the swelling and pain from Suanna's surgery was temporary. They thanked God, Father, and Creator, while Suanna tried to sort things out.

It had been emotional for them—and for her. She kept telling her parents in vivid detail about her experiences with the Gunas and how she had been counted on to help save her community from the Sky Dragon. Suanna explained with pride that she and others with albinism were considered closer to Earth Mother than the majority of the natives. Moon children were vital to Guna safety and survival.

Elizabeth recognized the Guna people of Panama from her anthro-pological studies. She was familiar with them for having the highest rate of albinism in the world, but she'd never learned about their culture in such personalized detail to the extent that Suanna was sharing. Eliza-beth was perplexed as to how her daughter could have learned so much. Had Suanna, unbeknownst to Elizabeth, watched a documentary or studied social media about this Caribbean tribe from Central America?

•

Suanna, at first reluctantly, told the story of the greys. It was unsettling to her. She stopped and started, and was told not to rush, that there was no hurry. It was a dark place, but she revisited it. She looked for con-firmation from her parents that it was only a dream, that there weren't places in the world that actually murdered children for being albino.

Elizabeth and Joe wanted to deny that reality. They wanted to tell her that those evil people and places didn't exist, except in nightmares. But, as Suanna grew tired, they minimized the evil, telling her that in Africa there were some superstitious people who did such things. They assured her that in Kansas and throughout the U.S., she was safe from harm.

Suanna confidently informed her parents that she wanted to learn about how "her people" were treated around the world. She wanted to help, if possible. She didn't know what she could do, but she knew she could do something.

•

Elizabeth and Joe had their own ideas about the detailed, colorful dreams that Suanna kept describing to them. Elizabeth theorized how Suanna's connection with the cultures that had a high rate of albinism mirrored Suanna's physical condition while unconscious. The dream about the mutilations in Tanzania could have reflected Suanna's worsening condition, while her dream with the Gunas from Panama may have paralleled her growing strength just prior to her wakening.

Joe agreed that the dreams were extremely important. He compared Suanna's stories to his own search for guidance when he was fourteen: a trip to the wilderness that had been a rite of passage. It had helped Joe understand that dedicating himself to becoming a world-renowned boxer was an opportunity for him to influence and improve his Indian community. Suanna's dreams were undoubtedly a vision about her future opportunity to connect with others, especially people with albinism. It was no coincidence that her visions had occurred as she fasted and suffered in isolation. In puberty, Suanna found her guardian spirit and was now prepared to serve.

Both Joe and Elizabeth found a noticeable difference between their old Suanna and their new, awakened daughter. Her dreams had certainly influenced her world. When Suanna talked about "her people," she no longer meant only those of Indian blood, the Nez Perce tribe, or the Colville Confederated Tribes Reservation. She meant people like her with albinism.

"Suanna, remember the summer camp I told you about that's for kids with albinism?" asked Elizabeth.

"The NOAH camp?"

"Yes, you might be more interested in it now. Before your accident you only wanted to know about your Indian side, but now you sound like you want to explore your albinism."

"Yeah, I want to learn everything about us."

"I'll bring your tablet tomorrow and you can have a look at some websites. At NOAH (National Organization for Albinism and Hypopigmentation) they help you embrace your identity through education and other people."

"I've looked at the site where teenagers are in the spotlight."

"Many of those students want to be role models for children with albinism," advised Elizabeth. "They believe that if a person can't fit in, then they can stand out."

"I don't remember if they tell about albinism in Africa," remarked Suanna.

"Not much, but there's another organization that might be of interest to you. It's called Under the Same Sun. It advocates for people with albinism, especially in Tanzania, but all over Africa. They fight discrimination through education."

"That's what I want to do."

"We'll have a look tomorrow." Suanna was fighting to keep her eyes open. She needed rest.

Joe had more questions for Suanna, but he decided to wait until after she had some sleep. He wanted to know about Grandfather's medicine bag that had been stored in his trunk with the totem Rabbit Chief Joseph. What had become of it?

•

Joe and Elizabeth held hands and swung their arms on the way to the cafeteria. Joe gave fist bumps. Elizabeth exhaled.

"Suanna's back!" declared Elizabeth. "Can you believe it?"

"It's sinking in. When you told me on the phone, it took me a couple of seconds to comprehend."

"The blood on her nose didn't make sense to me."

"I still can't believe it! We get another chance to raise our daughter," said Joe.

Elizabeth closed her eyes, took a deep breath, and shouted, "Yes! Let's celebrate with ice cream!"

"And potato chips!" added Joe.

"We'll spare no expense!" laughed Elizabeth.

After purchasing celebratory food, Elizabeth and Joe discussed their family's future.

"Do you still want to live on a reservation?" asked Joe as he crunched another potato chip.

"That wouldn't be the Colville you're talking about, would it?" asked Elizabeth as she licked the sides of her ice cream sandwich.

"You still want to interview elders?"

"Well, for starters I want to interview your mom, but I don't want to live with her. *Comprendes?*"

"I understand."

Elizabeth kicked off her shoes and wiggled her toes. "What would you do all day on the reservation? Hang out at casinos?"

"Ha-ha. I've got my horseshoeing, but there might be time for some fishing. I'll ask Officer Billy Goodenough to share his secret spots."

"But for you to start your farrier trade, you'll need customers. Why would anyone trust a foreigner from Kansas to hammer nails into their horses?"

"Don't push it or I'll spread the word you're F.B.I!"

Elizabeth ran a hand through her long blond hair. "Go ahead," she said with a laugh, "but I don't think anyone would believe I'm a Full-Blooded Indian."

"Finally, Suanna will get her wish," said Joe.

"And, I'll get mine."

"Elizabeth, I'm so sorry it took a tragedy for me to get past my ego. I've been selfish. Suanna's accident reminded me to take advantage of what we have."

"Well, I know you can't be hurried! You've always been on Indian time. Once Suanna's ready, I'll be ready."

"What about the school at Nespelem?"

"It was good enough for me," bragged Joe.

"Yeah, but I still want us to visit. I need to meet the teachers."

"And I want to meet the principal."

"Suanna will want us to start packing before she's even released from the hospital. We're going to have to take this slowly."

"We'll be careful," said Joe. "She's on her way to full recovery."

"Even the neurosurgeons don't really know what will happen. Full recovery is always a guess, especially with the brain."

"Honey, let's just celebrate her progress."

"All right. Sometimes, I get ahead of myself."

●

Joe thanked Creator for giving Suanna a second chance and then he thanked Grandfather for making Rabbit Chief Joe for Suanna. He also thought about how blessings were sometimes offered in disguise.

Had God given up on him, or had he given up on God? It took Suanna's critical accident to save him. Her lack of improvement in the hospital forced Joe to reach for the help he'd abandoned. He found hope in the old ways and rediscovered optimism in himself. From this point forward, he promised to stop beating himself up and to no longer hold himself responsible for the collective health of an entire reservation of people. He was ready to return home with his family and his faith, rediscover his culture, and once again to become part of the Indian community.

It was past time. Joe and Elizabeth asked each other unanswerable questions about their daughter's prognosis. Even the neurosurgeons didn't really know. Full recovery was always a guess, especially with the brain.

Before Suanna woke up again, Joe and Elizabeth agreed that they would all move to Washington as soon as it was safely feasible for Suanna. They had heard about the many risks and potential problems of TBI (traumatic brain injury) and post-brain surgery. They would be careful. Even though the neurosurgeon had reported there were no complications, it was also understood that even the healthiest bedridden patient had atrophied muscles in days after surgery. Gratefully, Suanna's speech was excellent, and she appeared normal. There were plans to get her up in the afternoon to test her balance.

•

"What are brain guppies?" Suanna asked the nurse.

"Whatever do you mean?" the nurse replied. "Like the little tropical fish?"

"When I was half-asleep, I heard some nurses or doctors talking about brain guppies blocking my drain," Suanna said.

"They might have been talking about your drainage tube having been blocked," said the nurse, "but you must have misunderstood them about guppies. No pets allowed in this hospital."

"Oh, okay, thanks," said Suanna as she tightened her grip on Rat, hidden under the wrinkled bed sheets.

But the nurse knew Suanna had heard correctly. Some neurosurgeons, after surgery, referred to brain matter, bone, and blood as "brain guppies," especially when a drainage screen got clogged with the mobile miniature particles. She smiled at the young woman's curiosity.

•

Elizabeth and Joe waited for Suanna to wake up. They were assured by the nurse that she was sleeping, not in a coma.

Joe picked up Rabbit Chief, the wooden totem that his grandfather had sent him years ago to give to Suanna.

Elizabeth watched silently.

After his critical injury, he had questioned, "Where is God?" but he was ecstatic when Suanna was born. He gave God the credit. When Suanna suffered her brain injury, Joe regressed, confused about his ambivalent spiritual faith.

He had searched for Grandfather's medicine-pouch gift because he wanted better odds, greater spiritual coverage. The recovered rabbit totem became his personal connection to the eternal spirit and his ancestry. If there was more than one God—which of course didn't make sense because God was the creator and ruler of the universe—then Joe wanted to enlist all available eternal spirits to help his daughter.

"Your rabbit *uchu*," said Suanna, awake. "You brought it to protect me?"

"Yes," he replied. "Bud was playing with it by the tree house before they left town. He told me where he got it."

Suanna squeezed her eyes shut. "I showed him and Catalpa your powwow stuff. Sorry."

"Did you also find the medicine pouch inside one of my old moccasins?"

"Yes, but I put it back after opening it and reading Grandfather Charlie's letter."

"Letter? In the pouch?" Joe asked with narrowed eyes. "Did it hold any sacred items? I never opened it."

Petting Rat, Suanna answered, "Just the letter."

"Do you still have it?"

"I put the letter and rawhide bag back where I found it," explained Suanna as she held Rat tighter.

"It's missing now. I never looked inside the medicine pouch. I was saving it to give to you someday."

"And I put it back in your trunk because I knew you weren't ready to give it to me, but I don't understand why you waited."

"Well, that's difficult to answer. When Grandfather sent it to us to give to you, I knew it wasn't a working medicine pouch yet, but when you got hurt, I was desperate for help. Now, I believe your rabbit totem has helped you recover."

"What did Grandfather's letter say?" Joe asked Suanna, still curious.

"Oh, he just told me welcome to our world," answered Suanna. "Told me that Chief Rabbit Joe was a doll he made for me, and he said that someday I might want to gather my own spiritual items to carry in the rawhide pouch. He said he couldn't give me important stuff because I needed to find my own.

"I'm going to wear my pouch around my neck the way Uncle Carl does," continued Suanna. "I've already found things. I have some fluffy feathers from Hubcap and some horsehair from Lady."

"Suanna, don't tell me any more about what you're going to put in your sacred pouch. That's only for you to know. But where's the bag? I couldn't find it."

"Like I said, I put it back in the trunk because I didn't want to tell you about it yet. I was waiting for you to give it to me when you were ready," explained Suanna.

"Well, I'm ready now, but it's missing. I didn't give it to you because I wasn't sure of myself. Since I didn't feel like a tribal member anymore, it didn't seem like I was worthy to welcome anyone else to the nation. I let my running away from the reservation affect you, and I'm sorry. Now, I'm going to do my best to make it up to you."

Elizabeth and Joe exchanged a glance and couldn't stop smiling. Then they told her.

"Suanna," said Elizabeth, as she massaged her daughter's feet, "you can go to school with other Indian kids and we'll live near dad's relatives."

Suanna's mouth opened wide and her eyes lit up. "Is this a dream too? Am I hearing right?" she asked, tilting her head and pausing.

"If you still want to move to the Confederated Tribes Reservation," said Joe, "then we're ready and eager to make that happen."

She raised her bedsheet as though she were ready to jump out and get dressed. "Oh, Daddy! Mom! Yes! When can we go?"

"When you're stronger," said Elizabeth.

"Thank you for granting my wish!" Suanna squealed as she nearly danced in bed. "Grandmother can help me learn to speak Indian!"

"*Cikli-tecix*," Joe said in Nez Perce. "We're going home."

Pass the Relish 32

The Jennings family arrived at the Morningclouds' ranch house for the evening in a sticky-August mood. Maybe they were dehydrated by the day's record heat and humidity. Maybe they were irritated by the invasion of gnats and blood-sucking mosquitoes. While they had all looked forward to the visit to the Morningclouds, the closer they got to their destination they grew nervous about being first-time visitors.

As Tom prepared to turn into their driveway, the business sign stood out: "Morningcloud's Farrier Service." The letter *u* in Morningcloud was a real upturned horseshoe that had been nailed to the sign to visually reinforce its message. It worked.

•

Elizabeth and Suanna met them at the front door and changed their mood.

Suanna was wearing a black skullcap that tied in the back rather than her standard western cowgirl hat. She was still covering her craniotomy scar until her hair got longer. But she looked ready to ride in a purple, plaid western shirt, boot-cut jeans, and brown, flame-stitch cowgirl boots. Her solid-brass belt buckle showed a bucking horse and rider. It credited the Kansas Department of Corrections First Annual Prison Rodeo. She bounced on her toes. "Julia, Hannah, come see Rat!"

All three girls quickly scurried down a hallway like gerbils in a maze searching for edible rewards.

"Thanks for coming," welcomed Elizabeth. "Tom, Joe's minding his fire. Just follow the path to the patio."

Tom left for the back yard with food on his mind, while hungry mosquitoes buzzed his appetizing head.

"How are you, Jesse?" asked Elizabeth, giving her a long hug.

243

"We're so pleased that Suanna continues to make steady progress," Jesse said in a bubbly voice, "but are you really moving?"

"Come in. We'll talk. I'm in the kitchen."

"Yes, we're all excited about our upcoming move," said Elizabeth as she proceeded to the crock pot and opened its lid, inviting Jesse to look.

"The beans smell delicious. What kind are they?"

"They're a small, white, heirloom bean from Mexico called *alubia blanca*. Would you like a taste?"

"Please."

Elizabeth poured a half-ladle of the creamy beans into a small bowl. "Here," she said, handing the bowl and a spoon to Jesse, "see what you think. There's salt, pepper, and olive oil right here for seasoning."

Jesse took a spoonful and closed her eyes in order to concentrate on the taste. After a few seconds she said, "This is heavenly."

"Sometimes I'll just have the beans with seasoning, but I've made this with mirepoix for flavoring."

"Yes, it's sweetened nicely and adds to the texture. Perfect."

"Joe's doing his brisket for the adults. The kids get hotdogs and hamburgers."

"Good plan. The girls will devour them. When did you decide on moving?"

"While Suanna was in the hospital, Joe and I talked a lot about what was important in life. Since first grade Suanna's wanted to live on the reservation in Washington. We figure now's the time for all of us to take advantage of our opportunities."

"Do reservations have schools? Is there one nearby?"

"If we live near Nespelem there's a public school that has kindergarten through eighth grade. Over the years I've spoken to Joe's relatives about the school and it's a mixed bag. Most importantly, I'm concerned about its academic standards."

"Are there good teachers? How does it compare to our school?"

"Reservation schools are often underperforming for a couple of big reasons besides limited funding. Many families suffer from intergenerational trauma and poverty.

"Academically the students at Prairie Grove are performing much better than in the Nespelem district. Since Suanna loves learning, we're not sure how this will work."

"We have poor families here in Prairie Grove," said Jesse. "It must be hard on everyone. A friend of Julia's started at another school after her family was evicted from their home. One day the student just disappeared. She didn't show up in Julia's classroom and then a couple of weeks later we learned she was across town at another school."

"That's right," agreed Elizabeth, "and when the children are raised in poverty, their basic needs like food and housing become priorities over homework and studying for tests. It makes sense. On the Colville Reservation the extremely high rate of students eligible for free or reduced lunch is an indicator that relates to academic performance. I checked it out last night on the school's website.

" Online, I also found a pretty nice house that includes acreage for our horses. It's on the Columbia River within ten miles of Joe's family, including Carl and Tina's house."

"Great! What's the house like?"

"Just a minute; let me find the video on my phone. It's pretty new, but there are only two bedrooms. We'd want to add on if we get it. We'll also need a barn and fencing for the horses."

"If it were mine, there'd be a sculpture studio and large windows with a majestic view! Have you called the realtor yet?"

"Not about this new listing, but we need to. There's a basement, so that might help with space. Joe needs to learn more about the pasture and drainage on the site."

"It never hurts to call. Are there a lot of houses on the market?"

"That's the best one with land, so this may be a chance we don't want to miss. We may not have enough time to move before school starts, but Susanna could possibly live with family in Nespelem until we get settled."

"I don't see a for-sale sign in your yard yet," kidded Jesse.

"Oh, we don't even have to wait to sell this! My parents were shocked when we told them we're moving, but they admit that they've had Suanna nearby for her entire life. They said that they'd purchase it from us if we don't sell it quickly. So, our move's not dependent on selling this house. Joe has already informed his customers so they can start looking for another farrier. Good ones are hard to find, but Joe has a couple of recommendations.

"I'd like some dedicated space for my research," continued Elizabeth. "After all these years I'm going to dump genetics and get back to my first love, cultural anthropology!"

"I'm excited for you! So, you'll find a school for Suanna and a barn for Joe's horses and horseshoeing, and you'll create space for you and your research," summarized Jesse.

"That's our plan. I don't know how easy it will be for me to get hired to do indigenous research since I'm not Indian. Meantime, I'm going to start having fun interviewing Joe's family members. Carl's wife, Tina, has already been my gatekeeper whenever I have questions about the reservation or the different tribes. You'd like her. She's creative with her hands—does embroidery."

"I'd like to meet her. You said Joe's family lives on the reservation; does that include his parents?"

"His father died years ago from a logging accident. I'm going to approach his mother and ask her if she'll let me interview her. We haven't talked about family traditions as much as I'd like. As long as she doesn't blame me for taking Joe away, we'll be all right. With Joe finally home, I hope I can get a new Indian name."

"What is it now?" asked Jesse.

"It's kind of long," said Elizabeth as she laughed. "She says it in Niimiipuu, the language of the Nez Perce, but it means Wicked-White-Woman-Who-Steals-Indians-Off-Reservation."

"Well, at least you're returning him—with child."

•

Julia and Hannah followed Suanna into her bedroom, and she closed the door. Suanna took them to Rat's ten-gallon glass cage, popped off the lid, and had him cupped in her hands before the visitors knew it was a gerbil. Sitting on the floor, the girls created a circle and let Rat crawl around the human ring, moving from arms to shoulders and necks. With a few shrieks and shudders from the visitors, Rat was quickly accepted as ticklish but harmless.

"Do you want to see my worms?" asked Suanna.

"Your worms?!" said Julia. Her eyes opened wide.

"Yeah," Suanna replied as she pulled out a plastic tub from under the table that held Rat's cage. Suanna flipped off the lid, turned it over, and looked at its underside. There was some moisture and brown matter with skinny worms slithering around. Suanna picked up each little worm with her finger tips and dropped them one by one into the worm bin to join their brethren, a multitude inching toward security in the subterranean darkness. They quickly disappeared into the brown abyss mixed with strips of damp newspaper and rotting food.

"These worms are pretty small compared to the ones in our yard," said Julia.

"It doesn't smell," offered Hannah.

"Yeah, these are *Eisenia fetida*, red wigglers," said Suanna as she pulled up a handful of the ground-like debris. This exposed a myriad of wiggling worms, many balled up in the shell-like skin of half an avocado.

"You play with them?" asked Hannah.

"Yeah, here," Suanna said as she divided her handful between Julia and Hannah.

"What do you do with them?"

"Mostly I just watch them, but they make compost for my mom. She uses it for her plants."

"Our mom buys bags of compost from the store," said Julia.

"I ordered the worms online from Pennsylvania. They eat our kitchen scraps and newspapers. They love old coffee grounds too."

"What's the brown stuff?" asked Julia.

"Worm castings," replied Suanna.

"Worm castings?"

"Worm poop," Suanna explained.

"Oh!" said Julia.

"Eeewww!" said Hannah.

"Do you want to go meet Lady Bonita, my horse?"

"Yeah!" Julia and Hannah eagerly replied, while depositing their worms and worm castings back into the bin. They repeatedly rubbed their hands and fingers together in an attempt to get the excess gooey poop off their skin, but it had unusual sticking power. "Can we wash our hands first?" asked Hannah.

As they walked out of the bedroom, Suanna continued her narrative. "I can't ride her until I'm stronger, but you can pet her if you want. Then we can look for Hubcap."

"Is Hubcap a horse?" Julia asked.

"Hubcap Houdini is our rooster," said Suanna. "He fights! Do you have roosters?"

"No, but we have three cats and three dogs at our house," said Julia.

"No, Julia, three cats and two dogs. Kudzu's gone."

"Yeah," agreed Julia, "two dogs."

"Let's go!" said Suanna.

•

Tom heard music outside emanating from Joe's patio and was welcomed by Willie Nelson's singing. He immediately recognized the words to the song, "Always on My Mind," and thought of how he'd been treating Jesse unfairly. While he was working he had let his job, not her, be always on his mind. He no longer treated her or loved her or held her the way he once did. Now, his job was gone, but he still flashed back to killing Odessa-Smith. Instead of the sound of bullets, the smell of gunpowder, and the sign of blood, Tom wanted Jesse to again be the first one on his mind. He had nearly lost her due to his unhealthy obsession with work and his drinking. He wanted one more chance to keep her satisfied, for her to be on his mind.

"Tom, welcome!" greeted Joe as he finished wrapping the brisket that had been cooked on the gas grill. Wearing a brand-new, white T-shirt with "Property of Nespelem Eagles" printed on the front, Joe continued: "Thanks for joining us. I thought you'd enjoy some Willie Nelson since you like country-western music. Elizabeth's told me how years ago you used to DJ on Country KZOK. These songs are on his best songs playlist."

"Thanks, Joe. Yeah, ten-four, those were good times."

As usual, any dog within sniffing distance found Tom Jennings. The Morningclouds' cocker spaniel, with a white patch on his brown chest, trotted up to Tom and nudged his hand, inviting petting. Each eyebrow was similar to a fluffy caterpillar or a beard on one of Jesse's tall bearded irises.

"Well, who's this?" Tom asked.

"That's Brownie," Joe explained. " Everyone loves him."

Just then, Suanna and Tom's girls bounded out of the house. Suanna invited Tom to meet Lady Bonita and Hubcap Houdini. He and Brownie followed the girls as they headed toward the stable.

"Are you sad about losing your job?" asked Suanna.

"Yeah, but I'm actually more angry than I am sad about being fired," answered Jennings as he petted Brownie's neck and chest.

"You told us in class that when you're angry you usually talk to your wife because she's one person you trust."

"You're right. I did say that. I need to talk with her some more."

"I hope you didn't get fired because of my injury at the bank. I'd like to apologize to you for causing the accident."

Tom cocked his head in disbelief. He almost asked her to repeat what she'd said.

"It was my fault for not looking," she continued.

"And I'm sorry to you, too," Tom said in a shaky voice as he rubbed his eyelids. "I wasn't looking either."

"That's okay. Who was the officer that found Rat? My mother told me a police officer brought him home in a Golden Dragon to-go box! All he had to do was put him in his pocket; Rat wouldn't have run away. Do you want to meet him? He's inside the house."

"Thanks, I'll meet Rat later. Officer Schmedley, from school, was the officer who dropped Rat off, but a lady FBI agent found Rat."

"Will you thank Officer Schmedley for me?"

"Sure, I'll let him know."

"I've never met anyone from the FBI. What's her name? Can she stop by today? I'll thank her personally."

"Agent Jones lives pretty far from here," explained Tom.

"Do you still get to see Kudzu? I remember at the school assembly when he found the hidden drugs."

"I haven't seen Kudzu for almost two months. Since he has a new handler, I don't want to confuse him. It's better for me not to visit."

"Girls!" yelled Tom, just as Julia started climbing up some two-by-four boards that were nailed into a tall cottonwood, functioning as steps on a ladder. Hannah was right behind her, as usual, ready to follow.

"What?" said Julia.

"What do you think you're doing?"

"We're climbing up to Suanna's tree house."

"No, you're not. The boards look rotten. It's not safe."

"It is too!" yelled Julia. "Suanna said she still goes up there. Well, before she was hurt."

"You girls are not going up to the tree house because I want you to be extra safe."

"Dad! You're treating us like babies again! I'm ten years old!"

"Okay, I'm treating you like babies again."

"Suanna's dad made this tree house for her, so you know it's safe."

Tom didn't reply.

"Suanna's the one that was hurt," continued Julia. "Why punish us?"

Julia and Hannah marched away with their arms pumping up and down and their hands clenched like unhappy soldiers. They were headed for the Morningclouds' back door to go inside and complain to their mother. Their dad was being unfair again—what Mom called "overprotective."

"Do you know that we're moving?" asked a grinning Suanna.

"No!" answered Tom. "Stay here. Don't move. I'm just getting to know your parents better. Your dad promised me a chance to ride your horse today. He said you couldn't ride yet and that your horse needed some exercise."

"He did?"

"No, just joking. But he said I'd be perfect on a Percheron."

"Officer Jennings! You're funny!" she said, getting the giggles. "A Percheron is a giant horse! We're moving to Washington where my dad was born. We try and visit there almost every summer. I've got relatives there. It's an Indian reservation. We're going to take our horses with us, including Lady Bonita, of course, and Hubcap. Washington has a state fair, just like us, only it's not as close like Hutchinson. Dad told me that Washington's fair has some of the same type of displays as Kansas. They have carnival rides and 4-H competition and poultry open entry and a butter sculpture and the-largest-pumpkin contest; they also have a rodeo. Mom likes to look at the quilts that people sew with fabric, the barn quilts that are painted on boards, and the photography exhibit. Dad said he'd be happy with horses, a hypnotist, and demolition derby."

Running her mouth at Indy-500 speed, Suanna sounded like a five-year-old sucking sugar cubes. Her brain and speech certainly appeared to be working on all cylinders. Tom, drenched in sweat from the heat, wiped his brow with his handkerchief, and watched her as she took another deep breath. She continued listing her plans as she paced in the yard, her body in constant motion.

"My dad's been asked to teach boxing at the community center near Nespelem. He's considering doing it if they have classes for boys *and* girls. He told me that I could help him. I know I can't participate because of my brain injury. My mother's against the idea of me even being an assistant. I heard them arguing.

"Next summer I can be in the July 4th parade on the reservation," Suanna continued, her face in the shade, but beaming light. "Right now my doctor has ordered me to stay ten feet away from horses. He says I can't even be on a horse carousel; that's a merry-go-round. Holly said she wants to visit! Do you and your family want to come see us for a vacation at our house by Nespelem? I'll go to school there. It's got to be better than here. Or, if you want, there's a hotel and casino in Omak called 12 Tribes, but that's pretty far away from our new house.

"The twelve tribes include my dad's family from Chief Joseph's Band of the Nez Perce. But I've learned the other tribes too: Chelan, Colville, Entiat, Lakes, Methow, Moses Columbia, Nespelem, Paulus, San Poil, Southern Okanogan, and Wenatchi.

"Oh, and guess what! There's a summer camp for children like me with albinism in New Hampshire. It's too late this year, but next year, if I want, my grandparents said that they'd take me there in their RV. It's way across the country! It sounds like it's really neat, but the camp's in July at about the same time as the rodeo, so I'll have to decide."

"That's wonderful, Suanna." Tom gave thanks that he was able to watch Suanna get excited about her future. Listening to her speed talk was a real joy. Until her recovery from the subdural hemorrhage and brain surgery, no one knew if she'd even have a tomorrow.

"I wonder if the Washington State Fair has bacon funnel cakes or fried, white cheese curds," said Tom.

"Every year we get the homemade chicken noodles and then ice cream for dessert," Suanna remarked. "If you let your beard grow longer, maybe next year you can compete in the mustache and beard competition, but it's too short right now."

Tom, with his trademark shaved head, rubbed it, then scratched his scruffy beard, (growing since the grand jury ended), and said, "Unlike you, I sure don't know what I'll be doing a year from now."

•

Tom drank tea as he watched Joe prepare to cook the hamburgers and hotdogs on the backyard grill. The smoke screen confused the gluttonous mosquitoes that smelled blood.

"Tom," said Joe, "I want you to know that Carolyn Odessa is making plans to sue you and the department. She's working on a wrongful death case over her son being killed. She tried to get us on board because of Suanna's injury."

"My attorney told me to expect it from Odessa, but thanks for letting me know. It's one more thing to deal with. I'm just glad Suanna is doing better. Her recovery means everything to me."

"Carolyn and Shawn know Elizabeth's parents," Joe explained, "so Carolyn talked with my mother-in-law, Ruth. Carolyn tried to get her support after the grand jury cleared you of any wrongdoing. Ruth promised to pass the message on to Elizabeth, but you should know we're not interested in a civil suit. That's why we have insurance."

"Joe, do whatever you need to do to take care of Suanna. We'll understand. Again, I'm so sorry this happened."

"Suanna has surprised the doctors. No seizures, no memory loss, or headaches. Her speaking hasn't suffered, but she's getting physical therapy. We're fortunate. Since she still gets easily fatigued and occasionally suffers dizziness, she's going to need to be careful for a while."

"Jesse tells me you're moving. I wouldn't blame you if your purpose was to put Prairie Grove behind you."

"On the contrary, Suanna has motivated me. We're moving back to Washington where our lives were interrupted a dozen years ago. I'm going home, not running away from it."

"Oh! Good for you!" said Tom.

•

The beef, hamburgers, hot dogs, sweet corn, baked beans, potato salad, and coleslaw were ready. Sliced watermelon waited in reserve, s'mores a possibility. The Morningclouds and their guests, the Jennings family, sat down in the humid summer shade and swatted mosquitoes. They had so much to be thankful for. Almost two months earlier the adults were nearly strangers, but in a short time they had grown to be friends. They were linked for life after a traumatic event.

The gathering, with bowed heads, listened as Joe prayed: "Dear Father, We're grateful for the food you have provided us, for new friends, and for the opportunities you offer us to show our faith in you every single day. You give us life so that we may understand death, and you give us death to understand life. You give us joy and sorrow. We continue to do our best to understand you, each other, and ourselves. Amen."

Amens followed.

There were good reasons why Tom Jennings had a reputation, complete with nicknames, for eating large quantities of food. Like his shoulder tattoo advertised, he was "Taz," the Tasmanian devil, who gorged on all edibles. He also answered to "Lunchbox," and "LB," for seriously chowing down during the time he worked in the county jail. When Jennings was called "Pork Chop," the nickname referred either to his love of pork or as the derogatory term "pig," meaning police officer. The Morningclouds, not unfamiliar to miracles, witnessed another spectacle occur before their very eyes. It all started innocently enough when Tom, sitting at their patio table, politely asked Suanna, "Would you please pass the relish?"

•

"I'm canceling my counseling appointment," said Tom

"Why?" asked Jesse.

"I don't need it anymore!" he said in a bubbly voice.

"How come, Tom?"

"Earlier, Suanna apologized to me for running into my car!"

"Oh! Tom!" said Jesse as she clasped her hands to her chest.

"Yeah, and I apologized to her. I'm going to be all right now. My guilt just shrank a whole lot."

"Good for you, Tom."

"If that girl can be over this, then so can we."

"She's quite a girl."

"Yes, she is," said Tom. "She's ready for her next chapter in life."

"So am I," concluded Jesse.

The Chief 33

Jennings entered the law enforcement center at the public entrance. He still recalled the numbers for the interior key-padded doors, but he recognized he was a civilian, not a uniform. He no longer had free range to the back office. Instead, he looked into the camera, picked up the phone, and identified himself to a familiar voice. Instead of an escort appearing, the door buzzed and unlocked. "You know the way," she said, and he hung up, entering his former life.

Tom followed the aroma of the cinnamon and nutmeg with olfactory memories of good cheer from an apple-pie childhood and adult, boozy, eggnog parties.

"Welcome back, Tom!"

"We've missed you!" another voice echoed.

"Are you here for some apple pie?" asked Candy, remaining behind her desk.

"It's great to see you again," answered Tom, "and even though you can't tell, I've lost a few pounds from avoiding these delicious daily treats. Who made the pie?"

"Me," said Sherry as she approached Tom, ready for a hug. "There's whipped cream, too. Help yourself."

"Let me see the chief first," replied Tom. "He called. Maybe later, thanks."

•

"Glad to hear the grand jury voted against indicting you," said the police chief, remaining at his desk. Nothing but business, he didn't rise or offer his hand. "It's good for you, and it's good for the department."

"Thanks," replied Jennings. "Does that mean I'll get my job back?" he asked, pushing his luck.

"Now, I invited you here for another reason, but still I'm happy for the decision. The city firing you is another matter that is best left up to the attorneys. We did what we had to do."

"Okay, you know we're appealing it. I deserve to get my job back. Just more waiting."

"Yeah, that's what we do, isn't it? We do our best and then we wait to see if others agree with us. That's my job too. The city council second guesses me more than you'll ever know."

"Yeah, ten-four," Jennings said, "I know they agree to abide by the decision of arbitrators after our FOP goes to an impasse on wages, but then they ignore the findings. They're politicians, no matter how little they get paid."

The chief picked up three small plastic bags from his desk, examined the bullet fragments, and asked, "Do you know if Jesse still wants this bullet back?" The chief sounded thoughtful, even caring.

Jennings was caught off-guard. He replied, "Last time we talked about it, yes, she wanted it back."

"Well, here's the twenty-two-caliber slug that was removed from the ceiling; here's the largest piece of the bullet casing found on the floor; and then this last one is the small ragged piece of brass casing that was collected after Jesse's surgery."

Jennings examined the bullet fragments. "This one bullet started a domino effect in my life and the lives of so many others."

"That's the truth," the chief responded.

"I'd love to take the bullet back, but I know I can't undo what's happened. Ever since the bank I've thought about my police academy training when Bill Peters told us to be careful before firing our gun, to be sure of our target, because we can never take a bullet back. I never dreamed the same thing could be true about simply putting a bullet in my pocket."

"You're not the first officer to ever lose track of a loose bullet. I've never told anyone this besides my wife—and I've sworn her to secrecy—but early in my career I was responsible for a bullet going off in our washing machine. A couple days after I'd been to the firearm's range, my wife washed my sweatshirt and jeans. Somehow, a loose round must have got caught in the clothing I was wearing. I apologized to her and then I replaced the washing machine with a top-of-the-line model. It taught me to count my rounds."

"Thanks for telling me," said Jennings, "and I appreciate you getting me this. I'm surprised. I figured the evidence custodian would have it forever."

"Well, I heard that Jesse didn't want to give it up at the hospital. But the criminal investigation is over. It's hers if she still wants it."

"Actually," said Jennings, "she's had an idea for using it in her art."

"I've heard of sculptors who have used confiscated guns that judges have ordered destroyed, and the artists have turned those swords into plowshares, so to speak."

"Yeah, ten-four. I don't know what she can do with this since it's so small. We'll see," Jennings added.

"Here's another thing that should have been returned to you or we could have shredded," said the chief, as he held a sealed brown envelope. "You filled this out years ago. I don't know if it's been updated anywhere else or not, but it's the paper work we keep in case an officer is ever killed in the line of duty. I've been told it comes in handy at funerals."

"Ten-four, I vaguely remember those questions. It will make for some good reading. For my sake, I'm glad you couldn't use it."

"Yeah, me too," agreed the chief.

•

Back home, Tom gave the bullet fragments to Jesse. She was caught off guard to see that the police chief had kept his promise. But, she was still upset that Tom had been sacrificed after his years of dedicated service to the city.

"I don't work for him!" said Jesse, as she raised her voice. "I've been hoping to run into that coward chief at the grocery store and tell him what I think he's done to the department."

"Yeah," Tom concurred, pleased to have his wife's support. "He still won't admit to firing me; blames the city attorney and the council."

"That's why I don't understand you fighting to get your job back," said Jesse, sweeping her arms into the air. "Could you ever work for him again?"

"If we win the appeal," said Tom, "we can get my back wages, maybe I get Kudzu again, and my record is cleared of ever being terminated."

Biscuit, with labored breathing, rested on the couch, but lifted her head at the sound of Kudzu's name and looked around the room. Gravy, standing in front of Tom, held a drooling tennis ball in his mouth. He dropped the ball to the floor, inviting Tom to play. Butch, the stubby-tailed Manx, was dozing out of reach, near the top of the cat tree. Across the room was a dusty bookshelf that held distant memories. There were sets of bookends in the shape of cats and dogs and a sculpture of a sexy looking woman with partially closed eyes and an inviting pout. Finally, music from another room stopped, followed by talking. The DJ from KZOK radio introduced the next song, *Somebody Pick Up My Pieces*, classic soul, by Bettye LaVette.

Jesse raised her chin. "But you'd still go back and work for him?" challenged Jesse, eyes narrowing, trying to understand her husband's reasoning. "They'd just find another way to fire you again. You know how I feel about it."

"You make it sound like it would be worse on you than on me."

"It's not just you or me, it's our family. Just like in the military, people forget the families. Yes, I feel like we've sacrificed enough. Don't you?"

"The chances of me getting back into policing aren't good. Who would want to hire me? I'm fat, I'm fired, and I'm in the middle of an appeal to get my job back."

"You're forgetting your health. Every day you have pain in your back. Your diabetes is acting up due to your stress and the way you eat. Could you even pass a physical? Are you forgetting what the doctor said? But, you know, someone will hire you if that's what you want. You're a dedicated officer."

"Despite the stress, the officers, not the administrators, are like family to me; most of the time the job is rewarding. Now that Suanna has gotten better, I can do this work again. I can rebound. And I know you're tired of me saying this, but it's how we make a living."

"Like family!" Jesse's nostrils flared and her face grew red. "Rewarding? If you're being treated like family, then it's a dysfunctional family, like ours right now. Cops out drinking and telling war stories; reliving the last shift. And your reward for this is to spend our savings on attorneys."

"Most of the expenses are being covered by the FOP. But what would I do if I wasn't a cop?" he asked.

"Remember the job offer from Ephesians Body Armor," Jesse recalled. "They emphasized they hire ex-police officers who have been injured in the line of duty."

"Their jobs are for officers who have been shot and disabled."

"They said you qualify to be hired in sales or tactical firearms training. It's your choice."

"Yeah, they're top-notch people with excellent products, but I don't know about it yet."

"They made you the offer; that means they want you."

"They're ready for me, but I'm not ready for them," Tom concluded.

"You talk about how working with the guys feels like family, but as part of your family I can tell you that it doesn't feel right for me. I can't do it anymore. I can't be the police spouse at home who imagines everything is going to be okay. And I've watched what it's done to you, too. Look at yourself. You need to know that I can't continue putting myself through this anymore. You need the job, but I need a change."

"What does that mean?"

"I can't change you, and I won't try."

"But you want me to quit trying."

"I need you to understand that I'm not asking you to leave law enforcement, but I am telling you that I can't live with you if you continue to choose policing. I can't do it any longer, day after day, night after night."

"You're not telling me what to do, but you're going to leave if I get my job back?"

"I'm no longer willing to compromise when it comes to your work. The shooting clarified things for me."

"I thought your counseling had helped?" asked Tom.

"It's helped me get back to who I am," explained Jesse. "I'm not just a mother or a police spouse; I'm me, too."

"We can go to marriage counseling. We can work this out," he promised.

Jesse rotated her wedding ring and said, "Marriage counseling is about understanding each other and making compromises. I'm no longer willing to compromise."

"I was a cop when we got married."

"That was a long time ago."

"I still love you."

"And I love you."

"What about the girls?" asked Tom.

"They know things between us aren't right. They're old enough to know things have changed around here. They need to grow up with less stress in their home."

"It's this way because of the bank, but we can make it better," promised Tom. "Time will help. I'll start counseling again."

"I don't think it's about counseling because you've chosen your profession despite its harmful consequences."

"So, you're saying that as long as I'm a police officer you don't want to live together, to be married? Do you want a divorce? Is that what you're saying?"

"I didn't say I wanted a divorce, but I can't watch you do the job anymore. I can't be a part of it on a daily basis."

"And if I give up my career?"

"You see, I'm not asking you to do that! I don't want you to give it up for me. If you gave it up for me, then things wouldn't be any better for us or the girls. Right now, I get it; you need the career, the interaction with your police family. You trust your guys. I'm just telling you the way I see it. We aren't a healthy family anymore."

"Honey, you've always been more important to me than my job. The girls mean everything to me. You don't want to break up our family."

"Me! It's already broken."

"I don't know what I'd do if I wasn't a cop, but I don't know what I'd do if we weren't together anymore, and the girls need us."

Phoenix 34

Tom eyed the police department's parking lot and the entrances to the station as he drove by his former home away from home, hoping to see a familiar face, a wave, or a nod. Jesse was used to the route whenever they were in town together.

Julia, with Hannah in the back seat, asked, "Mom, who's gonna be at Gino's Pizzeria besides Suanna and her parents?"

"Carl; his son, Storm; and Catalpa. We'll have a lot to talk about."

It was a last-minute celebration at the conclusion of the Morningclouds' manic race to leave town in time to arrive in Nespelem before Labor Day. Carl had recently driven back to Prairie Grove with his youngest son, Storm, and Catalpa Morningcloud, Joe's niece. Bud was not with his sister. Instead, he was back at the reservation with Carl's wife, Tina, and their three other children. Carl was helping the Morningclouds move. Within a day or two they would make the final road trip as a caravan from Kansas to Washington. Joe, Elizabeth, Suanna, and Carl wanted to say a final goodbye to Tom and Jesse Jennings. They were meeting at Gino's.

Carl greeted Jesse and Tom with warm hugs. Jesse squeezed Elizabeth's shoulders before sitting down next to her.

Before ordering food, introductions were made to the group of ten people sitting around the banquet table. Storm was the four-wheelin' daredevil; Catalpa, partial to reptiles, had a garter snake at home named Bolt. Julia's long hair, perpetually wet all summer, was evidence that she lived at the community swimming pool; and Hannah, already creasing a paper menu, was an expert in origami, the Japanese art of folding paper.

After the group ordered five pizzas and one salad, they collected their own drinks. Carl sat down and handed Tom the latest *Tribal Tribune*, a weekly newspaper from the Colville Confederated Tribes Reservation.

On the front page, circled in pen, was the first part of an article about a grant that had been received by the business council for the tribal police department.

"Tom, you might be interested in this job opening," said Carl. "The tribal police got a grant to purchase an arson dog because of all the fires on the reservation a couple years ago. They'll need a dog handler, too."

"I don't know anything about investigating arson," claimed Tom as he shook his head and raised his open hands as though he had nothing to offer. "The fire department investigates suspicious fires."

"But you know about training dogs," replied Carl, "and the business council understands the millions of dollars in timber revenue they can lose from wildfires. The North Star fire and Tunk Block fire were crippling to so many families and to the tribal budget."

As Tom read, Carl turned to Jesse. "You're looking good. I don't even see a scar on your beautiful face."

"Yes, I'm fine. Thanks again for helping me in my time of need."

"You know," said Carl, seriously, "if I recall correctly, you were trying to get me to disrobe for you in the bank until the gunfire interrupted us."

"In your dreams!" said Jesse as she flashed him a deep smile. "That scenario is wishful thinking. Actually, I recall some claim you'd made about being a famous warrior who traveled country roads pulling a horse trailer, fighting for truth and justice while auditing books at Indian casinos."

Carl grinned. "Sounds good to me!" he said.

"Here's your salad with Greek dressing," stated the waitress, as she placed the bowl in front of Elizabeth. "May I get you anything else?"

"Do you have ketchup in a bottle?" asked Tom.

The waitress hesitated before asking, "Ketchup?"

"Yeah, if you have any, I'll add it as a topping when you bring our pizzas."

"I'll check in the kitchen," replied the waitress before moving on to another table.

Julia and Hannah each gave a muted, embarrassed laugh. Then Jesse said, "Tom smothers everything in ketchup. I don't know why I bother seasoning his food."

Jesse was not disappointed. Tom answered: "Ketchup is seasoning."

"Julia," said Elizabeth, "what do you enjoy best about swimming?"

"Diving is my favorite."

"She dives off the high board and she's only in the fourth grade!" bragged Hannah about her big sister.

Julia thrust her chest out and had a gleam in her eye.

"Julia, did you know that Elizabeth used to compete on her college swim team?" asked Joe.

"Really?" asked Julia.

"Yes," said Elizabeth, "my favorite event was the butterfly, but I was pretty good in the breast stroke, too."

"If you weren't moving, I could show you how I can dive backwards," added Julia.

"Tom," said Joe, "if you're interested in the job, then come up with your family and visit us. We'll put you in the RV that Elizabeth's parents have loaned us. We purchased a house near Nespelem. After Elizabeth found it on the Internet, Carl sent us more video of the property; he even did a house inspection."

Carl's posture improved as he moved his shoulders back and raised his chin. He gave a knowing grin.

"We visited, signed the papers, and talked with the principal at the school," added Elizabeth.

"Are you saying that the tribal police would hire someone who's not American Indian?" asked Tom.

"Yep, that's right," said Carl, "you don't have to be a tribal member. The department employs people of different races. No Indian blood required. You won't need to prove your great-grandmother was Cherokee or an Indian princess," he joked. "My sister Diana's a 911 dispatcher and her white husband is an officer. Of course he's got an Indian name which probably helped him get the job," laughed Carl.

"His name is Billy Goodenough!" Suanna blurted out.

"I don't like him," said Storm.

"How about you call yourself Tipi Tom?" Joe suggested.

Elizabeth didn't laugh. Instead, she recommended they avoid slang names and stereotyping. She could have also urged Tom to find a different vanity plate than his football driven "Go Chiefs!" but she chose to wait and see where this tribal police talk was going. It sounded like Tom was considering the invitation. She would especially welcome Jesse as a neighbor.

Carl explained to Jesse that if he could lure Tom to the reservation to become a tribal police officer that he'd also be willing to pose for her artist sketches. "Do you draw children?" he asked Jesse. Then he offered up Storm and Catalpa as additional live models. "You could draw them on horseback," he suggested, "and sell the art."

Storm and Catalpa visibly shrank, worried about being volunteered to do anything, but Suanna saw her opening. "Me, too! I'm Indian!"

Hannah, who had been trying to show her sister how to make a paper crane, stopped her folding. Julia hesitated from playing a game on her phone. Both waited to see if they were going to be used as additional bargaining chips.

"Now's not the time or place," said Elizabeth, 'but there's a law dealing with the authenticity of Indian arts and crafts when they're sold. As long as the item isn't claimed to be Indian-made, then there should be no problem."

"I like your barcode tattoo," said Storm to Jesse. "I want to get one, but my parents . . . ," he looked at his father, "say I'm too young."

"Think before you ink," Carl automatically responded. "When you consistently make better choices, we'll talk about it."

"I got this tattoo when I was in college," shared Jesse as she massaged her bare neck. "Instead of beautiful, colorful art, why did I choose a black barcode?"

"You don't like it anymore?" asked Storm as he leaned forward awaiting her answer.

"When I decided to display the barcode," said Jesse, "it was a protest about our corporate society and how individuals were accepting treatment like mindless lemmings."

"To me a barcode means that anyone in today's world—no matter who they are, no matter how young—can be instantly connected and counted, anywhere, even on a reservation," said Storm.

"Then people who get the tattoo today see it differently than the way I did seventeen years ago," replied Jesse. "If I had chosen a flower, maybe a tall bearded iris, it would still represent natural beauty. Its meaning wouldn't have changed."

"My dad told me about a friend of his from the Army Guard who had a tattoo removed because it was the name of a girlfriend who dumped him," said Storm. "The guy didn't like the memory and his wife didn't appreciate it either."

"Yes, that's called a regretful tattoo," said Jesse, breaking into a smile. "Don't get your girlfriend's name put on your arm. By the way, my barcode tattoo doesn't scan anymore," said Jesse. "I tried it awhile back when I was shopping."

"You mean your tattoo scanned? I want one that scans!" said Storm as he again looked at his dad for approval.

"Over time the ink has changed and so has my skin," Jesse offered and laughed. "I never believed I'd age."

Tom listened to Jesse respectfully converse with Storm and he felt pride in her ability and willingness to really communicate. He also smiled at the thought of Jesse aging. He recognized that she was still the same stunning beauty he had met in the lobby of the law enforcement center so many years earlier. Her bright red hair still created a sustained luminous glow; her sparkling gray eyes resembled fireworks; and her cheeks displayed faint, captivating freckles like fading starbursts. Tom caught his breath.

Storm thought it was remarkable that Jesse would have a conversation with him when she had other adults to talk to.

Carl looked at Jesse but resisted rolling his eyes. Any good parent knew that to expect rational behavior from an adolescent was always wishful thinking.

"Are you looking forward to the new school year?" asked Elizabeth, clearly ready to change the subject away from a family controversy.

"No," Storm replied.

"Well, what do you like about your school?"

"Basketball and friends," he quickly answered.

"How many students are there in your grade?" asked Elizabeth, knowing the answer.

"Eight or nine."

"Suanna," said Storm, as he turned toward her, "you've visited the reservation during summer, but you don't know how bad our school is. If you go there, you'll regret it."

"Don't tell her that," snapped Carl. "You don't know what her experience will be."

"I know what my experience is," said Storm. "I'm just telling her how I see it. You told me to talk to her; that's what I'm doing."

"Suanna," said Carl, "you know our other children: Angel, Maggie, and Albert. They did fine at the school. It's just that Storm struggles."

"Dad!" said Storm. "It's not about being stupid or smart; it's about being an outsider."

Having completed reading the article, Tom interrupted Carl, "Are any of the tribal officers overweight?" It was obvious that Carl's invitation had caused Tom to reimagine his future.

"My brother-in-law, Billy, is good-sized," said Carl. "He once entered a competitive hot-dog eating contest in Seattle, but was slaughtered by the international Japanese competitor, Nao Danshita of Nara."

"I'm serious," said Tom. "It's not about eating; it's about being able to do the job."

"I don't know what the hiring standards are," said Carl, "but we've got some 4-X size officers working both on patrol and in our detention center. Like me, they were raised on five-minute noodles, fry bread, and pop."

"So," said Jesse, "you don't know if they even require a physical?" she asked Carl while staring at Tom. As Jesse listened, she began to pull at her wedding ring to see if it would come off.

"Guys, I don't know, but I can call Billy right now if you want. He'll know," said Carl, as he reached in his pocket for his phone.

"Carl, thanks for showing me this article," said Tom as he returned the newspaper. "It's interesting, but I'm hanging up my badge so I can do something else. Thanks anyways."

Jesse stopped fidgeting with her wedding ring.

"Here are three of your pizzas, so you can get started," the waitress said as she cleared space on the table. "We have a pepperoni, a hamburger, and a cheese with ham. Careful, the cheese is really hot."

"Oh, I almost forgot," the waitress added as she reached into her deep apron pocket and pulled out a bottle of ketchup. She handed it to Tom and said, "For your pizza!"

As soon as the waitress turned to go, the hungriest of the bunch reached for the steaming pizza. Each time a slice was claimed, the cheese stretched like a rubber band and it became obvious that eating was a two-handed operation. Before long, Tom was the center of attention because his beard appeared to have been targeted by someone with a spray can of cheese confetti.

"If you get hungry later," said Joe, "you'll have something to eat."

Everyone laughed, Tom included.

•

After a majority of the pizza-parlor group had finished eating, their napkins wadded up and their chairs pushed back from the table, Jesse addressed her friends and family. "Part of the reason we're here is to celebrate Suanna's remarkable improvement."

Suanna straightened up. She hadn't been forgotten.

Out of her purse, Jesse retrieved and held up a thin, silver, necklace chain holding a miniature silver bird with outstretched wings. The feet and claws of the royal bird were standing amidst rising flames.

Catalpa, who had been sipping her drink through a straw, abruptly started coughing and hitting her upper chest with an open hand. Recovering, she fell still, leaned forward, and studied every detail of the silver necklace.

Tom dropped his head.

"Suanna, have you heard of the mythical phoenix bird, who, upon death is reborn from its ashes?" asked Jesse.

"No, not a phoenix bird," replied Suanna, "but we have mythical stories with our tribes."

"To Tom and me, this Phoenix represents your recovery as a new life, a new opportunity," said Jesse, then handed the necklace to Suanna.

"Thank you so much. It's beautiful," said Suanna.

"Jesse made it," said Tom. "She's a silversmith."

"Oh, my, now it means even more to me," replied Suanna. "Thanks again."

Tom's eyes welled up.

"Suanna, it's partially made from the bullet that injured me in the bank," said Jesse. "We want you to have it as a sign of our friendship."

"Oh! Can I give you a hug?" asked Suanna, as she pushed her chair back.

Jesse stood up. Tom joined her, his head still bowed, his body shaking. Suanna spread her arms to full extension like a soaring bird and unsuccessfully tried to grasp both Jesse and Tom.

Catalpa crossed her arms in front of her chest while her eyes froze in a cold blank stare and her lips curled. Inside, she was imagining the phoenix bird in her possession, knowing that she was more deserving of the necklace. Soon, it would be hers.

•

Tom, by habit, retraced his route home. But as they approached the police station he didn't feel the same urgency for peer recognition or companionship.

He heard the distant train with its horn sounding: long—long—short—long, and recalled UP train rides when he was a small child with his father, and Hal, the engineer.

"Are you seriously thinking about us moving?" asked Hannah to her parents, "because we want to live here, not on some Indian reservation!"

Jesse looked at Tom before answering, caught his eye, winked, and gave him a mischievous smile. She turned toward the back seat. "Hannah, where's your sense of adventure?"

"Mom!" Hannah recoiled. "We have a lot of friends here!"

"You already know Suanna. How about Carl's son, Storm? I enjoyed his conversation. Did you like him? He seemed nice."

Julia groaned and said, "Mother! This isn't funny!"

"I think I'm ready for a change of scenery, a new start, far away from the Cottonwood County Sheriff's Office and our bank," said Jesse. "It would be good for your dad, too."

"We could at least visit," added Tom as Jesse's idea gained momentum. "Joe invited us to stay in their RV."

"Carl's agreed to be the first of many Indian portraits for me," continued Jesse.

"We can take a scenic train ride to Spokane and then rent a car so we can check out the Indian neighborhood."

The girls looked at one another, their eyes open wide, their lips closed tightly.

"What about us?" asked Julia. "It's our lives! Don't we get to vote?"

"Yes, you get to vote when you're eighteen," Jesse answered.

Julia rolled her eyes. Hannah's were frozen, unblinking.

Tom turned his head to Jesse, his face lit up, excited about the possibilities. "I wonder if anyone has a K-9 training business near Nespelem or if there's any interest in dog agility courses? I've been enjoying working with Gravy again. He's such a smart Lab. I think I'm ready to help others train their dogs. It's something I'm good at."

Jesse slid closer to Tom. "I always knew that dogs were your first love. Do you remember at the art fair the day after we first met? You told me cats were of no use to you because you couldn't train them!"

Tom raised his right arm and put it around Jesse's shoulders. He gave her a light squeeze. "I'll never forget making that mistake. I thought I'd lost you before we ever had our first date."

"Well, I forgave you."

"Will you forgive me again? I can recover from the shoot and getting fired, especially if you'll give me another chance. I really need your support."

"I'm ready for a new start too, but this is about more than the shoot or you being fired. I was losing you emotionally years ago. The job changed you. I want the old Tom back who sings in the shower."

"Yeah, I let the job get to me. I became cynical and I started fighting the administration. I've been spiraling downward for a long time."

Jesse moved closer to Tom. She had to rise up off the seat to give him a kiss on his cheek. "With the job behind you, we can start over now."

"I'm ready to get my big butt in gear," said Tom.

"I need my art," declared Jesse. "My art helps me explore and grow. It teaches me who I am. Do you understand how important it is to me? I'm more than a housewife and a mother."

"I understand now. I'll help more so that you'll have extra time for your work. The girls can do more too." Tom looked into the rearview mirror so he could see both children.

They stared out the windows in silence. The decision had been made without them. There was nothing more they could say. It was as if they were being kidnapped by someone else's parents.

•

Appendix: Photographs

Jesse Jennings

Tom Jennings

Joe Morningcloud

Elizabeth Morningcloud

Suanna Morningcloud

Carl Warrior

James Odessa-Smith

Jonathan Odessa-Smith

July

Suhaila

Tina Warrior

Rabbit Chief Joe (totem)

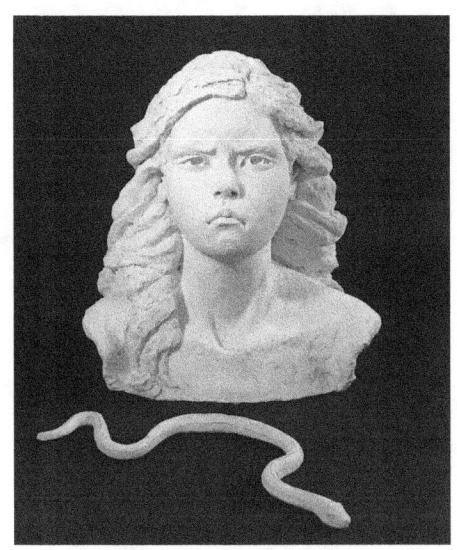

Catalpa Morningcloud
and Bolt

Le Chanteuse (The Singer)

Rabbit Chief Joe

Bookends

www.ingramcontent.com/pod-product-compliance
Lightning Source LLC
Chambersburg PA
CBHW071546110726
47908CB00007B/2009